Destiny's Journey

The Continuance

Richard K. Thompson

Bloomington, IN Milton Keynes, UK

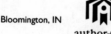

AuthorHouse™
1663 Liberty Drive, Suite 200
Bloomington, IN 47403
www.authorhouse.com
Phone: 1-800-839-8640

AuthorHouse™ UK Ltd.
500 Avebury Boulevard
Central Milton Keynes, MK9 2BE
www.authorhouse.co.uk
Phone: 08001974150

First published by AuthorHouse 3/7/2007

ISBN: 978-1-4259-8295-9 (sc)
ISBN: 978-1-4259-8419-9 (hc)

Printed in the United States of America
Bloomington, Indiana

This book is printed on acid-free paper.

To my friends, relatives and especially D. Hurff,
whose life and times have contributed
significantly to the writing of *Destiny's Journey*

Table of Contents

Prologue

During the days following an impulsive getaway he was supposed to have taken to Cabo San Lucas with Becky Parker, a woman he hardly knew, Neal Thomas found himself reminiscing on the beach behind his house trying to arrive at some reasonable explanation as to why that trip had been re-routed to Catalina Island.

Logistically, Catalina was a far better choice because it placed him closer to home, should an unforeseen emergency arise that would require his immediate return to the mainland. Additionally, the island also provided the comfort and privacy of a beautifully accommodated condominium overlooking Avalon Harbor. In this relaxing environment he could work at his leisure to complete a writing commitment he had made to Sterling Publishing Company before the voyage began. Still, the nagging question of what had prompted the change in destination bothered him, and suggested that he confront her on the subject whenever the opportunity presented itself.

As far as his novel was concerned, it was progressing well. Likewise, getting to know Becky and her friends was also improving by the hour. For this reason, he adopted the practice of limiting his writing regimen to mornings. By doing so, he could join them for the rest of the day to enjoy the social intercourse that, for some, carried into the wee hours of the next day.

Ever conscious of the pressure he was under to complete the novel, Becky respectfully avoided disturbing him during his working hours, until one morning several days after they had arrived.

Responding to a soft knocking on his bedroom door, Neal replied, "Come on in. I'm about through for the day."

"Good," Becky's somber voice said, as she entered the room. "There's something I must discuss with you."

"You sound uncharacteristically serious," he remarked cheerfully. "Is anything wrong?"

Walking across the room to stand in the warm ocean breeze entering through the balcony doors, she began to speak in a voice that was noticeably troubled. "I have just received word from my San Francisco office that an urgent matter has suddenly presented itself. Therefore, much as it upsets me, I must return to the city as soon as possible. I apologize for this untimely interruption, especially when our personal, as well as physical relationship, has become so wonderfully intimate. I was hoping the remainder of our time here would give us an incentive to see more of one another after this trip is over. Unfortunately, that will have to be postponed until another time."

"Does this urgent matter have anything to do with our not going to Cabo San Lucas?" he asked, grateful for the opportunity he had been waiting for.

"No, that was necessary to avoid a large storm that was headed in that direction. I felt it wiser to come here. It was the closest and safest place to have a good time. Regrettably, I'm afraid that time has been cut short."

Though the news was disappointing, his immediate concern turned to the problem of getting back home.

Anticipating that that subject would be foremost on his mind, Becky interrupted with a plan she had already worked out before coming to his room. "I have a friend who flies over here from San Diego to relax for a few days every now and then," she explained. "He's here now, and plans to fly back before dark. When I confronted him with my dilemma, he said he could drop you off at Palomar Airport without any inconvenience whatsoever, if getting back home is what's troubling you. Do you have any problem with that?"

"Only disappointment," he replied. "How much time do I have?"

Grateful for his bland acceptance of the awkward situation she found herself in, Becky replied, "Enough to pack up your things and have a leisurely lunch with me. I'll take you to the airport when the time comes."

"Give me a few minutes to save today's work," he remarked, sitting back down at the laptop computer she had provided him. "I'll get my things together and meet you downstairs in a minute or two."

"Take your time. No need to rush," she remarked calmly. "I'll have a drink waiting for you when you get there."

As the busy clicking of computer keys faded behind her, Becky returned to the kitchen and began preparing two drinks strong enough to take the edge off the disappointment she too was experiencing. Though the unexpected call from San Francisco was upsetting, she was well aware of the consequences that would result from ignoring it. There were times, she conceded with regret, when personal matters had to give way to higher priorities.

Arriving in the kitchen minutes later, Neal took a seat at the breakfast bar where Becky stood facing him. Toying with his drink for a moment, he suddenly raised it and smiled. "Well, like Bogie once said, here's looking at you, kid. Thanks for the buggy ride."

She laughed, realizing from his attempt to inject a little humor into the situation that he was making a valiant effort to avoid further comments on a matter over which she had no control. With only a few hours left before his flight would leave, she suggested that they have lunch at Antonio's Restaurant, before the strong drinks they were sipping teased them into an activity for which they had very little time, if any. In less than twenty minutes they were sitting in the restaurant enjoying their lunch, a glass of wine and a pleasant view of the boat-filled harbor.

Time passed quickly, with much of it spent conversing about events they had enjoyed together, and with her friends, most having already returned to her yacht to party, and prepare for their departure the next morning.

Unlike Neal, who was quite candid about his activities from boyhood to retirement, Becky preferred the role of listener, and cleverly avoided going into too much detail when answering his sometimes-probative questions, unaware that he knew more about her than she would ever have suspected. Tempted at times to divulge the information his friend Dusty Lewis had provided him with regard to her infamous past, he refrained for the time being, fearing it would have a detrimental effect on the relationship they had already consummated.

When their waitress arrived to clear the table, Neal excused himself to use the men's room, and waited in the hallway to intercept the young lady on her way to the kitchen. Handing her his credit card, he said, "Under no circumstances are you to accept any payment from my guest. This is my treat. Understood?"

"You're a little late for that, Mr. Thomas," she replied, with a grin. "Ms. Donaldson has already taken care of the bill. So relax and enjoy yourself. She can afford it."

Visibly surprised by the waitress' reference to the Donaldson name, he started to return to the table when he noticed a middle-aged man talking to her. He recognized him immediately as the Captain of her yacht and approached slowly to allow them time to finish their conversation. "Good afternoon, Captain," Neal said, extending his hand in a friendly gesture. "What brings you ashore this time of day?"

"I was just informing Ms. Donaldson that preparations for our departure to San Francisco tomorrow are near complete," he replied. "Sorry you're not going with us. I've enjoyed your company."

"Likewise," Neal replied. "Maybe another time."

"I hope so," the Captain said, saluting before he left.

A moment of awkward silence followed the Captain's departure, as the now openly identified Gloria Donaldson looked calmly out over the harbor and said, "I don't suppose there's much point in continuing this charade now that you've become aware of my true identity," she remarked, almost apologetically. "Betsy Parker is the want-to-be me. Tomorrow, unfortunately, or fortunately, depending on how you assess the situation, I'll become the real me again. I know this is all very confusing, but bear with me. I'm carrying a lot of baggage. You may want to rethink pursuing your curiosity, my friend."

Because her statement carried a sense of foreboding with it, Neal was almost tempted not to reveal what Dusty Lewis had told him. Her unexpected admission that she was living two different lives, however, forced him to ignore her friendly warning and reply, "I've been aware of who you really are for some time now, Gloria. But have hesitated to mention it for fear of jeopardizing whatever future relationship might develop between us. Now that that seems unlikely, given my eminent departure, who you are is of little consequence. For what it's worth, I like both of you. So, what name would you prefer I use if destiny should cross our paths again?"

"Lets play that one by ear," she replied, coyly. "I guess it all depends on whose territory I'm in at the time, yours or mine."

"Fair enough," Neal remarked. Glancing casually at his watch. "Don't you think we ought to be heading for the airport? It's almost time for your friend to leave."

Reluctantly, she agreed and fingered a number into her cell phone.

By the time they had finished their glass of wine and walked out of the restaurant, an over-sized, golf-cart-looking vehicle was waiting for them there. The driver was a handsome young man with wind-tossed blonde hair that capped his deeply tanned and smiling face. "Where to, Ms. Donaldson?" he asked, ushering them politely into the vehicle.

"The airport, Peter," she answered in a commanding voice. "This gentleman is hitching a ride back to Carlsbad with Jim Taylor, so don't dilly-dally along the way. Jim wants to leave before dark."

"No problem," Peter replied, respectfully. "We'll be there in plenty of time."

The road leading up to the airport was a winding one. From its crest it gave a travel brochure-like view of the entire Avalon Harbor, where a large cruise ship sat anchored and conspicuously out of place among the smaller sailboats moored closer to shore.

The picture revived memories of summer trips Neal and his friend, Ron Barns, had made to the island over the years to attend Dixieland Jazz Festivals in which their mutual friend Bud Winters and his band had participated. The band, humorously named *The Hyperion Outfall Serenaders*, derived its celebrated name from the Los Angeles sewage treatment system's offshore dumpsite, and was the source of much amusement to all who knew its origin.

Though the annual band competition at the Avalon Ballroom was entertaining, it paled in comparison to Saturday night's revelry in and outside bars all over the waterfront. The memory of those wild and overindulged-in days and nights soon faded, however, when Peter's cart arrived at the island's tiny airport. It was time for Neal to go home.

Shortly after the threesome arrived, another taxi cart pulled up with a single passenger who recognized Gloria immediately. Broadly grinning as he approached her, he said boisterously, "Hello, doll. How's my favorite hooker?"

"Never mind, smart ass," Gloria responded, calmly. "I'd like you to meet my good friend, Neal Thomas. He's the friend who needs a lift to Carlsbad. And, I certainly hope you show him more respect than you do me."

The man laughed good-naturedly, hugged her roughly, and then turned toward Neal, thrusting out his hand. "Pleased to meet you, Neal.

Jim Taylor's my name," he said, still smiling and holding Gloria in his arms. "How'd you ever get mixed up with this old broad?"

Neal couldn't contain his laughter any longer, especially while watching Gloria playfully struggling to free herself from his grasp. Shaking Jim's weather-beaten hand, Neal replied, "Likewise. I take it you two go back a long way."

"So far I'd have to shoot ya, if you knew," Jim replied in jest.

Finally breaking free, Gloria straightened her clothes and said, almost seriously, "Now that's enough, Jim Taylor. I think we can dispense with the history lesson. Besides, I have to get back to town."

Removing a business card from her purse, she placed it in Neal's shirt pocket and said, "Sorry our time together was cut short. But, I have a feeling we'll be seeing each other again in the not too distant future. Stay in touch, and don't pay any attention to what this character tells you. Despite his lack of chivalry, he's still a damn good pilot."

Thrusting her lips up against his in a parting gesture, Gloria kissed Neal hard on the mouth with a force and duration that left an unmistakable message: Till we meet again.

Turning and patting Taylor on the cheek, she said, affectionately, "Take good care of him, my friend. He's one of a kind."

Chapter 1

Back To The Future

The flight from Catalina Island took less than forty-five minutes in Jim Taylor's two-engine Cessna. Because of engine noise, conversation between the two men was limited until they landed at Palomar Airport in Carlsbad. Once on the ground, Jim taxied off the main runway and slowly turned the plane around near the terminal building so it was pointed back toward the main runway for takeoff.

It became obvious to Neal from Jim's demeanor that he was not going to waste much time in meaningless chatter, so he made ready to exit as soon as the plane came to a complete stop. After leaving the aircraft, Jim waited for Neal at the small baggage compartment door where he would unload Neal's bags. When Neal approached, he said, "Here's my business card. Give me a buzz sometime and we'll get together for lunch. There's a few things you should be aware of if you intend to pursue any kind of a relationship with Lady Donaldson."

Surprised by his remark, Neal took the card and shook Jim's hand, wishing for the first time that he had had more time to get to know the man. Something about him intrigued Neal, so he replied, "I'd like that very much, and thanks for the lift. I'll be in touch with you as soon as I get over this so-called vacation."

As Jim turned away to return to the cockpit, it suddenly dawned on Neal that he had neglected to give him a business card, so he shouted,

1

"Take this card with you in case you ever get back to my neck of the woods. I know a great place to eat at the marina. My treat."

Jim took the card, waving goodbye as he climbed back into the Cessna and buckled in. With a broad smile still gracing his weathered face, he gave Neal a friendly thumbs-up before slowly pushing the throttles forward, leaving Neal to hurry away from the propeller wind and head toward the terminal building. Before entering, he hesitated momentarily to watch Jim's departure, reminiscing about a day many years ago when he had taken off on his first solo flight in a small Ultra-Light airplane. At the time, it had been the biggest thrill of Neal's life, but one he could not continue to pursue in the midst of an impending divorce.

As Jim's plane left the runway and eventually faded from sight, Neal wondered about the strange set of circumstances that had brought them together, and the likelihood of their ever meeting again. *Only time could answer that question*, he thought, as he turned and entered the terminal building.

A short taxi ride later brought Neal to the front door of his beach-front home, tired and perplexed about how to face reality after chasing fantasies for almost a week. Had he known what was waiting for him inside, he might very well have thought, *to hell with it,* and escaped to a bar stool at the Village Pub. But his gut feeling made him accept the fact that the party was over. Resigned to accept whatever *Dame Fate* had in store, he put his bags down at the foot of the stairs and welcomed himself home.

Though glad to finally be there, the stale-air smell that invades a home when it has been closed up for several days hit him like a brick wall, so he hurried to open all the windows and doors. The inrush of fresh, ocean-scented air seemed to neutralize the odor almost immediately, quickly instilling the feeling of never having been away.

Knowing that his luggage was harboring a similar odor, he put all of his washables in the machine, sprinkled them liberally with detergent and activated the process. For whatever reason, the sound of the machine running, and the music he had turned on, gave him the feeling that, despite his return to the every-day routine of normal living, there was another adventure brewing out there in which he would soon become unavoidably involved – an adventure that would alter his life beyond the unimaginable.

I wonder when this merry-go-round is going to stop? Neal asked himself, as his footsteps led the way to a half-empty bottle of vodka that was beckoning him to celebrate his return to paradise. *Why not,* he decided, as he entered the kitchen, unaware that the light on his telephone answering machine was blinking.

Since he had already changed into shorts and a sport shirt, he slipped into an old pair of sandals and walked out to the bluff behind his house to witness the last remnants of a setting sun. For him, there was nothing left to ponder, other than whether or not to have another drink…or so he thought.

Returning to the kitchen, the blinking red light on his answering machine finally caught his eye. *Do I answer it now, or wait until tomorrow?* With some reluctance he pushed the *Play* button.

A soft feminine voice began to speak: "You have five messages… message one: Hi, Mr. Thomas. This is Jessica Sterling calling to inquire about the preliminary draft of our novel. My mother is also anxious to talk to you about a matter she prefers to discuss with you personally. So give us a call when you get this message. Thanks."

Jessica's message was all it took for Neal to remember that, although he had been chasing a moonbeam for several days, the cold wet hand of reality had just reminded him that he couldn't put a serious commitment on hold to suit his capricious lifestyle. Jotting down a quick memo as a reminder to call her in the morning, he deleted the message and proceeded to the next caller:

"Message two…Neal, this is Dusty Lewis. I have something important to tell you. Please call me as soon as possible."

After speculating for a moment about why Dusty wanted to talk to him, Neal concluded that it had to be related to the evidence Dan Hughes had asked Neal to give to the DEA before Dan and Donna Sanders fled the country. Making note of the call, he hit the *Delete* button and waited for the third message:

"Message three…Hi, Curly. This is Paula calling to let you know that poor old Franklin Potter died a few days ago. I will be in touch with you as soon as he has been put to rest. His lawyers have already contacted me about what he wanted done with the nursery. Hope you are well and happy. Talk to you soon."

Pausing briefly to sip his drink, Neal wondered how the old man's death would affect Paula's future. He smiled, certain that a dream was about to come true for a good-hearted woman he had shared his life with for almost ten years. No one deserved it more.

"Message four… Hi, Neal. *This is your sister, Carolyn. Just thought you'd be interested in knowing that I'm finally settled into my condo here in Florida, and would like to know if you'd be interested in coming to a family reunion to celebrate the event. Give me a call when you get this message and we'll talk about it. Love you."*

His sister's message came as welcome news. Having been aware for several months that she had been planning to relocate, he experienced a sense of relief knowing that she had finally sold her home and moved to the Sunshine State. Offhand, he thought there didn't appear to be anything that would prevent him from attending the reunion. With that thought in mind, he listened with renewed interest to the last message:

"Message five… Hello, Neal. *This is Janet, or Madame X, as you so lovingly put it. Since you're going to be in this area tomorrow, anyway, stop by for a drink. I have some disturbing news to tell you about my sister's husband, Walter. I hope you had a good time on your trip. See you tomorrow."*

Now what, he wondered, wishing he were someplace else. Frustrated by the fact that it was too late to respond to any of the five messages, he locked the doors, turned off the lights and wearily climbed the stairs to his empty bed thinking, *hopefully, things will look better in the morning.*

A restless night of tossing and turning, coupled with trying to figure out the substance of the five telephone messages he had received the previous day, Neal found himself tired and irritable when the dawn of another day began to illuminate his bedroom. It wasn't until he had shaved and taken a shower that his mind and body began to approach some degree of normalcy.

Following a hearty breakfast, mixed with several cups of strong coffee, he read the mail that had accumulated during his absence, most of which were bills and junk mail. One letter-sized envelope, however, was not from any one of those sources. It was conspicuous by the names on its return address: HENDERSON & HANCOCK, P.C.

Allen Henderson had been one of Neal's college roommates who had formed his own law firm in the greater Chicago area after graduating from college, and completing his tour of duty in the United States Navy. His only contact with Neal since college had been associated with Class Reunions, so it came as quite a surprise when he received an unsolicited letter from Allen after so many years of relative silence.

It came as an even greater surprise when he read that the purpose behind Allen's letter was to invite him to the annual gathering of the Sawmill Club, an elite, male members only organization located on a private lake in the tall timber country north of San Francisco. Since Allen's letter stated that he would contact Neal by phone to discuss the invitation in detail, he put it aside and concentrated on his first order of business – contacting Sterling Publishing Company.

Greeted by the familiar voice of the company's receptionist, Neal was put on hold for a moment, and pacified with canned music until Jessica Sterling came on the line. "Well, well, the wandering minstrel has finally returned," she remarked, almost sarcastically, "I hope you've used your time wisely, my friend. Otherwise, you have a lot of explaining to do."

"Not to worry, my dear," he replied reassuringly. "You and your mother meet me at Bully's in Del Mar this Friday at one o'clock. I'll deliver the completed first draft personally."

"I'm sure that can be arranged," she replied, with marked enthusiasm. "Hopefully, the luncheon crowd will have thinned out so we won't be rushed."

"Good," he answered, noting the time and place on his calendar. "Say hello to your mother for me."

"I will. She'll be pleased that you called."

Now, what the hell does Dusty Lewis want? Neal wondered with growing anxiety, as he punched in the DEA Office number.

Unlike the cool reception he had just gotten from Jessica Sterling, Dusty's receptionist, Ginger Spyce, greeted him with spirited enthusiasm. "Hi there, Mr. T. Sure is good hearing from you again. Let me get Mr. Lewis on the line. He's been waiting for you to call for days."

Moments later, Neal heard the click of Dusty's phone being picked up, and his gruff voice stammer, "Man, am I glad to hear from you. Where the hell have you been?"

"Chasing rainbows," Neal replied, sarcastically. "Now, what's all this urgency about?"

"I can't discuss it over the phone, but I need to talk to you as soon as possible," Dusty replied anxiously "Can you come to my office tomorrow morning around ten o'clock? It's urgent."

"What, not even a clue?" Neal asked, a little irritated by the cloak and dagger stigma Dusty was placing on the situation.

"Sorry, it's confidential," he replied. "You'll hear all about it tomorrow."

"Whatever you say," Neal remarked before hanging up. "I'll be there."

With no urgency associated with the calls he had received from the previous messages, Neal decided the rest of his day would be more productively spent reviewing the manuscript of his book so it would be as good as he could make it. Wondering what could be so important that Sandy would only discuss the matter with him, personally, Neal put his curiosity aside and went to work.

The clock on his computer screen read 3:15PM by the time Neal finished editing what he knew would only leave him a few hours to complete by Friday. Though there were those of his friends, and critics, who were skeptical about him ever completing a novel in the first place, it was with an intense feeling of pride and accomplishment that he clicked on the *File-Save* and *Print* commands. As the dozen or more pages of his day's work were methodically extruded from the printer, he looked wistfully around his studio and realized that his literary creativity seemed less dramatic without someone there to share it with. Determined not to let his progress go by unheralded, he shut down the computer and drove to his favorite watering hole to unwind.

Unlike most Mondays, the parking lot behind the Village Pub was unusually crowded. Smokers were gathered outside, chatting and joking with pretty young hair stylists from the salon next door, who took a break there between appointments.

Neal's arrival was met with enthusiasm and friendly gestures, as he made his way through the happy mix and into the crowded bar. What greeted him was a bumper crop of male and female revelers who had gathered to celebrate the bartender's birthday. Every seat was occupied, and the single aisle connecting the front and back doors was almost impassible by people lining the wall.

The bartender was an attractive woman in her late twenties. Her physical persona left little to the imagination, and was seductively enhanced by the bare flesh of her hips. Her belly button, in which a pea-size gemstone had been implanted, sparkled like a diamond in the rough. At times, her movements from one end of the bar to the other seemed to trigger nerve ends in the eyes of male customers, leaving little mystery as to what the brain behind those eyes were thinking. To be sure, every male in the place was infatuated with Anita Cassidy, and she knew it.

Though perpetually busy, and at times irritated by suggestive re-marks made by the more unsavory characters that frequented the place, Anita remained calm, cool and collected most of the time. Unlike the vast majority of her female predecessors, whose tenure generally lasted only as long as it took to find a job making more money, Anita was a lo-cal resident who lived alone in a small studio apartment over a two-story garage just a few blocks away, thus eliminating the expense of owning a car. And, as far as everyone in the place knew, she had no significant other, and had made it quite clear to some of the more aggressive males that she was in no way interested in having one. She was, as many of the patrons had summed her up, a woman of mystery.

It wasn't until a friend who was leaving asked Neal to take his place at the bar, that Anita became aware of his presence. Smiling, and shak-ing her head in dismay, she went to the draft beer station, filled a glass to the brim, and sat it down in front of him. "How long were you going to sit there before getting my attention," she asked, playfully scolding him. "You must not be very thirsty today."

"Au contraire, my dear," Neal replied, winking over the rim of his glass. "I understand today is your birthday. Cheers! I too have some-thing to celebrate this afternoon."

"Oh, and what are you celebrating?" she asked, raising her eyebrows in feigned surprise.

Before he could reply, the sound of a train passing through town attracted everyone's attention. Though a seemingly insignificant event, its loud whistle made it known to everyone that the Village Pub's famous *Train Beer* was now available for purchase. Pressed into action, Anita put her question on hold, rang the large brass bell that hung on the wall nearby, and took orders for the one dollar, paper-cup-size beer that was the Pub's hallmark. It took a few minutes to fill all the orders, but she managed. Returning to the sink in front of Neal to continue washing glasses, she inquired, "Now tell me, Mr. T., what are you celebrating today?"

Given the gradually mounting affect the beer was having on him, Neal fell victim to Anita's provocative attire, and the partially exposed breasts that hung like melons beneath her low cut blouse. Aware of his preoccupation with them, but flattered by his chivalrous attempt to hide it, she broke the spell and asked again, "And you are celebrating what?"

Recognizing her tactic, he smiled timidly and replied, "Well, for one thing, the sun came up this morning. Secondly, in four days I will be delivering the preliminary draft of my first novel to my publisher. Where it goes from there is anybody's guess. I'm just glad the writing will be over soon, so I can relax for a while."

"How exciting," she remarked, after rinsing the last glass and standing erect. "I had no idea you were writing a book. Why haven't you mentioned it before?"

"Well, to tell the truth, I never took the matter very seriously until my publisher commissioned me with a check not too long ago. Somehow, the smell of money, and an unexplainable urge to become a best-selling author, suddenly made it clear that those kinds of opportunities were too few and far between to be taken lightly."

Pausing briefly, he drank the remainder of his beer and pushed the empty glass across the bar to her. "One more for my fifteen minutes of fame," he said with a grin. "Then I better get out of here."

"Train beer or regular?" she asked, seemingly disappointed that he was not intending to stay until after her shift ended.

"What the hell," he sighed with uncertainty, "might as well make it a *Full Monty,* my dear. Nobody's waiting up for me."

"Pity," she replied humorously. "I hope you have a good book to read."

After she left the man next to him chuckled, and remarked, "I'd sure hate to be on her shit list, Mr. T. She doesn't look like she takes any prisoners."

Neal got a chuckle out of the man's remark, and replied, "Yeah, and I certainly don't intend to get captured."

They were both still laughing when Anita returned with Neal's glass filled almost to overflowing. Eyeing the two of them suspiciously, she remarked, "You guys are having way too much fun. It's my birthday, you know."

"Then get the hell out from behind the bar and enjoy it," Neal said, recognizing a familiar face coming in the front door. "Here comes your relief!"

Picking up the ten-dollar bill Neal had placed on the bar, she waved at the young man who had just entered. When she started to leave to get change, Neal said, "Keep it, honey. Happy Birthday!"

Surprised by his generous tip, she blew Neal a kiss and said, "Thanks! And please don't leave before I have a chance to talk to you...promise?"

Neal nodded affirmatively, wondering what in the world she could possibly want to discuss with him. *Oh well,* he thought, *what did it matter.*

While he continued to chat with the man next to him, Anita glanced at him, periodically, to monitor when his beer had approached the last-swallow level. When it did, she pushed her way through the crowded aisle as Neal was apparently getting ready to leave. "Oh no you don't, you sly old fox," she said, taking him by the arm. "I want to have a word with you before you go. Let's go out in the parking lot where there's not so much commotion."

Like a bad little boy being led to the principal's office, Neal obediently followed her outside, where she suddenly turned and confronted him. "Are you okay to drive?" she asked, in a quiet and genuinely concerned voice. "I don't want you on my conscience if you aren't."

Blinking with surprise, he replied, "And just what do you propose to do if I'm not?"

Her momentary silence, and the penetrating look in her deep blue eyes, brought home the message that she was genuinely concerned. Rather than play games with her sensitivity, he grasped her gently by the shoulders and said, "Thank you for your concern, my dear, but I'm fine. Though I still would like to know what you were going to do if I had responded differently...call the cops?"

Her face softened. Looking self-consciously away from him, she replied, "Not hardly. But I did have something in mind that I now think is best left to your imagination. Now, go home and think about it, while I go back in that zoo and act like I'm having a good time."

"Good advice." he admitted, "And again, Happy Birthday. I won't ask how old you are."

"I wouldn't tell you, even if you did," she said with a laugh, turning to walk back into the bar. "Some things are best kept a secret."

With that thought in mind, Neal got into his car and headed for home, more than willing to kick back and relax until bedtime. By the time he turned into the driveway, however, the thought of a hot soak in the Jacuzzi became more and more appealing. Stopping only to mix a drink, he removed his clothes, grabbed a beach towel and walked out onto the patio deck, never noticing that the red light on his telephone answering machine was blinking.

Though soothing, the hot swirling water that glowed in the moonlight like a giant searchlight only served to remind him of the evenings he used to spend waiting for his faithful companion, Paula Dillon, to return home from work and join him for what often times resulted in an impulsive, dinnerless interlude of intimacy. *Ah, yesterdays,* he remembered, *would they ever return?* Not likely, he concluded. Especially in light of what could happen if he should become a published author. What might that do to the carefree and uncomplicated life he enjoyed before Dan Hughes entered the picture? To avoid any further thoughts on the matter, he rose from the water. After toweling dry and putting his clothes back on, he returned inside, thinking, *I should get something to eat.*

Returning to the kitchen, he began making a sandwich. It was then that he became aware of the blinking light on his telephone answering machine. Looking at his watch, he reluctantly pushed the *Play* button and listened with amusement to the animated voice of his good friend,

John Pauly: "Hey Neal, this is John. Stop by tomorrow after you shoot pool with the boys. You won't believe what my two favorite daughters have cooked up for us. Trust me, you'll love it. See you tomorrow."

Smiling, he finished preparing his sandwich and sat down to watch television, wondering what kind of mischief John Pauly was going to spring on him the next day. His curiosity was cut short, however, when the eleven o'clock news commentator repeated a story from earlier that day that involved a DEA investigation into drug trafficking in Virginia's Tidewater Area.

Suddenly alert, Neal put his tray aside and watched with growing interest as DEA Director Raymond Bronson repeated what had been said on an earlier broadcast that day: "After further review of information relating to members of a suspected drug trafficking cartel operating in the Tidewater Area of Virginia, the DEA has come to the conclusion that the information was mostly circumstantial, and could not be used in court without verification by someone familiar with the information's source. Thus, our investigation has been temporarily put on hold until we can locate that person, or persons, to verify its authenticity. Any information you may have relating to this matter I can assure you will be held in strictest confidence. Thank you."

Stunned by the implications imbedded in Bronson's words, Neal slumped back in his chair and thought, *now I know why Dusty Lewis wants to talk to me.*

Though the urge to have another drink to help drown away the thought that Dan Hughes had knowingly dragged him back into the same situation he had just gotten out of, Neal decided against it. Putting his dishes in the sink, he turned out the lights and wandered upstairs, as if in a trance.

Oddly enough, considering everything else that had taken place that day, the last thought on his mind was the one Anita Cassidy had planted there only a few hours ago: *some things are best kept a secret.*

Chapter 2

Surprise, Surprise, Surprise

The morning after his brief but memorable participation in Anita Cassidy's birthday celebration found Neal Thomas sitting on the edge of his bed trying to remember the order of events that were to take place that day. First and foremost on the agenda was his ten o'clock meeting with Dusty Lewis. A flashback to the previous evening's television news broadcast sent a shiver up his spine trying to imagine how the consequences of that meeting could impact his relationship with Sterling Publishing, as well as other events taking place concurrently. Realizing that he was wasting valuable time trying to predict the future, he shaved, took a shower and dressed casually to deal with the other events that, to him, were just as important.

Because ten o'clock was only an hour away, Neal decided to eat on the run by getting a Breakfast Jack at MacDonald's rather than cook at home. Minutes later, a dark, brown-eyed Hispanic woman at the drive-in window handed him his order and wished him a pleasant day. He nodded and drove away, uneasy about what was waiting for him at the DEA office.

When he arrived almost an hour later, Dusty's receptionist, Ginger Spyce, greeted him less personally than she had on previous visits. Her demeanor, he observed, was somewhat overly professional. "What's the matter, aren't you glad to see me?" he said in jest, hoping for an unforced smile.

"Please take a seat, Mr. Thomas. I'll let Mr. Lewis know you're here," she replied, without making eye contact.

Neal went mute, realizing that she was either not feeling well, or something, or someone, had caused her to react that way. Deciding to *let the sleeping dog lie,* he excused himself and took a seat, wondering *what the hell is going on here?*

A few minutes later, the door to Dusty's office opened. With a noticeable lack of cordiality, he motioned for Neal to come in without offering to shake his hand. Once inside, he closed the door behind them and said, "Have a seat."

By this time Neal was becoming more and more irritated by the general lack of friendliness and decided to find out why. "What the hell's going on around here?" he finally blurted out, after taking a seat across the desk from Dusty's scowling face. "Did someone die around here?"

"That's what you're here to help us find out," Dusty replied sarcastically. "For your sake, let's just hope you're not an accomplice."

Neal sat back in his chair with an angry expression on his face, and replied, "You'd better explain yourself, Dusty. I don't like the way this conversation is going."

"Then let me put it this way. When one of my friends makes the head of the DEA look like an ass by giving him bogus information, ruining an investigation that took months to conduct, I think that friend owes me an explanation."

"What bogus information?" Neal asked, dumbfounded by the accusation.

Dusty sat silently for a moment nervously twiddling his thumbs. "Well, for starters," he continued, "that tool box Dan Hughes gave you to give to the DEA was supposed to contain irrefutable evidence that could be used to convict leaders of the Tidewater Drug Cartel. Guess what? None of it can be used in court, because all of it is circumstantial. Didn't you watch CNN yesterday?"

Helpless in the wake of what he should have suspected from the beginning, Neal slouched back in his chair, realizing that he might have been used. "When I got your telephone message the other day, I suspected it might have had something to do with Dan Hughes, but I put it out of my mind until I saw the news last night. What can I say? I've been duped."

Silence continued for the next few moments. It was Dusty who spoke first. "Don't beat yourself up over this, Neal. Realistically, all we can charge you with is poor judgment. We'd all be in jail, sooner or later, if that were a crime. However, there is an alternate approach to this situation that my boss is willing to consider, if you agree to locate Dan and convince him to testify for the DEA."

Like a gust of fresh air that had suddenly rushed in through an open window, Neal took a deep breath. For the first time since arriving there that morning, he began to relax. *How sweet the smell,* he thought. Rather than admit that he didn't have a clue about where Dan was, he stroked his chin and said, "Don't tell me the DEA hasn't already begun looking for Dan. I thought you guys could find a needle in a haystack?"

"We could, if we knew where the haystack was," Dusty remarked aggressively, "But we have good reason to believe he's left the country...at least for the time being."

"Well, I sure as hell don't know where he is, if that's what you're implying," Neal fired back.

During the few seconds of silence that followed, Neal's thoughts flashed back to the day when he returned from Virginia and discovered the tape Dan Hughes had mailed to him, along with the toolbox full of evidence and money that had accompanied it. To admit to having received the tape, he concluded, would automatically result in Dusty demanding that he turn the tape over to him. Which, in turn, could prove that Dan Hughes had given Neal a sizeable amount of money to act on his behalf. Reluctant to open that can of worms, he chose to remain silent in order to force Dusty to reveal what he wanted Neal to do about the dilemma.

Neal's unwillingness to voluntarily come forth with a solution to the delicate situation finally forced Dusty to lay his cards on the table. "What I'm asking is, that you use your influence with Dan's family, friends and associates to help us find out where the hell he is, and, most importantly, to encourage him to step forward and testify in court on behalf of the DEA. In exchange for that testimony, the DEA is prepared to offer him a full pardon for any past affiliation he may have had with that drug industry, providing he swears never, and I mean never, to have anything to do with that organization again. Violating such an oath, you understand, would nullify the pardon and put him behind bars for the rest of his life. Do I make myself clear?"

With everything else that was going on in his life at the time, Neal was reluctant to commit to anything that would jeopardize the completion of his book. To deny the DEA his help, on the other hand, was not a politically correct thing to do, given the circumstances. So, as a gesture of compromise, he replied, "Yes, I understand. Give me a few days to look into this matter on my own. I know a few people who may be able to shed some light on Dan's whereabouts. When I find out, one way or the other, I'll call you immediately. Fair enough?"

Dusty stood and offered his hand in a friendly gesture of acceptance, replying, "Fair enough. I'll be waiting for your call."

Passing through the outer office, Neal made no effort to communicate with anyone, especially Ginger Spyce. It wasn't until he approached the elevator and pushed the *Down* button that a voice behind him shouted, "Mr. Thomas!"

Turning around, he was surprised to see the shapely figure of Ginger Spyce walking quickly toward him. Looking up and down the hall in an apparent effort to assure their privacy, she said, "I didn't want to leave you with the impression that I was purposely avoiding talking to you. Since you were here last, surveillance cameras were installed in the office as a security measure. They have everyone a little nervous around here about acting in anything but a professional manner, especially between men and women. That's why I must have seemed a little impersonal when you entered the office. I just wanted to let you know that I'm sorry, and to thank you for returning all your expense money after you came back from your last trip to Virginia. Most people would have found some excuse to keep it."

Neal smiled, as he encircled her shoulders with one arm. "I'm sure glad you acted the way you did, my dear, because I had every intention of hugging you when I arrived. How would that have looked on camera?"

"You're so full of it, Mr. T," she giggled. "I wish I could accommodate you right now, but we're on *Candid Camera,* in case you haven't noticed."

Scanning the hallway ceiling, Neal observed that two cameras were strategically placed at both ends, providing full coverage of everything that went on. Whispering secretively, he said, "I guess that will have to wait."

Though brief, the humorous interlude had managed to calm the irritability Neal had been victimized with in Dusty's office. Looking at his watch, as he came out of the elevator at street level, he came to the conclusion that the day was still young enough to continue work on his book, make a few phone calls, and still make it to Ron Barns' house by mid-afternoon. Surprisingly energized by what was happening, he returned home with a variety of different thoughts churning around in his head like numbered balls in the State Lottery machine. *Things were happening.*

Back in Dusty Lewis' office, things were also happening. Ginger had returned to her desk satisfied that Mr. Thomas' confidence in her had been restored. Dusty's phone, she noticed, had remained busy from the time she left the office until she returned. Thinking it odd that the phone should be tied up that long, she flicked on the *Listen* switch to confirm that it was actually in use. She overheard Dusty Lewis' voice say, "He took the bait, Ray."

Speculating that her boss could only be talking to Raymond Bronson using those words, she shuddered and thought, *Oh my God. What are they up to?*

Back at home, after several hours of uninterrupted work, Neal rocked back in his chair, satisfied that his editing had considerably improved the remaining chapters of his book, and guaranteed that he would make his Friday deadline. With that pressure relieved, he decided to place a phone call to Henry Hughes to determine if Henry had seen or heard from Dan. After several rings, Henry's deeply accented southern drawl finally answered and expressed his genuine pleasure in hearing from Neal. "After what that crazy son of mine has put you through, I am truly surprised that you called me. What can I do for you?"

Masking the real reason for his call, Neal replied, "Believe it or not, I'm writing an adventure novel in which Dan's life plays a major roll. I was hoping you could tell me how to get in touch with him. I need his input to clarify some of the facts regarding certain events in his past. Have you any idea where he is?"

Immediately suspicious that there was more than just a casual interest in where his son was, Henry purposely muddied the water by answering, "Your guess is as good as mine. I haven't seen nor heard from him for several weeks. I suspect he may be hiding from the real world at his goofy timeshare property in Costa Rica."

"Does he have a phone there?" Neal asked, surprised by this strange turn of events. "I really do need to talk to him."

"Not that I know of," Henry replied. "He doesn't want to be bothered when he's down there. I suspect his place, wherever it is, goes back to the days when he was flying Marijuana all over Mexico and the Caribbean." Pausing a moment to take a swallow of what Neal suspected was a cocktail of some kind, he continued. "Or, he could be in Florida. His former wife and daughter live there."

"Can you give me their number?" he asked in desperation. "Maybe they know how to get in touch with him."

"Rather than call her," Henry cautioned, "let me give you the number of his best friend. He's a local boy and has known Dan since they were kids. If anyone knows where he is, it would be Cliff Bennett."

A moment or two passed while Henry looked up the number and gave it to Neal. "If Cliff is reluctant to help, tell him he'll have to answer to me. He owes me, big time."

"Thank you, Henry. I think both you and Dan will be pleased when I'm able to put all the facts together. In the meantime, stay in touch, especially if you hear from Dan before I make contact. It's imperative that I talk to him."

"I will," Henry assured him. "And thanks again for your concern."

As soon as Neal hung up the phone, he knew instinctively that Henry was privy to more than he was willing to share, however wise enough to put the monkey on someone else's back to avoid becoming overly involved. *What a sly old fox,* he thought, checking his watch. It was time to leave for Ron Barns' place. Scribbling down a reminder to call Cliff Bennett in the morning, Neal secured the house and left, hoping that locating Dan Hughes was now only one phone call away. Though optimistic, something in the way Henry Hughes had responded to Neal's inquiry seemed to convey the impression that locating Dan was not going to be that easy.

Putting the matter aside in favor of spending the afternoon with his friends, he took the usual exit off I-5 to pick up Joey Siegel, whose eyesight had gradually deteriorated over a six-month period, leaving him legally blind. Because of it, Neal had volunteered to pick him up every Tuesday afternoon as a token of their friendship, so Joey could continue to enjoy the company of his friends at least one day a week.

As usual, Joey had left the front door ajar. Pushing it open, as he was instructed to do, Neal entered, loudly announcing his arrival. Because of Joey's poor eyesight, Neal found him bent over his cluttered dining room table, intently looking at some document through a magnifying glass. The picture of him sitting there somehow reminded Neal of scenes from the television series, *Sherlock Holmes*, that he remembered watching as a boy.

Within easy reach was a bottle of vodka and an empty glass, which Joey filled with ice so Neal could join him for a drink before leaving to shoot pool. It was during that first drink that Joey shocked Neal with news that he had been diagnosed with cancer, and had elected to start chemotherapy the following week. Had it not been for the unemotional tone of Joey's voice, Neal might have over-reacted, but Joey cut him off by saying, "Hey, being bald doesn't bother me, but being bald and legally blind at the same time... that really pisses me off!"

When the hour finally dictated that they leave, Joey placed the empty glasses in the sink and remarked, "I guess we better get going before Ron starts wondering where the hell we are. Don't say anything to him about what I just told you. I'll tell him myself later on this afternoon. Okay?"

Neal nodded his concurrence and waited outside while Joey put a pint of vodka and a bottle of tonic mix in his booze bag. While they walked across the small parking area, Neal couldn't help but be amused by the cartoon-like character Joey seemed to impersonate. Khaki trousers covered bowed legs he had acquired through too many years of playing tennis on already damaged cartilage. An old cane dangled from his left hand, helping to steady his gait. An old golfer's cap topped it all off. Dark sunglasses shielded his failing eyes, helping to complete the picture of the celebrated cartoon character, *Mr. Magoo*.

In measures of time, it only took about fifteen minutes to complete the short freeway hop to Ron Barns' place, which was already playing host to a number of familiar, and not so familiar cars. For a Tuesday, there appeared to be more going on than just shooting pool. Mutually curious about what was taking place, Neal and Joey walked across the yard full of weeds to join the unexpected mix of merrymakers, all of whom Neal recognized immediately.

"Surprise," they all yelled in unison, as one by one they came forward to embrace the two latecomers, hugging them affectionately with wine bated breath.

Moments later, Jane Lennox, who at one time had been a colleague of both Neal and Ron Barns, put her arms around Neal's neck and kissed him full on the lips. "Go get a drink, Mr. T." she coaxed. "We've got a lot of catching up to do."

"Where's your husband?" Neal asked, surprised that she had come to San Diego alone.

"Pat's in Russia trying to help them develop safety guidelines for operating their Commercial Reactor Program," she replied. "I guess the Chernobyl incident convinced them that they really needed our expertise."

"That's a long way from home, girl. How long will he be gone?"

"Long enough to visit my sister before she moves to Hawaii," Jane answered, with a touch of melancholy. "I'll be leaving San Diego this coming weekend."

By the time Neal finished fixing his drink, Jane's longtime friend Janice Burrows had joined her and was whispering something in her ear. As Neal approached, she backed away and offered her arms in a hugging gesture that he was only too willing to accept.

"Are you two ladies going to shoot pool with us this afternoon?" he inquired. "Or are you planning some other mischievous activity?"

"Heavens no," Janice replied, quite emphatically. "Even if we were, we certainly wouldn't tell you guys. Right Jane?"

"Absolutely! What they don't know can't hurt them. Eat your heart out!"

While Neal continued his dialogue with the two ladies, Ron stripped the cover off his bumper pool table, and motioned for Joey to join him for a game. That invitation was all the two women needed to hurriedly bid the boys goodbye to pursue whatever feminine frivolity they had conjured up for their own amusement that evening. Bidding all the men a friendly goodbye, the two ladies left in their own cars, beeping their horns several times as they drove away.

Almost immediately following their departure, Johnny Holland and his bride of only a few months arrived to resume their weekly participation in the pool shooting competition. Following their recent return from several weeks on a cruise ship honeymoon in the Bahamas, they were eager to challenge the establishment. Noticeably tanned, and decked out in colorful matching shirts, they exploded onto the scene, laughing happily and carrying their signature bottle of red wine.

Once greetings were exchanged and the wine poured, the partner selection process began by turning over five numbered pennies. To his noisy delight, Ron Barns and Johnny's wife, Tina, ended up being partners, leaving Neal, Joey and Johnny as their opponents. Under normal circumstances, the competitors might have seemed somewhat one-sided, but Ron enjoyed the challenge of coaching Tina through almost every shot and expressed himself accordingly.

Despite the apparent one-sidedness of the match-up, Tina had developed a great deal of skill on her own during the relatively short period she had been playing. Thus, with Ron's watchful eye tracking her every move, the game score that day ended in a tie at two games each. Though it was getting late, Ron, heavily fortified by his canning-jar-size gin martini, insisted that they play out the rubber game. Reluctantly, everyone agreed.

Twenty minutes later, each team had one ball left on the table, with Joey and Tina competing for the win. It was Tina's turn to shoot, however, her ball was positioned in a corner about four inches off each cushion. A direct shot at the bumper-guarded hole, even for her partner, was very doubtful.

Joey's ball, on the other hand, lay protected by the center-table bumpers on the opposite side, making a defensive shot by Tina impossible. Though straight in from where his ball was positioned, Joey's failing eyesight posed a definite disadvantage.

With *what the hell do I do now* on her mind, Tina opted to shoot directly at the protected hole. It was then that Ron's voice rang out, "Tina, why not try Neal's favorite shot off the lead bumper."

Having seen Neal sink that same shot more times than not, Tina cringed and remarked, "Are you kidding? I've never done that."

"There's a first time for everything," Ron remarked, slurring his words slightly. "I'm going to put my finger on the bumper right where I want you to hit it. I'll line up your cue stick so all you have to do is shoot."

Tina hung her head and laughed, as Ron placed his finger on the rim of the bumper, at the same time coaching her right arm until the cue stick reached its critical angle. "Right there!" he shouted. "Medium speed."

Sighting on his finger, Tina slid the stick forward, struck the ball and watched it travel across the table. Unexpectedly, it struck the bumper exactly where Ron was still holding his finger, angled off in direct line with the hole and fell in. Her reaction was slow to express itself, almost as if she couldn't believe what she had done. Then it came. Her knees buckled as she arched backward, and her screeching voice yelled at the ceiling as if she were experiencing a giant orgasm, "Yes! Yes! Yes!"

"I'll be damned," Joey said quietly, scratching his head in bewilderment, while Tina's husband shook his head in disbelief, mumbling, "Hell of a shot, my dear."

About that time, Ron smugly remarked, "Looks like you've got some competition, with that shot, Mr. T. Now, what do you say we all go to Bully's and celebrate Tina's well-earned initiation into the now fragile world of what used to be called, a man's game. Looks like she's got balls, gentlemen."

"Excuse me," Tina replied, giggling at the rather inappropriate analogy.

"No offense intended, my dear," Ron replied, somewhat embarrassed. "I only meant to say that you've earned your place at our table. Sorry if I offended you."

"No offense taken," she replied, struggling not to laugh. "I just like being a woman."

Remembering that he had already promised his friend, John Pauly, that he would stop by on his way home, Neal finished his drink and asked Joey if he was ready to leave. Johnny Holland, however, interrupted and said, "Don't worry about Joey. We'll make sure he gets home safely. Besides, he says he'd like to go to Bully's too."

"Fine," Neal remarked, relieved not to be obligated. "Have a good time everyone, see you next week."

Outside, the afternoon sky over the ocean had already begun to turn yellow when the three cars pulled away from Ron's house. For an instant, as he approached the freeway on-ramp going north, Neal almost regretted not joining his friends. A more rational head prevailed, however, when he accepted the fact that even stopping at John Pauly's condo was an act of contradiction, let alone going to Bully's. Content that he had made the right decision, he continued onto the freeway and headed in that direction.

As was usually the case when he arrived, John was alone, watching television and talking on the telephone. Motioning for Neal to come in, he rose to greet him, after explaining to whomever he was talking to that an old friend had just arrived. An excuse he frequently used when he wanted to end a conversation. After he hung up, John welcomed him and began to explain the message he had left on Neal's answering machine. "While you were away doing your thing for the past several days, I received a phone call from my devil child, Linda. She wants you and me to fly up to Utah for a birthday celebration being organized by her best friend, Connie Davis. Her husband's turning fifty this month."

Neal scratched his head trying to put a face with the name, but couldn't. John gave him a reminder by saying, "You remember Connie. She's the gal who was all over you when you played the piano at Adolph's the first time we went there."

"Ah yes. Sweet Connie," Neal sighed, finally recalling the incident. "If only she weren't married."

"Well, she is," John reminded him, laughing at Neal's moonstruck expression. "But let's forget about that. Would you like to go?"

"When's her husband's birthday," Neal asked, as he considered the possibility.

"Not until the middle of next month. But Connie needs to know the body count right away, because she needs to get things squared away with the restaurant where the party's going to take place. She's going first class; live music, free beer and wine, buffet and plenty of unattached women, all the magic ingredients, so to speak."

Without taking into consideration the repercussions that might arise from his current effort to locate Dan Hughes, and the impending publication of his first novel, Neal replied, "Sure, why not? Tell her we'll be there. By then, I'll probably be ready to spread my wings and fly away from here. I can feel a serious case of cabin fever coming on."

"Fine. I'll call Linda tonight and have her tell Connie we'll be there with bells on," John remarked with a devilish grin. "I think this is just what the doctor ordered for the both of us; a welcome opportunity to get the hell out of Dodge!"

Two drinks later, Neal looked at his watch and decided it was time to head home, never anticipating how complex his life was going to become as soon as he got there.

Observing the wall clock as he walked into the kitchen, he realized it was too late to try to contact Cliff Bennett, but made a notation on the calendar to call him the next day. *All I can do is hope he's there,* he mumbled to himself, as he began preparing something to eat.

He hadn't progressed very far when the phone rang. Irritated by the interruption, his curiosity got the better of him so he picked up the receiver. The voice on the other end was the familiar voice of his former wife. "You can run but you can't hide," she said, sounding tired. "I hope you're sitting down. I have some rather unpleasant news to share with you."

"Don't tell me you're pregnant," he joked, certain she had been drinking and would enjoy the humor. "Go ahead, make my day."

Her laughter persisted for a few seconds, forcing her to dry her eyes before continuing. "At my age? Not hardly," she replied. "I talked to my sister today. She informed me, with understandable concern, that her ex-husband is going to sell his condominium out here, and wants you to take charge of shipping everything back to Virginia, including his SUV. Apparently, he's been diagnosed with prostate cancer and will be undergoing treatment very soon. How's that for brightening up your day."

Neal was stunned into silence for a few seconds. To ease the situation he called upon his sense of humor again, and replied, "Get in line, lady, I've been had by experts today. Moving Walter Douglas back to

Virginia is a piece of cake compared to what the DEA did to me this morning."

"Don't tell me you're getting involved with that crazy Dan Hughes again?" she asked. "He's been in some kind of trouble all his life. You'd better stay away from him before he drags you there."

Neal realized immediately, as he had during the final years before their divorce, that continuing to discuss the matter would only lead to angry words being exchanged between them, so he changed the subject, and said, "I'll call Walter to determine when and what he wants me to do. That way, nothing will fall in the crack."

Janet struggled to keep from giving her former husband advice that she knew from experience would only fall on deaf ears. Accepting the fact that he would handle the matter in his own way, regardless of anyone else's opinion, she replied sarcastically, "I'm sure you'll do it your way Mr. Know-it-all. Sweet dreams."

Following their brief conversation, Neal returned to preparing his dinner, poured a glass of milk and settled into his recliner to ease his thoughts away from the growing complexity of events that were beginning to threaten the lifestyle he had only recently begun to enjoy. Fed up with cop shows that seemed to have taken over evening television, he clicked onto the *History Channel*, where *Modern Marvels* was presenting a documentary on the construction and renovation of skyscrapers in various parts of the world. The history of the Chrysler Building's renovation was being presented when the phone rang again. Annoyed again by another interruption, he clicked on the *mute* button and went into the kitchen to answer it.

"Hey, Doofus. This is Allen Henderson calling," a friendly voice announced. "Did you receive my letter?"

"Yes I did," Neal replied, and then asked, "What the hell is this Sawmill Club all about. Never heard of the place."

Allen laughed, realizing that Neal hadn't the foggiest notion about what he was up to. "Do you remember that portrait you drew of me when we were roommates?"

"Yes I do," Neal replied, surprised that something that had happened so long ago was now resurfacing. "What's that got to do with anything?"

"Well, believe it or not, I still have it," Allen explained. "My wife, Kay, came across it when she was searching through a bunch of boxes we've had stored in our attic for years. She wants to have it framed so she can hang in our den."

"That would be nice," Neal remarked, still not sure what the portrait had to do with Allen's invitation. "I don't get the connection."

"I'm getting to that," Allen replied.

A moment of silence followed during which Neal overheard voices carrying on a conversation at Allen's end of the line. Seconds later, Allen resumed his explanation. "Finding that portrait reminded me of what a good friend you had been to me, and all our other roommates at the time. When I happened to mention the portrait to one of the club members the other day, he suggested that I bring you along to our annual meeting as my special guest. Are you interested?"

"When, and how long?" Neal asked, ever conscious of the growing number of commitments he was making.

"How does four days beginning one week from this coming Saturday sound to you," Allen replied. "Your only expense will be airfare to and from San Francisco, and Friday night in a reserved room at a nearby hotel. A chartered bus will meet you there the next morning, and drive you to the Sawmill Club site. Everything on site will be free. Now, tell me you're going to say no to that kind of a deal."

Having no legitimate reason for not accepting such a generous offer, Neal replied, "What, you think I'm crazy? Hell no I'm not going to turn it down. Thank you for inviting me. In my wildest imagination I never thought that portrait would bring us to this bend in the road. I'm really looking forward to seeing you again. It's been quite a while."

"Too long," Allen remarked. "I'll get the ball rolling at this end right away. You'll be receiving a schedule of events and other information in the mail around the first of next week. So go ahead and make your airline reservations right away. I'll be waiting for you at the Sawmill Club entrance when your bus arrives. Glad you can make it, my friend. You're going to have the time of your life."

"Can't wait," Neal replied enthusiastically. "I'm really looking forward to this."

The *History Channel* episode he had been watching when Allen called had ended during their conversation, and was now covering the

Japanese attack on Pearl Harbor during World War II. Having seen the documentary many times before, he turned the television off and concentrated on finishing his dinner.

With what he had had to drink that day, it didn't take long for his satisfied appetite to pull the lids down over his eyes, and end a day that had set the stage for the beginning of an adventure that would complicate his life beyond his wildest imagination.

Chapter 3

Voices From The Past

Early the next morning steadily falling rain coaxed Neal from the sleep he had hoped would give him the enthusiasm to continue working on the final pages of his book. Lingering effects of the previous days activity, however, had left him intellectually numb and physically tired. Not a good combination to fire up the creative juices necessary to complete the dramatic and page turning ending to a story he had worked so hard to perfect. Rationalizing that he was over reacting to a condition that pretty well typified most mornings, he decided things would look a whole lot better after a shower and something to eat.

As he dressed and busied around the kitchen, he could feel his energy gradually beginning to return. First order of business, he was reminded with some measure of curiosity, was to determine why Walter Douglas, had suddenly decided to sell his western retreat, a place he had been visiting twice a year when weather conditions in Virginia became less than desirable. Anxious to determine the specifics of this sudden change in routine, he placed a call to his home in Virginia.

After many rings without an answer, Neal expected Walter's message machine to kick in, but on the sixth ring someone on the other end picked up the receiver. The fragile voice of a woman said, "Hello. This is the Douglas residence. May I ask who is calling please?"

There's no mistaking that voice, Neal thought. "Is that you, Mary Jo?" he asked.

"Yes, Lord," she answered, immediately recognizing Neal's voice. "I am so glad you called. Walter has been trying to get a hold of you for days."

A moment later, a voice that Neal had become accustomed to hearing periodically over the years, said, "It's about time you called, you old fart. Where the hell have you been, out chasing some young chick?"

"I wish," Neal replied, "but she'd have to fall down for me to catch her. I don't think they have much to worry about from either of us."

Walter laughed weakly, then asked, "Did Janet finally get a hold of you?"

"Yeah, last night. She told me you were planning to sell your condo. Anything wrong?"

During the moment of silence that followed, Neal could hear muffled voices talking in the background that appeared to have distracted Walter. When he finally came back on line, his gradually weakening voice was barely audible. "Neal, old buddy, I've been diagnosed with prostate cancer and have been undergoing radiation therapy. For that reason, I doubt that I'll be traveling to California much anymore, so I need to ask you a favor."

Shocked by his admission, Neal stuttered, "I'll be glad to do anything I can, Walter. You know that. How long have you been undergoing treatment?"

"Shortly after I returned from my last trip out there," he replied. "Right now they've got me doped up with pain killers for my back. So before I lose it again, let's talk about what I'd like you to do for me."

"Go ahead, I'm listening."

"First of all, I've given all the furniture in the condo to a select group of friends and relatives back here. I'll let the rental agent out there know when the moving van is coming to get the stuff so she can let them in. That's one thing you won't have to worry about. When you notify me that my personal things have been shipped, and the place is empty, I'll contact the agent and tell her to have it cleaned, painted, and put on the market. Any questions?"

"Just one. How long do I have?"

"As long as it takes. I'm in no hurry," Walter replied, sounding more tired with each word he spoke. "I'll reimburse you for your time and expenses when the job's done. Fair enough?"

"I'll start as soon as I can, probably in the early evenings when I have time to kill. It will give me something to do besides falling asleep in my chair. Oh, by the way, what should I do about your van?"

Before Walter could answer his question, Mary Jo came on the line. "Sorry, Neal, he's fallen asleep again," she said. "Poor thing, they've got him so doped up he can't stay awake for very long. I'll have him get in touch with you when he's rested. If you need anything, give me a call at home. I'll make sure he gets the message."

"Thanks, Mary Jo. Ask him what he wants me to do with his van."

"I sure will. You take care now, and stay in touch."

Though the news of Walter's cancer came as a total shock, Neal took some consolation in the fact that Mary Jo was there to look after him. Walter's children, much as they loved their father, were very busy managing their own lives. Guardianship of his financial empire was handled by a brilliant attorney and dedicated friend that Walter had grown up with.

Because Walter was a millionaire several times over, he enjoyed the added advantage of being able to afford the very best medical care, which was carefully supervised by the local medical center's director, also a close friend. Though cancer would be considered a devastating and expensive illness to the average citizen, Walter had the means to fight it with a distinct advantage.

While he sat in the kitchen finishing his last cup of coffee, Neal began thinking about the many friends he had known over the years who had either died from some form of cancer, or were still alive and suffering with it. *How lucky I am,* he thought, as his ears picked up the sound of an airplane passing by overhead. It jolted him with a reminder that he had not yet ordered his tickets to San Francisco. Cursing for being so absent minded, he picked up the phone and spent the next few minutes making reservations that assured him of convenient departure and arrival times. Satisfied that the initial leg of his journey to the Sawmill Club was now under way, he proceeded to his studio to finalize the last chapter of his book. One thought nagged at him on the way; *How many shipping cartons will I need to accommodate all of Walter's personal belongings?* The answer was obvious – he had to look for himself.

Four hours later, blurry-eyed and tired, Neal let out a satisfying sigh of relief, as he saved the final chapter of his first full-length novel into the computer. After printing a hard copy to put with the rest of the manuscript, the feeling of relief was so overwhelmingly satisfying that he celebrated the achievement with a well-deserved drink. That, in turn, set the mood for contacting Cliff Bennett. If his timing was correct, he would find Cliff at home watching television.

Still wallowing in the pride of self-satisfaction, and a little buzz of self-inflicted reward, Neal dialed the number Henry Hughes had given him, anxious to put some finality to a situation that was becoming more complicated by the hour.

After four rings, Cliff Bennett's heavily accented southern drawl came online, and mumbled, "Yeah, this is Cliff."

It wasn't too much of a challenge for Neal to determine that Cliff was drunk. Rather than hang up and lose a rare opportunity to speak with him, Neal opted to take advantage of his condition, and said, "Cliff! This is Neal Thomas, Toni Lee Douglas' uncle from San Diego. I have an important question to ask you about Dan Hughes, so get your act together and pay attention to what I have to say."

"What's her mother's name?" Cliff shot back, rudely.

Realizing that Cliff was testing his identity, Neal replied, "Candy Douglas, and her father's name is Walter. Satisfied?"

"Sorry, Mr. T," Cliff replied. "You're the last person I ever expected to hear from tonight. I apologize, I've had a few."

"Sounds like it, but no offense taken," Neal replied. "Now listen carefully. Do you know where I can reach Dan Hughes?"

Again, silence followed. But Neal could hear a woman's angry voice talking in the background. Concerned that his question might have placed Cliff in an awkward situation, he said, "Cliff! Just say yes, or no. We can go from there."

Hesitantly, he replied, "Yes."

Sighing with relief, Neal asked, "Do you have someone there that you don't want to discuss this in front of?"

"Most definitely!" was Cliff's slurred reply.

"If I call you back in an hour, will you be alone?" Neal asked, desperate for some positive response.

"Afraid not," was the disappointing reply.

"How about tomorrow night about this time?" Neal suggested, with growing impatience. "You can't imagine how important this is. I have to talk to Dan!"

"Yeah, that would be okay," he replied. "At least I'll be sober."

Thank the Lord for small blessings Neal thought, as he questioned how reliable a man Cliff Bennett really was. "Don't let me down, Cliff." Neal continued. "There's a lot riding on this. I must get in touch with Dan."

"Call me. I'll be here."

Disappointed by having to wait another day to find out where Dan was hiding, Neal hung up, contemplating what to do with the rest of his day.

For the lack of anything other than yard work to occupy his time, he decided to drive by Walter Douglas' condominium to assess the magnitude of what he had agreed to do for him. The task would also give him a reason to drop in on John Pauly to discuss their future trip to Utah. And, as long as he was in the neighborhood, why not stop by his ex-wife's place. That would give him an opportunity to fill her in on what he was doing for her brother-in-law. Placing his empty glass in the sink, he secured the house and left.

Though he had no key of his own, Neal gained access to Walter's condominium by using one that Walter had hidden in the hot water heater compartment. It had been weeks since Neal had visited Walter's condo, and it smelled accordingly. Fortunately, opening the sliding doors to the balcony overlooking the swimming pool allowed an inrush of ocean air that freshened the inside almost immediately.

While evaluating what would be needed in the way of packaging containers, he was astonished by the inordinate amount of clothing Walter had accumulated in the few years he had been visiting there. *If you've got it, spend it* came to mind, as he opened and closed closets and drawers in every room in the place. Items that posed the biggest challenge were Walter's desktop computer and it's accessories. Scratching his head, he estimated he could scrounge enough odd boxes from Costco's supply of giveaways to properly package them. *What have I gotten myself into?* Neal thought, as he began searching through drawers and cabinets in the kitchen.

It came as no surprise when Neal witnessed the vast assortment of pots and pans Walter had accumulated, nor the equally large collection of dinnerware and accessories occupying all the overhead cabinets. The shocker came when he opened the bar and found a large assortment of every kind of booze imaginable. He shuddered at the thought of having to package them. Overwhelmed by the enormity of the overall task, he considered having a drink, but the unpleasant thought of having to spend every free moment of the next week there, soured any desire he had to remain. So, he locked up and left. All that made the whole ordeal worthwhile was the thought that he was helping a good friend who had more than enough to worry about. It was time to visit John Pauly.

Responding to footsteps climbing the outside stairway to his second floor condominium, John Pauly left the chair in which he had been watching television to greet his friend, Neal Thomas, as he reached the front door. "To what do I owe this unexpected visit?" John asked, surprised to see Neal. "Come on in, I'll buy you a drink."

Tired and frustrated, Neal helped himself to a double shot of vodka from an open bottle that John had already been nipping from. When they were comfortably settled in the living room, Neal answered John's earlier question. "I've just come from Walter's place. He's going to sell his condo and wants me to make arrangements to ship all of his stuff back to Virginia."

Surprised at Neal's reply, John asked, "What ever possessed him to do that? Is he sick or something?"

"I'm afraid so," Neal replied somberly. "He's just been diagnosed with cancer and is trying to get his estate in order. I suppose he's trying to prepare for any eventuality. Poor bastard, he didn't sound so good when I called him this morning. He was at home and heavily sedated. His lady friend, Mary Jo, was with him. Remember her? Tall and good looking."

"Yeah, I remember. A true southern belle, as I recall. How is she holding up under all this?"

"Better than anyone I suspect," Neal replied. "Walter fell asleep before I could ask him what he wanted me to do with his van. Mary Jo promised to remind him to call me when he felt better."

"Doesn't sound too good, does it?" John remarked, heading for the bar. "Want a roader?"

"Thanks, but no thanks," Neal replied. "I'm going to stop by Janet's to explain what Walter wants done with his things. I'll be in touch with you soon."

John accompanied Neal to the door and watched him descend the stairway. Half way down John called out after him, "My daughter said the crowd in Utah is really looking forward to us coming up for the birthday party celebration. They have something special planned for us. She wouldn't tell me what it was."

Neal turned and gave John a smiling thumbs-up, and replied, "Tell her I like surprises, as long as they're female "

As John watched Neal drive out of sight, he thought, *be careful what you wish for, my friend.*

Three blocks away Neal pulled up in front of the home he had purchased for his family over thirty years ago. There was a car parked in the driveway that he recognized immediately as belonging to his youngest daughter, Laura. *What a delightful surprise.*

As he walked through the entranceway, the bark of a butterscotch-colored Great Dane announced his arrival, as she ran to greet him with wagging tail and a toothy grin on her face. A moment after pressing the doorbell, Neal's former wife, Janet, arrived to let him in. Holding the big Dane back, she remarked jovially, "Well, this is one female who will always be glad to see you, Mr. T. What brings you back to the hen house?"

From the kitchen, the sound of his daughter's reprimanding voice shouted, "Mother!"

Neal laughed and grabbed the dog by the neck, scratching her roughly behind the ears. "I've just been up to Walter's condo trying to assess what it's going to take to get his belongings shipped back to Virginia." he replied. "I thought you might appreciate knowing what this move is all about."

Before he could explain further, Laura walked hurriedly from the kitchen and hugged him affectionately. After kissing him on the cheek, she turned and headed toward the front door, remarking, "I'm sorry I can't stay to chat with you, Daddy. I have to get home right away. Paul and I are going out to dinner. As usual, I'm running a little late. Love you! Bye Mom!" She was gone.

"Aren't you glad you're not that young again?" Janet remarked, as Neal walked over to the liquor cabinet and helped himself to a drink. "All that energy. I wish I could bottle it. I'd never have to pay another bill for the rest of my life."

While Janet poured a carefully measured Scotch and water, Neal looked pensively down at his drink and said, "Walter has cancer. That's why he's selling the condo."

"I know," she replied, unemotionally. "My sister called a few days ago and told me he was diagnosed with cancer and was undergoing treatment. I thought you'd want to know. That's why I called you yesterday. Looks like the devil's finally getting his due, doesn't it?"

Recognizing the condescending tone of her voice, Neal purposely avoided commenting on her remark, and said, "From what I just saw a little while ago, I'm going to need a lot of cardboard boxes to package what Walter wants shipped. I've got a few, but not nearly enough."

"There are some in the garage you can have," she mentioned. "A neighbor offered them to me when they moved into the neighborhood several months ago. They were too good to throw away, so I had my yardman put them up on the rafters, out of the way. They're yours if you can use them."

Hoping they might serve his purpose, Neal walked out into the garage and climbed a stepladder to have a look. Their size and strength far exceeded his expectations. Returning to the den, he told Janet that they were just what he was looking for. "You sure have made this job a whole lot easier," he said, "I'll pick them up when I come back to start packing. Okay?"

"Whenever," she replied. "Just call first to make sure I'm home. If I'm not, I'll put a spare key under the front door mat so you can let yourself in. And for goodness sake, don't let the dog out."

Neal helped himself to another drink, teasing the dog as she licked her chops for a taste of the cheese and crackers Janet had put on the table for Neal to snack on. Despite her warning against feeding the dog table food, Neal snuck her a cracker when Janet left to freshen her drink. The dog was delighted.

When Janet returned, Neal coaxed the dog away from the table and resumed conversation. "Mary Jo was with Walter when I called him to discuss the move. He sounded doped up, and fell asleep near the end of our conversation. Mary Jo said she would keep me informed of his progress."

"She will," Janet commented reassuringly. "She's a well-intentioned person, having known Walter all of his life. I'm glad she's there for him."

Neal looked at his watch and decided it was time to go home. All that could be done that day had been done. Thanking Janet for her hospitality, and especially the cardboard boxes, he patted the dog gently on her snoozing head and left, reassured that Walter's request could now be fulfilled more easily.

Traffic on the freeway was surprisingly light that evening, permitting Neal's thoughts to wander back in time to an event that had taken place many years ago. Another friend had asked Neal for a favor. One similar to the one Walter Douglas was now asking of him. Though it had been for an entirely different reason, the circumstances were just as emotional:

❖ ❖ ❖

Neal Thomas and his friend, Billy Newman, were sitting in Billy's den watching a football game between the Washington Redskins and the Baltimore Colts when the phone rang. Billy answered it. A moment later he handed the receiver to Neal, and whispered, "Robby."

"Hey, old buddy. Why aren't you over here watching the ball game with us?" Neal asked.

For the next minute or so, Billy kept one eye on the television and the other on Neal, watching Neal's normally happy face turn from a smile into a somber look of concern.

Seconds later, Neal handed the phone back to Billy, and said, "I've got to go. Robby needs to borrow my van."

"Can't it wait until after the game's over?" Billy asked, surprised that Neal would react so spontaneously. "What the hell is so pressing?"

While he gulped down the only drink he had had at Billy's, Neal tried to explain why he had to leave. "When Robby got home last night he found a note from his wife, Kitty, saying she no longer loved him, and was going back to her home town to try and sort things out. Not only that, she took everything they had with her, except for a few of Robby's personal things."

"That bitch!" Billy cried out. "I never did trust her."

"I've had my doubts too," Neal remarked, "but that's neither here nor there. He needs our help to get moved into his cousin's place until he finds another place to live. Poor bastard, she's really dumped on him!"

"Grab that bottle of vodka off the bar, and some mix," Billy said. "He's probably drunk up every thing he's got. I'll go with you and help, if I can."

"Thanks," Neal replied. "I think Robby's going to need it."

When they arrived at the small bungalow where Robby and Kitty had lived following their whirlwind courtship, and eventual marriage, they found Robby sitting alone on a stool in the kitchen, a near-empty bottle of booze on the floor beside him. His eyes were bloodshot and swollen from the tears that still hung in droplets from his chin, as he joked about his predicament. "Most of the furniture was hers, anyway," he said, pitifully drunk. "So I guess you could say I really haven't lost that much."

In less than an hour, with half the bottle of vodka they had brought with them gone, Neal and Billy put Robby in the van, along with what little he had accumulated over his brief marriage, and drove him to his cousin's house.

"He's really got a snoot full, ain't he?" the cousin remarked, as he helped Neal and Billy maneuver Robby into the house. "You can put the rest of his stuff in the living room. I'll sort it all out tomorrow after I pick up his car. Thanks for looking out for him. That bitch never really loved him."

Back at Billy's house, Neal remained in his van just long enough to make sure Billy made it safely into his house. When the lights came on, he honked the horn twice and left, wondering what kind of a greeting was waiting for him when he arrived home.

❖ ❖ ❖

The memory of what had befallen poor old Robby Sherman was still on Neal's mind when he pulled into his driveway. The truth of the matter was, Neal had been the person who had introduced Robby to his wife in the first place, making the eventual divorce even more regrettable. Rather than dwell on the unfortunate event, he decided to take a walk on the beach to cleanse away what was left of the guilt he had carried with him over the years. Removing the kitchen telephone remote from its receiver, he strolled out to the bluff and descended the beach access stairway.

He was returning from the lifeguard stand that marked his one-mile turn around point when the remote phone hanging from his belt sounded. Surprised, he pushed the *Send* button and said, "This is Neal."

"You mean Mr. T., don't you?" Dan Hughes' unexpected voice corrected from the other end. "I understand you've been questioning Cliff Bennett about my whereabouts. He said you wanted to talk to me about something very important. So, start talking."

"First off, where the hell are you?"

"I can't tell you that," Dan replied, "and neither can Cliff Bennett. What's so important that you had to bother him? He doesn't know anything but my cell phone number."

"Your father gave me his phone number. I suspect Henry doesn't want anything to do with whatever he thinks you're up to, so he put the monkey on Cliff's back."

"Probably," Dan remarked. "Now, what's so important that you went to all this trouble to talk to me personally?"

Struggling to find the appropriate words, Neal replied, "I've been contacted by the DEA, because the information you gave me to give to them is all circumstantial without your documented validation. Therefore, if you will agree to testify in front of a Grand Jury, my friend Dusty Lewis tells me the DEA is prepared to give you a full pardon, as compensation for your testimony."

From the prolonged silence that followed, Neal guessed Dan's brain was working overtime to weigh the acceptability of what had just been proposed to him. His response came with a laugh: "If you believe all the crap those crazy bastards have been feeding you, I've got some water-front property in Mexico I'll sell you real cheap. I wouldn't trust those characters any further than I could throw them."

"Is this the way you want to spend the rest of your life?" Neal fired back angrily. "What about your family and friends? And, what about me? You've put my ass in one hell of a crunch with the DEA."

"I'll tell you what, Mr. T," Dan remarked, after thinking over what Neal had said, "you bring me a signed affidavit from the DEA Director that the pardon is guaranteed, and I'll come back to testify, but only if you arrange it. And, absolutely no Feds are to be involved! That's a must!"

Neal's head snapped back. He was dumbfounded. "Why me for Christ's sake?" he asked angrily. "I can't provide you with any protection. I don't even own a gun!"

"No need to," Dan assured him. "I'll take care of all that. You just get the signed affidavit, and I'll make the necessary arrangements. When you have it in hand, call Cliff Bennett. He'll get the information to me. I'll call you as soon as I hear from Cliff and we'll proceed from there. Got it?"

"I guess," Neal replied, scratching his head. "You sure have an uncanny way of screwing up my life. Is this a lifetime ambition of yours?"

Neal could hear him laughing. "Imagine what life would be like if I had married one of your daughters," Dan answered. "So count your blessings."

"I am," Neal sighed. "There's just one more bit of information you should be aware of before we end this conversation."

"And that is..."

"I'm going to San Francisco for four days one week from this coming Saturday. I won't be able to travel until I return, so keep this in mind. I'll stall the DEA by telling them something they want to hear. In the meantime, please inform Cliff Bennett of my schedule so he'll make himself available when I return."

"No problem," Dan assured him. "I'm not going anywhere until I hear from Cliff, so do whatever it takes. We'll talk when you get back."

"Thanks," Neal replied, and ended the call.

The sun was almost down by the time Neal returned home. Hot and sweaty, he rinsed off under the hose, and soaked in the Jacuzzi until hunger pains told him it was time to eat.

While toweling himself dry, a thought about his meeting with the Sterling ladies the next day made him realize for the first time that he was entering a segment of society about which he knew virtually nothing. Hopefully, his time with the ladies would amount to little more than an informal turn over of his manuscript, a pleasant lunch and a few glasses of wine. *What could be less complicated than that?* he thought, never realizing what a complicated mess he was getting himself into.

)

Chapter 4

The Plot Thickens

Unlike most Southern California mornings he had wakened to in the past, Neal Thomas's eyes were quick to squint at the bright mix of early morning fog and sunlight that hung like a curtain outside his bedroom window. Un-accustomed to sleeping past sun-up, he stretched and sat up on the edge of his bed, glancing casually at the clock radio. It was almost 9:00 a.m. *I must have needed that sleep,* he thought, as he prepared to shave.

During the process, the memory of his conversation with Dan Hughes the previous evening reminded him to call Dusty Lewis to bring him up to date on what progress he had made locating Dan. *No matter what I tell him, he's not going to like it* he thought. Especially, after hearing the conditions Dan wanted met before re-entering the United Sates. Never the less, he felt he owed Dusty the courtesy of a call before meeting with the Sterling ladies that day, if for no other reason than to put the matter behind him.

While showering, a thought struck him: *What if Dan was right about not trusting anyone.* Neal had not considered the possibility that the DEA might have misled him with respect to the pardon they were prepared to offer Dan. That the DEA could find a way to renege on that promise, once they had Dan in their custody, suddenly shook his faith in the word *integrity.*

43

Minutes later when he entered the kitchen the phone rang. Hearing the voice of Ginger Spyce on the other end of the line almost took his breath away. Assuming that she was calling him from the DEA office, he said, "What a wonderful way to start the day. I truly am flattered."

"Let's just hope you feel that way after you've heard what I have to say," she remarked. "Are you alone?"

The question raised goose bumps on the back of his neck, prompting him to reply, "Of course. Why do you ask?"

"Relax, Mr. T. I'm not in my office," she replied. "I called in sick today so I could speak with you freely about something I think you should be made aware of."

"I'm listening."

"The other day when I said goodbye to you out by the elevators, I returned to my desk and found Mr. Lewis' phone light on. When it remained on for over a minute, I thought maybe Dusty hadn't put the receiver back on the cradle properly, so I listened in to see if they were still talking. What I overheard is the reason I'm calling you."

"You're starting to worry me, girl," Neal remarked. "What specifically did you hear?"

"The words, *he took the bait, Ray.*"

Suddenly, Neal felt as if the whole world had caved in on him. Not wishing to upset Ginger with an outburst of angry words, he held back and said, "Please, as a favor to me, forget you ever heard Dusty Lewis utter that statement. As far as I'm concerned, we never had this conversation. I'll swear to it in court, if that's what it comes to. Do you understand?"

"I could lose my job over this, Mr. T," she replied nervously. "but believe me, my lips are sealed."

"Good," he said, chuckling a little to lighten the mood. "Now, go see a movie or something. That's what sick leave is all about."

She laughed for the first time and said, "Thanks, I will."

Following Ginger's call, Neal sat for a moment trying to digest the implications in the statement she had overheard. No matter how hard he tried to disbelieve that Dusty Lewis would intentionally take part in a conspiracy against a friend, the reality of what was taking place created an upset feeling in his stomach that forced him to calm it with two antacid tablets.

After the nausea subsided, he placed a call to Cliff Bennett, fully anticipating that he would not be there. He wasn't. So, Neal left a message for him to contact Dan Hughes and tell him it was imperative that Dan get in touch with Neal that evening, no matter what time it was. Satisfied that he had done all that could be done, Neal turned off his cell phone and walked out on the bluff, breathing deeply until his head cleared.

Sometime later, considerably refreshed and eager to see Sandy and Jessica Sterling, Neal returned to the house, gathered up his manuscript and drove to Del Mar, leaving the grim business of Dan Hughes and the DEA behind him.

An attractive waitress he had known for years was serving Neal his first glass of wine when the Sterling ladies arrived. Rising to greet them, they each gave him a friendly embrace and took their place beside him in his favorite corner booth. Waiting until the ladies had been served their own choice of wine, Neal raised his glass and gave a toast: "I hope this day makes you both as happy as seeing you again makes me. To your health, wealth and prosperity."

"I'll drink to that," Sandy said. "Especially the part about wealth and prosperity."

"Roger that," Jessica added. "We are really looking forward to reading your manuscript, aren't we Mother?"

"Indeed we are," she replied.

Reaching down on the seat beside him, Neal came up with a thick, letter-size manila envelope and placed it in the middle of the table. "There it is, ladies," he announced with pride. "I hope your editor has a sense of humor and the patience of Job."

Before her mother could make an attempt to examine it, Jessica quickly moved the envelope over beside her and opened it. Withdrawing the manuscript, she flipped through several pages, grinning occasionally. When her curiosity had been satisfied she handed it to her mother and said, "This is going to be fun."

"Let's hope so," Sandy remarked, "We could use a best seller right about now."

Seconds later the waitress approached to take their order. "I don't know about you two ladies, but I'm starved," Neal said. "I didn't have any breakfast this morning!"

"That makes two of us," Sandy remarked supportively. "We can discuss the book later."

When the orders had been taken and the waitress left, Neal turned toward Sandy and said, "Jessica mentioned earlier that you wanted to discuss something with me in private. Is this an appropriate time?"

Knowing what that something was, Jessica said, "Excuse me, folks. I think it's time for me to powder my nose."

Now that she had Neal's undivided attention, Sandy looked around the restaurant briefly and said, "As the head of a successful publishing company, I occasionally meet people in the film industry who are continually searching for good story material. Based on what I remember hearing about your adventures when we first met, I believe this story of yours is exactly that kind of material. Would you be interested in exploring that possibility?"

With all that was happening in his life at the moment, Neal was reluctant to take on another commitment, but appreciated the wisdom in always protecting one's future by keeping the door to opportunity open, so he replied, "Why don't we wait until after you've read the entire story before moving in that direction. That way, I'll be sure you mean it."

Impressed by his clever diplomacy, and agreeing with its wisdom, she replied, "Mr. T, you've got a deal."

Moments later, Jessica returned. She eyed both Neal and her mother as if she were expecting one of them to tell her what they had been talking about during her absence. Contrary to the emotionally charged responce she expected, Sandy said, "We have our work cut out for us, my dear. By next week at this time, Neal is asking us to read his entire manuscript before committing to an opportunity I am trying to interest him in."

"I don't get it," Jessica replied with surprise. "Why should that involve me?"

"Because I want you to read the entire manuscript also," Sandy replied. "It goes to the logic that two heads are better than one. Wouldn't you agree?"

Before Jessica could respond, Neal interjected a comment of his own: "Actually, you might as well make that two weeks from now. I'm going to San Francisco at the end of next week and will be gone for five days. That should give both of you enough time to form an opinion about the future use of my story. After all, you have a sizeable investment in it already. Don't rush to judgment."

"He's right you know, Mom," Jessica remarked in support of Neal's logic. "We could even ask our chief editor to give us an unbiased critique. We are biased, you know."

"I'm afraid so," Sandy admitted. "We'll do it your way, and get back together with Neal in two weeks. That makes better sense."

An hour later, pleasantly full of Bully's Luncheon Special, Sandy and Jessica said goodbye, and returned to their offices in La Jolla to begin their individual analysis of Neal's manuscript, unaware of the complications that were about to beset their promising new author.

Despite Neal's effort to put the saga of Dan Hughes' impending return out of his mind, the phone call he had received from Ginger Spyce that morning still persisted. He now realized that Ginger's suspicion about a conspiracy being planned within the DEA to take Dan into custody when he showed himself was forcing Neal to address the question, *who is the DEA really after, Dan or the Cartel?*

With nothing else to do, except go home, Neal decided his time would be put to better use by picking up the packing boxes his ex-wife had offered him, and taking them over to Walter Douglas' condo. By doing so, the boxes would be readily available whenever he had time to pack Walter's belongings. As Janet had suggested, Neal called her on his cell phone to make sure she was there. A harried, "Yes, I'm here, but wish I wasn't," answered his question.

Minutes later, he pulled into Janet's driveway and found the garage door already open. After a brief conversation concerning Walter's condition, Neal stacked the boxes in his car and started to leave, when Janet said, "I'd invite you in for a drink, but I have to leave in a few minutes and won't be back until later on this evening."

"That's okay. I'm in a hurry too," he replied. "As soon as I get these boxes over to Walter's place, I'll be heading home."

Thanking her again, he drove the short distance to Walter's place and began planning how to pack them. Though most were sturdy enough to accommodate clothing and fragile things, there was still a need for a few more that were strong enough to ship the computer's hard drive, monitor, speakers, a Fax machine, and a printer.

Also needed was packing material such as newspapers, Styrofoam peanuts and tape, which he knew were readily available from a number of sources. Satisfied that he had, or could purchase, all that was needed to complete the task, he sat down to rest before leaving.

During that brief period he remembered how much of a packrat Joey Siegel was and decided to stop by his place to ask if he had saved any of the boxes his computer equipment had come in. Knowing how depressed Joey had become after being told he had cancer, Neal knew his visit would come as a welcome break from the almost sightless and painful world Joey now lived in.

Before leaving Walter's condominium, Neal made a quick check of the place to make sure it was secure. While doing so, he noticed that Walter had recently purchased what appeared to be a mobile chest of drawers. Upon closer inspection, however, it turned out to be a very expensive, two-piece, solid oak tool chest on wheels. Though the upper chest drawers were easily opened, the lower ones were held tightly closed by a vertical piece of wood that was key-locked to the cabinet frame. *How strange,* Neal thought, as he wondered what Walter had in there that was so valuable it had to be under lock and key. *Probably porno flicks,* Neal guessed with amusement, knowing what a womanizer Walter was.

Still smiling over the discovery, Neal locked the front door, placed the key back in its hiding place and left for Joey Siegel's apartment, ever hopeful that Joey's frugal nature would be Neal's bonanza.

Though slow to let him in, Joey was pleased to see Neal, and joked, "What are you doing here? Today's not Tuesday."

"Can't a fellow visit a friend when he wants to?" Neal replied. "Truth is, I'm thirsty, and need to ask you a question."

As they carefully made their way through Joey's living room, Joey remarked, "Giving you a drink is easy. What's the question?"

After Joey brought him a glass of ice and a bottle of tonic, Neal added a liberal shot of vodka from the bottle that was always sitting on the cluttered dining room table, and said, "Walter Douglas has decided to sell his condo. He wants me to take charge of shipping all of his belongings back to Virginia," he explained. "Do you have, or do you know where I can find, some boxes for shipping his computer equipment?"

"You're in luck, my friend," Joey answered. "The old grouch who just moved in next door threw all of his boxes in the dumpster. I picked out the good ones and put them in a storage locker that's only a few blocks from here. Take what you need."

"Not today," Neal replied. "How about next week before we shoot pool. I'll come a little early so you can take me there. Is that okay with you?"

"Sure, I'd be glad to."

Sometime later, just before Neal decided he should leave for home, Joey asked, "If you don't mind me asking, why is Walter Douglas selling his condo. I thought he loved it out here."

Realizing the sensitive nature of what he would have to tell Joey, Neal decided not to be totally candid, and replied, "When Walter had his deformed knee replaced, the straightening process put a terrible strain on his back, and he's been suffering with it ever since. That, and other complications, have left him pretty well dependant on medical care that he can only get back there. Traveling, he told me, was no longer an option, so he's straightening up the books, so to speak."

"Too bad," Joey remarked. "We sure had a lot of fun when he came to town. I'll miss him."

"Me too," Neal confessed, and said goodbye.

Though his visit with Joey had been pleasant and fruitful, the reminder that two of his closest friends were suffering the pain of predictable death left Neal with a sadness that made the journey home somewhat depressing. All he could think about was, *who's next?*

Being safely home, and as yet unaffected by the variety of maladies plaguing some of his friends and relatives, Neal sought solace in a vodka-flavored highball while he waited for the microwave oven to warm up a concoction of leftovers he had put together.

It was almost nine o'clock when he finished eating. Though he had entertained the thought of going directly to bed, the phone rang, putting that plan on hold for the time being. Remembering the message he had left on Cliff Bennett's answering machine earlier, he guessed that the person calling was Dan Hughes. He was right.

"What's up Mr. T?" Dan asked in his unmistakable southern drawl. "I didn't expect to hear from you so soon. Cliff Bennett said you left a message on his machine that said you had something very important to tell me."

Neal hesitated a moment trying to get his thoughts together, then said, "I got a call from someone inside the DEA this morning who told me something I think you should know before we start making any plans for your return."

"And that someone said…?"

"That she heard part of a telephone conversation between San Diego Agent, Dusty Lewis, and DEA Director, Raymond Bronson, which said, and I quote, he took the bait, Ray."

The prolonged silence that followed made Neal think that something had gone wrong with their connection, so he asked, "Dan! Are you still there?"

"Yeah, I'm still here," he replied in a grumpy voice. "I'm just trying to figure out why you keep referring to that someone person. Doesn't that someone have a name?"

"Yes, but I'm protecting it!"

"Think of it this way, Mr. T; having someone you trust inside the DEA could be very beneficial to both of us, and very financially rewarding to the someone you're protecting. As for me, I'm more worried about the Cartel than I am the DEA. I seem to be between that proverbial rock and a hard place."

"Yes, and guess who the guinea pig is?"

"Maybe. But let's take a hard look at what Agent Lewis meant by you taking the bait. Sounds like he's putting the monkey on your back to deliver my pardon, so the Cartel will be fooled into thinking that the DEA is planning to deliver it. Kind of a fake hand off, as you old jocks refer to it."

After considering Dan's logic for a moment, Neal asked, "Are you safe where you are for a while longer?"

"For the time being, yes," Dan replied. "But that won't last very long if someone like Miguel Ramirez finds out where I am. The tentacles on that octopus stretch a long way."

Convinced that any plan for Dan's safe return could not be formulated without a validated pardon in hand, Neal said, "I'm going to call Dusty Lewis Monday morning to determine the status of your pardon. If it's a done deal, then I believe I can get you back here safe and sound without anyone, including the DEA, knowing about it. In the meantime, just sit tight until I relay you a call through Cliff Bennett next week. Okay?"

"Seems like my options are pretty limited, Mr. T. I'll be here."

For just a little while before retiring that night, Neal sat in his living room listening to a CD recording by Jimmy Buffet, titled *Banana Wind*. The music sounded remarkably familiar to the music he could hear in the background from wherever Dan had placed his call. As he continued to listen, a smile came across his face, along with the self-satisfaction of figuring out where the call must have come from. Unmistakably, it had to have come from one of the Bahama Islands, a place where Dan had spent a major portion of his younger years transporting marijuana throughout that area, and up and down the southeastern coastline of the United States.

Logistically, the Bahamas were ideally located to provide Dan safe haven until his future was settled, and close enough to the American Coastline to return whenever the opportunity presented itself. He had planned his getaway well, Neal admitted, as he climbed the stairs to call it a day. *Lets hope his return goes as well.*

Before falling asleep, a question he had intended to ask Dan suddenly returned to taunt him: *was Donna Sanders, the woman Dan had rescued from the clutches of Miguel Ramirez, still with him?*

The answer to that question would have to wait. His mind no longer cared.

While eating breakfast the next morning, Neal considered for the first time in more than a week, that he had two days to spend any way he wanted. Mulling over his options, he decided that getting an early start on packaging Walter Douglas' personal belongings was a far wiser choice than anything else he could think of. Before he could set the plan in motion he was interrupted by a phone call from his sister, Carolyn Hynes. "Didn't you get my message?" she asked, sounding a little irritated.

Realizing that he hadn't responded to the phone message she had left while he was in Catalina, he replied, "Sorry, Sis, I completely forgot about it."

"That's okay, Bro." She replied. "When I didn't hear back from you for a couple of days I started worrying. You are okay, aren't you?"

"I'm fine," he replied, "but I am embarrassed for not returning your call. This is about our family reunion in Florida isn't it?"

"Yes," she replied. "I'm trying to get things organized to suit everyone's schedule, and it's a nightmare. So, I've decided to hell with it! I'm rescheduling for sometime in September, so don't change any plans. I'll let you know when I firm things up."

"This sure takes the squeeze off my schedule, Sis," Neal replied, relieved by the news. "I would sure hate to miss an opportunity to see you and Joel, no more than we see each other any more."

"Good. Go about your business, and I'll let you know when I have a firm date. Okay?"

"Sounds great, Carolyn. And thanks again for reminding me of what a great sister I have."

She laughed. "Yeah, and what a poor memory you have."

Though there was some disappointment in learning that the family reunion was being rescheduled, Neal felt relieved that he was no longer under pressure to make another commitment in the wake of those he had already made. Eager to get started on the first one, Neal called Joey Siegel to ask if he would mind getting the boxes needed that day, rather than waiting until Tuesday. Joey agreed.

Gathering together packaging tape and other supplies he had on hand, Neal drove to Joey's home and took him to the storage locker where the heavy-duty boxes he had promised were stored. In keeping with Joey's appraisal, the boxes were more than adequate to protect the delicate electronics of Walter's valued computer equipment. After returning Joey to his apartment, Neal thanked him for his generosity and proceeded on to Walter's condominium to begin work, confident that he could complete it in a minimum amount of time.

Because the computer equipment was fragile, and demanded the highest level of care in handling, he very methodically began disconnecting all the power cables and interconnecting wiring. Most were easily accessible on the floor underneath the corner-style equipment center. During the process, a small electrical shock caused him to jerk his head up and hit the underside of the center drawer. The blow was of sufficient force to dislodge a small key that had been hidden there. Surprised by the discovery, he picked up the key and stood up, examining it closely.

As he sat on the side of Walter's king-size bed rubbing his sore head and examining the key, he wondered why it had been hidden there. After trying all the desk locks without success, his peripheral vision was drawn to a lock bar attached to the mobile, two-piece tool cabinet he had admired on his first visit. Curious, he inserted the key and turned it. The lock opened. Removing the bar, he inspected every drawer. All but one contained an assortment of tools and other paraphernalia. The odd one contained a small, Zip-Loc bag containing a dirty green, tobacco-like substance, a fully loaded, 45-caliber automatic pistol, and a hinged wooden box. One whiff of the Zip-Loc bag contents confirmed that it was marijuana. Why Walter kept a loaded pistol in the place remained an unanswered question, until Neal lifted the lid on the box. Inside were bank records and investment statements that documented his multi-millionaire status. Photographs of a number of attractive, unidentified women, and several bundles of one hundred dollar bills, were also part of the contents.

Rationalizing that Walter had purchased the pot to ease the lower back pain he had suffered with for months, Neal couldn't help wondering who the supplier was. Reluctant to consider that it might have been Dan Hughes, he secured the cabinet and re-hid the key exactly where it had been hidden, content in the knowledge that it would soon be in a moving van on its way to Virginia.

It was late in the afternoon when Neal finished taping the last box of Walter's computer equipment. Commending himself on the progress he had made that day, he helped himself to a drink from Walter's liquor cabinet. Seeking the fresh open air of the living room balcony to enjoy a rapidly disappearing sun, he decided that a fitting end to his day would not be complete without having a beer at the Village Pub. Satisfied that his day had been well spent, he locked up the place and left.

Though he tried to dismiss it as he drove north along the Old Coast Highway, the thought of discovering Walter's stash of marijuana brought back a grim reminder of the only time he had actually been tempted to try it:

❖   ❖   ❖

After Neal and his wife had finally separated, he rented a bedroom in the home of a friend and colleague who had been divorced for a number of years. Unlike most divorcees, Todd Manning had been fortunate enough to win possession of the house as part of the settlement, and was glad for Neal's company.

As was true of most men who found themselves suddenly unshackled from the bonds of matrimony, Neal engaged in casual relationships with a number of single women he knew - and some he didn't - at local bars, dance clubs and odd places where singles gathered. At one such place he met an attractive, free-spirited brunette by the name of Bonny Sheldon who worked in a local real estate office, or so she said. After several failed attempts to contact her, he finally succeeded, failing to heed the old bromide that warned, *all that glitters is not gold.*

After being questioned by well-meaning friends about his newly found feminine interest, Neal was forced to address some of the questions they had been asking regarding Bonny's past and present history, all of which she cleverly managed to avoid. Overly naïve, and blinded by the sexual gratification she was only too eager to provide, Neal ignored the concerns of his friends until he received a phone call from her one day inviting him to join her for lunch.

"Where shall I meet you," he asked, delighted for a break in the routine of eating lunch at the company Cafeteria every day.

"I'm house sitting a friend's place in Del Mar," she explained. "I thought we could share a pizza."

"Fine." he replied. "How do I get there?"

After writing down the directions, Neal looked at his watch and decided to leave that instant. Smiling, he thought, *I haven't had a nooner in years. Might as well take the time to enjoy it.*

Following the directions Bonny had given him took Neal to a neighborhood not too far from homes of friends he had socialized with as a married family man. Being there gave him a feeling of uneasiness that lessened some of the excitement he had brought with him, and cautioned that he be alert to familiar faces. Fortunately, the address he was looking for turned out to be a condominium complex that had a small parking lot behind it that was partially hidden by tall, long established trees and shrubbery. Seeking their shade, he parked and walked hurriedly to the rear door of the unit where Bonny said she was staying. After two soft knocks the door opened, revealing the almost naked body of his luncheon date, Bonny Sheldon.

For an instant Neal stood frozen in place until Bonny grabbed his necktie and pulled him inside. "Whom did you expect to find, Grandma Moses?" she giggled. "I wanted to surprise you."

"You did," Neal gasped, as she grabbed both of his arms and pulled him into hers.

"Nobody's here but the two of us," she assured him, "so get comfortable while I pour us a glass of wine. Compliments of the owner."

"You do realize I have to go back to work, don't you?"

"One glass won't hurt you," she replied, pouting a little. "Besides, I want you relaxed for another little surprise I've been saving for you."

Not knowing quite what to expect, Neal stripped down to his shorts and sat down on the couch to wait for her to join him.

Moments later, she sat the two glasses of wine down on the coffee table in front of him and snuggled her warm body against his. After they had each consumed several swallows, Bonny removed the skimpy outfit she had on and began the quest for what she had invited him there for. He was powerless to resist.

After the passion subsided, Neal glanced anxiously at his watch. Bonnie pulled away, somewhat irritated by the gesture, and lit what Neal thought was a hand rolled cigarette. Having been a smoker himself for many years, he could tell by the way she inhaled and exhaled that it was not a cigarette. Several short puffs later, she handed him the butt, and said, "Go ahead, silly. It will relax you while I warm the pizza."

Reluctantly, in an attempt to rectify the untimely time check he had made, he took the nub and inhaled several times, holding each one several seconds to show her he knew what he was doing.

Minutes later, dressed in an almost transparent teddy, she returned with four pieces of hot pizza on a paper plate. Thinking he was waiting for the marijuana to kick in, she proceeded to eat a bite or two before looking up to check on him. What she saw made her choke on what she was chewing.

Made dizzy by overdoing what he had no business doing in the first place, Neal had attempted to walk off the dizziness, but staggered and fell motionless on the floor.

Alarmed, Bonny dropped her pizza and rushed over to help, but Neal reacted like a drunken person, awake but sloppy and unmanageable.

Desperate to revive him enough to get him dressed and out of the house, she started to apply plastic bags of crushed ice to the back of his neck. After several minutes, Neal finally shivered a little and rolled over with his eyes half-open. Relieved that he appeared to be recovering, Bonny sat back, covered her face with both hands and cried like a baby.

Conscious now, but still a little groggy, Neal reached up and fondled one of her breasts, and asked, "Why are you crying?"

Breaking away to get a napkin to wipe her eyes, she replied, "Because I thought you were dying, you big dummy!"

"Not quite," he remarked, realizing how much he must have scared her. "Give me a chance to get my sea legs back and I'll get out of here."

While she watched him slowly regain his equilibrium, as he put his clothes back on, she said apologetically, "I can't tell you how sorry I am about all this. Had I known you were a virgin I never would have encouraged you to try it. It takes time to build up a tolerance, which you obviously haven't acquired yet."

"And never intend to," Neal assured her. "That's one mistake I won't make again."

Putting on a lightweight bathrobe in an attempt to lend some dignity to what was fast becoming a very awkward situation, Bonny said, "That seems to have an air of finality to it, Mr. T. Will I ever see you again?"

By that time Neal was fully dressed and looking at his watch again. Taking her in his arms, he replied, "In all conscience, I can't blame you for my stupidity. I came by that naturally. Truth is, the company I work for has offered me an opportunity to work in North Carolina as a field engineer for several months, and I accepted. Truthfully, I need the extra money right now."

"Ah, the almighty dollar," Bonny remarked, sarcastically. "What would we do without it?"

"Remain in debt," Neal answered, reaching for his car keys. "And I'm tired of that."

Bonny pouted and opened the door. The goodbye was friendly, but hardly as warm as their meeting. Watching him walk away, she knew she would probably never see him again, so she yelled after him, "Thanks for the buggy ride!"

Without turning around, he waved and yelled back, "Thanks for lunch!"

❖ ❖ ❖

Entering the City of Carlsbad, the memory of that incident reinforced Neal's determination to visit the Village Pub, whose red neon sign beckoned in the distance as he turned the corner off Old Coast Highway. It had been a tiring day, and no one was at home worrying about whether he got there or not, so he headed for the parking lot, unaware of the life-altering surprise that was waiting for him.

The first thing he noticed when he entered the bar was an entirely different clientele. The after-work gang had arrived.

Having finished her shift, Anita Cassidy was sitting at the bar talking with two young women that looked vaguely familiar. One of them, who was facing Neal when he walked toward the only empty seat in the place, tapped Anita on the shoulder and pointed in his direction, giggling something he couldn't make out. Ignoring whatever the three apparent friends were up to, he ordered a beer from the friendly young male bartender he only knew as Wes.

As he sat waiting for his beer to arrive, Anita left her friends and limped toward Neal to say hello. "Aren't you a little out of your time zone, Mr. T?" she remarked. "You're usually a day-timer."

"I had some business to attend to down in Del Mar today, and decided a beer would taste good before I went home." Looking down at her bandaged ankle, he asked, "How'd you hurt your ankle?"

"I was trying to find out why the food in my refrigerator was spoiling, and slipped in a puddle of water that had dripped on the floor. Nothing serious, just a little sore."

"I know how that feels," Neal remarked, remembering his younger years playing football. "Did you mention the refrigerator to your landlord? He's responsible."

"No. He'd expect something in return," she answered, somewhat awkwardly. "I thought I'd ask one of the guys here to take a look at it."

"Wouldn't he expect the same?" Neal asked, looking suggestively over the top of his glasses.

"Yeah, I suppose. What's a poor girl to do?"

Hesitating a moment to let her sit down, he said, "May I make a suggestion?"

"Sure," she replied. "What did you have in mind?"

"Why don't you let me drive you home so you don't have to walk on that sore ankle." He suggested. "I had a similar problem with my refrigerator not too long ago, and fixed it myself, once I determined what the problem was. Maybe yours has the same one."

"Would you do that?" she asked, wide-eyed.

"Of course. Let's go take a look."

After saying goodbye to her friends, and listening to their silly innuendos, she followed Neal to his car and guided him to her small studio apartment. It was located over the garage of an ocean view apartment building that Neal recognized as one he had driven by for years on his way to the beach. *What a coincidence,* he though, never suspecting what he would discover inside.

Despite what he imagined the interior might look like – considering Bonny's generation and lifestyle – the rooms looked as if Martha Stewart might have had a hand in its decoration. Complimenting her on its cozy livability, he made his way to the small kitchen and opened the refrigerator's freezer compartment door. "My goodness!" he exclaimed. "No wonder your food is spoiling."

Curious, Bonny came over and looked in. "What's the problem," she asked.

Neal laughed, and explained, "The entire back of the freezer compartment is covered with ice, and has shut down the fan that feeds the lower compartment with cold air. That's your problem."

"Can you fix it?" she asked, hoping for a positive reply.

"I think so," he replied. "Do you have a hair dryer?"

Anita laughed, as if to say, *what a silly question to ask a woman.* "Of course I do, you ninny. Doesn't a hobby horse have a wooden asshole?"

"Then go get it," Neal laughed, wondering where she had heard that line.

While she was gone, he removed the frozen food and ice trays from the freezer, then took a short tour around the small apartment to examine a number of odd decorative items and framed photographs that had attracted his attention. When he got to the chest of drawers where her small television was sitting, a silver-framed photograph captured his eye, causing him to stop and stare as if he recognized something.

Assuming that Anita had had to use the toilet when she went to get her hair dryer, Neal picked up the frame and examined the picture closely. It was a color shot of a middle-age couple standing at the wheel of a fairly large sailboat. In the background the familiar structure of the San Francisco Bay Bridge loomed majestically. There was no mistaking the woman; she was Gloria Donaldson, alias Becky Parker.

When he heard the toilet flush, Neal quickly sat the picture back down and returned to the kitchen, anxious to hear what Anita would say when he questioned her about the photo.

"Sorry about the delay," she said, handing him the dryer. "I had to use the john."

"No problem," he laughed. "Can you get me a towel to soak up the water when I use this thing?"

"Sure can." Seconds later, she threw him one from a drawer, and asked, "Can I fix you a drink? I could sure use one."

"Got any vodka?" he asked, laying the towel down inside the freezer compartment and turning on the dryer.

Shaking her head and laughing, she said, "Like I said before, Mr. T. Has a…"

"I know, I know," he interrupted. "Got any tonic?"

"Got that covered too," she replied, pulling one from a six-pack in one of the cupboards. "Anything else?"

In minutes, melted ice was flowing freely down the back wall of the freezer compartment and onto the towel, exposing the circulator fan. As he suspected, it was not rotating. Rather than manually force it, Neal directed the hot air flow from the dryer directly onto the motor assembly until the fan shaft suddenly freed itself, and began spinning normally. "Bingo!" he shouted jubilantly. "Houston, we have ignition."

"Here's your drink, Einstein," Anita remarked, noticeable relieved. "You really have earned this one."

After taking a long swallow from what he didn't realize was a very strong drink, he grimaced and said, "I'm glad you don't serve those at the Pub. You'd have to provide ambulance service."

"You'll survive," she remarked. "Relax for a while. I'll clean up the mess."

Sitting down at a small table nearby, Neal watched her busily dry out the freezer compartment and replace its contents. The timing was right so he asked, "Whose the handsome couple on the sailboat?"

"Technically, they're my parents," she replied, un-emotionally. "My father died some time ago. Mother is just a bad memory, so let's just let it go at that."

"Fine." Neal remarked, realizing he had touched a tender spot. "I didn't mean to be nosey."

Turning away from the refrigerator, Anita tossed the wet towel she had been using into the sink and sat down at the table with him. "I don't mean to be a pain in the ass about the subject, Mr. T, but I'm carrying a lot of baggage when it comes to discussing my parents. Maybe I can share it with you someday. Right now, I just want to enjoy your company and say thanks for what you did for me tonight. I really do appreciate it."

Recognizing that he should go before an awkward situation developed, Neal checked the time and said, "Except for my three daughters, I seldom get the opportunity to come to the rescue of so lovely a young lady." Handing her his business card, he added: "If I can be of any help in the future, please don't hesitate to ask. Good night, and good luck."

"I'm impressed," she joked. "Come see me soon, Mr. Thomas. Beers are on me."

Lying in the semi-darkness of his moonlit bedroom, Neal thought about all of the personal involvement he seemed to be getting into almost on a daily basis. *When is this all going to end?* he silently asked.

An answer never came, nor would it. Sleep had put it on hold.

Chapter 5

Outfoxing The Fox

Having accomplished more than he had expected to over the weekend, Neal had every intention of spending most of the upcoming week packaging the remainder of Walter Douglas' personal belongings so it wouldn't conflict with his forthcoming trip to San Francisco. A calendar notation by the phone, however, reminded him of his promise to call Dusty Lewis at his DEA Office that morning. Although reluctant to do so, Neal placed the call because he had promised Dusty an update regarding the whereabouts of the elusive Dan Hughes. Complicating matters further was Dan's suggestion that Ginger Spyce might be tempted to act as a double agent, a suggestion that Neal knew could possibly come back to haunt him if she refused.

Several rings went unanswered before Ginger picked up the phone. After Neal identified himself, she whispered excitedly, "Man, am I glad to hear from you. I'd chat, but Agent Lewis has been pacing the floor waiting for you to call, so I'd better put you straight through to him. Sorry, we'll talk later."

Dusty came on like *Gangbusters*, "I hope you have something positive to tell me, Mr. T," he said with forced control. "Old man Bronson has been calling me night and day ever since I talked with you last. Did you locate Dan Hughes?"

"Not exactly," Neal replied evasively, "but I have talked with him."

"What do you mean, not exactly," Dusty barked back. "Are you playing games with me?"

"Not at all," Neal calmly replied. "Do you think Dan is dumb enough to reveal where he is without assurance that he's not going to be scooped up by the DEA as soon as he shows himself?"

"Have you mentioned the pardon?"

"Yes I have," Neal replied. "But what you don't realize, Dan is more afraid of the Cartel than he is of you guys."

"Hell! We'll provide him with all the protection he needs," Dusty said reassuringly.

"Yeah, like you provided the Kennedy brothers, Lee Harvey Oswald and Ronald Reagan?" Neal asked sarcastically. "Thanks, but no thanks."

"That was the FBI," Dusty countered angrily. Several seconds passed before Dusty asked, "What the hell does Dan Hughes want from us?"

"Something we can't discuss over the phone," Neal replied. "But I'll explain it to you tomorrow, if that's okay with you."

"Ten o'clock tomorrow morning?"

"That'll be fine."

Neal hung up and waited several minutes before placing another call to the DEA office. When Ginger answered, he said, "I have a ten o'clock appointment with Dusty tomorrow. Will you have lunch with me afterwards? Just say yes, or no."

"Yes."

"Good. We'll talk then,"

Tearing off a piece of paper from his note pad, Neal wrote down Cliff Bennett's phone number, placed it in his shirt pocket and walked hurriedly through the garage to his car, glad to be going someplace where he knew the phone wasn't going to ring.

It was a sunny day. Neal purposely avoided the freeway in favor of Old Coast Highway, so he could reminisce about the days when he and his friends used to Scuba-dive the many kelp beds along the way, and ogle the pretty young women who gathered there when he and his fellow divers emerged from the ocean. *Ah, to be young again*, he thought, turning inland toward the cluttered reality of Walter Douglas' soon to be vacated condominium.

While Neal waited for the balmy ocean breeze to replace the musty smell that had settled in overnight, Neal withdrew the notepaper that held Cliff Bennett's phone number and called him. Expecting a *no one's home* recording, he waited for it to end and left a message: "Cliff, this is Mr. T. Please call our mutual friend and tell him it's important that I talk to him before nine o'clock tomorrow morning, Pacific Coast Time. I repeat, this is very important."

For the rest of the afternoon, Neal worked tirelessly to pack and label all of the boxes that contained Walter's belongings. Based on what he had accomplished that day, he figured he could ship them by mid-week. At that point, he could tell Walter to send in the movers to pick up the furniture whenever it suited him.

As for what to do with Walter's van, Neal decided to postpone that responsibility until after he returned from San Francisco. Taking Walter's medical condition into account, he assumed Walter would not be permitted to drive for quite some time. To allow for the possibility that Cliff Bennett might have already contacted Dan Hughes, Neal drove immediately home in a hurried attempt to arrive before Dan called. He was in luck. For once, the red light on his message machine was not blinking when he entered the kitchen. Relieved, he mixed a tall drink, clipped the portable phone to his belt and walked out onto the bluff to watch the sun go down.

Only half of an orange sun was visible on the horizon. The surf was far calmer than he had ever witnessed. Beach walkers had stopped to view its splendor, frozen like stakes driven into the orange sand, their black shadows lying down behind them.

What an odd coincidence that the phone should pick that particular moment of splendor to shatter the beauty of it all. Dan Hughes had resurfaced once again.

"I just received Cliff's message," he remarked, sounding as if he had just been awakened. "What's up?"

"The ball's in your court, Danny Boy," Neal replied. "The DEA wants to know, and I quote, what the hell does Dan Hughes want from us?"

"Is that pardon they're offering me for real?" Dan asked. "I'm not going anywhere until I have it in writing."

"I'll make sure of that," Neal assured him. "I have a ten o'clock meeting with Agent Lewis tomorrow to discuss a plan for your return. After that meeting, I have a luncheon date with Lewis' secretary to test her willingness to act as an informant. If she rejects the proposal, then I'm afraid we'll have to fall back and re-group."

"Nonsense," Dan chuckled. "She's a woman isn't she?"

"What's that supposed to mean?"

"Come on now, Mr. T, how many women do you know that don't like money?"

"Not many?" Neal laughed. "Actually none!"

"So, tell your friend if she cooperates with us, she'll never have to work another day in her life. That's my promise to her."

Hesitating for a moment to think of a way he could avoid having to involve Ginger at all, Neal finally accepted the fact that Dan's safe return required her participation. "That's very generous of you, Dan," he said finally. "Assuming that she goes along with my proposal, and I receive an official pardon for you tomorrow, I need the following information before I can proceed."

"Fire away," Dan remarked. "I'm not in a position to argue with the only person I can trust."

"Is Donna Sanders there with you?"

"No!" he replied, most emphatically. "She jumped ship as soon as we were far enough away from Virginia for her to feel safe. I gave her enough money to go wherever she wanted to. I haven't seen nor heard from her since."

"Good! That's one problem we don't have to worry about. Now, where the hell are you. I know you're somewhere in the Bahamas, so don't try to bullshit me."

"Damn!" Dan exclaimed. "How'd you figure that out?"

Neal laughed, and replied, "Well for one thing, I heard Calypso music in the background the last time we talked. Two and two puts you back on an island where you still have friends…right?"

"Bet you can't tell me which one," Dan challenged.

"Doesn't matter. You're not going to be there long enough for me to give a damn. Is your boat there?"

"Sure is." Dan replied. "I wouldn't go anywhere without her. She's the only woman I know who can keep her mouth shut."

"Roger that!" Neal laughed. "Now, what's your damn cell phone number? This business of having to rely on Cliff Bennett every time I need to talk to you takes too much time."

Reluctantly, Dan gave Neal his new number, explaining that his father had worked a deal with their service provider to have Dan's calls billed against Henry's real estate business until Dan returned to the States permanently.

"I figured your father knew more about your whereabouts than he was willing to admit when he told me to contact Cliff Bennett," Neal remarked. "He was protecting you."

"Yes he was," Dan admitted openly. "I just hope I live long enough to make things right between us, though I surely don't deserve it."

"You'll get your chance," Neal assured him. "Here's what I have in mind…"

By now the sun had disappeared and Neal's glass was empty, so he left the bluff and walked quickly back toward his house, asking Dan along the way, "Wherever you are, can you pick up and leave whenever I ask you to?"

"Yes, but I'll need at least a few days notice," Dan replied. "When and where do you want me to go?"

"I have to leave town for a few days," Neal answered. "I will contact you as soon as I return. After I have lunch with Agent Lewis' secretary tomorrow, I'll know whether or not I can rely on her to keep me informed on what the DEA is up to. In the meantime, sit tight and don't breathe a word about this to anyone, especially Cliff Bennett and your father. Understood?"

"Loud and clear," Dan replied.

When their conversation ended, Neal couldn't help thinking about the interrelated incidents that were slowly drawing him into a situation in which he could easily become a victim. His only consolation was that in a few days his burdensome responsibility to Walter Douglas would be over. That thought alone prompted him to seek the soothing comfort of his Jacuzzi for a little while before getting something to eat. It was there, with only another drink to keep him company that he drifted into a state of melancholy, which he begrudgingly attributed to not having had an intimate relationship with a woman since his brief rendezvous with Gloria Donaldson on Catalina Island. That in turn gave rise to a spasm of wishful thinking that he might meet her again during his trip to San Francisco. That such a coincidence had any chance of happening caused him to snicker, "In your dreams, stupid."

Sometime later, refreshed and casually dressed for the evening, Neal descended the stairway from his bedroom looking forward to a bite to eat while watching television. He had no sooner removed several items from the refrigerator when the phone rang. Tempted to ignore its bothersome ringing, yet concerned that the call might relate to his current activities, he picked it up.

"Hi, Curly!" an excited voice greeted him. "Guess who?"

Neal stood speechless for a moment, completely surprised at hearing the voice of his dear friend, Paula Dillon. "Well, well, if it isn't my favorite Tootsie!" Neal replied in humorous recognition. "I was thinking about you just a little while ago."

"You were in the Jacuzzi, weren't you," she teased.

"As a matter of fact…"

"Yeah, I know," she giggled. "Spare me the details."

What a breath of fresh air Neal thought, as he asked, "How are you?"

"Compared to what?" she answered, sounding frustrated. "Between old man Potter dying, running his nursery twelve hours a day, and fighting lawyers over what he left me, I haven't had much of a life until just recently."

"Oh, what happened?"

Hesitating a moment to catch her breath, she replied, "Yesterday I signed the last piece of paper that made the nursery legally mine. Franklin Potter held true to his word and left it to me in his will."

"Congratulations," Neal said enthusiastically. "How's your family reacting to all this?"

"I'm not sure," she answered. "On the one hand, they are thrilled about my good fortune and financial security. On the other, they fear I will eventually want to move into a place of my own."

"That sounds reasonable," Neal commented, "Why would they object to that?"

"Because they've all become used to my being there," she replied, sounding frustrated. "And, I'm available in the evening to look after the girls when they want to do something socially. Plus, they've provided me with a free place to live. That's the bottom line."

"Makes sense to me. At least you'll have someone to come home to."

"Which gets to the real reason I called," she said, coyly.

"And that is…?"

"Mike wants to take Ellen and the girls on a cruise to Mexico next week before the school year starts," Paula explained. "I was wondering if you and I could get together for dinner some evening while they're away. You could spend the night and take a tour of the nursery with me the next day."

"When?" he replied, fearful that his trip to San Francisco would deny him the opportunity to see her again.

"They will be gone for a week beginning the middle of next week," she replied. "Can you come up on the Saturday of that weekend?"

Looking at the calendar where he had marked his travel days to and from San Francisco, he grinned and replied, "Yes I can. What time?"

"Seven o'clock. I should be back from the nursery by then. I'll call you the night before to confirm it."

"Good," Neal replied enthusiastically. "But don't try to call me before then because I'll be out of town visiting an old college roommate for a few days."

"I understand," she said, with a touch of skepticism. "Doing the guy thing, I suppose."

Following their conversation, Neal fixed a drink and contentedly went about preparing his dinner. He felt more relaxed than he had for days, and enjoyed the elevated mood that Paula's invitation had left him with. The thought that his previously perceived feelings of being tired, and at times irritable, had its origin in a need for sexual gratification was now confirmed. It pleased him immeasurably to think that a woman could be equally as affected, and take the initiative to satisfy those cravings. It had been a long time for both of them, he remembered with some remorse. But the promise of resurrecting their mutual lust for one another put a smile on his face. As he stretched out in bed not long thereafter, the smile lingered for a while, but soon disappeared as his eyes closed and darkened him into a deep, undisturbed sleep.

When he awakened the next morning, a lazy glance at his bedside clock signaled a reminder that in three hours he would be entering Dusty Lewis' office to initiate a series of events that would change the course of his life from that day on.

Following a much-needed shave and an invigorating shower, Neal dressed appropriately for his meeting with Dusty Lewis, and prepared a light breakfast to tide him over until his luncheon date with Ginger Spyce. As he drank his coffee and glanced haphazardly through the morning paper, certain words and subtle phrases kept side tracking his concentration, prompting him to toss the tabloid aside. It was time to leave.

With no way of anticipating what questions would be asked when he arrived at Dusty's office that morning, Neal concentrated on developing a plan he had contrived while showering that morning; a plan that Dan Hughes had unwittingly given him when he acknowledged that he still had his boat, and Donna Sanders was no longer with him. Her absence simplified matters considerably, because now Neal only had Dan to contend with, and not the emotional upheaval and unpredictability that Donna represented. As he approached the door to the DEA office, a calm feeling of having total command over the situation suddenly came over him. Bolstered with self-confidence, he opened the door and entered.

Ginger Spyce's eyes peering over the top of her nose-riding glasses was the first picture that greeted him. A faint smile showed itself, but only for a moment. Recognizing that she was under the scrutiny of security cameras, Neal formally introduced himself and asked to see Agent Lewis.

Moments later, the door to Dusty's office opened and he came out to greet Neal looking seriously troubled about something. Hesitant to ask any questions in the presence of others in the room, Neal accepted Dusty's hand cordially and followed him back into his office.

Rather than confront Neal from behind his desk, Dusty walked to a window that overlooked the city and waited there for Neal to open up a dialogue. Finally frustrated by Neal's reluctance to do so, Dusty asked, "Have you heard from Dan Hughes yet?"

"Yes I have, but he still refuses to identify his specific location for what he thinks are obvious reasons."

"Obvious to whom?' Dusty snapped back, almost angrily. "How can we protect him if he won't tell us where he is?"

Neal shook his head in silent disbelief that his friend of many years could be that naïve. "Your protection could get him killed, for God's sake," Neal replied, becoming more emotionally charged. "Putting your men anywhere near Dan would be like painting a target on his back for every Cartel hit-man to take a potshot at. That's what Dan's afraid of, not you guys."

Before Dusty could respond, Neal added: "That pardon you're offering isn't going to do him much good if he gets killed trying to use it."

"Does he have a better idea," Dusty asked, "or is this where you come into play?"

Dusty's question opened the door that Neal had been looking for since their conversation began. Seizing the opportunity, he said, "Give me a copy of that signed pardon and I'll explain what I believe will satisfy both Dan and the DEA."

With a stern look on his face, Dusty walked over to his desk and handed Neal a sealed manila envelope, remarking, "Now, let's hear this plan of yours."

Satisfied with the envelope's content and authenticity, Neal slipped it immediately into his briefcase. After setting the lock, he turned toward Dusty and said, "You're too young to remember this song, but there's a line in it that says, '*do nothing till you hear it from me.*' That pretty well sums it up, my friend. I'll be in touch."

"Not so fast, Mr. T." Dusty remarked, as Neal attempted to leave. "I believe that line ends with the words, '*and you never will*.' That's totally unacceptable."

"Touche," Neal replied, in a more friendly tone. "You surprise me."

Sitting back down, Neal continued: "I'm going on vacation for a few days beginning this weekend. I'll be returning the middle of next week. At that time, I will tell you in more detail where and how Dan will present his testimony to the Congressional Committee investigating this case. I can assure you it will contain enough information to bring formal charges against all key members of the Tidewater Drug Cartel. Their lawyers will have no other recourse than to comply."

Dusty held his eyes fixed on the man he had admired from the very first time he met him, and said, "I've never known you to overstate your case, Mr. T., so here's my hand. I'll keep the departmental wolves at bay until I hear from you. God help you if you don't live up to your word."

"Not a chance," Neal replied, as he shook Dusty's hand and left his office.

Deep in thought, he almost passed by Ginger Spyce's desk when her voice called out to him, "Would you please fill in the sign-out register, Mr. Thomas. It's a new office policy. Sorry."

Neal grinned and obliged her, unaware that the reminder was Ginger's way of delaying him long enough to slip a note into his hand. Crumpling the paper as he filled in the data, he casually stuffed it into his pocket, shook her hand, and left with only a courteous goodbye. Once seated in the privacy of his car, he retrieved the wrinkled note and read its message: *The café at Balboa Park – one hour.*

Pleased that all indications thus far were favorable for gaining Ginger's willingness to participate in his undercover plan, Neal left and drove to the park. It was now eleven a.m. Aware that it had been years since he visited the area, he walked leisurely through several of the museums, content to be alone and gaze in awe at the beautiful paintings and artifacts that were exhibited there, ever conscious of the time that was passing. When his watch finally reached 11:45 a.m., he decided it was time to leave.

Somewhat disappointed, he knew he could not afford to delay his rendezvous with Ginger Spyce a moment longer. Ever mindful of its importance in terms of how it would benefit his plans for Dan Hughes, he left the museums and walked to the café in time to sip a glass of wine while he waited. His glass was only half-empty when Ginger walked into the café and spotted him sitting at the bar.

"Why did I know you'd be sitting in here?" she remarked, in good humor. "I'd join you, but I only have time to eat something and head back to work." Taking Neal by the arm, she said, "Shall we?"

While walking behind her through an area of the Café that Ginger was obviously familiar with, Neal recognized a certain similarity in the movement of her body that reminded him of Vicki Daniels walking up the aisle during his flight to Washington's Dulles Airport weeks ago. He was still grinning when they sat down opposite one another at an out-side patio table. Having seen him eyeing her backside via a large window they had passed to get there, she asked, "Did you enjoy the view?"

Neal couldn't help being amused, and replied, "As a matter of fact, I did. You remind me of an airline stewardess I once knew."

During the laughter that followed, a waitress arrived to take their order. When she left, Ginger took the initiative and said, "Agent Lewis placed a call to our home office right after you left today. I don't know what was said because he placed the call on his hot line, which by defi-nition means it was highly classified. I suspect it had something to do with your visit. Is that why you've asked me to lunch?"

She's good Neal thought, as he shifted nervously in his chair. "I guess I might as well spread the cards on the table where you can see them," he replied. "All I ask is that you do not tell anyone what we discuss here today. Is that understood?"

"It was before you asked," she answered calmly. "I didn't think we were here to discuss the weather."

"Good," he said, still not sure that she would be receptive to what he was about to propose. "In order for Dan Hughes to testify against the infamous Tidewater Drug Cartel, he has demanded a Presidential Pardon, which Agent Lewis gave me in his office today. However, the pardon is of little value if the DEA is setting him up to be taken into custody as soon as he shows his face."

"I think I know where this is going," Ginger remarked, "but do continue. I want to know the whole story, not just the first chapter."

Before Neal could continue, the waitress arrived with their orders, filled Neal's wine glass and left. Reinforced by Ginger's outspoken curi-osity, Neal continued: "Actually, its not the DEA Dan is worried about, it's the Cartel. If they get wind of his return, he's a dead man, and Dan knows that. But I have a plan that will give the DEA what they want, without having to worry about some crazy hit man killing Dan."

Ginger looked across the table, her eyes glistening with woman's intuition, and asked, "What do you want me to do, Mr. T?"

Choosing his words carefully, Neal replied, "Just keep me informed about any surveillance activity that your boss and Director Bronson might use to track me, and especially Dan Hughes."

"I could wind up losing my job, and even be prosecuted," Ginger remarked while eyeing her watch. "The DEA doesn't take it lightly when an employee turns snitch."

"I'll deny under oath that you were ever involved, if that becomes an issue," Neal replied. "That's a promise."

"You've made a lot of those recently, haven't you," Ginger commented, as she stood up to leave. "I hope you're not over extending yourself. A promise made may not always be a promise kept. But I will watch your back. That I can promise."

"Thanks," Neal said, placing a fifty-dollar bill on the table.

Outside, where they had more privacy, Neal said, "Dan Hughes wanted me to let you know that your help in this matter will not go un-rewarded. If nothing else, he is a man of his word."

"Let's hope he lives to keep it." Ginger replied, pessimistically, "I've heard that song before."

As Neal made a move in the direction of the parking lot, Ginger stopped and cautioned him not to follow her. "Just to be on the safe side, let's leave separately. Being seen together, especially under these circumstances, would only arouse suspicion if the wrong person were to see us. So, thanks for lunch and good luck with your plan. I'll watch your back as best I can."

"And I'll watch yours," Neal joked, "There's no mistaking that identity."

Shaking her head with amusement, Ginger disappeared into the parking lot wondering what she had gotten herself into.

Neal, on the other hand, was jubilant. He had gained an ally that was in an excellent position to warn him in advance if anyone threatened to jeopardize the plan he was now prepared to initiate on Dan Hughes' behalf. Encouraged by how well things were working out, he decided to spend the rest of the day packaging the last boxes of Walter Douglas's personal belongings and arrange to have them all shipped.

By five o'clock that afternoon the last carton was taped and addressed. The task was finished. Neal was enjoying a well-earned drink on the balcony when he heard a door close inside. Curious, he walked back inside to see who had come in and saw the attractive sales and rental agent, Pamela Andrews, standing there.

"I saw your car parked behind Walter's van and figured you were up here, so I thought I'd drop in and see how you were getting along. Judging from the looks of things, and all these boxes, I'd say you're done."

"Yup," Neal replied, confirming her observation. "Shipping is all that's left."

"Well, I guess this is where your job ends and mine begins," she sighed.

"Your job?" Neal said with noticeable surprise. "I thought Walter was expecting me to arrange for that."

"You were," she continued, "that is until Mr. Douglas' lady friend called this morning and told me to relieve you of that burden. That's why I'm here."

Thank you, thank you, Mary Jo. "Her generosity comes at a very opportune time," Neal remarked. "I'm going on vacation soon, and can certainly use the extra time to get ready. Glad you stopped by."

"Me too," Pamela said excitedly, "Now I can start getting it ready to sell. There's a waiting list for these places, you know."

"I'm well aware of that," Neal replied, checked the time. "Now, if you'll excuse me, I have other business to attend to. It's been a pleasure seeing you again. I hope you prosper from all this."

"Oh, I will," she remarked confidently.

While Pamela began to survey the place for work that still needed to be done, Neal said goodbye, gathered his materials and left, overjoyed that his commitment to Walter Douglas had finally been fulfilled. All that remained to be done that day was to ask Ron Barns if he could drive Neal to the airport on Saturday, a request Ron had yet to deny him during all the years they had been friends.

When Neal pulled up in front of his house, Ron was watering his avocado trees and hollered for Neal to go inside. Since unexpected visits were a common occurrence there, Neal went in, fixed a drink and watched one of the several televisions that were all on different programming until Ron appeared in the doorway.

"You showing up here at this time of day makes me think you're up to no good, my friend. What is it this time, something female?"

Neal laughed and replied, "I wish. Truth is, I need a ride to the airport Saturday afternoon. I'd like to leave my car here, if that's okay with you."

"No problem," Ron answered, undisturbed by Neal's request. "Where are you off to this time."

Rather than violate whatever code of privacy might apply to the Sawmill Club's location, Neal simply said, "I've been invited to join some of my college roommates in San Francisco for a few days. I will be returning at one-thirty next Tuesday afternoon in time to shoot some pool. Can you pick me up?"

"Of course," Ron replied. "I was afraid you were going to tell me you couldn't make the game. Now you can tell us all about your trip."

Relieved, Neal finished his drink, thanked Ron and left, anxious to return home to call Dan Hughes and fill him in on what went down during his meeting with Dusty Lewis and Ginger Spyce .

Finally, things are beginning to fall into place he thought, as he drove onto the freeway, and began thinking about how to get Dan Hughes safely back into the United States.

It took him all the way home to reach the conclusion that the only foolproof way to give the DEA what they wanted, and still not jeopardize Dan's safety, was to find a place where he could secretly film Dan answering specific questions put to him by a certified DEA representative. *But who and where* was the question. As he strolled toward the sea bluff behind his house, the gray silhouette of Catalina Island hit him like a bolt of lightning. "What better place." he chuckled out loud. "Dusty Lewis, I'm going to make you a hero!"

Convinced without question that he had *outfoxed the fox*, Neal hurried back to the house where he placed a call to Dan's cell phone. Hopefully, the time difference between California and the Bahamas would catch him partying on the beach, or in some swinging bar where the likelihood of being overheard by threatening types would be unlikely. His hunch was right. Several rings later Dan came on line. "Yeah, this is Dan."

"This is Mr. T., Dan. Can you talk freely?"

Dan didn't reply immediately, almost as if he were seeking out privacy. "You caught me in a compromising situation," he finally admitted. "I had to come out on the beach where we couldn't be heard. What's up?"

"Have you been drinking?" Neal asked. "What I have to tell you is very important to both of us, so pay attention."

"I've had a couple of pops, but not enough to mess up my head," Dan assured him. "What's so important?"

"First of all, I picked up a copy of your pardon in a meeting with Dusty Lewis this morning. Secondly, I had lunch with his secretary following that meeting. The bottom line is, she doesn't trust them any more than you or I do. For that reason, she's willing to advise me of any deviation from what we now assume to be only your protective custody during the congressional hearings."

"Bullshit!" Dan cursed loudly. "I'm not going anywhere with those bastards, let alone a congressional committee "

"Hold on," Neal interrupted. "Let me explain."

"I'm listening."

Calming himself, Neal continued: "The DEA is planning a media leak as a diversionary tactic to sidetrack the Cartel into thinking you are actually going to testify before a congressional committee. While the Cartel is busy trying to track you down back there, you're going to be filmed live at a remote location here on the West Coast. Your testimony will only address questions scripted by the DEA about details pertaining to that evidence you gave me to give to them. You won't have to deal with anyone but one DEA agent who just happens to be a friend of mine. All I have to do now is tell him that you have agreed to this proposal and we can get on with it. So…?"

Having no good reason to contest Neal's proposal, Dan asked, "When does this plan of yours go down?"

"As soon as I get back from San Francisco next week," Neal told him, "but I've got some important things for you to do while I'm gone."

"I thought you might," Dan remarked. "How can I help?"

Caught up in the excitement of the adventure that was unfolding, Neal asked, "Do you know two people who you would trust enough to return your boat to the Back Bay Marina in Virginia when I give you the word?"

"Why not let me do it?" Dan replied. "I'm the owner."

"Because you'll be on your way to California. Can you slip away from where you are right now without attracting too much attention?"

"Have you forgotten who you're talking to, Mr. T," Dan answered. "At one point in time I did that for a living, if you'll recall?"

Amused by Dan's smug reply, Neal remarked, "Yeah, let's just hope you haven't lost your touch. It could be costly."

"Not a chance," Dan replied with gutsy self-confidence. "You just let me know when and where to go and I'll be there."

"Good. Don't breathe a word about this to anyone. I'll call you when I have the when and where figured out. I have to run this past the DEA, but they're hardly in a position to give me a hard time, all things considered."

"Don't take anything for granted, and watch your back," Dan countered. "I wouldn't trust them with a mentally retarded goat!"

"That's why we have Ginger Spyce on the payroll," Neal remarked in closing. "And keep your cell phone with you at all times."

Following Dan's somewhat less than enthusiastic acceptance of Neal's proposal, Neal settled back in his chair and concentrated on his next priority. With the whole of his plan hinging on the DEA's list of evidence-related questions, he decided to put that burden of responsibility on Dusty Lewis' shoulders. Anticipating how slow the process would be, Neal figured he would be back from San Francisco before Dusty could get it completed and approved, so he called him.

Several rings later, Ginger Spyce's voice greeted him in a business-like manner and transferred him directly to Agent Lewis. "I hope you have something of redeeming value to tell me, Neal," Dusty said rather dryly. "Ironically, I just got off the phone with Ray Bronson. He was anything but polite when he asked me what progress I had made toward locating Dan Hughes."

All to well, Neal remembered what a crusty old curmudgeon Bronson had been when their paths first crossed early on in the original quest for Dan's whereabouts. "Well, tell him this," Neal replied, rather arrogantly: "What happens next depends entirely on how willing he is to follow my lead."

"Would you mind telling me exactly what that is?" Dusty asked sarcastically. "I'm not a mind reader, you know."

Realizing that Dusty was probably on Ray Bronson's shit list, Neal began to explain his plan: "Dan was not all that relieved when I told him that I had his pardon. His main concern is still the Cartel's hit men, so I came up with this idea: First, you and Bronson are going to draft a list of questions that Dan would normally be asked if he were to testify before a Congressional Investigating Committee regarding the toolbox full of questionable evidence I gave you. Secondly, when that list is complete and in your hands, I will have you taken to a remote location where you and Dan will be filmed asking and answering those questions. Both of you will be taken to this remote location separately to avoid any chance of Dan's entrapment by either the Cartel or the DEA. Any questions so far?"

Dusty strained to contain his anger, and asked, "Do you think Ray Bronson is crazy enough to present the President of the United States with such an outrageous plan? What the hell were you drinking when you dreamed this up?"

"Stone cold sober, my friend," Neal replied seriously. "You know I never mix business with pleasure."

"If you say so," Dusty remarked sarcastically. "Now, tell me, where the hell is Dan Hughes?"

"I don't know." Neal answered, truthfully. "Somewhere in the Bahamas, I think. But I get the feeling from talking to him that he won't be there long. He likes my plan. In fact, he told me to tell you and Bronson that it's the only one he'll go along with, if you want his testimony."

"Damn it!" Dusty cursed. "Let me see what I can do. I'd subpoena your ass, but you have me over a barrel. When are you getting back from San Francisco?"

"Next Wednesday."

"Call me the next day," Dusty said in closing. "Hopefully, I will have some clear direction by then."

"I will," he replied, confident that he had successfully implanted the diversionary tactic his call to Dusty was supposed to have accomplished.

Tired and thirsty, Neal mixed a drink and walked out on his bluff to enjoy the setting sun with one thought on his mind: *It's time to get the hell out of Dodge.*

Chapter 6

Strangers In The Night

The day after telephoning Dusty Lewis regarding his proposal to film Dan Hughes' testimony, Neal lingered in bed trying to remember if he had overlooked anything that would interfere with his invitational trip to the Sawmill Club. As he struggled with getting out of bed, the phone rang. Ironically, it was his host, Allen Henderson.

"Good morning, Doofus," he said, more cheerfully than that time of the morning warranted. "Are your bags packed?"

"Hell, I've got to get out of bed first. Do you know what time it is out here?"

"Don't get out of bed on my account," Allen laughed. "I just wanted to make sure you knew which hotel to go to when you arrive in San Francisco."

"As a matter of fact, no," Neal replied. "I've been expecting you to call with that information. I've already made my airline reservations. I get into San Francisco International Airport around three o'clock in the afternoon."

"Good. Take a taxi to Little Bohemia. It's an artsy community not too far from the airport. You can relax there, meet a bunch of interesting people and eat some outstanding food. There's a popular Bed and Breakfast place there called Emma's Loft where I've booked you a reservation. A limousine will pick you up the next morning at eight o'clock sharp, and drive you to the Sawmill Club. Got all that?"

"Yes, I wrote it all down," Neal assured him, "Once again, I want to thank you for inviting me. You can't imagine how much I'm looking forward to getting away from this place for a few days."

"Glad you could make it. I'll see you tomorrow."

Following his usual shave and shower routine, Neal spent his time preparing a light breakfast and reading the paper. He was in the process of cleaning up when he heard the doorbell ring. Surprised by having visitors at such an early hour, he went to the front door. It was Dusty Lewis looking nervous and agitated.

Oh, oh, Neal thought, opening the screen door to let him in. "Aren't you a little off the beaten track this morning, my friend?" Neal asked, a little un-nerved by Dusty's unannounced arrival. "Your the last person on the planet I expected to see this early in the morning. Am I in some kind of trouble?"

"Not yet, but you could be."

Jumping to the conclusion that his lunch date with Ginger Spyce might have been witnessed, Neal asked, "Are you going to tell me why you're here, or are we going to play twenty questions?"

"Relax! I'm here to discuss that filmed interview idea you've dreamed up to exonerate Dan Hughes. Don't ask me why, but Ray Bronson thinks it's a good idea. He has directed me to assist you in any way I can, making it very clear, however, that it was not to be discussed with anyone, especially those in our office. That's why Bronson told me to come here unannounced to personally to tell you this. Absolute secrecy has to be maintained."

For the first time in his dealings with the DEA, Neal felt that he had gained the degree of respect he deserved, and worded his remarks as diplomatically as he could. "Considering the animosity Dan Hughes has toward government intervention of any kind, I believe the wisest course of action is to allow me to proceed completely on my own until such time as Dan is safely back in this country. With all due respect to you and the DEA, too many cooks have a tendency to spoil the soup, as the saying goes."

"Ray Bronson anticipated you would react this way," Dusty said calmly. "That is why he is prepared to let you handle the operation as you see fit. However, he and I agree that in order to pacify certain members of Congress who are very close to this investigation, we should be given the courtesy of being informed periodically as to what progress is being made. After all, the authority you are being given is somewhat unprecedented."

Neal's immediate reaction was to grab Dusty and hug him, but he held back in favor of a more professional response. Extending his hand in a gesture of acceptance, he replied, "Thanks. You and Bronson have my solemn word that I will contact you as soon as Dan is back in the United States."

"What about your activity between now and then?" Dusty asked, still dubious about the amount of latitude Neal was being given.

"As you know, I am leaving for San Francisco this afternoon to enjoy a little R&R in the California wilderness," Neal explained. "During that period I am going to give Dan instructions on how and where to re-enter the United States. When he is in that location, I will contact you. In the meantime, use the time I am away to prepare the questions you want Dan to answer. Make them simple and to the point. That's all I can tell you at this time. Any questions? I have a plane to catch."

"You sure picked one hell of a time to go on vacation!" Dusty remarked, noticeably frustrated. "I still question my boss' sanity, but that's none of my business. He's still the boss."

"There's much more to this than just my vacation," Neal said, as he walked Dusty to his car. "When this is all over, you'll be a hero and probably get a promotion. So relax and go on to work. I'll call you when I have something to report."

"You'd better," Dusty remarked. "Enjoy your trip!"

After watching Dusty disappear in the early morning mist, Neal returned inside and spent the next hour packing for his departure, never suspecting how the next four days would alter the course of his life.

Drinking the last of his third cup of coffee, Neal rinsed his cup and looked at his watch. It was time to leave. Assuring himself that all the necessary security precautions were in place, he picked up his travel bag and briefcase, locked the front door and headed south on the freeway, relieved that he was finally on his way.

When he arrived at Ron Barns' place minutes later, Ron had re-parked his pickup truck in front of the house, so he backed into the driveway, transferred his baggage and started to walk toward the front door when Ron appeared. "No time for a *roader* today," he yelled excitedly. "There's been an accident on northbound I-5 that has southbound traffic all screwed up because of all the damned gawkers. We better get a move on or you might miss your flight."

Having already experienced similar delays on trips to the airport in the past, Neal was only too willing to follow his friend's advice. It didn't take too many miles down the highway to find out that his advice had been wise. When they approached the accident area, traffic had slowed considerably, costing them almost twenty minutes delay. Angrily cussing the gawkers, Ron did manage to weave his way through them eventually, and resumed his faster than usual rate of speed. Although nervous about his country-boy way of driving, Neal remained silent and kept a firm hand on his door grip, appreciating that Ron had developed his driving skills on two-lane country roads in the Midwest where he grew up.

Must have been fun at the time Neal thought, as they approached the airport terminal exit. "I gotta hand it to you, Ron," he remarked, as they eased into the curbside baggage check-in station. "I was afraid for a minute we had pressed the envelope too much, but you made it with almost an hour to spare. Now all I have to do is change my underwear."

Ron laughed and said, "You're going to have a lot of explaining to do in the men's room. Have a good time. I'll be here when you get back. Give me a call the night before you leave to remind me when to pick you up."

"I will. And thanks for the lift."

Minutes later, his bag and briefcase in hand, Neal passed uneventfully through the terminal security station and proceeded directly to his departure gate, content to finally sit down and relax.

It was a beautiful day. Much of the flight was spent within viewing distance of the coastline, giving passengers on the starboard side of the aircraft something beautiful to look at for most of the trip. It was when the right wing dipped slightly, and the jet engines changed pitch noticeably, that Neal realized the Captain had begun the first leg of his approach to San Francisco International Airport.

Remembered from cross-country trips he had made recently, the beginning of a landing approach usually gave rise to increased activity in the passenger cabin. The emotional relief of knowing that in minutes the traveler would be on the ground must have been the impetus that prompted the attractive middle-aged woman sitting next to him to inquire, "If I may ask, what brings you to San Francisco, business or pleasure?"

Considering the fact that the woman had been reading a book and nodding off occasionally, her question came as not only a surprise, but seemingly quite out of character. Not wishing to appear unapproachable, he smiled and replied, "Hopefully pleasure. San Francisco is my one night stop over before continuing on to a wilderness retreat called the Sawmill Club for a few days. Ever heard of it?"

Her reciprocal smile and laughing eyes gave visible indication that she had some knowledge of the Club. "Have you ever been there before?" she asked, expressing amusement.

"No, I'm the guest of a college roommate of mine. I haven't a clue about where I'm going, or what I'll be doing when I get there. Just a babe in the woods, so to speak,"

His reply brought an instant outburst of laughter, which she quickly muffled with her jewelry-laden hand before she responded. "Pardon my curiosity, but I find it difficult to believe that a man of your maturity hasn't heard about the Sawmill Club. Where did you and your roommate go to go college?"

As she spoke, Neal couldn't help admiring her beautiful teeth. Watching her smile reminded him of lifting the keyboard cover on a Steinway grand piano. Hoping to amuse her further, he answered, "Yale University. You know, where they learn to make padlocks."

Her reaction was just the opposite from what he had expected. "Now you're making fun of me," she said, pouting a little.

"No-no-no," Neal was quick to respond. "It was a joke to make you to laugh. You have such a beautiful smile."

"Thank you," she said, smiling again. "What's your name, by the way?"

"Neal Thomas. And yours is…?

"Kimberly Prentice," she replied, eyeing Neal suspiciously and offering her hand. "And you've honestly never heard of the Sawmill Club?"

"Scouts honor," he replied, looking her straight in the eyes. "Why, is there something I should be aware of?"

Realizing that Neal was being genuinely honest, Kim grinned and looked out of the window at the gradually approaching runway and replied, "Well, Mr. Thomas, you'll find out soon enough! Damn if I'm going to spoil it for you."

From that moment until the jet's wheels screeched onto the San Francisco Airport runway, Kimberly laid her head back and rested quietly with her eyes closed.

Neal, on the other hand, gazed thoughtfully out the window wondering what the lovely women next to him meant by, *not spoiling it for him*. He hadn't a clue. Maybe she knew someone who was a member of the Club, or had read something in the newspaper. Remembering how serious his friend Allen Henderson had been in advising Neal not to publicize his visit to the club, or discuss its activities with anyone, it was doubtful that whatever Kimberly Prentice knew didn't come from a public source.

What did it matter, he thought, as the big jet came to a stop at the terminal building, setting the mad scramble to deplane in motion, and separating the two of them in the process.

Thus, it was not without a measure of surprise when Neal found Kimberly waiting for him when he entered the terminal building. "I was afraid I'd lost you," he muttered clumsily. "Can I buy you a drink before we go our separate ways?"

"Thank you, I'd enjoy that," she replied. "Follow me. I know just the place."

Minutes later, as the hustle and bustle of people moving in every direction continued around them, Kimberly headed for a door that bore the name, *Executive Lounge*. "This is where I spend my time between flights when I have to travel," she explained. "It's less crowded as a rule."

The lounge was only partly occupied when they entered. Kimberly led the way to a table in front of a large tinted window where San Francisco Bay glistened in the distance. A well-dressed waiter attended to them almost immediately, and left just as quickly. Comfortably alone, Kimberly asked, "Where are you spending the night, Mr. Thomas?"

Her directness caught Neal by surprise, causing him to carefully consider his reply. "I was told to take a cab to a place called Little Bohemia, wherever that is. A limousine will pick me up in the morning and take me to the Club. That's all I know."

Kimberly struggled to keep from laughing and then said, "Based on your unfamiliarity with what the Sawmill Club is all about, I have to assume that you are just as unfamiliar with what goes on in Little Bohemia. Is that a reasonable conclusion?"

"I'm afraid so," he replied, starting to feel as if he were being cross-examined. "Why don't you fill me in on what to expect so I don't make a fool of myself when I get there."

Aware that Neal was becoming increasingly uneasy, Kimberly tried to ease the tension by saying, "Your friend would be very upset with me if I told you what to expect. So relax and enjoy the excitement of it all!"

Before Neal could follow up with a question about how she had become so well acquainted with the Sawmill Club, the waiter arrived with their drinks. After toasting one another, Neal asked, "How about telling me a little about yourself. Are you married? Where do you live? What do you do for a living?"

After mulling over the questions for a moment, Kimberly looked wistfully out over the bay and replied, "No, I'm not married. I'm a widow living alone in Sausalito. What I do for a living is no one's business but my own. So, for now, Mr. Thomas, that will have to do."

Feeling a little guilty for having invaded her privacy with questions of a personal nature, Neal caught the eye of their waiter and signaled for two more drinks. "Sorry, I didn't mean to pry into your personal life," he apologized. "And please, call me Neal. I hope we've progressed further than just ships that pass in the night. Or, have I overstepped the boundaries again?"

"Absolutely not!" she replied. "I'd be the first to let you know if you had. Now, why don't you tell me a little about yourself?"

During the next few minutes, Neal summarized his career in engineering, his life as a family man, his divorce, and what he was doing currently, omitting any reference to his involvement with the infamous life of his friend, Dan Hughes. When he finished, Kimberly glanced at her watch and said, "I really must go now. Here's my card. Give me a call when your book is available. I'd love to read it, especially now that I know the author."

Neal took her card and signaled the waiter for the check, as she excused herself to use the ladies room. When the waiter arrived, he explained that the Executive Lounge was a members only club, and as such, billed its members monthly.

Amused by having been out-foxed by a very foxy lady, Neal placed a ten-dollar bill on the small silver tray the waiter was holding, and joked, "Don't spend it all in one place."

"Thank you, sir," the waiter replied, grinning broadly. "Please tell Ms. Prentice we enjoyed seeing her again. I hope you both have a pleasant evening."

Following the waiter's departure, Kimberly came out of the ladies room and motioned for Neal to follow her. Retrieving their carry-on luggage from the small storage facility near the entrance, they left the lounge and went to the ground transportation station outside the terminal building. A chauffeur standing near a large black limousine waved as if he had been waiting for her. After telling Neal goodbye, she got in and disappeared behind the limo's heavily tinted windows. As it maneuvered into the exit lane, Neal caught a glimpse of the rear license plate. It read: **California FOXYLDY**.

Amusement by how promising the first day of his vacation was progressing, Neal was finally successful in waving down a taxi. "Emma's Loft in Little Bohemia," he directed the cabby, not having a clue about where he was going.

"Where?" the driver asked, looking curiously at Neal in the rearview mirror.

Neal repeated the address a little louder.

"That's what I thought you said," the cabby laughed. "You're the fourth guy I've taken there today. What's going on, a convention?"

"Your guess is as good as mine," Neal answered. "I'm a stranger in town."

"Obviously," the cabby joked while merging into the heavy traffic. "I hope your health insurance is paid up!"

"What's that supposed to mean," Neal asked, starting to feel a little uneasy.

"Just kidding, Sir," the cabby replied, "Excuse me for asking, but aren't you a little out of your element."

"And just what would that element be?" Neal remarked, hoping for a little clarification.

"I'm from back east, Sir. Believe me, you've got Ivy League written all over you. Not that that's a bad thing, but you're going to stand out like a priest in a whorehouse in Little Bohemia."

"Thanks for the graphics," Neal jested in reply. "I believe I get the picture."

For the rest of the time it took to reach Little Bohemia, Neal and the cabby conversed back and forth on the merits and demerits of the California lifestyle, and its influence on everything from sexual behavior to who was residing in the Governor's mansion. It wasn't until they drove under a large overhead latticework of ornamental ironwork bearing the name *Little Bohemia* that Neal began to comprehend what both Kimberly Prentice and the cabby were talking about. He was speechless.

Driving slowly over the beautifully patterned cobblestone roadway that wove its way through what Neal estimated to be a large city block of Disney-like structures, he was captivated by the variety of casually dressed people who were congregated there.

Some were standing or sitting in groups. Others were by themselves, or walking with a companion in different directions, much like what Neal remembered from times when he and his former wife had treated their three daughters to a trip to Disneyland.

In the center of a large circular roadway that they had to drive around to reach Emma's Loft, an old fashioned bandstand stood surrounded by people listening to a Dixieland jazz band. The band members were colorfully dressed men and women of varying ages and ethnic backgrounds. One in particular caught Neal's attention because of her unique piano playing style. Had she not been a woman, Neal would have sworn he was hearing Fats Waller at the keyboard, which prompted him to ask the cabby to pull over and park until she was finished.

While they listened, a black man dressed similarly to those in the band approached and said, "Hey, boss, if you gonna stay here for a spell, how about turning off that stink pipe. We already got enough smokers around here."

Neal apologized and asked the driver to continue on to Emma's so he could change into more comfortable clothes and return to listen to more music. Had he known his overnight lodging was only a stone's throw away, he might have paid the cabby and walked. But he didn't, so he relaxed for the remainder of the way, totally captivated by the people and places they passed.

Emma's Loft was like no other place he had ever seen, except possibly in some e-mail pictures he had once received from an old friend who had attended Mardi Gras festivities in New Orleans.

The building itself was three stories of red brick, whose façade was geometrically divided into three horizontal sets of wrought-iron balconies at each level, all having access from within through a set of white French doors.

To enter, Neal climbed up several flights of stairs that were separated in the middle by a wrought-iron handrail with banisters at the top and bottom. Stairways down to a cellar-level restaurant flanked those he had just climbed that bore the name, **The Cave**.

As he reached the top thinking about what the inside of the restaurant looked like, he got the impression that he was entering a mini-version of *Gone With The Wind's* famous plantation named *Tara*. Unlike the movie, several not so glamorous couples had gathered there to enjoy the music he had just left. Eager to get settled, he approached the check-in counter and announced his arrival to a buxom young woman attendant. "Pardon me, young lady, my name is Neal Thomas. I believe you have a reservation in my name made by Mr. Allen Henderson."

Smiling pleasantly, the woman clicked her way into a computer file and confirmed the reservation. "May I see your driver's license, Mr. Thomas?" she asked politely.

After confirming his identity, she said, "It is our policy for one night guests to pay in advance, Mr. Thomas. That way, you may leave at whatever hour you choose. Would you prefer cash or credit card?"

Neal couldn't help being pleasantly amused by her professional demeanor, despite the contradiction her attire represented. Being a guest and a stranger, he simply asked, "How's the food downstairs?"

"Best in the Bay area," she proudly replied. "Our clientele represents some of the area's most successful citizens and celebrity entertainers. Tony Bennett was here for dinner a few nights ago and sang a song or two. Mostly because he has the highest regard for our regular pianist, and the charity work we do for our homeless citizens."

After concluding their business, she added, "Stop by there tonight. The Cave really swings on weekends."

"Can I leave a wakeup call for five-thirty tomorrow morning?"

"No need," she replied. "Just set the room clock alarm before you go out and enjoy yourself. You won't be disappointed."

Thanking her for her thoughtfulness, Neal picked up his things and walked to the elevator across the small lobby. Minutes later, he stood on the balcony of his room sipping on a vodka tonic from the lock-up bar. Lights and the activity below tugged at his curiosity, begging him to explore what was happening all over this crazy little dot on the map. Two drinks later, he did just that.

One hour later, toting a shopping bag full of souvenirs and postcard reminders, Neal returned to his room to freshen up before going to The Cave for dinner. During the process, he was reminded of what the desk clerk had mentioned about wakeup alarms being in all the rooms, so he set it for five-thirty a.m. and left for The Cave, eager to explore her recommendation. As he passed through the lobby, the cute little desk clerk who reminded him so much of "Abby" on TV's NCSI remarked, "Have a nice evening, Mr. Thomas."

Neal waved back and descended the winding stairway to The Cave, where an evening he would never forget was about to begin.

His first surprise came when he approached the entrance. Unlike any other doors he had passed through over the years, the upper halves were leaded glass mosaics of cave men and women dressed in skimpy animals skins, and embracing one another in a jungle-like environment. The effect of lighting and movement within the restaurant gave an aura of animation to the glass, as an electronic device sensed his approach and triggered them to open. Once inside, a time delay signal triggered them to close, leaving him captured by the grandeur that lay within.

Uniquely different from the carnival-like setting of the village environment he had visited earlier, the restaurant's posh interior was specifically designed to attract an affluent clientele who could let their hair down without being bothered by police, media reporters and celebrity seekers.

What the hell am I doing here? Crossed his mind when a man dressed in a leopard skin tuxedo approached. "May I seat you at a table, sir? Or would you prefer the bar?"

"I'd like to have dinner, thank you," Neal replied. "Do you have a small table where I can enjoy the entertainment?"

"Of course, monsieur," the maitre d' answered. "Follow me, please."

As he walked behind the man, Neal took note of the restaurant's layout and became fascinated with how cleverly the architect had arranged the seating to provide maximum visual access to a semi-circular stage where a concert grand piano sat waiting for whomever was scheduled to provide the evening's entertainment. After being seated, he took the opportunity to ask the maitre d' what sort of entertainment they were featuring that night. He replied, "We have a three-piece ensemble beginning in just a few minutes that plays dinner music until nine o'clock. At that time, other musicians will join them to provide dance music until one o'clock. Now, make yourself comfortable and enjoy the music. Your waitress will be with you in just a moment."

During the interim, Neal's attention was drawn to an area several tables away where a small group of women sat at a larger table that was partially hidden by a piece of decorative latticework. Based on what he could overhear, they appeared to be celebrating an event of some kind. Amused by the fun they were having, he failed to notice an attractive waitress approach his table and clear her throat to get his attention. Somewhat startled, he looked up and smiled sheepishly at the Playboy-style outfit that clung to the woman standing there.

"Would you like a drink before you order, Sir?" she asked.

"I sure would," he replied eagerly, nodding in the direction of the party going on nearby. "Looks like I'm way behind."

The waitress laughed. "Don't try catching up," she cautioned. "They've been at it for quite a while. From what I gather, one of Ms. Donaldson's business partners just returned from a political convention in San Diego. Evidently, she prospered very well."

Her reference to the Donaldson name sent a shiver through Neal's body that challenged his curiosity immediately. "That wouldn't be Gloria Donaldson, would it?"

"Sure is," she waitress answered, with eyebrows raised in surprise. "Do you know her?"

"Let's just say we're acquainted," he replied coyly. "Now, about that drink…you'd better make it a double!"

During her absence, Neal's mind continued to replay the scene at the airport when Kimberly Prentice left him in the **FOXYLDY** limousine. Could it be that Kimberly was Gloria Donaldson's business partner? While he puzzled over the possibility, the waitress arrived with his drink, followed by a woman he failed to recognize.

Between the first large swallow of his overly fortified drink, and the beginning of dinner music, Neal never noticed the woman that had walked up to his table and asked, "How long were you going to sit there before coming over to say hello?"

Recognizing who it was immediately, Neal stood up and awkwardly replied, "First of all, to whom am I speaking, Becky Parker or Gloria Donaldson?"

"You're in my territory now, Neal Thomas. You'd better call me Gloria."

"Gloria it is," he said, taking her willingly into his embrace. "It's good to see you again. I've missed you."

"Thanks. The feeling is mutual. Won't you come and join our table? You look so lonely and out of place over here."

Neal looked around frantically and said, "Let me find my waitress so I can tell her where I've wandered off to. Then I'll join you."

Gloria giggled. "Come along, silly. She's our waitress too."

Hand in hand, Gloria led him to the table where she introduced him to her small gathering of attractive females. One in particular he recognized right away as Kimberly Prentice, the woman who had befriended him on the airplane that day. Obviously a little tipsy, she turned un-steadily toward the others and said, "This is the charming man I was telling you about earlier that sat next to me on the plane today. Now do you believe me?"

When the laughter subsided, Neal sat down next to Gloria and looked over at Kimberly. "Just what did you tell these charming ladies, Ms. Prentice?"

A hush came over the table as all eyes focused in her direction, waiting expectantly for her reply. Realizing she had unwittingly put herself in an awkward situation, she laughed and replied, "Only that you were the only man I had ever met who had never heard of the world renowned Sawmill Club."

Suddenly, every one at the table looked wide-eyed at one another and then at Neal. Realizing that Kimberly had cleverly dodged his question by putting the burden of a response on his back, he said, "Having spent the better part of my life on the East Coast, I willingly admit to ignorance on this matter. Kimberly is right. I have no idea where I'm going tomorrow, or what will happen when I get there."

His admission brought on an avalanche of laughter, whispered comments and a unanimous request for another round of drinks. It was then that Gloria spoke up. "One more while we eat, ladies. Our guest, Mr. Thomas, is going to need his nourishment. After all, he has to get up early tomorrow. So, be good little girls and leave him alone."

Excusing herself using the premise that she needed to use the Lady's room, Gloria disappeared into the mix of activity taking place all around her to mask a detour to the bandstand. Following a brief conversation with the pianist, she slipped him a sizeable gratuity and continued on to the ladies room, un-noticed by Neal and her playful companions.

After applying a token brush of lipstick, Gloria returned to the table. Fresh drinks had already been served, along with menus. During the ordering process, Neal heard the trio of musicians end the song they were playing, and the pianist announce that they were going to take a fifteen-minute break. Before leaving the stage, however, he approached the microphone and announced, "Ladies and gentlemen, word has reached me that we have a fine pianist visiting with us tonight. How about a nice round of applause to bring Neal Thomas up here to play a couple of numbers for us."

Overwhelmed by the audience's response, Neal stood up and accepted the invitation. Before leaving the table, however, he turned and used the applause to muffle his remark to Gloria: "I'll get you for this."

She just laughed and replied, "I certainly hope so!"

Before beginning to play, Neal figured a little praise for the attention he had been given by local citizens and the Loft's staff was in order, so he picked up the microphone and made a short announcement. "Here's to Little Bohemia and every one here at Emma's Loft. I think what I'm about to play says it all."

Placing his eager fingers on the keys, he began playing *I Left My Heart In San Francisco* with all the skill and grace it had taken years to achieve. When he finished, the applause was immediate, lasting fifteen seconds or more. Tempted to let it go at that, he started to get up when a voice from behind him said, "Don't quit now. My guys want to join you for a number or two."

As Neal sat at the piano racking his brain for a song he hoped they would know, the guitar player and drummer returned to the stage and sat down. "Do you know, *How High The Moon?*" the guitar player asked.

"Not if it's at Les Paul's tempo," Neal replied apologetically. "These old hands can't play that fast any more."

"We'll cut it in half for you." Looking over at the bass player, the guitarist said, "Give him a lead in, Tommy."

The bass player walked his strings while the guitar man chorded enough melody for Neal to pick up the tempo. Four beats later Neal's fingers hit a chord that started the ball rolling. Spurred on by the rhythmic clapping of the audience. Neal though, *I've died and gone to heaven.*

Back at the table, Gloria and her friends were captivated by what was taking place. All thought of eating had been put on hold in favor of watching Neal perform, as they drank freely from the magnum of vintage champagne Gloria had ordered to celebrate the occasion. At that very moment, unfortunately, Gloria's enjoyment was interrupted by the arrival of their waitress, who handed her a cell phone and whispered something the other women couldn't hear. Irritated by the untimely interruption, Gloria excused herself and sought the privacy of the lady's room to take the call.

Minutes later, emotionally upset almost to the point of tears, Gloria returned to the table and informed her friends that she had to leave, explaining that an emergency had arisen that demanded her immediate attention. Trusting her to explain the situation to Neal, she asked Kimberly to tell him to call her on his way home from the Sawmill Club. Kimberly agreed and walked Gloria to the lobby. While waiting for the taxi to arrive, Gloria insisted that Kimberly return to The Cave and whispered instructions she wanted followed when the evening was over.

Unfortunately, by the time Kimberly arrived at their table, Neal had already finished his brief session with the band and was enjoying a cocktail while he looked over the dinner menu. Disappointed by Gloria's unexplained departure, he took solace in the fact that he was still in good company, and did his best to keep them all entertained with funny stories from his past. When the stories finally ran out, he glanced at his watch and remarked, "I don't know about you ladies, but I'm hungry."

There were no objections. Everyone went immediately to screening the menu for a favorite dish, talking back and forth in a continuous stream of meaningless babble. Minutes later, the waiter arrived and patiently helped with everyone's order. After he left, Neal leaned back in his chair and said, "Pardon me for asking, but where are all you lovely ladies staying tonight? I hope you're not thinking of driving anywhere."

All five looked at one another with visible amusement, then turned toward Kimberly Prentice, assuming she had been delegated the responsibility of primary spokeswoman during Gloria's absence. Befitting that responsibility, she replied, "When Ms. Donaldson was unexpectedly called away, she took a taxi and left her limousine here for us. All we have to do is call the chauffeur's cell phone number and he will come to pick us up. So don't be concerned, Mr. T. We're in good hands."

Relieved that he wasn't under any obligation to assist the five women, Neal relaxed in the knowledge that he was where he was going to remain that evening. While he sat listening to them talk among themselves, he was reminded of what Dusty Lewis had uncovered about the infamous past of Gloria Donaldson, coming to the conclusion that he was presently sitting in the company of five of her most attractive prodigies. Amused by it all, he couldn't help wondering what they were celebrating before he arrived on the scene. *Oh well,* he thought, *what did it really matter?*

Another thought that crossed his mind was the photograph he remembered seeing in Anita Cassidy's apartment when he repaired her refrigerator. Gloria not being present to approach her on the incident, prompted him to make a mental note of it so he could discuss it with her when he passed through San Francisco on his way home. What puzzled him most was the difference in the two women's names. If Anita Cassidy was really Gloria Donaldson's daughter, why did she change her last name to Cassidy? Then it struck him; Anita kept her married name, even after he mother had it annulled. *A piece of the puzzle had finally fallen into place.*

One hour later, Neal looked at his watch as another waiter was clearing the table. During the process, Kimberly took that opportunity to address the other women. "I think the time has come for us to start thinking about calling our chauffeur, ladies. Mr. Thomas has an early departure time in the morning, so why don't we all freshen up a bit and meet upstairs in the lobby."

Reluctantly, one by one, they came to Neal and said goodbye, hugging him affectionately before leaving. When they were all out of sight, Kimberly said, "Gloria's last words to me were not to allow you to pay for any part of our bill. So, Mr. T, as Gloria sometimes refers to you, you're free to go. I'll take care of things here and make sure they are all safely in the limousine before I retire for the evening."

"You're staying here tonight?" Neal asked with surprise.

"Yes," she answered casually. "I'm flying back to San Diego in the morning, so I decided to stay here tonight. It's conveniently close to the airport."

"Well, maybe I'll see you in the morning before I leave," he remarked. "If I don't, please tell Gloria how much I enjoyed myself. And, I will definitely call her when I return next week."

"I will," she said, smiling peculiarly as she walked away.

Returning to the privacy of his dimly lit room, Neal stripped down to his under shorts and was brushing his teeth when he heard a series of soft knocks on his door. "Who the hell can that be?" he mumbled.

Irritated by the intrusion, he walked over to his chain-locked door and cracked it open slightly. Surprised beyond words, he found Kimberly Prentice standing there in a knee-length silk robe. Relieved that he wasn't being burglarized, he thought he would have a little fun. "Having trouble finding your room, lady?" he whispered.

"I know where I'm going, wise ass," she laughed back. "Now, open the damn door before someone sees me."

Forgetting that he was almost completely naked, Neal slipped the chain lock from its track and opened the door. "Is there an emergency, Madame?" he continued to joke, as she tiptoed into the room.

"You might say that," she replied in a similar whisper, as her hand reached up and flicked off the light switch. "I forgot to mention the other thing Gloria wanted me to take care of. I hope I'm not too late? Looks like you were expecting someone,"

Neal stood in dumb silence as he watched her silken bathrobe come apart and fall to the floor, revealing the shapely nakedness he could only have imagined earlier that evening. Powerless to resist, he gave in willingly to the hand that fondled him into bed and aroused the manhood he was beginning to think would never fully return. He was wrong.

Chapter 7

Wilderness Adventure

When Neal's alarm sounded the next morning, Kimberly Prentice was no longer lying beside him. Thoughtfully aware that she would only have interfered with his early morning departure, she had decided to return to her own room after their romantic interlude had spent itself. Though the temptation to stay the night was strong, she let discretion be the better part of valor, as she too had a commitment that could not be ignored. Thus, they were each prepared to go their separate ways as dawn approached, with only fond memories of the brief physical bonding they had enjoyed. That they might see one another again was never mentioned.

As Allen Henderson had promised, a shiny black limousine was parked in front of the Loft when he came down the steps at seven-thirty that morning. *What a way to start the day,* he though, wondering, *what's next?*

Several men had already gathered on the curb next to the limo when he arrived, each presenting a formal invitation and driver's license to the black-suited chauffer before they were allowed to enter. Witnessing the formality, Neal opened his briefcase, withdrew his invitation and stood in line with his wallet in hand until he too had been processed. Several minutes later, all five men were in the limo talking amongst themselves about the overly dramatic security measures that they had just been subjected to.

"Hell, that was as bad as an airline terminal inspection," one joked.

Another remarked, "What's next, a pat-down?"

When the door closed and locked behind them, the chauffer turned and said, "This identification check might seem a little extreme to some of you, but once you've become exposed to what the Sawmill Club is all about, I'm sure you will agree that making sure you are who you say you are is a good security precaution. Please help yourself to the choices that are available in the bar, or the coffee pot. If you are into early morning news programming, there is a satellite television available. The clicker is in the pocket next to it. For your privacy, I am going to close the window that separates us. If you need to communicate with me, push the window control button on your armrest. My name is Rudy Bates. Now, please fasten your seat belts and we'll get this show on the road."

Considering his previous night's activity, Neal's interest in doing anything more than closing his eyes was all he wanted to consider. The other men, obviously less hung over than he, became immediately adsorbed in a televised golf match and helped themselves to the vodka and Bloody Mary mix, which that was in ample supply. At the risk of being labeled a *party-pooper* by his fellow passengers, Neal gave in to their chiding and joined the revelry that would become the modus operandi for the next four days.

Because the golf match was becoming the focus of everyone's attention, Neal did not notice how dramatically the landscape was changing as they drove further north. It wasn't until they stopped at a roadside park facility to use a public restroom that he realized they were entering mountainous terrain. Were it not for an area map that was encased in a glass case outside the rest rooms, Neal wouldn't have known where he was. A red-circled area, however, placed them at the entrance to Plumas National Forest, a wilderness area he was totally unfamiliar with.

An hour after turning off the main highway onto a winding gravel road, the limo came to a stop in a clearing that appeared to be in the middle of nowhere. Were it not for the large, ten passenger helicopter idling in the middle of that clearing, it might just as well have been nowhere.

Thank God for those Bloody Mary's Neal thought, as the chauffer unloaded their baggage and led them to the open door of the chopper.

"This is where we part company gentlemen," Rudy shouted over the noise. "Your pilot's name is Jordan Pikes, JP to you. Enjoy yourself, I'll be waiting for you when you return."

As soon as Rudy Bates had walked beyond the whirling blades of the chopper, the pilot throttled the engine and lifted them up to a vantage point where they could more clearly see the ground below. Except for the winding road they had just traveled to get to the clearing, there was nothing to indicate that they were in any way connected to the civilized world. Three hundred and sixty degrees of endless acreage covering the earth beneath them was nothing but ravines and canyons covered with heavy concentrations of trees. Occasionally, the sun's reflection gave witness to a few small lakes hidden there, or a stream winding its way down the mountainous terrain. The scene was reminiscent of a time when Neal and two other officer candidates were dumped from a military vehicle during map-reading training in an uninhabited part of the wilderness property surrounding Fort Benning, Georgia.

An apprehensive glance at his watch made Neal aware that he and his companions had been airborne for approximately thirty minutes. He could tell from the expressions on their faces that they too were beginning to experience some uneasiness. However, that soon ended when their pilot pointed to the high ground they were approaching, and shouted, "We're almost there!"

Curious about what lay beyond the ridge they were about to cross, everyone's eyes focused forward. As the chopper's belly passed over the jagged ridge, they stared in awe at the large crater-lake that lay hidden there, its calm water shimmering in the morning sun. Neal estimated it to be about half a mile in length, and half that distance in width. Unlike the uninhabited landscape they had been flying over for what seemed to have been hours, the lake revealed a large, two-story structure sitting majestically about half way down the east side of the lake's shoreline. As its structural details became more visible, the men could make out a wide walkway supported by large wooden pilings paralleling the shoreline. From its midpoint, a pier projected out into the lake to provide mooring slips for small pleasure boats.

It became apparent from the choppers angle of descent that the pilot was headed straight for a large white circle painted on the square platform at the outboard end of that pier. Nearby, their sponsors stood anxiously waiting for the chopper's cargo of guests to arrive, anxious to begin the four-day series of special events that their guests were given the rare opportunity to be a part of.

Before leaving the chopper after it landed, Neal hesitated at the door long enough to thank the pilot. "I've never been up in a helicopter before," he admitted. "I'm sure I'll be a hell of a lot less nervous when you come back to pick us up. Thanks again."

Jordan Pikes gave Neal a friendly smile and replied, "Thanks, but I'm not going anywhere. It's part of my job to stay here in case there's an emergency. One hasn't happened yet, but that's no guarantee it won't. Have a good time."

Neal shook JP's hand, picked up his things and began walking toward the group where his travel companions had gathered when he heard a loud voice call out, "Hey Doofus, over here!"

It was his friend, Allen Henderson.

Experiencing a wave of relief as he walked in that direction, Neal shook Allen's hand excitedly, and said, "Man, am I glad to see you. You're not going to believe what happened to me last night!"

"Oh yes I will," Allen laughed. "But first, let's get you registered at the lodge, then you can tell me all about it over a drink. Looks like you could use one."

"You can say that again," Neal remarked, agreeably excited. "Lead the way."

As they walked the pier together, Allen gave Neal a condensed version of the Sawmill Club's history, and how it had progressed to its present day status of exclusivity.

"Going back to day one, it's hard to believe that this lake was the site of a sawmill owned an operated by a rugged, pioneer-spirited easterner by the name of Frederick Donaldson. He ventured out here and bought acreage as far as the eye could see for its endless supply of timber. He was a wealthy old codger gifted with an uncanny ability to see beyond the gold that brought on the California rush. He knew that the building industry was where the real gold was, so he had a lumber-processing mill built on the shore of this lake where he could cut and ship lumber to wherever it was needed."

The name, Donaldson, stopped Neal in his tracks. "Did he have family?"

"One of California's wealthiest," Allen replied. "They're spread out all over the state from San Francisco to Los Angeles, and in all the major industries, including banking, real estate and construction."

"Would your club have a record of the Donaldson ancestry?" Neal inquired. "I'd like to look it over if they do."

"Are you kidding?" Allen quickly replied. "We have a library that contains historical records of all members, past and present. Of course, that information is not for publication outside the organization. Your registration signature documents your agreement not to do so. Any problem with that?"

"None whatsoever," Neal assured him. "I was just curious to know if your records contain any reference to a friend of mine whose last name is also Donaldson. Wouldn't that be a coincidence if she turned out to be an apple on the Donaldson family tree."

Although it was not a long walk to reach the club's main entrance, it did give Neal an opportunity to make several observations along the way. One was a large bronze placard imbedded in the surface of a tall, natural stone monument at the building's entrance. It read:

Sawmill Club

Original site of Donaldson Lumber Company, whose dedicated employees helped pioneer the building of the great State of California. This monument is dedicated to their sacrifices. May they rest in eternal peace and happiness.

Frederick R. Donaldson
Founder

"Quite a remarkable man," Neal commented, as they approached the clubhouse. "Was he ever involved in politics?"

"Not in California. History tells us that he came out here from Virginia because of his outspoken views on the way the Federal Government was being run. Those opinions put him in disfavor with many of his colleagues. According to books I have read, he was a crusty old curmudgeon. Kind of a Randolph Hearst type, you might say."

"I still can't get over the enormity of this structure," Neal remarked, as he and Allen began to climb the wide flight of stone steps leading to the front entrance. "It must have taken years to construct back in those days. How many rooms are there?"

"Over two hundred," Allen replied. "But don't be fooled into thinking it was built back when old man Donaldson was still alive. After we get you registered, I'll take you on a tour to give you a little history on how and when this all came about."

Neal's biggest surprise came when he and Allen entered the main lodge building. On either side of the short hallway leading into the main reception area were state of the art administrative offices where they stopped briefly for Neal to register. A casually dressed young man in his mid-twenties took Neal's bag and briefcase, explaining that they would be waiting for him in his room. Neal made an attempt to tip the young man by reaching for his wallet, but Allen's quick hand held him back. "You can take care of that when your visit is over," he explained. "Everything else is paid for, so don't attempt to tip anyone. Just enjoy yourself and forget about money."

"It's been quite a while since I've heard anyone say that," Neal replied, with an element of surprise. "Now, how about that tour."

Leaving the office, Allen led Neal into a huge room whose walls rose all the way to the ceiling of the second floor. A wide balcony at the second floor level looked down on them and others who were gathered there. It was then that Neal remarked, "I haven't seen a room this big since my friend Ron Barns took me and a group of our friends to visit the Hearst Castle years ago. Old man Donaldson was way ahead of his time, I'd say."

"You mean one of his grandsons was," Allen corrected him. "This place wasn't built till years after the old man died."

"What happened to the lumber business?"

"Several factors contributed to closing down the old man's sawmill," Allen began to explain. "The most dramatic was a fire that destroyed nearly half the timber acreage, but not the property bordering the lake, fortunately. Another was a prolonged drought that dried up rivers that fed the lake, preventing them from transporting logs to the mill. When the money finally ran out, most of the loggers left to search for gold.

That's when the mill was shut down and abandoned. Without a steady supply of timber the property was useless."

Scratching his head as if confused, Neal finally asked, "Where did he get the money to build this place?"

Inviting Neal to sit with him near a massive fireplace at one end of the room, Allen said, "A waiter will be here shortly to bring us a drink. In the meantime, let's take a break while I get my second wind. Okay?"

Neal agreed, using the time to let his eyes wander around the room and marvel at what he saw. *I still don't believe this place* he thought, as his focus came to rest on a large framed portrait hanging over a similar fireplace at the opposite end of the room. He was about to ask Allen if the painting was a portrait of one of the Donaldson clan when a young man arrived to take their orders.

"Now that's service," Neal remarked, after the young man left. "Is everything around here this prompt?"

Allen smiled and replied, "You haven't seen anything yet, Doofus."

Picking up the Sawmill Club history where he had left it, momentarily, Allen continued with his explanation of how the present Sawmill Club had come into existence.

"Following the events that put the Donaldson Lumber Company out of business, the family lost all interest in the property, until one of Frederick Donaldson's grandsons, named Randolph, hired a seaplane and flew up here with a group of his wealthy friends to go fishing. Randy, as the family had nicknamed him, was a very popular San Francisco playboy at the time, and used the money his father had left him to take over a small shipyard located in the Bay Area that built luxury yachts for the very wealthy."

Before Allen could continue, the waiter returned with their drinks, giving Neal an opportunity to think about what he had heard thus far. The more he thought about it, the more he was convinced that a connection was developing between Gloria Donaldson and the playboy Randy Donaldson. Rather than confuse Allen with that aspect of the Donaldson family history, Neal sat back and waited for the waiter to leave, content with the drama that Allen was unwittingly contributing to.

"What prompted Randy Donaldson to fly up here to go fishing?" Neal asked when the waiter had gone. "Did he know something his friends didn't?"

"He sure did!" Allen answered assertively. "According to the old man's will, the property was divided equally among his heirs. As it turned out, none of them knew what to do with it because the fire had destroyed its value. On top of all that, it was virtually inaccessible. To develop it for commercial resale would have required construction of an access road and other development costs that none of them wanted to get involved with. So, it just sat here. Randy, on the other hand, had always had the uncanny ability to see potential where others couldn't and offered to buy them out. They, of course, leaped at the opportunity."

"That's a lot of acreage," Neal commented. "Certainly he was not in a position to assume such an expense on his own."

"Ah, hah!" Allen remarked, with raised eyebrows, "Therein lays the difference between success and failure, my friend – doing the unexpected."

"And that was…?"

"Randy called the same friend who had flown him to the lake on that fishing trip I mentioned and asked him to fly up here to survey the property before going ahead with what he had in mind. What he discovered was a wilderness paradise covered with fresh new growth, and the lake filled to original capacity. There were streams feeding the lake again and fish were jumping. The isolated beauty was all the incentive Randy needed to turn his creative imagination into this wonderful reality."

"That would explain the original fishing trip." Neal remarked with a chuckle. "What was the bait this time?"

"An investor's share in the new Sawmill Club," Allen replied. "You can't imagine how many San Francisco millionaires Randy rubbed elbows with. They leaped at the opportunity to invest in the development of this place. The current membership is well into the hundreds, so you can imagine the amount of money this place represents."

"What about the Club's membership?" Neal asked. "How does one become a member?"

"There's a review board that investigates all the nominees. The vote is secret and has to be unanimous or you won't be accepted. No questions asked."

"How about guests?"

"You wouldn't be sitting here if you hadn't passed muster," Allen remarked, as he finished his drink and stood up. "Now, let me show you where our room is before we continue the tour. We still have a couple of hours before dinner."

As the two men climbed the wide stairway to the second floor, Neal remarked, "I still don't understand how this place could have been built without an access road to deliver building materials and whatever else was needed. Certainly it wasn't flown in here."

"Not hardly," Allen replied. "A road was built specifically for that purpose, and still exists, but is only used during special occasions like this by employees and maintenance staff. Because of the Club's stringent policy regarding privacy, a busing system was created to bring members and guests to and from the lake by picking them up at a parking facility at the main entrance. Baggage is tagged and delivered directly to assigned rooms by members of the staff. You, however, arrived by helicopter, so yours didn't get handled until you registered."

"No cars on the premises, right?"

"Only battery-powered golf carts driven by employees are permitted." Allen explained. "And they are only used to assist the physically impaired. Other than that, it's strictly foot power. I hope you brought some comfortable walkers."

"Yes I did," Neal replied. "I had a hunch we'd be walking a lot."

The room that Allen and Neal would share for the next few days had four beds; theirs, and two that had not yet been claimed.

"Looks like our other roommates are late getting here," Neal commented, as he opened his suitcase to change his shoes. "Anyone you know?"

Allen inspected the identification tags on each of the other two beds and replied, "Only one of them. The other must be a guest."

Neal's inquiry about the other two roommates prompted Allen to mention a subject he should have addressed earlier concerning a members right to privacy. Giving his statement careful thought, so as not to offend Neal, he said, "As a general rule, the Sawmill Club is all about leaving the world we live in as far behind us as possible. That way, everyone can lose their identity for a few days and have a good time any way they want to. So, in your conversation with members and their guests, try not to get too personal. Some of these characters get pretty touchy when you do. And above all, whatever you see or hear over the next few days, please keep to yourself. Do I make myself clear?"

Loud and clear! Neal thought, recognizing the doctrine of silence. "Of course," he replied, amused by his friend's seriousness. "Sorry, your name was…?"

"Never mind, smart ass," Allen chuckled. "Now, let me get you acquainted with a few things."

After leaving their sleeping quarters, Allen led Neal to a pair of louvered doors that opened into a tile-covered room housing six individual shower stalls, wash basins and toilets. "Obviously this is our bathroom facility," he remarked. "Strictly G.I."

"Reminds me of the Officers Candidate School at Fort Benning, Georgia," Neal commented. "I noticed each one of our beds was made, and had a towel and wash cloth on it. Who does the housekeeping around here?"

"We have a staff of young college men who monitor all the rooms," Allen replied. "It helps them earn a little money during their summer vacation. They also serve as waiters at meal time."

"Are they live-ins?"

"No. They're bused in at six a.m., and bused out at ten p.m. Only members are allowed to stay here overnight."

As they left the bathroom and walked toward the stairway that would take them back to the ground floor, Neal stopped occasionally to look at the collection of paintings and statuettes that adorned the hallway. "Did Randy Donaldson collect all of this beautiful artwork?" he inquired.

"Oddly enough, he and his grandfather were both obsessed with the arts, and collected the best of their individual generation's work. As part of the family legacy, Randy had it all shipped here for safe keeping when construction of the Club was complete. There was a proviso in his will stipulating that everything was to be given to his wife, Gloria, when he died."

Mention of Gloria Donaldson's name for the second time over the past two days reminded Neal again of the photograph he saw in Anita Cassidy's apartment the night he fixed her refrigerator. She had stated at the time that the two grownups in the photograph were her mother and father. Ironically, looking back on the incident, Anita's mother bore a remarkable resemblance to the woman he knew at the time as Becky Parker. Only recently had he discovered that she was also Gloria Donaldson, a woman he had been intimate with on Catalina Island only a week ago. Because Anita had willingly claimed the couple as her parents, Neal had to conclude that the man in the photograph was Gloria's deceased husband, Randolph Donaldson.

How crazy is this? Neal's thoughts kept repeating. Allen finally stole his attention by saying, "If you're wondering why all this artwork still remains here, I can ease your mind by telling you that Randolph Donaldson's widow recently changed her will to bequeath all of it to the Sawmill Club. It was her way of preserving her husband's memory."

Still anxious to determine if there was an indisputable link between the Gloria Donaldson he knew and the one Allen had been referring to, Neal asked, "Did Randy Donaldson and his wife have any children?"

Allen waited until they had left the main lodge before answering Neal's question. "I wasn't ignoring you," he explained. "I just wanted to be away from my fellow Club members before I answered. That subject is a very controversial one around here, especially to those of us who were close friends with the Donaldson family. To answer your question, yes they did have a child. A girl they named Anita after Grandmother Donaldson, a real beauty in her time, and a constant worry to Grand-father Donaldson."

Though he didn't show it, Neal felt like his heart had skipped a beat when Allen mentioned Anita's name. Despite the urge to question him further on the child, Neal remained silent in the hope that Allen would voluntarily expand on the family relationship. His patience was rewarded when Allen stopped a few yards short of the next building they were about to enter to avoid getting too close to the crowd of men who were gathering there. Turning his back toward them, he continued:

"One of the most prestigious social events in San Francisco is the Debutante Ball. To parents, it represents a sizeable expense just to introduce their daughters to society. A society that they could enjoy and prosper in, once they had achieved the level of education that was consistent with their family's aspirations for them. Randy and Gloria Donaldson were no less expectant of Anita when they enrolled her in a highly accredited university in New England, hoping its reputation would eventually land her a job with one of San Francisco's successful business professionals."

Before Allen could continue, Neal grunted and said, "Say no more, I know exactly what happened."

Allen scowled at being interrupted, and said, "Okay, wise-ass, tell me what happened!"

Pursing his lips, as he grinned and looked out over the lake, Neal said, "Anita met a guy in college, fell in love and got pregnant. They got married so as not to embarrass the families, and she brought him home to meet Mommy and Daddy during Christmas break as a well-intended surprise. How am I doing so far?"

"There's more," Allen remarked, somewhat disgruntled by Neal's uncanny accuracy thus far. "Care to comment on the outcome?"

Because Allen did not know that Neal had first-hand knowledge of Anita's whereabouts, Neal took a less aggressive stance and replied, "Her mother probably arranged to have the marriage annulled and the baby put up for adoption. Most mothers of Gloria Donaldson's background would go to any lengths to preserve her daughter's reputation, regardless of the consequences. The father was probably kept intentionally out of the loop because his love for his daughter prevented him from dealing with the situation in a rational manner."

Suspecting that Neal's uncanny ability to describe the Donaldson family's tragic history was not purely coincidental, Allen decided not to pursue the subject any further, suggesting that it could be discussed in more detail when they were alone.

Neal couldn't have been more agreeable, and welcomed the opportunity to join the large assembly of men inside the Timberlake Tavern that Allen explained was built to honor all the men who had worked and died at the original Sawmill Club.

"The original tavern was a far cry from this one," Allen remarked. "Stories passed down from survivors over the years confirm that Frederick Donaldson was a drinking man's drinker. He built the original bar on this site for the sole purpose of keeping his men happy and less inclined to quit. Occasionally, he even had women horsed in from a mining camp not far from here to make sure his men's physical needs were taken care of. Even paid for it out of his own pocket."

"Was that why Grandmother Donaldson became a constant worry to the old man?" Neal asked. "She must have become terribly lonely with him up here all of the time."

"We'll discuss that situation later," Allen replied in a whisper, as they entered the tavern. "Right now we've got more exciting things than conversation to occupy our time."

When they entered the tavern, Neal's memory flashed back immediately to a time when he and his best friend, Billy Newman, had been invited by another close friend to attend an all-male gathering at a privately owned hunting club near Billy's summer home at the beach. *What a day that was!*

◆ ◆ ◆

As was often the case when the Newman and Thomas families gathered for a weekend at the beach, the women and children spent their time sunning, gossiping and splashing in the surf.

Billy and Neal, on the other hand, always managed to find some kind of mischief to get into, which usually involved drinking at someone else's house, or at the small beach community's only restaurant and bar. This particular Saturday afternoon, however, had a much different twist to it.

A friend of Billy's by the name of Eddie Marizano saw Billy and Neal having a drink at that bar just before noon. Since they were by themselves, Eddie invited them to stop by the Duck Hunter's Lodge later on that day where he and his employees were having their beauty salon's annual picnic. Without hesitation, Billy and Neal accepted the invitation, unaware of what they were getting themselves into.

The Lodge, as everyone in the beach community referred to it, was an eight-room, ground level structure located near the entrance to the small community. It had been built by a group of doctors who only occupied it during the duck-hunting season, renting it out through an agency during the off-season to defray their expenses. Being a local resident, it was the perfect place for Eddie to have the event, and a day Billy Newman would never forget.

The party was well underway when Billy and Neal arrived, with cocktails galore, live music and a buffet of specially prepared seafood dishes to charm everyone's pallet. As a group, everyone seemed to be having a good time. Though it was common knowledge among patrons of Eddie's salon that all of his beauticians were gay men, it was not very well known outside the Virginia Beach business community. So, to add a little humor to the mix, and enhance his reputation as an unscrupulous prankster, Eddie asked *his boys* to attend the festivities dressed as hookers. They, of course, thought it was a hilarious idea and agreed to it unanimously.

Needless to say, the hookers soon became the center of attention as the afternoon wore on. The combination of swing dancing and alcohol broke down all inhibitions and brought unlikely partners together on the dance floor. One such couple was Billy Newman and one of Eddie's hookers, who appeared to have impressed Billy romantically.

It wasn't until Neal noticed Eddie laughing at Billy from across the room that he realized Billy had become drunkenly infatuated with the hooker. Reluctant to embarrass his friend by taking him aside to explain how he had been duped, Neal stood in silent amusement until the dance was over. As Billy and his partner left the floor, Neal witnessed the partner's hand caress Billy's backside before slipping coyly into the crowd to join the other cohorts, laughing all the way.

Disappointed by his partner's sudden departure after flirtatiously coming on to him, Billy lumbered across the dance floor to where Neal stood desperately trying not to laugh. Slurring his words a little, Billy mumbled, "Man, I'm in love."

Laughing with friendly pity, Neal said, "Take the hook out of your mouth, my friend. You've been had big time."

Looking up at Neal with his eyes half-closed and a dumb look on his face, Billy muttered, "Scuze me?"

"Never mind." Neal said, realizing it was neither the time nor place to tell him anything. "I'll explain it all on the way home. You stay right here while I thank Eddie, and then we'll get the hell out of here."

Eddie was still laughing when Neal approached him with an outstretched hand. "Thanks for the invite, you nutcase," Neal remarked, laughing a little himself. "I better get Billy home before he proposes to that fake hooker of yours. Jennifer's going to kill him."

"Glad you could make it," Eddie chuckled. "Tell the little guy I'll see him next week. He probably won't remember much, but that could be a blessing."

"Hopefully," Neal remarked, as he turned and walked away.

Billy sat without uttering a word until they were within eyesight of his cottage. Seeing Jennifer, Janet and all the children returning from the beach, dragging towels and other paraphernalia behind them, finally made him speak. "I suppose you think I'm crazy for trying to make out with that chick back at Eddie's party?"

"I hate to burst your bubble, numb nuts," Neal replied with a tired sigh, "but that chick is a guy."

Billy straightened up suddenly from his laid back position and yelled, "For Christ's sake, stop the car before they see us!"

Luckily, Neal was able to pull off onto a side street before their wives noticed them. "What the hell was that all about?" Neal yelled, after coming to a stop.

"I kissed that guy?" Billy choked, and spit out the window in disgust.

Amused by the sickened expression on Billy's face, Neal said, "Take it easy, lover boy. You've kissed uglier women. I doubt you'll be getting any calls. Eddie set the whole thing up as a joke, so don't think you're the only switch-hitter on the block."

"Son of a bitch! You knew all about this, didn't you?"

Neal laughed out loud this time, put the car in gear and turned around. "No, I didn't. But it was sure fun watching."

By the time the two men finally made it home, the humor in the whole incident had set in, and they were both laughing. Aside from them being a little tipsy, which in itself was a predictable outcome whenever Neal and Billy went off someplace together, both wives were in a good humor, and amused themselves by preparing dinner for the children until their husbands returned. Once again the age-old saying had proven true: *"All's well that end's well."*

❖ ❖ ❖

Neal was still lingering in the humor of his brief reverie when Allen brought him back to present day by continuing with his history narrative: "Randy Donaldson felt so strongly about his grandfather's dedication to the men who had worked for him, he had this place built on the original site of the old bar to preserve its memory, and carry on the tradition."

Observing that Neal had become somewhat preoccupied with the interior design of the restaurant and bar, Allen asked, "As a designer of some merit yourself, what do you think of the place?"

"I wondered what this building was used for when we flew in this morning," Neal answered. "I certainly didn't expect to see anything like this. How many people does the tavern accommodate?"

"About half the membership," Allen stated. "It varies, depending on how many members show up, and how many days they stay. It's all pre-arranged well in advance of opening day. Let's find out what table we'll be sitting at before we hit the bar."

That accomplished, Allen led Neal into the bar where they waited in one of the three lines that had formed. There were three bartenders on duty, so the lines moved fairly rapidly. Once served, Allen suggested that he and Neal resume their previous conversation regarding the Donaldson family history on the patio deck where they could expect a reasonable amount of privacy. Neal agreed.

Given his increasing interest in that subject, Neal was eager to make further inquiries in order to prepare for the possibility of making contact with Gloria Donaldson again when he passed through San Francisco on his way back home.

When they were comfortably seated, Allen said, "You asked me previously if I thought Grandfather Donaldson's wife, Anita, might have rebelled against Frederick for being gone so much when the lumber business was operating at its peak. Were you implying that she might possibly have been having an affair?"

"Wouldn't your phrase, *a constant worry,* almost imply that?" Neal replied. "After all, you did use the words, *a real beauty in her time.*"

Allen looked over at Neal rather suspiciously and said, "Much of Frederick Donaldson's personal history reveals that he was primarily a man's man, and not very comfortable with the intimate side of married life. Thus, he used his lumber business as a convenient excuse to minimize that part of the marital relationship."

"From what you told me a little while ago about paying women to come up here to keep his troops satisfied, it would appear he may have had a yen for that type of woman, instead of the prim and proper type that were indigenous to San Francisco high society at the time."

Allen smiled, rolled his eyes skyward as if to say, *your perception of the old man is almost clairvoyant.* Then he said, "Let me ask you a personal question, Doofus. Does any of old man Donaldson's personal history touch a spot of personal sensitivity with you?"

Shaking the ice in his empty glass to indicate that he was ready for a refill, Neal replied, "No, not me personally. But my past is full of friends and acquaintances whose spouses could double for any one of the Donaldson family members. In fact, I'll bet you a free visit to San Diego that I can tell you how this situation between old man Donaldson and his wife played out."

After Allen had waved down a waiter and ordered two more drinks, he turned to Neal and said, "Based on your success rate thus far, I'd be a fool to challenge you. But I haven't been to San Diego since I was an officer in the Navy. So, go ahead. Make my day."

Neal chuckled and began: "The truth is, Anita Donaldson couldn't have cared less if Frederick was gone for long periods of time. She had plenty of money, and a very active social life with women who lived pretty much the same way. It was her passion to have a child that forced her to seduce her husband. So, to bait the hook, she planned a social gathering at her home that would turn out to be the talk of all San Francisco, and one that she knew Frederick wouldn't embarrass her by not attending."

"Do you have a crystal ball hidden somewhere?" Allen remarked, with a hint of sarcasm. "I can almost say with certainty that visiting San Diego anytime soon appears to be just wishful thinking, but please continue."

"Think about it for a moment, Allen. Suppose the shoe was on the other foot. What would you do under those same circumstances?"

"I'd spoil the hell out of her for a few hours," Allen replied, with a devilish grin, "then I'd spike her drink with a small drop of aphrodisiac. Hopefully, her gratitude, or the horny potion would bring her around to my way of thinking."

"Yes, that might do the trick, but the drug could backfire and put her out of commission. Especially if it didn't mix well with the booze."

"Okay, Mr. Wise Guy," Allen shot back, "Tell me how she did him in?"

"Simple. After the last guest left the party, Anita went on the offense and acted just like one of the broads her husband paid to take care of his men. How does that old adage go: *fight fire with fire?*"

"Funny you should mention that," Allen commented. "A San Francisco historian wrote a book about the Donaldson family some years ago that implied the same thing. According to the book, Frederick Donaldson hired a foreman to run the lumber company right after that social event took place, and stayed home to help raise all the children they eventually had. Anita Donaldson, it turns out, was quite the foxy lady."

"Yes, and I'll bet her daughters were too," Neal added. "But that's another story, Allen. Right now, I'd like to hear about what you've been doing all these years."

Before Allen could respond, a voice from the speaker system announced that dinner would be served shortly, initiating a mass exodus from the bar to tables in the dining area. Shortly after Allen and Neal were seated, Allen made an attempt to answer the question Neal had just asked, but the opening of a curtained stage at one end of the large dining room interrupted him again. Gathered on the stage was a small, casually dressed orchestra, and a pianist who was about to address the gathering.

"First," he began, "I would like to welcome all of my fellow members and their special guests to the annual Sawmill Club summer outing. Though I love the City of San Francisco, I do look forward to these few days of relaxation without the pressure of concerts and recording sessions that demand so much of our time. That said, let's get on with the music and have some fun!"

The applause that followed rocked the room. "Is that who I think it is?" Neal asked.

"Sure is," Allen replied proudly. "Toby Tanner and his band were great friends of Randy and Gloria Donaldson back when Randy was building yachts on the bay. He played at the Debutante Ball when Anita Donaldson made her debut, and at Randy's funeral when he died. They were the closest of friends."

With the sound of background music muffling his voice, Neal leaned closer to Allen and whispered, "Which brings up the unpleasant subject of how Randy Donaldson died?"

By now, dinner was being served. The increased level of conversation around them made it comfortable for Allen to continue the Donaldson saga. "To continue from where I left off, young Anita Donaldson was not all that happy with becoming a mother at her tender age, so she gave in to her mother's insistence that she have an abortion and have the marriage annulled. To squelch any objection the young husband might have had, Randy Donaldson paid the young man off by giving him enough money to finish his college education, with the condition that he never attempt to contact Anita again.

Begrudgingly, Anita finished her education in a very fashionable private school near San Francisco."

"So, what does all this have to do with Randy Donaldson's death?" Neal persisted. "I don't get the connection."

"You would if you had suffered a heart attack as a result of all the emotional trauma that Anita had stirred up," Allen remarked. "Randy passed out at work one day and was rushed to a hospital, but never regained consciousness."

"Leaving mother and daughter to blame one another for his death, I suppose," Neal added.

"Those close to the family have implied as much," Allen suggested. "Which all goes to support the theory that Anita ran away from home to get away from the constant friction that existed between she and her mother. No one has seen or heard from Anita since."

"How could she survive?" Neal asked, in an attempt to probe further. "Was she working at the time?"

"She had a menial job at her father's shipyard so he could keep close tabs on her," Allen explained. "It was Anita who discovered her father slumped over in his office chair one day after work. She had gone there to ride home with him, as she did every day. I believe the shock of finding him that way pushed her to leave home as soon as he was put to rest."

"How could she support herself?" Neal asked, "Surely her brief tenure at her father's shipyard couldn't have provided her with much of an income."

"That's where the story ends, I'm afraid," Allen replied. "Unfortunately for her, she left without knowing that her father willed her a sizeable sum of money that's just sitting in a bank in San Francisco accumulating interest. Her mother refuses to liquidate the account in the hope that she might return some day."

Moisture began to appear on Neal's forehead from the emotional rush that Allen's detailed accounting of the Donaldson family history had generated. That, and the alcohol he had consumed, made him giddy thinking about what the next few days might reveal. Excited by the prospect, he turned toward Allen and said, "I can't thank you enough for giving me the opportunity to visit this extraordinary place. You'll never know how much I appreciate your generosity. In return, I'm offering you and your lovely wife an open-ended invitation to visit my home any time you can make it. And that you can take to the bank!"

As their glasses clinked together in a toast, Allen grinned and said, "Thanks. You're good company, Doofus. What do you say we get a breath of fresh air so I can give you a run down on what we'll be doing for the next few days?"

"Lead the way, my friend, I'm all ears."

Their walk back to the open patio was interrupted frequently by many of Allen's friends who welcomed Neal enthusiastically. "Nice bunch of guys," Neal remarked, when they were back on the patio deck. "I thought I recognized some of them."

"Probably on television or in the tabloids. The room is loaded with media personalities, politicians, musicians, et cetera. I can see why you might not recognize many of them. They're not dressed like you're used to seeing them in the public eye. They can get pretty casual at times."

Allen was just about to summarize the scheduled activities that were to take place over the next three days when Neal interrupted him. "What are all those lights on the other side of the lake?" he asked.

Allen looked with disinterest in the direction Neal was pointing and replied, "Do you remember me telling you that old man Donaldson used to horse in women occasionally to satisfy his men's urges?"

"Yes I do. I thought that was pretty generous of the old boy, I might add."

"Randy Donaldson thought so too," Allen remarked, "because he carried on the tradition, only in a little more grandiose style."

"Grandiose?"

"Well, if you ventured over there during the daytime, you'd find half a dozen, fully equipped bungalows that house a group of very attractive and accommodating women. Their sole purpose in being there is to provide those of our members who are so inclined with relief from those very same urges, if you get my drift."

Sparked by what DEA Agent Dusty Lewis had already told him about the infamous Gloria Donaldson on a previous occasion, Neal was now convinced that she was the late Randy Donaldson's wife. "Yeah, I get your drift," he replied. "Now, tell me, who supplies these women?"

"Don't ask me." Allen answered, purposely trying to avoid Neal's question. "Truthfully, I don't know anymore than you do."

Not wishing to offend Allen by pursuing the subject any further, Neal injected a little humor to smooth over what appeared to be a delicate matter: "You know, I get those same urges sometimes."

Allen let out a hearty laugh. "Sorry, Doofus. Members only."

While Allen spent a few minutes outlining the activities he and Neal would be engaged in over the next few days, Toby Tanner and his band quit playing in order to mingle with the diehards who traditionally were the last to call it a day. Toby was considered one of those stalwarts, and eventually made his way to the patio where Allen and Neal were sitting.

"I don't believe we've been introduced," Toby said, addressing Neal with an outstretched hand. "I can't say as I'm overly impressed with the company you keep, but to each his own, as they say."

Allen laughed, as Neal stood up to shake Toby's hand. "You should have seen this guy in college." Allen remarked. "Neal's the guy I told you about who used to play the piano before dinner to impress our dates. They thought he was so cool."

Toby seemed impressed. "Give us a tune before we turn in," he suggested. "I'd appreciate hearing someone else play for a change."

Encouraged by the clapping that came from some of the men who had overheard Toby's request, Neal walked up on stage and sat down at the concert grand piano he had been admiring all evening. Relaxed, and grateful for the opportunity to play, he chose, *I Remember You*, a song he had played frequently while in college. He could tell by the reduction in background noise that he had captured the attention of most of the men who were still there, so he continued with a medley of old favorites for a while longer, and then rejoined Allen and Toby.

The two men were still clapping when Neal returned to the patio. Toby offered his hand again and said, "You play beautifully, Neal. I was just telling Allen that I'd like you to sit in for me while you're here. Are you okay with that?"

Neal was deeply flattered, but reminded Toby that he played by ear, and in a bastard key.

Empathetic towards Neal's concern, Toby said, "That piano you just played on is equipped with an electronic key selector that will put you in any key you want to play in. Now, get some rest. We're going to have a lot of fun over the next few days. I'll be in touch."

Back in their bedroom a few minutes later, Neal and Allen were quick to strip down to under shorts and collapsed into their respective beds. Allen was asleep in seconds, leaving Neal to stare wide-eyed at the full moon shining down on him through the room's only window. Moments later, as Neal's mind raced back over the events of that day, his eyelids finally grew heavy from focusing too long on the image of the Donaldson family portrait that Anita Atkins had in her Carlsbad apartment. *What a reunion that's going to be!*

Chapter 8

The Adventure Continues

Sounds of others moving around in the bedroom the next morning gave notice that the second day of Neal's visit to the Sawmill Club had already begun. A quick glance at Allen Henderson's bed confirmed that he had not caused the commotion.

Aware that Neal was awake, an unfamiliar voice cheerfully said, "Rise and shine boys, a new day is born."

Struggling to sit up, Neal managed a painful, "Good morning. I'm Neal Thomas. That other body over there is Allen Henderson. What the hell time is it?"

"A little after ten o'clock," the man replied, offering Neal his hand. "My name's Jack Peters. The other bed belongs to my friend, Jim Taylor. He's taking a shower."

Without placing any particular significance on the name, Neal asked, "When did you guys get here? Those other two beds were empty when we finally turned in last night."

"Jim and I flew in from Alameda Naval Air Station a little while ago," Jack explained. "Sorry we woke you."

Despite Allen's attempt to go back to sleep, the conversation going on between Neal and one of the new arrivals brought him up on his elbows. "Don't you guys have any respect for the dead?" he said, still groggy from being awakened from a sound sleep. "I feel like I've been embalmed."

About that time, the door swung open and a naked body wrapped in a towel walked in.

"Speak of the devil," Jack remarked. "Meet Jim Taylor, the craziest pilot west of the Mississippi."

Neal's eyes blinked with surprise, as he realized he knew the newcomer. "Jim Taylor?" he shouted. "What the hell are you doing here?"

Squinting though the water that was still dripping from his hair, Jim walked further into the room and began to laugh when he recognized Neal. "Well I'll be damned! You're the last person on the planet I expected to run into in this God-forsaken place. I've forgotten your name, but not that face. You were with Gloria Donaldson on Catalina Island, right?"

Neal thrust out his hand. "Neal Thomas, Jim. You're right on target. Good to see you again?"

"Likewise," Jim replied, as he began to put on his clothes. "What the hell are you doing up here, if I may ask?"

During the cross-conversation that followed, Neal learned that Jim Taylor and Jack Peters had been pilots in the same squadron during the Korean conflict, and had kept in contact with one another after the war ended. Jack had gone back to school to obtain a master's degree in Political Science, while Jim finished his twenty-year hitch in the Air Force and retired to take over his father's flying school in El Cajon.

Looking at the other fellow, Neal asked, "Where do you live, Jack?"

"San Diego North County," he replied. "Rancho Santa Fe, to be more specific. Ever heard of it?"

"Heard of it! I could have bought a house in Rancho with the money I pissed away at Mille Fleurs." Neal replied. "I finally settled for Carlsbad. I'm divorced and officially retired now. Home is a quiet little place overlooking the beach that I rent from my oldest daughter and her husband."

"How about you?" Jack asked, looking in Allen's direction. "Where do you call home?"

"I'm the odd man out, I guess," Allen replied. "I'm a co-partner in a Chicago law firm. Neal and I were roommates in college. Like you, I spent time in the Navy during the Korean War. I'm semi-retired now with a large family. A grandfather, in other words."

"Well, I guess that pretty well does it for the who's who rigmarole," Jeff remarked. "Why don't we get together for lunch before the craziness begins."

"Good idea," Allen agreed. "Neal and I need a shower to get our motors running, then we'll join you in the dining room."

Jim Taylor had finally finished dressing and was about to leave when Neal held the two of them up momentarily by asking, "By the way, how did you two get here by plane? I didn't know there was an airport near here."

"That's the beauty of having Jim for a friend," Jack replied. "He's probably the only pilot around who has a re-built Grumman Goose to fly around in, except maybe Jimmy Buffett."

"I doubt that Jimmy flies his any more," Jim commented. "I spent a lot of money getting mine airworthy, but it was worth every penny. I'm welcome at all the Naval Air Stations, and I make a pretty good hunk of change flying people around to lake and ocean resorts. Pays for its upkeep, and it's fun to fly. I'll take you up in it before we leave."

"You're on," Neal responded excitedly. "I wouldn't miss it for the world."

Following Jack and Jim's departure, Neal and Allen concentrated on getting ready for what was beginning to look like a fun-filled day. It was while Allen was out of the room taking his shower that a totally unexpected incident occurred. Neal had all but finished dressing when his cell-phone chimed.

Questioning who the caller might be, he flipped open the cover. "Hello, this is Neal."

"Hello yourself, Mr. T," the unmistakable voice of Dan Hughes greeted him. "How's your vacation going?"

The sound of Dan's voice sent a quiver of uneasiness racing through Neal's body, as he wondered what could have prompted him to call. Expecting the worst, he asked, "Where are you?"

During the short pause that followed, Neal could hear the familiar sound of ice being dropped into a glass.

"I'm at the Rosarito Beach Hotel in Baja, California," Dan replied, "and lucky to be here, I might add."

"What's that supposed to mean," Neal asked, frustrated and angered by having been reminded of a world he thought he had escaped for at least a few days. "Are you okay?"

"Depends on your definition of, okay." Dan replied, slurring his words a little. "Yeah, I'm okay. At least for the time being."

"Quit dancing around the question, Dan. Tell me what the hell you're doing in Rosarito Beach?"

"Right after you left to go on vacation a friend of mine informed me that two suspicious looking characters were on the island making inquiries about me. Considering the possibility that they might be DEA agents, or Cartel assassins, I decided it was time to haul my ass out of there. After moving my boat to a safer location, I hopped a late flight to Tijuana and took a cab down here the next morning."

"Well, that sure simplifies my plans considerably," Neal remarked with a sigh of relief."

"So glad to be of service," Dan replied sarcastically. "What plan is that?"

"I can't tell you right now. Just stay put and don't get into any trouble," Neal said seriously. "I'll be back home in three days. I'll call you then to plan our next move."

"Don't hurry on my account, Mr. T. I'm beginning to like this place."

Irritated by the flippant attitude Dan was taking over the potentially dangerous situation he was in, Neal said, "Don't get too comfortable, sport. The real challenge is yet to come."

A few seconds after his conversation with Dan Hughes was over, the bedroom door opened and Allen Henderson entered the room. "Your turn, old buddy," he remarked, with noticeable enthusiasm. "Soap's in the shower."

On his way to the bathroom, Neal couldn't help thinking, *was Jim Taylor's presence here a timely coincidence that solves the problem of how to get Dan out of Mexico?* The more he thought about it, the more convinced he was that Jim and his seaplane were the answer to his dilemma over how to get Dan back into the United States. Now all he had to do was convince Jim to participate.

Refreshed by a shave and shower, Neal returned to the bedroom to find Allen dressed and stretched out on his bed reading a newspaper.

"Anything of interest happening in the real world?" Neal asked, for the sake of making conversation.

"As a matter of fact, there is," Allen replied. "On the front page of this paper there's a small headline that reads: **Suspected Drug Dealer Eludes Authorities Again.** The inside story mentions a resident of Tidewater, Virginia who narrowly escaped being apprehended in the Bahamas by DEA agents acting on information provided by an un-named source. According to this article, the DEA suspects someone inside their organization leaked confidential information about agents in the Bahamas Islands looking for a guy by the name of Dan Hughes."

After a slight pause, Allen continued: "Didn't you live in the Tidewater area at one time, Doofus? Ever heard of this guy, Dan Hughes?"

Hesitant to admit that he had, Neal merely replied, "Vaguely. But that's neither here nor there. Let's go get something to eat."

There were Bloody Marys sitting in front of both their other roommates when Allen and Neal met up with them in the main dining room. Considering their mutual belief in the mythical healing power of antiquity's classic remedy for a hangover, they sat down and ordered the same thing.

Light conversation about personal histories and middle-aged foolishness continued until the waiter came to take their breakfast orders. That done, the conversation turned to a brief discussion about the activities that were available to take part in that day. The list of options was varied and included archery and track and field events. Additionally, hiking mountainous trails surrounding the lake was particularly popular, along with swimming races held in a portion of the lake near the heliport.

"I wasn't aware that the Sawmill Club was being considered as a future site for the Olympics," Neal joked. "I hope they have awards for best spectators."

Neal's humor was well timed, prompting Jim Taylor to say, "I wouldn't mind winning something today. I understand there are some pretty nice prizes waiting for the winners over on the other side of the lake. Any one up for a canoe race?"

"Why burn up all that energy," Allen butted in. "All one has to do is get in that pontoon boat down near the heliport to be chauffeured over there and back free of charge."

"Does that include a prize?" Jim asked.

Allen smiled, looked at Jim and said, "Just don't forget your wallet, sport. Or you'll be swimming back!"

After breakfast, the four men walked leisurely up and down the shoreline working off the delicious meal they had just eaten. They lingered at times to observe some of the events that were taking place all around them.

"This sure is a busy place, athletically," Neal commented. "I had no idea these men were so competitive, especially the older ones."

"That's another tradition that got passed along by old man Donaldson," Allen commented. "There are photographs in our library that record the annual competition which Frederick promoted. They included speed sawing, axing logs, log rolling on the lake and other events, all of which represented sizeable cash rewards for the winners in those days."

"I don't know about the rest of you guys, but I'd like to see those pictures," Neal said, as they approached the stone steps leading to the main lodge.

"Been there, done that," Jack Peters remarked. Facing Allen, he suggested, "Why don't you take him? Jim and I will meet you down at the tavern when you're finished. We can watch the race from there."

"See you in forty-five minutes," Allen replied, turning toward Neal. "I know you have a special interest in seeing those pictures, Neal. So let's go to the library, while those two have a drink and wait for us."

"What race are they talking about?" Neal asked out of curiosity.

Allen stopped and pointed in the direction of the heliport pier. "See those sailboats tied up down there? Notice that they're all Lightning-class. Each year, those who wish to participate pair-up and sail around those red buoys you can see anchored at opposite ends of the lake. They sail twice around the lake from a dead stop at the start line. Only their jib sail is raised at that point."

Neal laughed. "How the hell can they get an even start if they're floating all over the place?"

It was Allen's turn to laugh. "Before the race begins, that big cabin cruiser out there ties a rope to its stern that has Styrofoam tubes strung onto it so it won't sink. The other end of the cable is attached to a cleat on one of the dock pilings down near the waterline. Then the cruiser pulls the rope into a straight line and drops anchor. Meanwhile, the two-man crew of each sailboat paddles into starting position by grabbing the rope and hanging on. Like maneuvering racehorses into a starting gate, for example."

"I'm glad it's a big lake," Neal joked. "What next?"

"When every boat is held fast to the starting rope, an official up there on the dock fires a starter pistol, and away they go. Simple as that."

"Wait a minute," Neal remarked skeptically. "What happens to the rope?"

"I knew you would ask," Allen replied, eager to explain what to him seemed obvious. "Remember, the only sail that has been hoisted thus far is the jib, and most of them are just fluttering because the boats are facing into the wind. During the time it takes for each boat to raise its mainsail, the cruiser has up-anchored and hauled ass toward the opposite side of the lake, dragging the starting line with it."

"Is determining the winner that goofy?" Neal asked, amused by the whole bizarre process.

"Nope, it's all recorded on camera," Allen replied, as he turned and started toward the lodge. "Now, let's get over to the library so we can get back to the tavern and enjoy the race."

Getting to the library meant passing through the main reception hall again in order to access its double-door entrance on the opposite side of the room. Once inside, Neal stood in awe of the floor-to-ceiling shelves that supported hundreds of photo albums locked behind glass doors. Closer inspection showed that each album was identified with the year in which the photographs were taken.

What a graveyard this turned out to be Neal thought, as his eyes scanned the albums for those dated in the early sixties.

"When you find the years you want to examine, let me know," Allen remarked. "I'll have to get the key from the front office to open the glass doors."

"The early nineteen-sixties," Neal replied.

While Allen went to get the key, Neal examined the many glass-topped cases that took up the entire center portion of the room. All were locked and contained a wide variety of artifacts – including old guns, knives, beads, jewelry, coins, and odd pieces, such as buttons, buckles, spurs, and a beautifully crafted nugget of gold that was inset with a ruby-red gemstone. As he stood wondering what significance the strange looking piece of jewelry held, Allen came back.

Observing Neal's fascination with it, Allen remarked, "To this day, no one's been able to figure out where that one came from, Sherlock. So don't get a headache trying to solve the mystery. It was found in the stomach of a decomposed bear that someone killed when old man Donaldson was still running this place. He thought it had some mystical power and hung it around his neck for years. Anita finally talked him into giving it to one of his sons. Guess which one?"

"Randy Donaldson's father?"

"You're pretty sharp today, kiddo," Allen remarked. "Randy wore it too, until his wife, Gloria, talked him into putting it in here for safe-keeping. Good thing she did, all things considered. Now, are you ready to start looking for whatever it is you hope to find in here?"

Neal put aside his preoccupation with the strange looking artifact and walked over to the shelves that held the albums beginning with the year 1960, and said to Allen, "Open this one."

The search began slowly. Fortunately, whoever cataloged the photographs had dated them. They had also written key words at the bottom identifying the event and/or person(s) being photographed. It wasn't until he was well into those taken in the mid 1960's that he came upon one titled, *The Randolph Donaldson Family*. His heartbeat quickened when he read the sub-title of that one: ***Randy – Anita – Gloria***. Unquestionably, they were the same individuals as those who were in the photograph Anita Atkins had in her apartment. His quest to learn the true identity of Gloria Donaldson was now finally over.

"Satisfied?" Allen asked, suspecting that Neal had found what he had been looking for.

"I sure am," Neal sighed with relief. "You'll never know what a wonderful thing you've done by inviting me up here. I shall be eternally in your debt, my friend. And so will some others I know."

"We'll work something out," Allen jested. "But for now, let's get back to the tavern so we can enjoy the race."

Neal was only too happy to oblige. After locking the case, they returned the key and left the lodge just as activity on the boat dock was getting underway. Jack Peters and Jim Taylor were drinking beer and laughing about something when Neal and Allen reached their table on the patio.

"Welcome!" Jack said in a somewhat subdued tone of voice. "Did you enjoy your tour through the archives?"

"More than you can imagine," Neal answered. "I've never seen history so well documented. The albums reminded me of a book I bought my father for Christmas back in 1950. It was called, *YEAR – Mid-Century Edition*. My mother gave it to me after my dad passed away. I still have it."

"I remember that book," Allen remarked, noticeably interested in Neal's recollection. "Charles Seymour was President Emeritus of Yale University at the time. He wrote the *Forward* to that book."

"Hmm, that's interesting, "Jack commented, as if he had suddenly been reminded of something. "I believe my parents also have a copy of that book. What a coincidence. I'll have to research that when I get back home."

"When are you and Jim planning to leave?" Neal asked. "I thought you were here for the duration."

"I was, until a few minutes ago," Jack replied, looking disappointed. "I've been called back to attend an emergency meeting of the Rancho Santa Fe City Council, which I can't ignore, unfortunately. I've already made arrangements to take the emergency chopper out of here in the morning. That way, Jim won't have to fly me back to San Diego. I've already booked an afternoon flight out of San Francisco, so there's nothing left to do but enjoy ourselves."

While looking out over the water to watch the sailboats gradually maneuvering into starting position, Neal noticed the concrete ramp where Jim Taylor's seaplane sat ready to enter the water. Prompted by the relief he felt in knowing exactly where Dan Hughes was for the first time, Neal looked over at Jim Taylor and asked, "Do you have any commitments after this shindig is over?"

"Not now," he replied. "It's just me and The Goose from here on out. Why, did you have something in mind?"

"As a matter of fact, yes," Neal said, "but we can talk about that later. I believe the race is about to get under way."

All four men immediately directed their attention to the line of sailboats that had one man each grasping the elevated starting rope. As they bobbed up and down like so many corks, a shot rang out and the starting rope dropped into the lake. Following its release, the anchor-men scrambled to hoist their mainsails, while the tiller men worked their rudders back and forth feverishly to catch the wind and start tack-ing. From a spectator's point of view, it was a hilarious spectacle that had everyone cheering madly and laughing like a bunch of football fans, adding validation to the typical female interpretation of such child-like behavior – *boys and their toys.*

By the time another round of drinks reached the table, the race was well under way. Some visible display of nautical savvy seemed to have turned the initial chaos into something approaching skilled maneuver-ing, as some sailboats were rapidly approaching the second and final lap of the race. It was then that Neal felt a hand settle on his shoulder and a familiar voice ask, "Enjoying yourselves, gentlemen?"

Neal turned and found Toby Tanner standing behind him with a drink in his hand, and grinning like a kid. Surprised by Tanner seeking him out so early in the day, Neal replied, "Won't you join us and watch the finish? It looks like it's going to be a close one."

"Thanks, but not right now," Toby answered. "I just stopped by to see if you were up to boating across the lake with me a little later this afternoon."

Surprised by the invitation, Neal took a few seconds to mull it over before responding. "I thought only members were permitted to go there? You guys aren't setting me up for something, are you?"

Each of the four men looked at one another and shrugged their shoulders in denial. Toby finally broke the silence. "Band members are excluded from that ruling, Neal. You are going to fill in for me later on, aren't you?"

"Sure beats the hell out of hanging around with us, Doofus," Allen remarked. "Go on over with him. We can live without you for a few hours."

Everyone clapped in support of Allen's encouragement, forcing Neal to ask Toby, "When were you planning to leave?"

"Right after the race is over," he replied. "A few of us volunteer to play a little music for the ladies during their cocktail hour. We do it every year. You'll have a ball!"

"Shall I change clothes?" Neal asked, still suspicious of what was going on.

"Why?" Allen laughed, slapping Neal on the shoulder "Relax, for bloody sake. It's a party, not a formal dance."

Everyone laughed, embarrassing Neal into accepting his fate. "Okay, I'll go!"

Amused by Neal's reaction, Toby pointed toward the heliport dock and said, "I'll see you down there at five o'clock sharp. And believe me, this is no joke."

After Toby left the patio deck, Jack Peters remarked, "You've been holding out on us Mr. T. Since when are you in cahoots with the infamous Cottage Kittens?"

"I swear to you on my mother's grave," Neal responded defensively, "I have no idea who those women are."

"Who cares?" Jack roared with delight. "Be sure to get some pictures."

Returning his attention to what was taking place on the lake, Allen remarked, "It looks like boat number seven has the lead. You might know. That's Hank Swenson's boat. He wins this race every damn year."

From where the four men were sitting the numbered flags atop each mast confirmed that Allen's observation was correct. After completing an extremely close passing of the lake's northern buoy, Swenson's boat tacked into a crosswind run for the finish line with both sails full and her mast heeled over about twenty degrees.

By the time all five boats were about two hundred yards from the finish line and nearly abreast of one another, the tiller on Swenson's rudder snapped unexpectedly, swinging his boat off course and out of control. Floating helplessly like a piece of driftwood, Swenson could do little more than watch the other boats pass him by and press on toward the finish line, number thirteen crossing first.

As spectators cheered loudly for the new winner, Swenson and his companion could only paddle helplessly back to shore with their sails flapping in the wind. Contrary to what many spectators were expecting from Hank because of his inglorious defeat, he leapt from his beached boat, sought out the winner and shook his hand vigorously.

"Congratulations, Sam!" Swenson bellowed with laughter, "If I had to lose the damn race, I'm glad it was to you."

Ironically, had Hank taken the time to inspect the tiller immediately after the race was over, he might have discovered that someone had drilled a small diameter hole half way up its under side, only inches from where it attached to the rudder. That hole eventually caused the stress fracture that cost Hank the race. Thanks to careless oversight by whoever replaced the tiller, Hank never knew he had been sabotaged. Such a discovery would have touched off an investigation that could have had serious consequences for the guilty party. But, as someone of questionable wisdom once said, *Shit happens.*

Part of the post-race celebration activity included a winner's lunch that lasted until almost four o'clock that afternoon. Becoming increasingly aware that his trip across the lake with Toby Tanner was less than an hour away, Neal decided it was time to take Jim Taylor aside and approach him on the subject of taking Jack Peters' place when Jim flew back to San Diego. By doing so, he would have an ideal opportunity to test Jim's willingness to use The Goose to fly Dan Hughes from Mexico to Catalina Island.

Since Jim had wandered un-noticed out onto the patio deck to get a breath of fresh air, Neal seized the opportunity and followed him. As Jim stood wistfully looking out over the lake, Neal approached and said. "A penny for your thoughts."

Undisturbed by Neal's intrusion, Jim's eyes remained fixed on the far side of the lake. "It's going to cost you a lot more than that, my friend," he replied thoughtfully. "I could get into a lot of trouble for what I'm thinking."

"Oh?" Neal said, surprised by the somber tone of Jim's voice. "Want to talk about it?"

"Not really. It's kind of personal," he replied. "Is there something you want to talk to me about?"

Suspecting he had interrupted a somber moment of personal reflection, Neal crafted his words carefully. "It concerns that conversation we had before the race began when I said we could continue it later."

"Well, it's later, that's for sure," Jim replied humorously. "What's on your mind?"

Sensing that Jim's mood had softened a little Neal said, "Since we're both going in the same direction after this gala event is over, I thought you might like a co-pilot to keep you company, now that Jack Peters won't be going back with you."

Jim remained silent for a moment and then replied, "This may come as somewhat of a surprise to you, but I've been thinking along those lines ever since Jack bailed out. Let's talk about this further tomorrow morning after he leaves. You're not going to be in any kind of shape to discuss much of anything after Toby and his boys get you back tonight."

Elated by Jim's willingness to fly him back to San Diego, Neal glanced at his watch and said, "I guess I better get going. Toby is probably wondering where the hell I am."

Following a friendly handshake, Neal turned and started to leave when Jim's voice called after him, "Don't do anything I wouldn't do!"

Several minutes later, Neal walked out onto the heliport pier where the Sawmill Club's pontoon houseboat was tied up with its engine idling. Inside, Toby Tanner and a few of his musicians were already seated, while a young man wearing deck sneakers, shorts, a red-striped T-shirt and a captain's hat looked anxiously at his watch. Amused by the picture, Neal approached and addressed the young man formally. "Permission to come aboard, sir," he said, saluting him in a sharp, military fashion.

The surprised young man snapped to attention, returned the salute and replied, "Permission granted, sir. Welcome aboard."

Toby laughed at the charade going on outside on the dock and shouted, "Okay, Captain, let's get this tub underway. Everyone's accounted for."

As the Captain released the mooring lines and jumped effortlessly on deck to take his place inside behind the wheel, he saw a man running down the dock shouting, "Hey! Wait for me!"

Seconds later, the man stepped clumsily onboard. Neal recognized him immediately. It was Jim Taylor. Breathing heavily, with drops of perspiration glistening on his forehead, he panted to the young captain, "Thanks for waiting."

"You're too old to be running like that," Neal remarked with concern. "Are you trying to kill yourself?"

Hesitating for a moment to catch his breath, Jim replied, "Allen Henderson and Jack Peters have decided to play in a bridge tournament this evening, so I got to thinking, why not hang out with you guys?"

"Can you play a musical instrument?" Tanner asked, as a joke.

"I played drums in a Dixieland jazz band when I was in college."

"You're on," Tanner said, shaking his head and laughing. "Won't the girls get a kick out of you two characters?"

Traveling across the lake took close to twenty minutes. A small bar, however, made the trip pleasurable, and helped heighten the anticipation of what was waiting for them. To Toby and his musicians, it was just another gig. But to Neal Thomas and Jim Taylor, it would prove to be an evening of unforeseeable surprises and far-reaching consequences.

Due to the mountainous terrain surrounding the lake, the late afternoon sun disappeared early, bringing on a premature nightfall. Thus, when the boat approached its destination, lights began to come on like stars beginning to twinkle in the deep-blue sky overhead.

What couldn't have been seen from the Sawmill Club before the boat left that side of the lake was now clearly visible. A small group of log cabin-like cottages were conveniently arranged around a clubhouse building, and connected to it with sidewalks like spokes on a wagon wheel. Neal observed that whoever designed the complex had conveniently distanced the cabins from one another to ensure the privacy of what went on inside.

Since neither Neal nor Jim Taylor had any prior knowledge of what social protocol was in place, they followed Toby Tanner like two little puppy dogs on a leash, carrying instruments to help the musicians tote everything into the clubhouse in one trip.

The first surprise came when they entered the building. Its interior was a men's club in every sense of the word – lavishly furnished with heavily upholstered leather couches and chairs, just like the main lounge at the Sawmill Club. Members who had been there for several hours were waiting to board the boat Toby's group had just arrived on, laughing and joking as they greeted the newcomers. A young man behind a beautifully crafted mahogany bar was feverishly working to make it ready for the new group. A few minutes later, he looked up and greeted them enthusiastically. "Gentlemen, the bar is now open for business."

Eager to start the ball rolling, Jim Taylor and a couple of the musicians who had already set up their instruments wandered over to the bar and ordered drinks. During their absence, Neal helped Toby finish setting up his electronic keyboard. Unable to contain his curiosity any longer, he finally asked, "When do the ladies arrive?"

Toby waited until after he had plugged in the speaker wires before answering. "This is typically their quiet hour," he explained. "Most of them just hang out in the bungalows, bathe, fuss with their hair and get dressed for the evening. You know, honing their charm, so to speak. They'll be here before the next boat arrives, though. You can bet your bottom dollar on that."

After ordering a drink, Neal stepped outside to see if the next boat was on its way. The lake was very calm, beautifully reflecting the constantly darkening sky above him. Just as the tiny white shape moving slowly towards the complex confirmed the approach of it's next cargo of revelers, so did the unmistakable sound of feminine voices entering the clubhouse behind him give notice that they would be there to greet them.

Having no idea what to expect when the boat arrived, Neal returned inside and was dumbstruck by the first thing he saw. Moving closer to the bar, he discovered Jim Taylor in the embrace of one of the women who had just arrived. Because she stood with her back toward him, Neal didn't know or care who the woman was. He did, however, experience a small twinge of envy at seeing his friend already so unexpectedly preoccupied. Neal had already made a move to distance himself from the scene when Jim's voice rang out, "Hey, Neal! Come on over here. I want you to meet someone."

Not knowing whom to expect, Neal turned and approached the couple just as Jim released her to greet him. The look of surprise on Neal's face turned quickly to one of *what do I do now, coach?*

"I'd like you to meet Kimberly Prentice," Jim said, "She's an old friend of the Donaldson family. I asked her to marry me once, and she never forgave me for it. Funny how that word scares some women."

Neal offered his hand without any attempt to express recognition. "Pleased to meet you, Kimberly. I'm Neal Thomas."

"I know," she replied in like fashion. "Toby Tanner mentioned that he was bringing you with him when I talked with him earlier today. He told me you were quite the pianist. I'm anxious to hear you play."

"Be careful what you wish for," Neal replied, in an attempt to lighten the mood.

"Oh, and modest too" she laughed. "I can't wait."

Before the conversation could progress any further, a horn sounded from the direction of the boat dock, signaling the much-anticipated arrival of the final group of Club members for that day. In an attempt to apologize for having to leave them, Kimberly turned in the direction of the front door and said, "Sorry boys, looks like it's time for me to go to work. Don't either of you leave without saying goodnight. And try to stay out of trouble, will you?"

Neal recognized the conflict of interest Kimberly was faced with, given the nature of her past relationship with Jim, so he decided to wait for a more appropriate opportunity to ask her to do him a favor.

Moments later the door to the clubhouse burst open, unceremoniously, and a small group of men sauntered in and grouped themselves at tables around the room and at the bar. Almost simultaneously, Toby Tanner and his small group of musicians left the bar and began playing to the boisterous cheering of the new arrivals. The scene reminded Neal of so many western movies he remembered seeing where riverboat saloons provided the backdrop for a mix of men and women flirting with one another at gambling tables and on the dance floor. Occasionally, when the evening was *getting a glow on*, pairs of men and women would slip away unseen to collect the favors the men had come there for.

That the woman he had felt so deeply about many years ago would willingly take part in such activity bothered Neal, until Jim Taylor explained what had happened to her early in her first and only marriage. According to Jim, she had been tragically widowed early in that marriage, and had made a solemn vow never to expose herself to that kind of unhappiness again. The rationale for what she was doing now was simple and straightforward – very lucrative. So, rather than upset himself with a situation over which he had no control, Jim fell out of love and limited his contact with Kimberly to this once a year get together.

When the band finished the song they had been playing, Toby Tanner leaned over his keyboard and addressed the noisy gathering. "And now ladies and gentleman, our first break of the evening will be complimented by two of your guests who have agreed to fill in for me and my drummer while we take care of an urgent calling." Following the laughter that ensued, he continued: "Neal Thomas, and his friend, Jim Taylor, are going to sit in for a few numbers. So, please welcome them with your applause and enjoy their music. I'm sure you will be impressed."

In response to Toby's announcement, an enthusiastic round of applause filled the room, coaxing Neal and Jim to put aside the trials and tribulations of their personal lives and come forward. After conferring with the remaining band members for a moment, Neal took his place at the piano while Jim settled down behind the drums. Neal's announcement that they would begin with a number titled *Ain't Misbehav'n* brought a burst of laughter, setting the mood for the next hour.

When Toby and his regular drummer finally returned, obviously the worse for wear, everyone in the place gave Neal and Jim a standing ovation, prompting Toby to joke, "Those two guys can swim home!"

When Neal and Jim adjourned to the bar, hands on the wall clock showed the time to be a few minutes before seven o'clock. Tired and thirsty, they quickly disposed of their first drink and were well into the second when Jim excused himself to use the men's room. During his absence, the thought of not being able to see Gloria Donaldson on his way home kept Neal preoccupied with how to let her know that flying home with Jim Taylor was of necessity a higher priority. A soft hand on his shoulder, and a voice he recognized immediately, gave him a possible solution.

"Where's Jim?" Kimberly asked.

"He went to the men's room," Neal replied, offering her his stool. When she accepted, Neal quickly asked, "Will you do me a favor?"

"Depends on what it is," she answered coyly. "What did you have in mind?"

"Seriously, I need you to contact Gloria Donaldson for me and explain to her that I won't be stopping in San Francisco on my way home. Something has come up that demands my immediate attention, so I'm bumming a ride back to San Diego with Jim Taylor. Just tell Gloria that

I will get in touch with her as soon as I get this mess I'm in straightened out. Will you do that?"

"I'll give you her cell phone number before you leave this evening. You can call her yourself," she replied, as she noticed Jim approaching in the bar mirror behind Neal. "Right now we've got company."

Recalling how childishly jealous Jim had been during there brief relationship, Kimberly eased away from Neal and turned around to intercept Jim before he could say anything foolish. "Ah, there you are," she said jovially. "I was just telling Neal how wonderful the music sounded when you sat in for Toby this past hour. The girls have been hounding me for some personal history on you two, but I very diplomatically advised them to discover that on their own."

Her ploy had worked. Jim's possible over reaction to finding Neal and Kimberly in close company with one another changed abruptly to a broad grin, as he patted her gently on the backside and said, "We did do pretty well for a couple of old farts, didn't we Mr. T.? That bass player sure knew how to put a bottom under us. What a hell of a musician!"

Satisfied that she had thwarted what could have been an embarrassing situation, Kimberly looked over at the bar clock and remarked, "Well, the bewitching hour is upon us, I guess. Toby and his group are packing up their instruments. I assume you'll be leaving with them."

Not wanting to consider any other option, Neal took the initiative and said, "I can't speak for Jim, but I'm bushed and hungry. So I think I'll take the boat back, eat dinner with the boys and hit the sack."

"Sounds good to me," Jim seconded. "I need a good night's sleep too. Flying The Goose with a four-day hangover is not a good idea, much as I would like to stay."

Feigning disappointment for Jim's benefit, Kimberly said, "Yes, by all means. I don't want my last recollection of you two characters to be pictures in an obituary column. Please, spare me that grief."

Both men laughed and hugged her warmly. As Jim walked away to help Toby Tanner with his equipment, Neal felt a warm hand quickly slide in and out of his left trouser pocket, leaving something behind. When they separated, Kimberly whispered, "Don't give that number to anyone. I'll be in enough trouble giving it to you."

Neal winked his understanding and left to help Toby. When they were ready to leave, Kimberly joined the men as they headed back to the boat. She remained on the dock for some time, waving at them as the boat slowly turned away and floated slowly off into the night.

Walking back to the noisy confines of the lounge, Kimberly had but one thought: *I'm going to miss this place.*

Allen Henderson and Jack Peters were standing on the illuminated heliport pier when the band returned to the Sawmill Club. Something about their presence there gave Neal an uneasy feeling that something was amiss. Concerned that it might involve Allen, he wasted little time in getting off the boat and hurried to where the two men were standing. "What's up?" Neal asked, looking directly at Allen. "You don't look so good."

Because Allen was obviously too upset to answer, Jack interceded for him. "Allen received word that one of his clients had committed suicide a couple of hours ago. As the man's attorney, Allen feels obligated to return home, but wanted to talk to you before he left."

"I'm sorry about all this, Doofus," Allen finally spoke up. "I hate to leave you on such short notice, but at least I got the chance to see you before that chopper pilot gets here. I called the lounge a little while ago to tell you what had happened, but they said you had already left."

For a moment, Neal and Jim Taylor stood speechless from the shock of it all. It was Jim who understood better than anyone what Allen was going through. Taking the initiative, Jim turned to Allen and said, "When that pilot does get here, you get your ass out of here. Neal's my responsibility now. I'll make sure he gets where he's going."

Allen managed a weak smile and expressed his thanks.

At that very instant, the helmeted figure of a man in khaki flight gear came running down the dock, gave a thumbs-up gesture and climbed into the chopper. Neal recognized him immediately as the pilot who had brought him to the Windmill Club – Jordan Pikes. Seconds later, the rotor blades began to turn, prompting Pikes to signal Allen to get in. Following handshakes all around, Allen walked out into the chopper's air-wash and climbed aboard. Moments later, with tears beginning to well up in his eyes, he disappeared into the night, while three friends waved goodbye from the heliport below.

Given Jack Peters plan to leave early the next morning, Jim Taylor found himself wondering whether or not staying there for another full day was in his best interests. Events scheduled for the next day were mostly of an academic nature, and held little interest for him when compared with the benefits he could gain from returning home a day early. Since Neal had already volunteered to keep him company, Jim concluded that Neal would be receptive to most any plan that furthered their mutual interests. With that thought in mind, he fell in step with the other two men and proceeded to their room to freshen up before dinner.

A half an hour later, Jack Peters suggested they leave for the dining room. Welcoming the privacy their absence would provide, Neal told them to go ahead because he wanted to make a phone call. When he was sure they were well on their way, he reached in his pocket and pulled out the slip of paper Kimberly Prentice had planted there. Activating his cell phone, he pressed in the number she had given him and waited. Four rings later, a woman's voice answered.

"May I ask who is calling, please?"

"Gloria? This is Neal Thomas."

"Who gave you this number?" she fired back immediately.

"Take it easy, will you. Just be glad it isn't the FBI or the CIA."

"That's not funny, Neal," she replied in a less challenging tone. "Judging from the trouble you must have gone through to get this number, I assume you are not the bearer of good tidings."

"Relax. It's not that bad," he assured her. "I'm calling to let you know that I will not be stopping in San Francisco on my return trip home."

Silence.

"Actually, I'm bumming a ride back to San Diego with Jim Taylor. I have something important to discuss with him that involves a friend of mine who's in trouble and needs my help."

"You couldn't have picked a better companion to get in trouble with," Gloria commented sarcastically. "You must be desperate."

"Truth is, Jim and that plane of his may be saving my friend's life, so give the devil his due, for Pete's sake?"

"You don't know him like I do," She replied, a little more calmly. "When am I going to see you again?"

"Soon, I hope. I'll call you when I get things figured out. I'm going to need your help also."

"Me? What can I do?"

"I can't discuss it with you right now."

"You'd better," she remarked, somewhat threateningly, "You at least owe me some kind of an explanation."

Realizing that either Jim or Jack could return to check on him at any moment, Neal cautioned, "Look, I'm going to arouse suspicion if I stay where I am any longer. I'll call you in a few days and explain everything. Fair enough?"

"I guess..."

Jim Taylor and Jack Peters were each sipping a glass of wine when Neal arrived at their table. Jim had placed a napkin on the chair next to him to reserve it and advised Neal that a drink had been ordered for him. The interim period between cocktails and dinner provided Jim with an ideal opportunity to discuss his intentions to leave the next morning.

To his surprise, Neal applauded the idea, admitting that he had even considered it himself, especially after Allen Henderson had been so unavoidably forced to leave. "I couldn't be happier with the way things have worked out," Neal remarked. "This has been a lot of fun for me, but it would appear that all of us have good reason to call it quits." Raising his glass, he invited the others to do the same. "Here's to the Sawmill Club, and all the wonderful memories it has created. Thanks for a marvelous time."

It was well past ten o'clock when the stewards began clearing the dinner tables, giving notice to those who still remained to either adjourn to The Tavern, or go to bed. As far as Jim Taylor, Jack Peters and Neal Thomas were concerned, the day was over.

Though Jim and Jack fell asleep almost immediately, Neal resisted long enough to weigh the consequences of Gloria Donaldson and Anita Atkins coming face to face at a point in time when he could arrange it. The scenario blurred as a picture of Dan Hughes laying on a deck chair at the Rosarito Beach Hotel flashed before his eyes, reminding him of the real challenge that lay ahead.

Chapter 9

The Alliance

When Neal's eyes cracked open the next morning he saw a diagonal wash of white light running down the wall behind Jim Taylor's bed that came to rest on his bare shoulder. Soft snoring and an occasional twitch of his body were ample indicators that he was still asleep.

Jack Peters, however, was missing, a subtle reminder that he had been true to his vow to be on his way home before first light of dawn.

Considering the overindulgence all three men had subjected themselves to the previous day, Neal took advantage of the early morning quiet to piece together a realistic plan for getting Dan Hughes out of Mexico and safely tucked away in Gloria Donaldson's condominium on Catalina Island.

Now that Jack Peters was out of the picture, Neal figured the ideal time to approach Jim was at breakfast that morning. To launch that plan he rose quietly and walked to the bathroom where he hoped a hot shower would revitalize him for the day ahead.

Two men were toweling themselves dry when Neal entered the room. Except for a polite "Good morning," they finished and left without further conversation.

After adjusting the temperature to his liking, Neal stepped behind the curtain and stood for what seemed to be a long time, letting the water beat on his head and run soothingly down the rest of his body. After a thorough soaping, he rinsed off and closed the hot water valve.

Seconds later, the lake's icy water hit him like he remembered it had when he was a teenager skating over thin ice on a meadow not far from his home. Equally memorable was the scolding he got from his mother, followed by being sent to bed without any supper after his father arrived home later that afternoon.

When he could tolerate the cold no longer, he quickly closed the valve and waited until the shivering subsided before throwing the curtain back and stepping out. Though it took a few moments to regain his normal body temperature, the shock had accomplished its purpose. With renewed enthusiasm he toweled dry and returned to his room where he found Jim Taylor sitting on the edge of his bed, yawning. "I was wondering where the hell you ran off to," he remarked while scratching his whiskers. "How's the water?"

"Just what the doctor ordered," Neal replied enthusiastically. "Sure worked for me."

"Good. A hot shower and a hearty breakfast ought to get us on our way in fine shape," Jim said. "Wait for me, I'll be right back."

During the interim, Neal made good use of his time by packing his bag and making sure he wasn't leaving anything behind. With bag and briefcase sitting on the foot of his bed, he thumbed through a magazine while he waited for Jim to return.

Several minutes later and still dripping, Jim entered the room and said, "Damn, that water's cold! Sure did the trick, though. I feel almost human again."

Neal smiled and thought *that's encouraging.*

The main lodge dining room was only partially filled when Neal and Jim arrived. Leaving their luggage in the foyer, they entered and sat at a table by themselves. After ordering coffee, they sat silently reviewing the menu until Neal put his aside and said, "I think it's about time I leveled with you about my real purpose in wanting to fly back to San Diego with you. I've waited until now to bring up the matter because I believed it would be unwise to mention it in front of others. Now seems to be as convenient a time as any."

A smile came to life on Jim's face as he continued to peruse the menu. "I'm listening," he finally remarked. "I suspected you had something on your mind ever since we returned from the other side of the lake last night. Go ahead. Get it off your chest."

Neal faltered for a moment. His respect for Jim's military background and training, however, gave him the assurance he needed to ask, "I suppose you've already figured out that Gloria Donaldson is involved?"

"I gathered as much. Gloria and I go back a long way, but that's neither here nor there. Please continue."

"I have a friend who has information relevant to drug trafficking in the Tidewater area of Virginia," Neal began. "The DEA desperately needs him to testify before a Congressional Committee to authenticate evidence he had already given them. Without his testimony, the DEA is powerless to close in on the Cartel."

"What's your friend's name?" Jim asked.

"Dan Hughes."

"Go on."

"I knew Dan as a child," Neal continued, "He was wild then, and still is for that matter, but he's not a bad person. When I saw him recently he treated me with genuine respect and generosity. So much so that he confided in me where he had hidden the evidence the DEA now has, but can't use because it's only circumstantial without Dan's testimony. Problem is, not only does the DEA want him, so does the Cartel. To escape them both he fled to the Bahamas where he still has loyal friends."

"Is that where he is now?" Jim asked just as their waiter approached to take their order.

Waiting until after the waiter had gone Neal answered. "No. He fled to Mexico when he received word from a friend that the Cartel had sent two goons to the Bahamas to get rid of him."

"Pardon my curiosity, but how did you come by all this information?" Jim asked. "You've been up here for the past couple of days."

"I got a call from Dan yesterday morning right after you and Jack Peters left the room," Neal replied. "He's at the Rosarito Beach Hotel in Baja, California waiting for me to tell him what to do."

Jim looked over at Neal with a furrowed brow and asked, "Is that guy nuts? What the hell does he think you can do for him in Mexico?"

Conceding that he could no longer keep his friend guessing about what was going on, Neal began explaining what he hoped Jim would agree to. "I have convinced the Director of the DEA that the only way to get Dan Hughes to testify is to film him answering their prepared questions at a remote location I have in mind. One where the DEA and the Cartel would ever think to look."

"Whoa! Back that up a little there, Mr. T," Jim interrupted. "How do you propose to get your friend out of Mexico?"

"I'm sorry, I guess I'm getting little ahead of myself. Let me tell you what I have in mind, since it involves you and one other person."

Neal's attempt to explain, however, was interrupted briefly when the waiter arrived with their meals. Following his departure Neal noticed that Jim had developed a scowl on his face, forcing Neal to re-evaluate Jim's role in the alliance he was hoping to establish. With no other alternatives available, however, and time running out by the hour, he thought *to hell with it*, and continued. "I'm sure you know that Gloria Donaldson has a condominium on Catalina Island. With her approval, I intend to use that location to film Dan's testimony."

"Are there any other people involved in this operation?" Jim asked, tapping his fingers nervously on the table.

"Actually, there's only one," Neal replied. "Dan and me don't count. That means the success or failure of this whole operation falls smack on your butt, Jamie boy!"

Jim's face gradually relaxed into a devilish smile, as he looked across the table at Neal and said, "You need The Goose, don't you?"

Realizing that Jim was much more perceptive than he had given him credit for, Neal countered with a statement that he hoped would appeal to the one-time jet pilot's sense of fair play. "Dan Hughes is sitting in a hotel in Mexico waiting for me to come up with a plan to help him maintain his citizenship in a system you risked your life to defend. Are you going to sit there and tell me he's not worth it?"

"Take it easy!" Jim replied. "I get the message. Let's finish our breakfast and get the hell out of here. You can tell me the rest of your plan when we're airborne."

Half an hour later both men picked up their luggage and walked to the main office to check out. Because he was a guest, Neal was asked to sign a confidentiality agreement that he would not discuss any of the Club's activities, once he left the premises. After doing so, he addressed the clerk and said, "My sponsor, Mr. Allen Henderson, said that I could express my gratitude to your staff at this time. Will two hundred dollars take care of it?"

"That's very generous, Mr. Thomas," the young clerk replied. "Thank you, and have a safe trip home."

On their way to the concrete launch ramp where The Goose sat waiting, Jim chuckled and said, "Can I help you with your bags, sir?"

Neal laughed, and flipped him a finger.

Climbing up into the side-entry hatch of the twin-engine seaplane, Neal looked around in surprise at the work Jim had done to make the interior comfortable. It had been cleverly paneled with lightweight material similar to that of a passenger aircraft. Two belted seats flanked both sides of the narrow passageway leading to the cockpit. Each had a curtained window. Aluminum cabinets deep enough to house emergency rations, water, ice and booze were built into the backside of the cockpit bulkhead.

After placing their luggage in the aft storage compartment, Jim led Neal into the cockpit and told him to strap himself in, as he flipped a series of switches to activate the plane's operating systems. Looking over at Neal he said, "Slide your window back and make sure there's no one milling around near the starboard engine."

Neal did as he was asked and replied, "All clear, Captain. Anytime you're ready."

Before Jim started the starboard engine, he handed Neal a set of headphones with a micro-speaker attached to it. "Here, put these on. We can communicate much better after the engines are up and running."

Less than a minute later, both engines were idling smoothly. Acting on a signal from Jim, the man responsible for removing the wheel blocks snatched them away and gave him a double thumbs-up. Releasing the brakes, Jim eased the two throttles forward until the engines pulled them slowly down the ramp and out into the water. Once afloat, the seaplane navigated effortlessly to the down-wind end of the lake like a giant swam. Turning slowly into the wind, Jim looked over at Neal and asked, "Are you ready for this, Mr. T?"

Grinning like a kid who had just been put in the front seat of a roller coaster, Neal replied, "Let'er rip, my friend. There's no turning back now."

In less than thirty minutes the glistening water of San Francisco Bay passed slowly beneath them, as they approached the Golden Gate Bridge. Moments later, Jim dipped his left wing and turned south toward San Diego. They had only been on that heading a few minutes when Jim asked, "I wonder what our friend, Gloria Donaldson, is doing this morning?"

"Probably just getting out of bed," Neal replied with a chuckle. "I don't see her as much of a morning person."

"How do you think she'll react when you tell her what you're up to?"

He's fishing for something Neal thought before answering. "Depends on whether or not I can tell her you've agreed to help me, I would imagine." Remembering Jim's statement about how long he had known Gloria, Neal added, "Just how far back do you two go, by the way?"

Giving into the urge to ease some of the anxiety Neal was experiencing regarding Dan Hughes' predicament, Jim replied, "First of all, you can stop worrying about my support. I was nearly captured by the North Korean's when my plane ran out of fuel just north of the 38th Parallel. Luckily, I managed to glide back to within a few miles of the border where I crash-landed. Fortunately, I was able to make it back into friendly territory without incident. So you see, I know what it's like to be hunted, just like Dan."

Stopping for a moment to take a sip from a canteen of water he kept onboard, he continued. "Secondly, my relationship with Gloria Donaldson began when I saved her husband's life years ago. He had accidentally fallen off their boat at Catalina Island's Avalon Harbor. I was a guest onboard and jumped in with a life preserver after Gloria screamed that he wasn't a very good swimmer. Her husband was pretty well waterlogged when we finally got him back onboard, but Randy survived." Pausing, thoughtfully, he concluded by saying, "Yes, we go back a long way, but that's as far as it goes."

A short time later, Neal picked up the conversation again and said, "The first thing I'm going to do when I get home today is call Gloria and ask her if I can use her condominium. If she's agreeable, I'll need your help to go get Dan and fly him directly to Catalina sometime next week."

"I was thinking about that while you were talking." Jim replied. "Considering the pressure you're under, and Dan's precarious situation, I can make myself available whenever you need me. My staff can run the business as well as I can. Just give me a day's notice."

Reassured by the way things were working out, Neal said, "I will call you over the weekend to explain the particulars of my plan. Hopefully, sometime in the near future Dan will be a free man again."

Jim looked thoughtfully ahead at Palomar Airport's gradually approaching runway and replied, "For your sake, I hope so."

Moments later, the wheels touched down on the main runway for a flawless landing. Smiling with pride, Jim maneuvered his way over to the terminal building and idled the engines. After locking the brakes, he accompanied Neal to the rear exit hatch, remaining there until Neal had climbed down onto the tarmac. When they shook hands and parted, Jim hollered over the engine noise, "You're a good man, Mr. T! Give Gloria my best wishes when you talk to her. I'll be waiting for your call!"

The taxi ride home was short and anti-climatic compared with what was going on in Neal's mind. Tired and grateful to be home, he paid the taxi driver and walked casually up the driveway until the sight of his front door brought him to an abrupt halt. Approaching cautiously, he observed that the front door screen had been torn away, and the wood around the main door lock mutilated. Pushing the door open with his foot before attempting to go in, he stepped carefully over the threshold and sat his luggage down on the cluttered floor. His heart sank like a bowling ball dropped from a two-story building, as he eyed the clutter that greeted him. Someone had broken in.

From where he stood he could see that every drawer had been opened and its contents strewn haphazardly on the floor. *Whoever it was, they must have been in one hell of a hurry.*

Looking through the second floor bedrooms revealed much the same thing, so he returned downstairs and looked in the garage. Contrary to what he expected to find, only a few items had been tampered with. What suffered the most damage was the filing cabinet in which he kept important records. From what he could gather from a cursory inspection, nothing had been taken.

Emotionally disheartened beyond recent memory, he raised his head to see if the old travel bag in which he had hidden the large sum of money Dan Hughes had given him was still there. *Thank God for small blessings.* By some quirk of luck it was.

Returning to the kitchen, his first impulse was to pour a stiff drink to neutralize the anger that was welling up inside of him, but a cooler head prevailed, at least for the moment. Aware that he was ill equipped to properly diagnose the legal aspects of the break-in, he picked up the phone and called DEA Agent, Dusty Lewis.

Before transferring Neal's call to Dusty's office, Ginger Spyce hesitated long enough to whisper, "We have to talk."

"Not right now," Neal apologized. "Is Dusty in. It's terribly important."

"I understand," she replied. "I'll call you at home tonight. There's something you should be aware of."

"Thanks. I'll make it my business to be there."

Seconds later, the phone rang in Dusty Lewis' office. Leaving the window where he had been watching the San Diego's skyline, Dusty walked over to his desk and picked up the phone. "This is Agent Lewis."

"This is Neal Thomas, Dusty. We have a problem."

"What's this, we shit," Dusty barked back. "My boss has been bugging me every day you've been gone for more information about your filming proposal. He's convinced the President that it's the only way we can be assured of busting up the Cartel without getting someone killed. You'd better tell me what I want to hear, or you're going to be the one with a problem."

Neal hadn't counted on Dusty's response being so emotionally charged, so he hesitated a moment in order to soften his reply. "Someone broke into my house while I was gone. I think you and some of your people should investigate this place for evidence before I start cleaning up. Or does that make too much sense?"

"Damn!"

Realizing he should probably listen to what Ginger Spyce had to say before Dusty investigated the matter, he said, "Look, it's getting late. Why don't you and your boys come up here around nine o'clock tomorrow morning when everyone's rested. There may be something here that will give us a clue as to who the invader was. Besides, nothing's going any place."

What have I got to lose? Dusty thought. "Okay," he conceded, "but don't disturb anything."

"I won't. I'm too damn tired."

After he hung up, Neal came to the conclusion that, except for the papers that were lying all over the place, there really wasn't a whole lot of tangible evidence that would point a finger at anyone. He had, however, gained enough time to contact Gloria Donaldson, whom he hoped would join his alliance, and end the madness he was gradually growing tired of. Checking the time, he picked up the phone and placed the call.

Growing doubtful that Gloria would answer after more than four rings, Neal made a move to hang up when he heard a harried voice say, "This is Gloria!"

"Hi there. This is Mr. T. Did I interrupt something?"

"Yes you did," she replied, sounding a little irritated. "I was taking a bath."

In an attempt to try and pacify her with a little humor, he replied, "It's about time you cleaned up your act."

"That's not funny, party boy. Did you have a good time at the Club? I understand Kimberly Prentice was there."

Caught off guard by that acknowledgement, Neal didn't know what to say. Rather than be caught in a lie, he replied, "Who do you think gave me your number?"

Gloria laughed. "At least you didn't lie. Kimberly had a guilty conscience and told me she had given it to you. And, I understand you hitched a ride home with Jim Taylor. I'd sure would like to have been a stowaway on that flight."

"I hope that's all Kimberly told you," Neal remarked sheepishly. "And yes, I did have a good time."

"Good! Now, are you going to tell me the real reason you called?"

Damn women, Neal thought when he sensed that she knew more than she was willing to admit. He was about to continue when he realized that his phone might have been tapped during the break-in, so he said, "I have a large favor to ask of you that I'd rather not discuss on this phone. Would you please hang up and let me call you back on my cell phone?"

Having been plagued by the demons of confidentiality for most of her adult life, Gloria was only too willing to comply with his request and signed off.

After retrieving the cell phone from his briefcase, Neal placed the call while sitting at the kitchen table with his first drink of the day. Seconds later, she answered.

Thanking her for her patience, he resumed their previous conversation. Essentially, he repeated everything he had told Jim Taylor, adding that Jim had already offered his help.

Her reaction was what he had anticipated, given the circumstances. "If Jim Taylor's onboard, so am I," she said reassuringly. "I'd follow that man down the mouth of a cannon if he asked me to. When do you need my condo?"

"Next week, "he replied. "Jim's available on one day's notice. All I have to do is contact Dan Hughes to tell him when and where to meet us."

"I hadn't intended to tell you this for reasons I would prefer to keep my own," she admitted. "But, considering the situation you are in, I think it is in your best interest to know that I'm in Catalina right now."

"You are? How long have you been there?"

"Since I last saw you at The Cave restaurant in Little Bohemia," she replied. "That's what that telephone call I received was all about. I came down here on my boat that evening, so make your plans. I'll help in any way I can."

What a stroke of luck Neal thought. "You can't imagine how much your being there is going to mean to the success of this operation."

Glancing at his kitchen clock, Neal felt obligated to tell Dan Hughes immediately what had developed since they last talked. Anxious to get on with it, he excused himself and said, "I have to call Dan Hughes before it gets too late. I'll call you when all of my plans have been finalized."

"That will be fine," she assured him. "Do what you have to do."

Pleased by her unexpected departure from the normally stuffy verbiage she used to express herself, Neal smiled and flipped down the cover on his cell phone, thinking, *Anita Cassidy is never going to believe this.*

Just as quickly, he pressed in Dan Hughes' number, hoping to catch him in a receptive frame of mind for the task that lay ahead. He was in luck. Dan's lazy southern drawl came on line loud and clear. "This is Dan."

"Can you talk freely?" Neal asked. "This is all about D-Day."

"You're in luck Mr. T., I'm just lying on the beach wondering when you were going to call. Do we have a plan?"

"Listen carefully, Dan," Neal replied over the faint sound of surf breaking in the background. "I have a licensed pilot and a twin-engine Grumman seaplane at my disposal for..."

"A Goose!" Dan interrupted excitedly. "I can fly that old crate. Jimmy Buffett taught me?"

"What I was about to say when you cut me off was, ...for getting you safely out of Mexico next week. Are you prepared for that?"

"That depends," Dan replied. "Where are we going?"

"To my friend's condo on Catalina Island."

"Who else is going to be there?" Dan asked suspiciously.

"You, me, our pilot and a DEA agent who doesn't know he's going yet. He has to be there to authenticate your testimony. If it makes you feel any better, he's a very trusted friend of mine."

By this time, Dan was on his feet walking toward an unoccupied stretch of beach where he asked, "When, specifically, is this pickup supposed to take place?"

"Tentatively, next Tuesday."

"Why next Tuesday? Can't we get this plan under way before then?"

"Patience Dan. There's still a lot of work to be done before we can pull this thing off without anyone knowing what's going on. Don't forget who chased you out of the Bahamas in the first place. I'll call you Sunday evening with specific instructions. Wear your cell phone wherever you go."

"Thanks a bunch, Mr. T," Dan remarked sarcastically. "You're not exactly making me feel any better about all this."

Neal laughed and assured Dan that, despite the seemingly ill-defined details of the operation, his freedom would soon be a reality.

With little to occupy his time until Ginger Spyce contacted him, Neal felt the need to purge himself of the frustration his homecoming had brought on. Grabbing a towel from the linen closet, he opened the sliding door leading onto the patio and activated the Jacuzzi. Returning inside, he mixed a strong drink to ease some of the anxiety that was still lingering while he waited for the water to heat up. Minutes later he stuck his foot in and found it comfortably hot. Throwing his towel aside, he started to step in when he heard the kitchen phone ring. Expecting it to be Ginger, he grabbed his towel and walked hurriedly to the kitchen, anxious to learn what she had to say. Another voice, however, greeted him instead. It was his dear friend, Paula Dillon.

"Hi, Curly. I couldn't remember when you were coming home, so I took a chance on calling to make sure we were still on for this weekend. You are coming up, aren't you?"

Caught completely off guard, he hesitated for a moment before answering. "I don't know," he replied honestly. "I came home a day early and found my home had been broken into. I don't know what they were looking for, but the place is a holy mess."

"Was anything taken?"

"Not that I know of. I called my friend, Dusty Lewis, at the local DEA office thinking it might be related to what I'm doing to help Dan Hughes get back into the United Sates. Dusty said not to disturb anything until after he and his men investigate the place for evidence. They're coming out here first thing tomorrow morning."

Sounding mildly disappointed, she said, "I'm sorry this has happened to you, Neal. But as long as you are in any way involved with Dan Hughes, trouble is going to follow you around like a dark shadow. I was hoping we could get together, but under these circumstances, I think it would be wiser to postpone our rendezvous until a later date. Call me when you're not so involved with that man."

"I'm sorry about all this," Neal apologized. "I was looking forward to seeing you again."

"I know," she replied unemotionally. "Take care of yourself."

Neal had no sooner placed the phone back on its cradle, than it rang again with an uncanny sense of urgency. It was Ginger Spyce. "Are you alone?" she asked.

"Unfortunately, yes," he replied unemotionally. "What's on your mind?"

"I don't know where you are with this Dan Hughes business," she said, "but I think you should know that your whereabouts are being monitored. I overheard a conversation between Agent Lewis and Director Bronson on that subject just recently and thought you should know. The only reason I'm calling you on your home phone is because I don't have your cell phone number. If I were you, I'd be using it for all of my personal business from now on, just to be on the safe side."

"I've already begun doing that," Neal assured her. After giving her his cell phone number, he said, "Thanks for the information. I'll conduct my future business accordingly. Especially where your boss, Mr. Lewis, is concerned."

"That would be wise. I'll be in touch."

The un-nerving news that his whereabouts were being monitored made it vividly clear to Neal that he could no longer trust anyone other than those with whom he had formed the alliance to repatriate Dan Hughes. The sinking feeling that came from realizing he was being manipulated by the government made him angry. Especially in light of what he had already done to help them apprehend the Tidewater Drug Cartel.

Tossing his towel aside, he slipped into the Jacuzzi and began examining all the options that were available to get Dan safely out of Mexico without involving the DEA. Given his commitment to Dusty Lewis, the possibility of that being a viable option seemed limited, until a thought struck him that took him back to the days when he and Ron Barns, along with three single women they worked with, invested in a mobile home in Rosarito Beach where they partied on weekends for almost nine years.

❖   ❖   ❖

In addition to the many friends and colleagues who came to Rosarito Beach to party with the five "Partners," as they were often referred to in those days, a number of English-speaking Mexican citizens soon befriended the group, helping them over the occasional embarrassment of not being bilingual. One such person was a bartender at a popular steakhouse located in the heart of town called *El Nido*. Neal and Ron

Barns spent most Sunday mornings there enjoying the bartender's signature Bloody Mary. His name was Ricardo Lopez.

Ricardo, in addition to being a personable mixer of drinks, was a working partner in a local fishing business during the week. As such, he spent a lot of time boating back and forth to popular sites where fish and abalone were plentiful, one of which was located off the southern tip of San Clamente Island called Pyramid Head.

On one particular occasion during those Rosarito Beach days, Neal asked Ricardo Lopez if he could recommend someone who would take him and a couple of his friends scuba diving off Pyramid Head. Ricardo, being the softhearted person he was, replied, "No one knows that spot better than I do. I will take you."

When the day arrived, Neal took his diving buddies to a cove just south of the city where Ricardo said he would be waiting. The boat, he thought would be more like a cabin cruiser turned out to be something resembling a small whaler with a large outboard engine bolted to the transom. Silently questioning the wisdom of boarding the undersized craft, Neal and his four friends reluctantly climbed in with their gear and prepared for the trip.

The first reason for concern came when Neal's dive buddy, Ben Chase, noticed water bubbling up through a small hole in the bottom after they were well out to sea. When he looked at Ricardo and pointed to it, Ricardo just smiled and handed him a large coffee can. Half way to the island Ben got tired of bailing, so he improvised a plug out of a stick match and jammed it into the hole, much to Ricardo's amusement.

In addition to normal concerns regarding the boats seaworthiness, their eventual arrival at Pyramid Head proved disappointing. Contrary to what Ricardo and other experienced fishermen had promised, the rocky reef where they would spend the next two hours gave up nothing more than two undersized abalone, and four small fish that were virtually destroyed by the three-prong pole spears that Neal and his diver buddy had used. Tired and frustrated, the group headed back to the mainland. What made the return trip somewhat exciting, however, was watching a killer whale in hot pursuit of a small school of seals that dove under their boat. The killer whale did the same thing, much to the nervous amusement of everybody onboard.

To avoid the embarrassing failure that the day's miserable catch represented, a brief stop at Ricardo's fish market provided enough excess to feed those who hungrily awaited their arrival, but not without a multitude of humorous innuendos.

◆ ◆ ◆

I wonder if Ricardo is still there? Neal pondered, while a new idea for getting Dan Hughes to Catalina Island began to take shape in his mind. Confident that he had solved the most challenging part of the plan, he left the Jacuzzi and prepared something to eat, hoping after that to relax in front of the television before going to bed. It suddenly dawned on him, however, that Dusty Lewis had been quite explicit about disturbing anything. Irritated and hungry, he put on the same clothes he had worn that day and made his way outside wondering where to go.

How about a cold beer and a hot dog a silent voice within him suggested. Intrigued by the possibility that Anita Cassidy might still be there, he propped a chair against the damaged front door, left all the lights on and exited through the garage.

The sun's fiery dome had just disappeared below the western horizon when he pulled into the Village Pub's crowded parking lot and entered through the rear door, surprised at the number of people who had gathered there, including Anita Cassidy. She remained unaware of Neal's presence until the evening shift bartender waved and called him by name, causing Anita to spin around on her stool and greet him. "Well, well, if it isn't Mr. T. Did you have a good time on your vacation, sugar babe?"

Neal smiled self-consciously, and replied, "It was cut short a day, but I had a good time. Met a lot of interesting people. How've you been?"

"I've been better," she answered, in a manner that hinted of being a little under the weather. "Some days it just doesn't pay to get out of bed."

"Tell me about it," Neal remarked. "I came home a few hours ago to find my house had been broken into, so I thought I'd cry in a beer and chew on a hot dog. I'm starved."

Without hesitating, Anita suddenly stood up and took Neal by the hand. "Me too," she said. "Drive me home and I'll fix you something to eat. I've had enough of this place for one day."

"Are you serious?" Neal asked, looking wide-eyed and embarrassed. "I didn't mean for you to…"

"Shush," she said, pulling him toward the rear entrance. "I haven't had a man over to my place since you fixed my refrigerator. Besides, I don't want to walk home alone. Can't you be my knight in shining armor for a little while?"

Neal sensed that Anita was reacting to something more serious than the loneliness that sometimes accompanies a little too much to drink, so he opened the passenger side door for her - bowing a little - and said, "Your chariot awaits, sweet princess."

A few minutes later, with little conversation having passed between them, Neal parked his car in front of her second floor studio apartment and escorted her somewhat unsteady body up the short flight of stairs. Once inside, she went directly to the refrigerator, removed some already prepared items of food and a bottle of wine. "Vodka tonic, right?" she asked, finally smiling and acting a little more relaxed. "Seems to me I remember that being your drink of choice."

"Your memory serves you well," he replied, still bothered by the preoccupation she seemed to be struggling with. As he watched her mix his drink, he finally asked, "Is that what's on your mind tonight…something you don't want to remember?"

His question froze her like an icicle, leaving her head bowed and her hands gripping the sink in order to maintain her balance. As he made a sudden attempt to steady her, she broke down in a torrent of tears, sobbing uncontrollably. The sudden grasp of his arms gave her the steadiness she needed to turn against his body and lay her tear stained face against his shoulder. She remained there motionless while he continued to pat her back. Aware that she might fall if he attempted to let her go, he guided her carefully to the living room couch and sat down with her still cradled in his arms.

Moments later Anita's sobbing quieted. Embarrassed, and trying to regain some sense of composure, she raised her head and said, "Please forgive me. That's been coming on for a long time. Thanks for being here when it did."

"Your not the first woman who's cried in my arms," Neal said, in an attempt to add a little levity to an awkward situation. "Do you want to talk about it?"

Anita laid her head back on his shoulder briefly and said, "I promised you something to eat, and that's what I'm going to do. Fix yourself another drink while I freshen up a little. We'll talk about this over dinner. Do you like tuna and macaroni salad?"

Neal burst out laughing and replied, "Are you kidding? I was raised on that stuff. I love it. My mother used to mix it with onions, celery, olives and deviled eggs when we went to the beach on picnics."

Walking toward her small bathroom she looked back and said, "Well, I sure as hell can't compete with that, but I'll try."

During her absence, Neal made it a point to reacquaint himself with the photograph Anita had admitted to him was of her parents. *There was no mistaking them now*, he concluded. They were the same family he had seen in the Sawmill Club library, but he felt hesitant about bringing up the subject until she voluntarily confided in him about her true identity.

Twenty minutes after Anita returned from her toilette, the kitchen table was set and a bowl of macaroni salad sat between them, topped with sliced cucumber and Paprika. As they chatted and sipped the wine she had poured, Neal wondered what could possibly have upset this attractive woman who now sat opposite him looking as though the incident had never taken place. Spurred on by his insatiable curiosity, he asked, "Why don't you tell me what's been troubling you?"

"My problem," she replied sullenly. "I doubt that your knowing about it would change anything."

"How will you ever know, if you don't share it?" he persisted. "What have you got to lose?"

Cupping her wine glass with both hands just below her freshly painted lips, she stared at him for a moment, and then said, despondently, "I have a rotten job, no boyfriend, no car, no identity and a mother who doesn't even know I exist. How's that for starters?"

Neal sat his glass down and leaned back against his chair, fully prepared to launch a verbal exchange that he knew might do more harm than good. "Whose fault is that?" he asked calmly. "Have you ever tried to get in touch with your mother? You obviously would like her to know that you do exist."

"What business is that of yours?" she asked, defensively. "And what makes you think you can do anything about it? You don't know the first damn thing about my family."

Without saying another word, Neal walked over to get the framed photograph he had examined earlier and returned to the table. Placing it in front of her, he said, "That's you as a child, Miss Donaldson. Your parent's names are Randy and Gloria Donaldson. Your father died of a heart attack. Your mother never remarried and still lives in San Francisco. I had dinner with her several days ago, believe it or not. We have become very good friends, I might add."

Both of Anita's hands were now covering her face. "How could you be so cruel" she cried out, angrily. "I hate you for this, you son of a bitch!"

"For what, trying to save your life?"

"No! For not telling me sooner," she sobbed. "How long have you known about this?"

"Since yesterday," he replied. "I didn't mention it because I really didn't know how you would react."

"You were in San Francisco, weren't you?" she asked, while serving the salad.

Observing that her mood was beginning to change from anger to curiosity, he continued. "Yes. I spent the night there in a section of the city called Little Bohemia. I accidentally ran into your mother having dinner with friends there. The next day I continued on to meet an old college buddy of mine at an all male wilderness retreat called the Sawmill Club. I suspect you know where that is."

"Yeah, I know where it is," she admitted. "I was pretty young when I first heard the name. Unfortunately, I later learned more about that Club than I wanted to, but that's another story. Why don't you elaborate more on what you think I ought to be doing with my life? Seems to me you're in a much better position to tell me what to do than I'll ever figure out on my own."

Neal remained silent for a moment, looking carefully into her eyes for some sign that would convince him she was sincerely asking for help. One word, however, gave him the simple encouragement he was looking for – "Please?"

With the door to her heart now wide open, he revealed what he had only recently learned regarding her father's will. "I was invited to take part in the Sawmill Club's annual meeting by my friend, Allen Henderson, who has been a member for years. Allen, I found out at the time, happens to be quite well informed when it comes to the Club's history. Part of that history deals with your father's death, and the terms and conditions of his will. Because your mother was concerned that you might squander your inheritance away foolishly, she arranged to have it put in a private trust account until such time as you matured enough to manage it more wisely. In the meantime, it has been sitting in a San Francisco bank earning interest ever since your father died. It is now a sizeable amount of money, I might add. Problem is, you've kept your married name to hide your identity. Consequently, your mother is the only person who can legally prove that you are Anita Donaldson, the legal heir. Do you have your old Social Security card, or a copy of your Birth Certificate?"

The news that she was an heir to anything shocked Anita into a state of starry-eyed disbelief, until Neal reached across the table and snapped his fingers in front of her eyes. "Hell-o-o. Anybody home?"

Unable to fully comprehend the life-altering consequences of what Neal had just revealed to her, Anita starred blankly across the table at him and replied, "Please tell me I'm not dreaming all this, Mr. T. I can't believe this is happening. Slap me! Do something!"

Reaching across the table again, he patted her gently on the cheek and said, "Anita, listen to me carefully. You are not dreaming. The reality of all this is, we've got to figure out how to get you back into your mother's good graces without her finding out what I just told you. Otherwise, she might misunderstand both of our motives."

"How the hell are we going to do that?" she asked in frustration.

"We won't have to," he assured her. "My best friend dates an attorney. I'll discuss the matter with her as soon as I can. She'll know what to do. In the meantime, live every day just like you have in the past. Most importantly, do not discuss this with anyone. And I mean, anyone!"

A quick glance at Anita's wall clock made him aware that he had stayed there well past the time he should have gone home. Though he was concerned about leaving her alone with all that he had burdened her with that evening, he thanked her for dinner, kissed her goodbye and left with one final remark to brighten her day. "Sleep tight, princess. Now you have a life to look forward to."

Chapter 10

A Change In Plans

The sound of automobiles entering his driveway the next morning alerted Neal to the early arrival of Dusty Lewis and his team of DEA investigators. Eager to begin the process, he went to the front door to greet them wearing a pair of surgical gloves Paula Dillon had left behind. Dusty noticed them right away and said, "You can get rid of those gloves if you want to. Your prints are probably all over the place anyway."

Following introductions, the two agents Dusty brought with him went immediately into the house and began their work. Dusty, however, had something else in mind. Motioning for Neal to follow him, he turned and walked over to the bluff where he said, "My boss wants to know where and when you are planning to film Dan Hughes' testimony. He insists on providing you with the protection he thinks you're going to need."

Recalling what Ginger Spyce had revealed to him the previous evening, he avoided answering that specific question by replying, "Protection against what? Until you find specific evidence to the contrary, my house could have been broken into by anyone who knew I was on vacation. And, as far as Dan Hughes is concerned, he's left the Bahamas, and will contact me from wherever he's going when he gets there."

"When is that supposed to be?" Dusty asked, getting progressively impatient with Neal's evasiveness.

Faced with the danger of revealing his entire plan to the DEA, Neal made a split-second decision to alter it based on his conversation with Gloria Donaldson the previous day. Considering the consequences of lying to a federal agent, he said, "Next Tuesday afternoon."

"Where?" Dusty persisted.

"At Pyramid Head on the southern tip of San Clemente Island."

"You better not be bullshitting me, Mr. T," Dusty warned. "My boss can be a real horse's ass when someone lies to him."

"As far as I'm concerned, that's my plan, Dusty. Tell your boss to relax and let me handle this. I'm not as dumb as he may think I am."

"Au contraire," Dusty remarked, as they walked back to the house together. "Ray Bronson respects you very much. Too much I fear."

Both agents were sitting on the front porch smoking cigarettes when Neal and Dusty returned, their faces expressing the simple message that they had found nothing. "Except for the mess, there's nothing to indicate that this was anything more than vandalism," one of the agents remarked. "I'd turn the matter over to the local police in case you discover something missing when you're cleaning up."

Dusty looked at Neal and said, "Something doesn't smell right here. If nothing's missing, what were the vandals looking for? Go ahead and clean the place up. If you find something relevant to our mutual interest in Dan Hughes, let me know. Otherwise, carry on with what you were doing."

Neal promised he would, shook Dusty's hand and said goodbye, glad that he and his agents were leaving so he could begin putting his house back in order. They had only gone a few paces when Dusty turned and said, apologetically, "Sorry, I almost forgot to give you this. I'm sure it will make Mr. Hughes a little more comfortable wherever he is." Handing Neal a sealed, letter-size envelope, he explained, "It's a copy of his pardon. Though I must warn you, it won't mean a thing if this plan of yours doesn't work out. I have my doubts, but good luck anyway."

Walking back into his house, Neal looked with curiosity at the envelope, suddenly wondering, *is this what they were looking for?*

It took most of the morning to accomplish the task, but by noon his house was back in order, with still no clue – other than the envelope he had just been given – as to why anyone would have wanted to break into his home. Tired and frustrated, he made a sandwich, cracked open a can of beer and went to his studio to begin reading his mail, when the phone rang. Hoping it was a junk call, he let it ring until a familiar voice began leaving a message. "Hi Neal, this is Sandy Sterling calling…"

Neal immediately grabbed up the receiver. "Sandy! I was anticipating a junk call. Sorry about that. How are you?"

"Fine. I trust you had an enjoyable time on your vacation."

"Yes, but it was way too short. What's on your mind?"

"Well, I'm calling to let you know that Jessica and I have finished reading the preliminary draft of your novel. We found it quite intriguing. So much so that we would like to discuss it with you over lunch tomorrow, if you are available."

Reflecting on Paula Dillon's timely postponement of their weekend together, he replied, "As a matter of fact, I am. May I suggest Bully's at one o'clock?"

"That will be fine."

Can things get any more complicated he asked himself, as he continued to sort through the mail that covered his desk. He was writing checks when his cell phone suddenly sounded. It was Jim Taylor. "I just wanted to let you know that things down here are pretty well back to normal now. How are you doing?"

"I'm glad you called," Neal replied, reflecting on Jim's timing. "I've had to rethink my original plan for picking up Dan Hughes, due to information I have just received from a reliable source inside our local DEA office."

"You don't need The Goose?"

"Oh yes," Neal assured him. "More so than ever." Thinking back to what Dusty Lewis had confided in him with regard to Raymond Bronson's intentions to provide some element of security for the rescue operation, Neal asked, "Can you fly up here next Tuesday morning around ten o'clock? I'll explain everything when you get here."

"No problem," Jim replied. "Can I bring anything?"

"I'll need a fairly large inflatable boat and a motor, if you have them."

Jim laughed and replied, "It's what the Navy calls emergency preparedness."

"Perfect!" Neal shouted. "See you Tuesday at ten o'clock."

An hour later, Neal completed his paperwork and had his bills in the mailbox. Longing for a breath of fresh air, he decided to stand out on the bluff and soak up some sunshine before making his next two calls, calls that would be essential to pulling off this deception of a lifetime.

Clipping on his cell phone, he opened a can of beer and sauntered out to the bluff where he let the ocean breeze fan his face for a few minutes. The break was rewarding, and brought a sense of adventure with it that he hadn't experienced for some time. Determined that he was not going to let the DEA dictate the conditions of Dan Hughes' return, he called Gloria Donaldson, the key to his altered plan.

Gloria was resting comfortably on her condominium's balcony when her cell phone jingled. Not wishing to reveal her identity, she simply said, "Hello?"

"Are you alone?" Neal asked.

"Of course I'm alone. Where are you?"

"Standing on the bluff behind my house looking in your direction. Are you at your condo or on the yacht?"

A broad smile raised her cheeks into a devilish expression. "That's for me to know and you to find out?"

"I wish I could, but the timing is bad. Listen carefully, I have something very important to tell you."

Leaving the patio, Gloria went to the refrigerator and removed a bottle of wine. Refilling her glass, she said, "Okay, Mr. T. What can I do for you today?"

Still fascinated by her uncanny ability to sense when she was going to be asked to do something, Neal replied, "First, let me tell you what has happened since our last conversation."

"Go ahead."

"As you know, Dan Hughes is currently staying at the Rosarito Beach Hotel waiting for me to tell him how he's going to be picked up. Originally, I told him to charter a fishing boat to San Clemente Island where Jim Taylor and I would pick him up in Jim's seaplane. From there I had planned to fly to Catalina and film his testimony at your condo."

"What changed your mind? Sounds like a good plan to me."

"It was, until I got word that the DEA was planning to oversee the operation. Dan would scuttle the whole thing if he found out they were involved."

"What do you plan to do now?" Gloria asked. "You seem to be between the proverbial rock and a hard place."

"Not if we can count on your help," he countered.

"Me! What can I do?"

Encouraged by her willingness to participate, Neal began to explain his strategy. "There's a popular restaurant and fish market community south of Rosarito called Puerto Nuevo. I need you to take your yacht down there and anchor off shore. I will instruct Dan to hire someone to take him out to your yacht, once you get there. When he's onboard, take him back to your condo and wait till Jim and I get there."

"No need to involve someone you don't know," Gloria advised. "I'm familiar with Puerto Nuevo. I'll send a couple of my men in to pick up Dan on the boat dock when we see him there. Make sure you tell him to raise his arms over his head and form a circle so we'll know it's him. Remember, I've never met the man."

"I will," Neal assured her, "He'll be on the dock at twelve noon next Tuesday. Take good care of him, he's precious cargo."

"So am I," she replied, as a reminder. "I hope the DEA isn't too upset with you when they find out you've deceived them."

"They won't have any reason to be upset with me if Dan fails to show up for his own rescue, now will they?"

"See you Tuesday, Sherlock. You can tell me all about it then."

Two down, one to go Neal thought, as he went over his strategy one more time to insure its achievability. Satisfied that there was no reason for it to fail, he punched in Dan's number and waited.

After three rings, Dan answered. Pleased that it was Neal, he said, "This better be good news, Mr. T. I don't think I can hack this place much longer. All these Mexican broads want to do is get married and move to the States."

Amused by Dan's notorious quest for women, he said, "You won't have to worry about that much longer, my friend. Make whatever plans are necessary to leave Mexico next Tuesday at noon."

"In what, a casket?"

"One that floats" Neal replied, returning the humor. "Now, pay attention. After you check out of the hotel, take a cab to Puerto Nuevo. It's a small beach community just south of Rosarito. Go to the boat dock there. A private yacht will be waiting off shore that will send in a boat to pick you up at noon. But first, signal it by placing your arms over your head so they form a circle. They won't pick you up unless you do."

"Has the yacht got a name?" Dan asked. "And who's the skipper? I damn sure don't want to end up in Hong Kong."

"The boat's name is The Wayward Wind. Its owner is a friend of mine by the name of Gloria Donaldson. Treat her with respect. She's a real lady."

"Where is this nice lady taking me, if I may ask?"

"To Catalina Island. I'll meet up with you there sometime that afternoon. I'll have a copy of your pardon with me."

"I'll say one thing for you, Mr. T," Dan said in closing, "you've gone to an awful lot of trouble to get me out of this mess I'm in. I don't know anyone else who would. I just want you to know how much I appreciate it. See you in Catalina."

It's done, Neal thought, as he left the bluff and returned to the house to take on his next challenge.

An onshore flow of air that periodically banged his damaged screen door took all doubt out of what his highest priority was now. Grateful for the opportunity to concentrate on something other than what waited for him on Tuesday, he grabbed his checkbook and drove to the nearest Home Depot. With the help of an attractive, well-trained female employee, he selected a steel framed screen door, and the hardware necessary to repair the damaged front door.

By mid-afternoon the replacement repairs were complete, including the addition of a heavy-duty slide lock and chain assembly. To reward his patience and bruised knuckles, it seemed prudent to get away from the threat of bothersome phone calls, so he secured the house and decided to visit his friend, Ron Barns. Being Friday, there was a good chance that others would be there looking for the same escape, friends whom he hadn't seen for some time.

When he arrived, however, his friends were uncharacteristically somber. They greeted him with the sad news that Joey Siegel, a regular member of Ron Barns' Friday afternoon social gathering, had been hospitalized and diagnosed with cancer. That, on top of Joey already having been legally declared blind, put a damper on everyone's normally animated behavior. After the usual round of handshakes and friendly embraces, Neal made his way to the cluttered kitchen and mixed a stronger drink than usual to ease the sadness he felt personally.

When he returned to join the others, it was Janice Burrows, a woman Neal had dated at one time, who approached him and said, "For what it's worth, Ron told me when I first got here this afternoon that Joey had called him earlier that day to say that he would be starting chemotherapy soon. Ron also mentioned that Joey still wants you to pick him up on Tuesdays, as usual."

"I will," Neal replied. "I'm just glad he's still up to it."

"I doubt he'll go down without a fight," Janice remarked. "He's a crusty old curmudgeon."

Moments later when the dialogue between them seemed to have run out, Janice said she had to use the bathroom and excused herself. As she turned to leave, the word *Tuesday* suddenly sounded an alarm. *My God, that's D-Day!*

Panicked by his own thoughtlessness, Neal immediately approached Ron. "Can you step outside with me for a minute," he asked, in a hushed voice. When they reached the privacy of the front porch, Neal said, "Janice Burrows just reminded me that Joey Siegel is expecting me to pick him up next Tuesday, but I won't be in town. I have something very important to take care of that involves Dan Hughes."

"Again?" Ron barked with surprise. "I thought you were rid of that guy." Watching Neal's face grimace with guilt forced Ron to question him further. "What's going on, Neal? Has that guy gotten you messed up again?"

"I can't talk about it right now," Neal replied defensively. "Can you get someone to pick up Joey for me?"

"Hell, yes," Ron assured him. "It wouldn't be the first time. I'm more concerned about what you've gotten yourself involved with this time. Anything I can do?"

"I wish I could tell you, old buddy, but I'm afraid it will have to wait until next week. Just pick up Joey for me this one time and I'll explain everything later."

For the next two hours Neal circulated among his friends, talking and laughing about people and events that now seemed like so much trivia in light of what he had to look forward to. Glancing around the room, he doubted very seriously if there was anyone there who would have voluntarily gotten themselves involved in anything remotely related to what he was about to do for Dan Hughes. Feeling strangely out of place all of a sudden, he finished his drink, said goodbye and left.

Approaching the 15th Street traffic light in downtown Del Mar, he glanced at Bully's and wondered what course his life would take after he met with Sandy and Jessica Sterling there the next day. Hopefully, a positive appraisal of his first novel would open a new and less traumatic future for him, so he could spend more time writing, walking the beach and occasionally sharing quality time with his three daughters. *You'd die of boredom* a voice from within commented. *Probably so,* he admitted, as he continued up the coast to have a drink with his friend, John Pauly. Predictably, the only person Neal could count on being where he was supposed to be – home alone watching television.

"Aren't you a little off the beaten track?" John asked when Neal walked in un-announced. "You usually don't show up around here until Tuesday."

"That's true, but I won't be here next Tuesday, so I thought I'd drop in to see you as long as I was in the area. How are you?"

When they were seated in his living room John looked wistfully out of the window and said, "I'm fine. I wish I could say the same for our friend, Walter Douglas. I got a call from his lady friend, Mary Jo Tyler this afternoon. Since you weren't at home, she called to let me know that Walter passed away peacefully early this morning. Apparently, his body just gave up from trying to fight off the cancer he's suffered with over the past several years. She wants you to call her when you get a chance."

Emotionally upset by the unexpected news, Neal closed his eyes and laid his head back against the couch. "Did Mary Jo mention anything about why she wanted to talk to me?"

"No, only that Walter had told her something before he passed away that she thought you should be aware of. It involves your friend, Dan Hughes."

Confused by this sudden turn of events, Neal finished the rest of his drink, picked up John's empty glass and walked pensively into the kitchen to freshen them. On the way back he remarked, "I wonder if Walter knew he was that sick when he asked me to pack up everything in his condo and ship it back to him? Being terminally ill never entered my mind."

"Me either," John admitted. "I still can't believe he's gone. I was getting ready to call you a little while ago to see if you had heard the news. That's when you showed up. Quite a coincidence, I'd say."

"Me too. I should probably stop by Madame X's to see how she's doing before I go home. She doesn't handle this kind of news very well."

Hurriedly drinking what was left of his drink, Neal stood up and said, "I'm getting a headache thinking about all this. Makes me wish I'd stayed in San Francisco."

John didn't comment and rose to accompany him outside. As he stood there watching Neal walk down the stairway, he yelled after him, "My daughters are still bugging me about when you and I are going to come up to Park City."

"Tell them to be careful what they wish for!" Neal hollered back. "I have a feeling it might be sooner than they think. I'll be in touch."

The short ride to his former home was just enough time to reach the conclusion that there wasn't much room left on the planet to escape what was rapidly turning his life into a dichotomy of conflicting emotions; damned if you do, damned if you don't.

It would help to keep your nose out of other people's business a silent voice advised, as he walked up the familiar entranceway to his former home. The screen door was locked so he called out, "Anybody home?"

Moments later, Janet Thomas and her two dogs appeared in the doorway to welcome him, her wet eyes and red nose bearing witness to the fact that she had been crying.

"Where have you been?" she asked, unlocking the screen door. "I've called your number several times to tell you Walter Douglas died this morning. I finally left a message."

"I already know. John Pauly told me when I stopped by his place a little while ago. How's your sister doing?"

"She's been divorced from him long enough to accept it without grieving," Janet replied. "I'm flying back tomorrow to attend the funeral."

"I'd go with you, but I have appointments I can't break."

"No need to," she remarked. "I'll represent the family. I've already sent a wreath."

Knowing that Janet was pressed to prepare for her trip back east in a few days, Neal graciously declined her invitation to stay for a drink. "I'm glad you're going to the funeral. I'm sure your sister will be pleased to see you. Let her and the children know that we are thinking of them. I'll stop by when you get back. Have a safe trip."

The late afternoon sun was falling rapidly when Neal decided to take the Coast Highway home. A Santa Ana condition had flattened the usually active surf into gently curling waves that flowed lazily toward the beach, robbing the usual gathering of late afternoon surfers of their late afternoon amusement.

Clearer than he had ever seen it, Catalina Island sat majestically on the horizon, taunting Neal with her promise of still another adventure yet to come, one that would alter the course of his destiny beyond his wildest imagination.

Just ahead, bathed in a pink wash of the setting sun, a familiar landmark came into view that triggered his curiosity. *I wonder if she still works there?*

Acting on a sudden impulse to determine if Maggie Jyles was still hustling drinks in the Hilton Inn lounge, Neal drove in and parked near the entrance. *Not much has changed* he thought, as his footsteps led him into the familiar surroundings he and Dan Hughes had frequented not so long ago.

Resembling the days following the Inn's grand opening, there was a scene of bustling activity when he walked through the main lobby and into the lounge. Unlike earlier days, two waitresses were now required to take care of the increased number of people, neither of whom bore any resemblance to Maggie Jyles. Somewhat disappointed, he decided to have a drink for old times sake and sat down at a small table near a window so he could watch the sunset. Moments later, one of the waitresses noticed him sitting there unattended and went over to take his order.

"I'm sorry, sir. I didn't see you come in," she said apologetically. "I can't imagine not noticing the most distinguished looking man in the room. What can I bring you?"

Oh boy Neal thought, struggling not to laugh. "It's not on the menu, my dear. So why don't you bring me a vodka tonic. That'll get the ball rolling."

Amused by his quick wit, she winked and replied, "We never put the good stuff on the menu, sir. It's too expensive."

A short time later, while Neal was preoccupied with watching the sun disappear, the waitress returned with his drink, and said softly, "Beautiful, isn't it?"

"Sure is," he replied, finally looking up. "Speaking of all things beautiful, what ever happed to Maggie Jyles? Did she quit?"

"I wish," the young woman replied, "They promoted her to Personnel Manager. She's my boss."

"Well I'll be damned," Neal blurted out. "Has she gone home yet? I'd like to say hello."

"No, she's in her office. I'll tell her you're here, mister…"

"T," Neal joked. "Just tell her Mr. T's here. She'll know who you mean."

Looking puzzled, the young waitress hurried off, leaving Neal grinning at the irony of it all.

In less time than it took to finish his drink, two female figures came into the Lounge and walked directly to his table. "Here he is, Miss Jyles," the young waitress said, still looking puzzled. "This is Mr. T."

Neal grinned at Maggie and stood up to give her a hug, as she floated into his arms and kissed him full on the mouth. Pushing him away at arms length, she said, "I couldn't believe my ears when Christa told me that a Mr. T. wanted to see me. Where have you been all this time?"

Feeling like a third wheel, Christa excused herself and started to leave when Maggie held her back. "Bring Mr. Thomas another drink, and I'll have a glass of Chardonnay. Put it on my tab. He's my special guest tonight."

For the next hour Neal summarized the major events that had taken place in his life, especially those related to the one person Maggie could relate to – Dan Hughes.

"I'm surprised he's still alive," she remarked. "When did you finally track him down?"

171

"I didn't," Neal replied. "He called me from the Bahamas recently to let me know he was still alive and kicking." Being careful not to mention anything further about Dan's whereabouts, he replied, "Wherever he is, he's better off there than here. Now, enough about Dan, what have you been doing since I last saw you?"

"There isn't a whole lot to tell," she replied, in a manner that suggested she wasn't willing to go into too much detail on the subject. "When I told the manager I had been offered another job with more money and benefits, he made me an offer I couldn't refuse. So, here I am."

A short time later, Neal decided it was the right time to call it a day. Checking the time, he said, "I'm going to have a heavy day tomorrow, Maggie. I think I'd better get on home. Thanks for a delightful evening. It's so good to see you again."

"The feeling is mutual, Mr. T. Let me walk you to your car. I could use a little fresh air."

As soon as they were outside, Maggie took a deep breath and said, "In case you need to get in touch with me for any reason, here's my cell phone number. I carry it with me all the time. By the way, I live here at the hotel now. It's one of the perks I received when I agreed not to quit. So drop in when you can."

After they embraced and went their separate ways, Neal drove immediately home to check his mail and settle down in front of the television with a sandwich and a glass of milk. But as he soon learned, *the best laid plans of mice and men often go astray.*

There were only a few envelopes and some ads in his mailbox when he arrived home. A quick scan of the return addresses showed nothing that demanded his immediate attention. However, a postcard showing the nation's capital building did arouse his curiosity because he thought it might be from his brother, Joel. A quick check of the message proved otherwise: *Please check your P.O. Box as soon as you receive this card.* No sender information was included.

Since the U.S. Post Office for his area was only a few blocks away, Neal got back into his car and made the short run, second-guessing its contents all the way.

Only one other car was in the dimly lit parking lot when Neal arrived. It appeared to be occupied by a young man and women engaged in what he remembered doing when he was that age. So as not to disturb or frighten them, he parked near the entrance, sought out his mailbox and opened it.

In addition to the usual amount of junk mail that had accumulated during his absence, he found a key to another box that indicated he had received an item larger than his regular box could accommodate. When he opened the larger one, he found a package roughly the size of a five-liter box of wine. It had been professionally wrapped and sealed. Again, no return address was visible. Eager to determine its contents, and the sender's identity, he placed it in the trunk of his car and returned home.

Before attempting to open the package, Neal's stomach sent him a message that it needed something in it, so he sat the package aside and made a hasty sandwich and poured a glass of milk. Not content to just sit quietly and enjoy his meal, he went to his studio and came back with an all-purpose box cutter to find out what it was that required so much secrecy and protection. Eating occasionally, he made a continuous cut around the packaging material on one side and lifted it off. What he found was a Styrofoam container whose lid was securely taped. *This thing must contain the Ark Of The Covenant* he thought, as he finally succeeded in removing it. Taped to the underside of the lid was a letter-size manila envelope stamped, **CONFIDENTIAL.**

Breaking the seal, he removed three documents; a formal letter addressed to Neal Thomas, a booklet of questions, and a thinner document titled, **Operating Instructions**.

Setting those aside, he removed the space-age looking camera from its Styrofoam container. "Where's 007 when you need him," he muttered, as he studied the object with intense curiosity. After examining it for a minute or two, he placed it back in the container and picked up the letter. It read:

Mr. Thomas,

The contents of this container are being sent to assist you in producing your live interview with Mr. Dan Hughes, suspected former member of the Tidewater Drug Cartel. Because we have reason to believe that there has been a breach in security relevant to this matter, I believe our interests would be better served if the DEA gave you complete authority to conduct the interview using whatever means you deem necessary. Otherwise, the evidence you turned over to us on Mr. Hughes' behalf will be meaningless unless it can be authenticated. For this reason, we are providing you with a special camcorder that will produce a high definition film recording of your interview without the risk off being detected and/or altered in any way.

In order for this agency to bring the individuals who are identified in Mr. Hughes' evidence package to justice, additional information is needed in the form of his answers to the questions I am sending you. He should answer each question truthfully, and in as much detail as possible, especially names, dates and places.

Read the Operating Instructions for this camcorder carefully and thoroughly. Return it directly to me in the same container it came in after the interview is over. The return address has been provided.

To insure this operation's success, do not share this letter with anyone. Good luck.

Raymond Bronson – Director

What's going on here? Neal thought. *Why didn't Bronson send this stuff via Dusty Lewis? And what's this breech in security all about?*

After placing all the contents back in its Styrofoam container, Neal searched the interior of his home for a safe place to hide it, but couldn't decide on one. Considering the recent break-in, the thought came to him that he was riding around every day in probably the safest place of all - his car. Grabbing the car keys off the countertop nearby, he proceeded to the garage and placed it in the trunk, pledging to spend the next morning reading the material Bronson had sent him more thoroughly. Satisfied that all was secure, he returned to the kitchen to put his sandwich fixings away when the phone rang. Though tempted to ignore it, the thought that one of his allies might be trying to contact him won out. "Hello?"

"Hi, Curly, it's me."

Surprised and happy to hear the friendly voice of his dear friend, Paula Dillon, Neal responded with a suddenly uplifted spirit. "Well, well, well, if it isn't my long lost playmate, Ms. Dillon. What have I done now?"

"I don't know," she replied. "I'm afraid to ask."

"Believe me, you've made a wise choice," he remarked. "What's new with you?"

"A guilty conscience, I guess. I was way out of line trying to tell you how to choose your friends, and I apologize. Truth is, I was upset about being stood up. I had great plans for us."

"I was looking forward to seeing you too. But this mess I've gotten myself into with Dan Hughes has complicated my life beyond belief. What makes matters worse is, I can't discuss it with anyone."

"And I'm not going to ask you to." Paula replied. "I just want to say I'm sorry for acting like a bitch the other day. Just call me when you have some time to share. I miss you."

"I miss you too, dear," Neal replied sincerely. "I'll call you when I finally get rid of this albatross that keeps buzzing around my head."

Paula laughed. "It sure doesn't look like that's going to be anytime soon, now does it. Just be careful, and be wary of those who offer unsolicited help."

Desperate for a few minutes of uninterrupted quiet time, he placed the remote back in its stand and sought the comfort of his easy chair. Though he had turned on the television, somehow Paula's closing statement interfered with his concentration, and forced him to reflect on the package he had just received from Raymond Bronson. Reacting to Paula's statement about being wary of those who offer unsolicited help, Neal was prompted to get the Styrofoam container from his car and inspect the camera device more closely.

After reading the operating instructions more carefully, he concluded that it was designed to operate, in principal, much like a mini-CD player. The one he held in his hands, however, had some additional features.

The most obvious was a sealed, plastic lockbox containing touchtone keys arranged exactly like a telephone. As the instructions stipulated, they were used to code in commands for the operating features. The access key had been taped to it.

Oddly, there were no access covers for installing or removing film. All that seemed conventional was a power cord connection, and its cord. Presumably, the filming medium was a CD, which Neal guessed had already been installed.

It was approaching the eleventh hour when he decided to have one drink before putting the device back in his car. As he sat enjoying the afterglow of the first swallow, his eyes wondered over to the device and came to rest on a small tapped hole that the pistol grip holder screwed into. Not having paid any attention to the holder before prompted him to attach it so he could get a feel for its weight. When the holder was almost seated, he felt a touch of backpressure and stopped to see if something had fallen into the hole. Using a small flashlight he kept in a kitchen drawer, he peered into the hole and gasped at what he saw. "Son of a bitch," he yelled out, and fell back against his chair.

Seconds later, shocked and emotionally upset, he looked back into the threaded hole. His worst fears were confirmed. Protruding slightly up from the bottom was a small, round-headed pin, which he diagnosed as a spring-loaded actuator. Examining all the possible applications for such a mechanism, he came to one conclusion – when the holder was screwed all the way in, it activated an electronic tracking signal inside the device that pinpointed its location without the user knowing it. Thus, the exact location of the Dan Hughes interview would be known as soon as the handle was attached. *How clever* he thought, while re-packaging the device and returning it to its hiding place.

Minutes later, while his tired eyes fought uselessly against closing, a thought suddenly flashed through his mind, and brought on a smile that pleasantly ended his day.

Chapter 11

Days Of Enlightenment

The sound of softly falling rain awakened Neal very early the next morning. Though rarely occurring at this time of year, he thought little of it when he remembered the sad news John Pauly had passed on to him the previous day – Walter Douglas had passed away.

As he walked naked into the bathroom, he tried to second-guess what Walter had told Mary Jo Tyler just before he died, but came up clueless. Given the three-hour time difference between East and West Coasts, he figured he could call her as soon as he took a shower and got dressed. The timing couldn't have been better. She answered after the third ring.

"I'm sorry I wasn't able to contact you personally about Walter's passing," she said apologetically. "I didn't know you were out of town, so I called John Pauly to have him relay the news."

"I'm glad you did," Neal replied. "I stopped by his place last evening for a drink. That's when he told me Walter had died. He also mentioned that Walter had something he wanted you to pass on to me. Could you enlighten me on that?"

"Are you using your cell phone?" she asked.

"Most of the time lately, just to be on the safe side."

"Good. I'm sure you don't want anyone to hear what I'm about to tell you."

"I'm home alone and it's raining, of all things. How safe can it be?"

There was a slight pause and the sound of a door closing in the background before she continued. "I'm aware of your well intended efforts on behalf of Dan Hughes. It was Walter's last wish that I inform you of some facts that he believed might help you in that endeavor, something I've pretty well figured out for myself over the years."

"Is anyone else privy to this information?" Neal asked with increasing interest.

"Absolutely no one!" she replied most emphatically.

"Well then, I should make a very captive audience for you. What is it he wanted me to know?"

"As you may remember, Walter became actively engaged in local politics soon after his father died. That involvement brought him in contact with a few State and Federal politicians whose struggle for power led them into an underworld of drug- related activity in Virginia's Tidewater Area where Dan Hughes grew up."

"Wait a minute!" Neal interrupted, "Are you implying that...?"

"Let me finish," she insisted, cutting him off abruptly. "Yes, your friend and mine, Dan Hughes, was a wild and adventurous individual during his younger years, using his flying skills to deliver marijuana and cocaine to the Tidewater Cartel. From there it was distributed locally and to other areas, including ours. To be perfectly honest, Walter was an undercover distributor of marijuana and cocaine for an elite group of Washington politicians who paid him handsomely for his cache."

"Do you know who those individuals are?" Neal asked.

"No," she answered with certainty, "but their names may be mentioned in papers he kept hidden in his mountain retreat. Walter and Dan used to go there periodically to take care of business. Off the record, so did Walter and I. I'll go up there and take a look around as soon as I can. I still have my key."

"I'd appreciate that," Neal replied encouragingly. "That information could put a whole new slant on things."

"I will. I'll call you back as soon as I find something that may be of interest."

By the time it was light enough to see the ocean from his bedroom window the drizzle had stopped. Patches of clouds were beginning to brighten, bringing hope that the sun would be shining by the time he met with Sandy and Jessica Sterling. Though seeing them again would bring a welcome departure from his ongoing involvement in Dan Hughes' turbulent life, Neal couldn't dismiss thinking about the deception Raymond Bronson was trying to pull off by sending him a bugged camcorder that cleverly concealed an electronic tracking devise. *Did Bronson really think that I could be that easily fooled?*

It wasn't until he sat down to eat breakfast that his preoccupation with the camcorder inspired a counter move so bizarre that it made him start laughing. "Well Mr. Bronson, two can play that game," he chuckled.

Bully's parking lot was beginning to thin out when Neal arrived, a good indicator that those who were cursed with the necessity of having to return to work were already on their way. As he approached the ramp leading up to street level, he heard a voice call out from a car that had just pulled in. Turning in that direction, he saw Jessica Sterling and her mother step from their car, each carrying a copy of his manuscript.

"Hi, Mr. T. How's my favorite author doing today?" Jessica asked, as she took his arm. "We've missed you."

"That's good to hear," he replied. "I missed you too."

"I'm afraid you've acquired a fan," Sandy remarked, showing some embarrassment over her daughter's aggressive behavior. "My sentiments too, by the way. Welcome home."

Entering the restaurant Neal was quick to recognize the manager, Tommy Camillo, chatting flirtatiously with his waitresses. When he saw Neal and his two female companions enter, he came over and said, "Ah hah! Don Juan returns with his senoritas. It's good to see you again, my friend. Are you having lunch today?"

"Yes we are, and three glasses of Chardonnay for starters." Neal replied, shaking Tommy's hand. "Good to see you again too."

"The front window booth is all yours, Mr. T. I'll send the wine over as soon as you are seated."

Shortly after the wine arrived, Sandy seized the opportunity to open the conversation. "As I believe I mentioned before you left on vacation, I gave a copy of your manuscript to my senior editor to get an unbiased opinion of your work. The good news is; she was quite impressed with the storyline and character development, as well as your clever use of dialogue. Her only criticism was grammatical correctness. She believes that strict adherence to fundamental rules of writing, such as punctuation, grammar and paragraphing, are synonymous with best-seller quality. Do you care to comment on that?"

Neal remained composed, even smiled a little when he replied, "I wasn't expecting a Pulitzer Prize. Actually, I was anticipating that kind of a critique, since I've only studied what prep school and college offered in their basic curriculum. I really welcome her comments. After all, my specialty was always sports-related."

"See, I told you, Mother," Jessica broke in.

Before Neal could ask what Jessica meant by her remark, Sandy interrupted him and said, "Let's discuss this after we order, Jessica. I'm satisfied with Mr. Thomas' reply."

Observing the eye movement going on between the two women, Neal came to the conclusion that he had become a third wheel in something they had discussed prior to their arrival, so he asked, "Do I get to play this game too?"

"Go ahead and tell him," Sandy remarked, as she saw their waitress approach.

"Are you folks ready to order now?" she asked pleasantly.

"I'll have a Chicken Salad with Ranch Dressing, please," Sandy replied.

"Make that two," Jessica said, refocusing on Neal. "Mother wanted to observe your reaction to constructive criticism before she gave you the real meat of our editor's comments. In other words, you were being tested."

Neal smiled, looking at each of them momentarily to build up a little suspense, and then addressed the waitress, "I'll have a bowl of Clam Chowder and a small salad, please. And another round of wine."

Sensing that there was business being discussed between the threesome, the waitress smiled politely and left. That was Neal's opening to look over at his guests and say, "Ladies, I've been tested by experts. Being upset over constructive criticism is like refusing crutches after you've broken a leg. I'm a big boy. Do you want your money back?"

Jessica had just swallowed her last sip of wine when Neal asked the question, causing her to cough and grab for her napkin.

Sandy, on the other hand, remained calm. "No, that's not the is-sue," she replied. "Although there's a good chance it might be if you're willing to consider a suggestion our editor has convinced us is worth looking into."

"Great!" Neal replied enthusiastically. "What's her name?"

"Norma Manning, "Sandy replied. "Very talented and well edu-cated. She's been with us for almost ten years."

"Recently divorced with no children," Jessica added. "And very at-tractive."

"And her suggestion is…?"

Before Sandy could answer the waitress arrived with their orders. When she left, Sandy continued, none the less enthusiastic for the in-terruption. "Norma thinks your story, and the colorful characters you have created, are ideally suited for developing a series of stories much like Mickey Spillane did in his Mike Hammer mystery books, or Ian Fleming in the 007 series. She's very interested in meeting you to discuss that approach. Are you interested?"

"Who wouldn't be?" Neal replied excitedly. "I love the concept. There's just one problem."

"And that is…?" Sandy asked, a little surprised.

"I won't be able to give the project my full attention until possibly the end of next week," he explained. "If you can live with that, I'll call you as soon as this other matter is behind me and we'll get to work on it. Fair enough?"

"Do I have a choice?" Sandy replied disappointedly.

Before he could respond, Jessica sensed that her mother was becom-ing a little annoyed with Neal's failure to recognize that he was finan-cially obligated to Sterling Publishing to fulfill his book commitment as soon as possible. Suspecting that Neal might feel like he was caught in the middle of a conflict of interest situation, Jessica asked him if she could have a minute with him in private.

Sandy made no effort to question Jessica's request, as the two got up and walked outside. There in the semi-private atmosphere of disin-terested passers-by she said, "Something tells me there's more going on here than meets the eye. In all fairness to mother and me, I think you owe us an explanation. Otherwise, I'll expect you to return the advance we gave you. Now, what's it going to be, Neal?"

Given her past history with the DEA, and her relationship with Dan Hughes when their paths crossed in Cuba, Neal realized he could confide in Jessica without fear of it jeopardizing his plan, so he replied, "Next Tuesday I'm going to smuggle Dan Hughes out of Mexico so I can film him testifying against the Tidewater Drug Cartel."

"Where is this filming going to take place?" Jessica asked, a little less agressively. "You are aware of who you're dealing with here, aren't you?"

"Oh yes," he assured her. "That's why I have been so damn careful to keep the whole operation a secret. Especially after I just found out how determined the DEA is to find out where Dan's testimony is going to take place."

"How many others know about this plan of yours?"

"Only three, including yourself."

Jessica chuckled and shook her head. "I've got to hand it to you, Mr. T. You sure know how to muddy-up the water."

Neal watched her silently concentrating on something that apparently had her amused, forcing him to remain quiet until she broke out laughing. "What?" he remarked, somewhat irritated. "This is not funny!"

"Oh yes it is," she countered, taking him by the arm. "We should go back and finish our lunch before mother thinks she's going to be stuck with the check."

Inside, Sandy had already finished eating her salad and was chatting with Tommy Camillo when Neal and Jessica returned. "Well it's about time," she remarked, showing signs of giddiness. "Thanks to Mr. Camillo, I was not completely ignored! What have you two been up to, if I may ask?"

Once again, Jessica interceded. "Unbeknownst to us, Neal has been doing research on a segment of his book that will take a few days to finalize. Since I have experience in that particular area, I have offered my services to help him with the details. He'll be much better prepared to meet with Norma Manning if we give him the extra time."

You are some piece of work Neal thought, as he sat down without uttering a word. Moments later, after flirting with Sandy in his typically playful manner, Tommy excused himself, leaving Neal and Jessica to finish their lunch while Sandy sipped her wine and wondered, *have I missed something here?*

It was approaching mid-afternoon when Neal gave their waitress his credit card, explaining to Sandy and Jessica that he had other business to attend to before going home. He could tell by the look Jessica gave him that, like it or not, she was now one of his allies, one who would soon be the deciding factor in determining Dan Hughes' fate.

Just as they were getting up to leave, Jessica excused herself to use the rest room. During her absence, Neal paid the bill and took her mother outside into the warm afternoon sunshine. Looking a little melancholy, she turned to Neal and said, "I will never be able to thank you enough for bringing my daughter back into my life. I couldn't stand to lose her again. So please, watch out for her while you're doing whatever it is you don't want me to know about. You two don't fool this old broad for one minute."

Amused by her statement, he started to assure Sandy that her daughter was not in any danger when Jessica came out of the restaurant and joined them. "Thanks for a lovely lunch," she said, offering her hand to Neal. "I think we accomplished quite a bit here today. Wouldn't you agree, Mother?"

"Someone did," Sandy snickered. "I'm just not sure who it was."

Neal laughed, as his palm felt the folded paper Jessica had placed there. "I'm looking forward to working with you two again," he said convincingly. "I'll call your office next week as soon as my research is concluded."

To avoid any further discussion along those lines, Neal escorted the two ladies to their car where he embraced them both and left. Once clear of the parking lot, he turned south in the direction of Ron Barns' house, thinking he might ask him to question his attorney friend, Nancy Shore, about the legal ramifications Anita Atkins' might face when she attempted to claim her inheritance. It dawned on him along the way that he was getting himself into the same situation he had been in when he reunited Jessica Sterling with her mother. *My nose is too big,* he mused. *I should learn to keep it out of other people's business.*

Approaching Ron's house, Neal noticed another automobile parked in his driveway that looked like the same vintage Cadillac that belonged to Nancy Shore, Ron's lady friend. *Now there's a coincidence,* he thought while he parked and walked toward the house.

"Well I'll be damned!" Nancy remarked, as Neal entered the house. "Speak of the devil."

Neal laughed and gave her a friendly hug, recalling how professionally she had represented his former wife during his divorce. "I see Ron has your car blocked in the driveway. Have I arrived at an inopportune time?"

"Yeah," she teased. "We're about to leave for the airport. I'm flying back east to see my father. He hasn't been feeling well recently."

"I'm sorry to hear that," Neal said. "I enjoyed talking with him the last time he came out here to visit you."

"Why don't you ride along with us," Ron suggested. "You can keep me company on the way back."

"Good idea," Neal replied. "I've been wanting to talk to Nancy about a legal matter that's come up. We can discuss it on the way."

"I'll send you the bill when I get back," Nancy joked. "Right now we'd better get going."

"I'll drive," Neal suggested, knowing how crowded they would be in Ron's pickup truck.

They had only been on the freeway a few minutes when Nancy asked, "What legal matter did you want to ask me about, Neal?"

Grateful that she had asked on her own, Neal described the situation that Anita Atkins was in when he told her about her inheritance.

Nancy remained silent for a moment, weighing the extent of Neal's relationship with both mother and daughter. As the airport exit came into view, she said, "Confront Gloria Donaldson with the photograph you saw in Anita's apartment. See how she reacts. Regardless of their past differences, no caring mother would walk away from an opportunity to see her only child again, especially after learning that she was alive and well. I'll bet you Gloria Donaldson has that very same picture in her own family album."

"What about the inheritance?" Neal reminded her. "Anita didn't know anything about it until I told her what Allen Henderson had told me."

"How did she react?"

"More surprised that I was a friend of her mother than learning she was heir to a large sum of money."

"Good. Tell Gloria Donaldson the same thing," Nancy advised, "The last thing you want is a greedy female going after what she thinks is hers, using a bunch of equally greedy lawyers. Have you figured out how to get mother and daughter together yet?"

"No, but I'm working on it," Neal replied. "I'll figure out something."

"I bet you will," she said dryly. "Just don't get yourself in the middle."

"Hell, I'm already there!"

"Call me if a problem develops between Gloria and her daughter," she advised when Neal came to a stop in front of her baggage check-in station. "That's soon enough to start worrying about legal recourse."

Thanking Nancy for her suggestions, he went to get her bags out of the trunk. During his absence, Nancy opened her door and got out so Ron could take her place up front. When the door closed behind him, she giggled and said. "You're going to have to shorten that guy's rope, my friend. He's strayed way too far from the barn."

During the interim, Neal returned with her two suitcases and carried them over to the luggage check-in station for her. Before leaving, he remarked, "I hope you're right about that mother/daughter thing, Nancy. The last thing I need right now is to be dragged into a lawsuit that's none of my business."

"I really don't think it will come down to that," she said reassuringly. "I've seen you handle too many women before to believe you can't pull this one off. Get in touch with me when I get back and let me know how things worked out. In the meantime, good luck, and don't make any promises you can't keep."

When Neal and Ron were about half way back to Del Mar, Ron broke the silence. "I think Nancy's idea about showing Gloria Donaldson that family photograph is a very clever way of avoiding what might turn out to be a very emotionally upsetting experience for her. After all, they haven't seen one another for quite some time."

"I couldn't agree more," Neal replied. "I just don't know when I should show Gloria the photograph."

"I'd get the photo from her daughter first," Ron suggested, "and then wait for the proper time. After all, you have no guarantee that Anita will go along with this plan."

Neal knew his friend was right. Encouraged by the suggestion, he exited the freeway and drove along the lagoon to the street where Ron lived. There in the cluttered comfort of his modest home they enjoyed a drink together and watched the day waste away one minute at a time.

The horizon was beginning to turn pink when Neal told Ron that he was going to take his advice and talk Anita Cassidy into loaning him her family portrait. Checking the time, he said, "Her shift doesn't end for an hour, so I'm going to leave now to see if I can talk her into letting me drive her home."

Throughout the many years they had known each other, Ron couldn't remember a time when Neal wasn't involved with someone else's problems, usually a woman's. Hoping that what he was attempting to do for Anita Cassidy didn't backfire, Ron yelled after him, "Good hunting my friend!"

It was obvious from the lack of spaces in the Village Pub's parking lot that weekend frivolity was well under way. Forced to look for a space somewhere else, he started to back out when the taillights on a large SUV came on. He was in luck. Someone was leaving.

The song *Luck Be A Lady Tonight* came to mind as he entered the rear entrance of the crowded bar and searched unsuccessfully for an empty stool. Left with but one place to stand, he leaned back against the wall and held up a ten-dollar bill hoping to attract Anita's attention. Finally, after passing him by several times, she noticed his uplifted arm, and shouted, "The usual?"

Amused by her un-characteristically hassled behavior, he nodded affirmatively and handed her the money, but she refused it and walked hurriedly away. Moments later she returned with his beer, hesitating long enough to say, "I get off in fifteen minutes. I need to talk to you."

Pleased that she appeared to be in a mood that leant itself to accepting a ride home, Neal drank his beer and passed the time by speculating on why she hadn't taken his money, especially in front of all the people who had witnessed her refusal. It was then that he noticed that Anita wasn't taking money from anyone. Turning to the young man next to him, he asked, "How come no one's paying for drinks?"

"Because that fellow in the funny looking hat down there just hit four out of five numbers on Super Lotto," he replied. "He gave Anita a hundred dollar bill and told her to keep giving drinks away until it was gone. How's that for luck?"

Never having won anything more than a few dollars in all the years he had played the lottery, Neal's eyes widened with surprise. "Hell, I couldn't make out in a whorehouse with a handful of fifty-dollar bills."

Maybe it was the amount of free beer the young man had consumed that caused him to double over with laughter, but Neal's humorous remark seemed to have struck his funny bone. Finally straightening up, he said, "Man, you really crack me up, Mr. T!"

Twenty minutes later, looking more hassled than he had ever seen her before, Anita came out from behind the bar carrying a mug of dark beer. Brushing aside a lock of hair that had dropped down over one eye, she said, "I don't know about you, but I'm all for finishing our beer and getting the hell out of this place. I'm pooped!"

Using that statement as an open door to suggest what he had come there for, Neal asked, "Can I give you a lift home?"

"I thought you'd never ask," she said, as she turned and headed toward the rear entrance.

Hesitating only long enough to drink his last swallow of beer, Neal followed her lead, confident that she would not deny him use of the photograph he thought would change her life forever, and possibly his own.

As they left the parking lot, Neal ventured to ask, "What is it you wanted to talk to me about?"

After nervously fidgeting with her hair for a moment, she replied, "I'm curious about what my mother did with her life after my father died."

Being careful not to disclose what little he knew about Gloria Donaldson's suspected involvement in providing corporate level call girl services, he used the question to lay the foundation for what he hoped would soon be Anita's reunion with her, and replied, "She's on the Board Of Directors of Donaldson Enterprises, which includes your late father's shipbuilding business, and a number of real estate holdings, one of which I believe you are familiar with."

"Ah yes, the good old Sawmill Club," she said, as he pulled up in front of her apartment. "Got time for a drink? I'm buying."

"I never turn one down if I can help it," he chuckled. "Besides, I've got something I want to talk to you about."

Moments later, Neal and Anita sat facing one another in her small kitchen, each with a drink of their choice. Smiling for the first time, she said, "Now, what's on your mind?"

"My best friend dates a female attorney by the name of Nancy Shore. I talked with her this morning about the situation you're in with your mother."

"And?"

Pointing in the direction of Anita's family portrait, Neal said, "Nancy thinks I should confront your mother with that photograph to see how she reacts before mentioning anything about your inheritance. Her instinct says that your mother will be so overwhelmed by learning you are alive and well that she'll do anything to see you again. In other words, let the subject of your inheritance come from her, so she won't have any reason to suspect you of having an ulterior motive."

Anita agreed and stood up to refill their glasses. "However, please believe me when I say that I had been thinking about my mother for sometime prior to you coming into my life. Call it maturity, or just plain being fed up with trying to blame everyone else for mistakes I made on my own. Thanks for giving me the opportunity to do something about it."

Neal reached across the table and touched his glass to hers. "That's all I needed to hear. Now I can proceed with my plan to re-unite you two."

Exercising her feminine curiosity to its limits, Anita asked, "When, where and how are you going to arrange for me to see my mother? I need to know so I can make arrangements for someone to take my place at the Pub while I'm gone."

To avoid further complicating his already scheduled plans for the following Tuesday, Neal decided to put Anita on hold until after Dan Hughes had been successfully picked up from Mexico. Without divulging any details relevant to that operation, he replied, "Tell your boss that you want to take next week off to vacation in Mexico with a friend. On Monday, pack a bag with everything you would normally take on such a trip. I will pick you up at three o'clock that afternoon and take you to my place to spend the night…in my guest room, of course."

"Of course," she mimicked him, trying not to laugh.

"I'll explain then where we go from there."

"I certainly hope so. This is beginning to sound like a James Bond movie."

Checking the time, he grinned and said, "Time to go, young lady. I'm no Sean Connery."

"Don't forget my family," she said, walking over to get the photograph. "I hope it brings us both luck."

Picture in hand, he patted her shoulder and started down the stairs, while she stood at the top and called after him, "Here's to Monday!"

Though the temptation to stop at the Hilton Inn was on his mind when he saw its lights twinkling in the distance, the fact that Maggie Jyles had been promoted to a manager's position seemed to make her less accessible on a drop-in basis, so Neal continued on his way home, resigned to read his mail and watch television with some leftover pizza. He was in the process of mixing a drink when his cell phone sounded. Reluctantly, he removed it from the charger and flipped it on. "This is Neal."

"Hi there. This is Mary Jo Tyler. Are you alone?"

"Yes," he replied, looking at his watch to determine the East Coast time. "You're up pretty late for a working girl aren't you?"

"Not really. This is the only time of day I can get anything done. Besides, I've found the information you asked me to look for. Do you have a FAX machine?"

"Yes I do. Can you send it right away? Time is of the essence."

"Unfortunately, it's in my office, but I'll send what I have the first thing tomorrow morning. Are you okay with that?"

"Are you kidding?" he answered excitedly. "You've certainly made my day."

"I must warn you, though. This information is highly volatile. In the wrong hands it could severely jeopardize the reputations and careers of a select group of Washington politicians who are well thought of on both sides of the aisle. Be extremely careful with whomever you share this information. It could come back to haunt you…and me."

"I will," he assured her, "And thank you again for all your help. As far as revealing where I obtained the information, you can rest assured that your name will never be mentioned in connection with what you send me. That's a promise."

"I appreciate that," she replied trustingly. "But just to be on the safe side, I plan to destroy the originals right after I FAX you copies. Better safe than sorry. Good luck. Let me know how all this turns out."

"You'll be the first one I call."

Excited with curiosity over what Mary Jo had uncovered, Neal took his drink upstairs to sip on while he changed into more casual attire. As he emptied his pockets onto the dresser, he noticed the folded piece of paper Jessica Sterling had placed in his hand when they parted company that afternoon. Upset with himself for not having looked at it sooner, he unfolded it and read: *Please call my cell phone number whenever you get home today. I believe I can help you with Dan Hughes.*

"Damn!" he shouted, hurriedly returning downstairs to look up her number. After placing the call, he waited until after the sixth ring before deciding she wasn't home and ended the call, disappointed at having to spend the night wondering what she was going to propose.

He had just turned on the television when he heard his cell phone ring. Rushing back to his office, he grabbed the phone from its charger and panted, "This is Neal!"

"If you had waited one more ring, I would have answered," Jessica Sterling's voice remarked. "I was in the bathroom."

"Sorry about that. Patience is not a virtue of mine," he replied. "Having raised three daughters, I'm all too familiar with the process."

Jessica appreciated the humor in his remark and said, "Our brief conversation regarding your strategy to get Dan Hughes out of Mexico got me thinking about how I might help."

"I need all I can get. What did you have in mind?"

"First of all, Dan trusts me. Secondly, I know how the DEA operates. I wouldn't trust them any further than I can spit. With my past experience as an agent, I could lend credibility to the taping of his testimony by asking the questions. With me in the film there wouldn't be any question about its authenticity?"

"You've got a rock solid point there. Do you think your mother will go along with taking a few days away from your office just to help me?"

"That's my job," she answered confidently. "Doesn't this fall under the heading of field research for your book?"

Again, Neal found no fault with her logic and replied, "In that case, pack a bag with what you'll need to spend a few days on Catalina Island. On Monday drive up to my place after work prepared to spend the night. I'll explain what we're going to do then."

"Are you propositioning me, Mr. T?" she asked, trying to add a little humor to an awkward situation.

"Not unless you're into ménage a trois," he replied. "Another woman will be joining us there too."

"Why you old fox!" she remarked excitedly. "Now you've really got my curiosity up. I'll see you Monday."

Although his reputation for smutty humor had long since proceeded him, the laughter he had enjoyed over Jessica's reaction to a time-worn French cliché was short lived when he glanced at the photograph Anita Cassidy had loaned him. "I hope your mother is ready for this," he said with an anxious voice. "Our day of reckoning is nigh."

Chapter 12

A Gathering Of Forces

While eating breakfast the next morning, Neal reflected on the mix of individuals and events that were destined to come together during the next few days. Seemingly unrelated, like differently shaped pieces in a jigsaw puzzle, each of them would be an integral part of a conspiracy to deceive a government agency into accepting its own fallibility by outsmarting them.

Eyeing the calendar that hung over his phone suddenly became a reminder of how quickly time had passed since his journey to the Sawmill Club. Considering what had already been accomplished, all that remained was to coach Anita Cassidy on what to do with the bugged camcorder the DEA had sent him. As he stood at the sink rinsing away the remnants of his breakfast, he thought, *Mr. Bronson, I do believe your cunning little deception is about to backfire.* Then, another thought struck him that made him dry his hands and go to his studio. As Mary Jo had promised, there was a small stack of typewritten pages sitting in the tray of his FAX machine, ominously waiting to give up information that would severely influence the intent of questions the DEA wanted Dan Hughes to answer. Eager to read what would soon prove to be a revealing history of Walter Douglas's undercover relationship with Washington's political aristocracy, he returned to the kitchen, fixed another cup of coffee and sat down to evaluate how the information could be used to benefit Dan Hughes' exoneration.

Contrary to Neal's long established opinion regarding Walter Douglas' lack of literary skills, a brief review of the information revealed the names and titles of individuals employed by various offices within the Federal Government, including the FBI, CIA, DEA, DOD, Executive Branch and others. A note at the bottom of each page read: *An asterisk (*) following a person's name denotes those who either used and/or distributed my services.*

When Neal finished reading the last page, it became immediately clear that he was holding a paper time bomb that could cause more devastation than the senseless destruction of the World Trade Centers in New York City and Hurricane Katrina combined. Politically, the consequences would be catastrophic. *Thank God Mary Jo destroyed the originals.*

Unable to imagine the far-reaching consequences of such a document, Neal rolled the pages into a cylinder, put them in a Zip-Loc bag and walked out into the garage to find a suitable hiding place. He was about to consider his metal file cabinet when he saw what had happened to it during the recent break-in, cautioning him to look elsewhere. As luck would have it, his eyes wandered to a shelf where he had stored a barbecue charcoal starter given to him by a friend. It was round and had a lid on it. *Perfect* he thought. *No one would bother looking in that thing.*

Outside, the late morning sun sparkled like jewels on the incoming tide, a sun that had already charmed surfers of all ages into challenging the rolling surf. As he watched their silent vigil, a thought came to him that changed his focus from wishing he were out there to verifying that the major players in his soon to be initiated deception were prepared for its arrival. Strapping on his cell phone, he grabbed a lounge chair from the patio and walked out to the bluff to begin the inquiry, calling Dan Hughes first.

Dan answered within seconds. The sound of his voice, and music playing in the background, made it clear that he was partying somewhere. "I don't know where the hell you are, Dan, but get the hell out of there so I can talk to you about Tuesday."

"I'm at the Beachcomber Bar and Grill," Dan replied, half laughing. "There's a piano player here who says he remembers you and your partners from years back. Can you believe it?"

Neal scowled. "Will you please walk out on the beach so we can talk without all that noise! And don't tell anyone there that it's me you're talking to."

"Okay, okay!" he replied, sounding irritated. Several seconds later, with the background noise noticeably quieter, Dan said, "Okay, I'm out in the parking lot now. What the hell is going on?"

"I'm just checking to make sure you know where you're supposed to be on Tuesday. There's a lot at stake here, Dan. Please don't screw it up."

"No way," he replied convincingly. "I've already checked out the pier at Puerto Nuevo. I'll be there at twelve o'clock high on Tuesday to meet your friend's boat. I believe you said it was The Wayward Wind, right?"

"That is correct," Neal answered, relieved that his worst fears were of his own making. "I'll see you Tuesday. There'll be a surprise waiting for you."

"I don't like surprises, Mr. T."

"You'll like this one," Neal remarked. "Now go on back to your party and keep our conversation to yourself. See you Tuesday."

Reassured that Dan wasn't foolish enough to jeopardize the effort that was being made to give him another chance at a legitimate way of life, Neal placed a call to the one person he was relying on heavily to provide the type of transportation that was essential to the entire operation – Jim Taylor.

"Taylor Flying Academy," a female voice announced after several rings. "This is Judy."

"My name is Neal Thomas, Judy. Is Jim there?"

"Ah hah," she replied, in a perky voice. "So you're the guy he's sprucing up The Goose for. Yes, he's here. Hold on while I transfer you over to Hanger B."

Seconds later, Jim Taylor came on line. "I was wondering if you were going to check in with me before Tuesday. Are we still on?"

"Are you?"

"All gassed up and raring to go," Jim replied enthusiastically. "I've already packed The Goose with everything I think we're going to need. How's it going at your end?"

"Right on target," Neal replied confidently. "I've had to make a minor change in my choice of recording equipment. Other than that, I'm ready."

Suddenly, as he was about to terminate the call, a thought struck him. "There is one minor item I forgot to mention."

"And that is…?"

Embarrassed by his own thoughtlessness, Neal added, "A former DEA agent by the name of Jessica Sterling will be joining us on Tuesday. She's a close friend of mine who has agreed to help me with Dan's interview."

Several seconds of unrecognizable sound followed before Jim was able to reply. "I sure hope you know what you're doing, Mr. T. Does she have any idea what she's getting into?"

"It was her idea!"

"Lord help us," Jim sighed. "See ya Tuesday."

Two down and one to go Neal thought, as the sun's heat began to bring beads of perspiration out on his forehead. Prompted to seek the shade of his Jacuzzi deck, he decided to treat himself to a cold beer before calling Gloria Donaldson.

The beer was cold, soothing the dryness that had parched his throat from too much talking over the past several days. Several swallows later, after a relaxing mellowness had crept over his body, he placed the call.

Gloria answered after the third ring. "Don't ask me why, but somehow I knew it was you calling," she said in a whisper. "Are we still on for Tuesday?"

"Most definitely," he replied, impressed by her enthusiasm. "I just wanted to make one final check to make sure everyone was on the same wave length."

"Is Mr. Hughes?" she asked, almost sarcastically.

"I just talked to him. He assured me he would be waiting for you as planned."

"Good. I'm getting kind of excited about all this," she replied. "It's not often I'm asked to participate in such a noble cause."

Neal did not comment on her remark immediately, because the mental image of Anita Cassidy's family photograph suddenly distracted his train of thought. Realizing that he would soon be determining the fate of two individuals who had willingly placed themselves in his hands, he finally said, "I hope you still feel that way when all of this is over."

"What's that supposed to mean?"

"Oh, don't pay any attention to me. I'm just nervous that's all. I'll feel much better when we can relax and enjoy ourselves again."

"I'm sure that can be arranged," Gloria said, giggling a bit, "See you Tuesday at my condo. Mr. Hughes and I will be waiting for you there."

So far so good Neal thought, thirsty for another beer. He had just pulled the tab back when his cell phone rang. *What now?* Setting his beer down he picked up the receiver. "Hello, this is Neal," he said with a touch of irritability.

"Why don't you go back to bed and try getting up from the other side," the voice on the other end suggested. "This is Jessica Sterling. Is Mr. Thomas available?"

"I deserve that," he replied, after realizing how rude he must have sounded. "I'm wound up tight as a banjo string today," he explained. "Please forgive me. I must be suffering from pre-game jitters."

"You're forgiven," she giggled. "Sounds to me like you need someone to pluck your banjo. Which brings up the reason for my call."

"Pluck away."

"I suggested to mother that she invite you to attend our annual employee dinner party here at our house this evening. Sounds like you could use a little relaxation."

"You can say that again. What time?"

"Be here around five o'clock. We have someone we want you to meet."

"You're not match-making are you?"

After a moment of muffled conversation with someone in the background, Jessica answered, "Not hardly. I was thinking that it would be an opportune time for you to meet our senior editor, Norma Manning. I know Mother will be pleased if she thought we were getting together to indulge in a little book-related conversation. Also, Norma is quite a talented lady. I've asked her to bring her cello so the two of you can entertain our guests for a little while after dinner, if that's okay with you."

Pleased with the whole idea, Neal replied, "Sounds like fun to me. I haven't played with anyone for years."

Jessica burst into laughter. "Don't tell her that!"

Neal caught the unintended metaphor and recanted, "I meant music, of course."

Still laughing, Jessica wiped her wet eyes and said, "Mr. T, you're something else! See you at five o'clock."

Following Jessica's unexpected phone call, Neal remained in the kitchen and finished his beer, reflecting on how capricious life could be at times when every effort had been made to maintain some semblance of order and predictability. Convinced that his life was becoming more or less a crapshoot, he welcomed the opportunity to spend an evening in the company of individuals whose lives were, for the most part, completely foreign to him. With nothing to do but wait for Tuesday's outcome, he welcomed Jessica's well-timed invitation.

Not having had the luxury of an afternoon nap for more time than he could remember, Neal picked up one of his more comfortable deck chairs and carried it out to the bluff. There, with a morning newspaper to keep him occupied, he read until his eyes grew weary and closed. A short time later, however, his cell phone chimed him back to reality. A familiar voice identified itself. "Hello, Neal. This is Ginger Spyce."

Although he was a little irritated by having his nap interrupted, Neal knew Ginger's call, especially on a Saturday afternoon, must have been prompted by something she felt was important. "It's good to hear your voice again, my dear. How are you?" he asked in a friendly tone.

"I hope you'll still feel that way after you've heard what I have to say," she replied. "Are you alone?"

Recognizing a tone of urgency in her voice, he replied, "Yes, I'm alone. Are you all right?"

"Yes, but I have information that may affect whatever plans you have made to pick up Dan Hughes this Tuesday."

"What, specifically?" he asked, alarmed that his plans might have been compromised.

"Dusty Lewis, asked me to work today," she began nervously. "I don't normally work on Saturdays, but I'm glad I did. He told me in confidence that DEA Director Raymond Bronson had made him personally responsible for tracking you down whenever you tried to use that camcorder device Bronson sent you."

Without revealing that he had already discovered the tracking mechanism, Neal questioned, "Has Dusty made any plans in that regard?"

"He knows where and when you are going to pick up Mr. Hughes, based on information you gave him," she replied. "But not the actual location where you plan to film the event. That's why I'm calling."

"To tell me...?"

"You've unknowingly set yourself up to be taken into custody after you pick up Dan on San Clemente Island, and take him to wherever you're going to film his testimony. No matter where you go, that camcorder Bronson sent you will set off a locator signal. That's when Dusty and his men will swarm in on you. All in the name of protecting Dan from the bad guys...yeah, right."

A smug smile appeared on Neal's face when she finished. "Not to worry, my dear. That situation has already been addressed. Thank you for confirming my suspicions. I owe you one."

"Make it a double, will you. I feel a hangover coming on."

Any notion that he could resume his nap disappeared as soon as he shut down his phone. Upset and angered by the thought that Dusty would deceive him, Neal paced up and down the bluff trying to figure out what to do next. Then it struck him. An idea so bizarre that it caused him to burst out laughing and return to the kitchen. Still grinning, he mixed a drink and took it upstairs to keep him company while he showered and dressed for dinner, thinking, *what a strange day this has turned out to be.*

To avoid traffic, Neal opted to travel the Old Coast Highway that afternoon because of an unexplainable desire to look at the elegant beach houses and condominiums that lined both sides of the road. Much of his fascination came from a curiosity regarding those who lived there. Where had they come from? And what had they done to earn the kind of money their properties represented. Being a lover of the sea, and the mystique that went along with it, Neal experienced moments of envy when he saw residents standing on their patio decks waiting to witness sunsets that had become legendary. *Maybe someday* he thought, as he exited Del Mar and began his ascent to Torrey Pines State Reserve, past Scripps Memorial Hospital and down La Jolla's beautiful Scenic Drive.

Security gates at the Sterling Estate were open when he arrived, allowing him to proceed directly to the main house. There, much to his surprise, were two young men in matching outfits standing near a small podium and a sign that read, **Valet Parking**.

After exchanging his car keys for a numbered tag, Neal proceeded directly to the large front doors he had entered during previous visits to the Sterling residence. *Seems like a long time ago.*

Ivan Olofson, Sandy Sterling's resident butler, greeted Neal like an old friend when he entered. "Good evening Mr. Thomas," he said, offering his hand and smiling. "It certainly is good to see you again. Please pass through the reception line on the patio. Ms. Sterling is eagerly awaiting your arrival."

Based on the number of people who were gathered on the patio, it didn't take Neal long to realize that he had walked into a much larger event than he had anticipated. As Ivan had instructed, he took his place in line and waited patiently to be introduced to the hostess. He hadn't been there long when a woman he was glad to see approached and asked, "Are you ready for this, Mr. T?"

"Why didn't you tell me I was going to the Queen's Coronation?" he replied in a whisper.

"I'll tell you after you've said hello to mother and her staff," Jessica answered authoritatively, placing her arm in his. "She's trying to show you off, you know."

It was only a matter of a few seconds before Neal and Jessica came face-to-face with Sandy Sterling, the first person of several in the reception line that Neal speculated were other corporate executives. Offering her hand, Sandy said, "Good evening, Mr. Thomas. I'm glad to see that my daughter already has you in tow. Be that as it may, welcome to our company's annual get together. We're all pleased that you could attend on such short notice."

"I am honored to be here," he replied politely. "You look lovely, as usual."

Lowering her eyes briefly to hide the blush she felt, Sandy turned to her left and addressed an unusually attractive brunette standing next to her. "Norma, I'd like you to meet our newest author, Neal Thomas. And, incidentally, your accompanist at the piano this evening."

Norma Manning raised her hand slowly until Neal's fingers engulfed it with gentle firmness, never letting her eyes wander from his. "I've been wondering when these two ladies were going to introduce me to the infamous Mr. T," she remarked pleasantly. "I hope we can talk about your book a little later on this evening. I've become quite fascinated with it."

Still captivated by the unusual attractiveness that separated her from any woman he had ever met, Neal wondered what ever possessed her former husband to seek a divorce. Eager to pursue her suggestion, he replied, "I'd say as soon as possible, but there's some personal business I must take care of first. Jessica will advise you when I'm available to discuss the book."

Norma shifted her eyes over to Jessica's and waited expectantly for a response.

Knowing she had no other recourse than to support Neal, Jessica said, "I'll make sure you're the first to know when he's free to return to the book."

Though disappointed by what she viewed as needless delay, Norma respected Jessica's judgment and accepted the situation. "I will look forward to working with you whenever it is expedient, Mr. Thomas. In the meantime, loosen up your fingers. I'm looking forward to playing with you later on." Realizing how easily her words could have been misinterpreted, she giggled self-consciously and added, "at the piano, that is."

Moments later, after they had run the gauntlet of formal introductions, Jessica hustled Neal over to a long table serving as a bar. Three older men in matching jackets were busily mixing drinks there. Waving her hand to get one's attention, she mouthed the words, *"Double vodka tonic, and a glass of wine… please."*

Several seconds later, the bartender thrust their two drinks past the other guests waiting to be served, and joked, "Nothing personal, folks. She just happens to be the boss!"

Following that little episode, Jessica led Neal to a quiet place where they could talk privately. "I asked you here today for a number of reasons," she began, "That is, if your interested."

"What, to get me drunk?" he remarked with a grimace, after sampling his drink. "Why would you want to do that…I'm easy?"

"No, silly," she countered. "For one thing, I thought it would draw mother's attention away from questioning me about what you and I are planning to do next Tuesday. She already suspects the worst."

"She's no dummy, you know."

"Well, to reinforce our ploy, I thought this annual company party would be an ideal time for you to meet Norma Manning. That was mother's idea, knowing you both played musical instruments."

"All I can say is, I hope Norma has a sense of humor."

"She has," Jessica remarked, giggling a little. "When we told her you could only play in one key, she laughed and said, good, that simplifies things considerably."

Amused, but needing to change the subject, Neal reminded Jessica that he had not given her any detailed information regarding what was to take place on the following Tuesday. Having already promised that he would do that when she came to spend the night, he re-thought that plan and said, "Before we get carried away with this gala event, I need to fill you in on a few of the specifics that are vital to Tuesday's operation while I can still think straight."

"I was expecting you to," she replied more seriously. "That's one of the reasons why you were invited. As you can observe, no one here gives a hoot about what we're talking about, so fill me in. I need to know everything you have planned in order to help you pull this thing off."

Encouraged by her straight forwardness, he began. "I have recently been advised by a reliable source inside the DEA that their agent, Dusty Lewis, has been given the responsibility of intercepting my filming of Dan Hughes' testimony after we get him out of Mexico."

"I thought Dusty Lewis was an old friend of yours."

"He still is, but not as far as this operation is concerned."

"Go on."

Hesitating briefly to put his strategy in logical sequence, he continued. "This coming Monday evening you will meet another friend of mine who is going through a situation much like the one you and your mother went through years ago. Her name is Anita Donaldson. Alias, Anita Cassidy. "

"And the plot thickens," Jessica remarked, rolling her eyes skyward. "What's her part in all this?"

"I'm trying to re-unite her with her mother."

"You've sure got a round about way of doing it," Jessica remarked. "Hold that thought while I get us another drink."

As he stood alone with his thoughts bouncing back and forth between the bizarre characters that seemed to be in control of his destiny, Neal caught sight of Ivan Olofson approaching, apparently looking for him. "Ah, here you are," he said, with a sigh of relief. "Ms. Sterling has asked me to inform you that dinner will be served in thirty minutes. She also expects you and Miss Jessica to join her and Ms. Manning at their table for dinner." Winking at Neal as he turned to leave, Ivan whispered, "A word to the wise."

In the wake of Ivan's departure Jessica returned with fresh drinks, "What did Ivan want?" she asked inquisitively.

"We're expected to join your mother and Norma Manning at their table for dinner."

"That's a given," she remarked nonchalantly, "but please finish what you were about to tell me a minute ago. You won't get a better chance than now."

Back-tracking to where he had previously ended their conversation, Neal continued. "Before you came into the picture, I had invited Anita Cassidy to spend Monday night at my place because I intended to take her to Catalina Island for a showdown meeting with her mother. She just happens to own the condominium where we are going to secretly film Dan Hughes' testimony."

"How were you planning to get there?" Jessica asked. "Fly?"

"Exactly," Neal replied. "While I was on vacation I made a good friend who owns a seaplane. Ironically, he turned out to be an old friend of Gloria Donaldson, Anita Cassidy's mother. I thought, why not take Anita along and reunite them. The same way I did for you and your mother."

"For that I shall be forever grateful. But how did Anita and her mother become estranged in the first place. Something's missing here."

"That's an entirely different story," Neal replied, somewhat apologetically. "I'll let her mother fill you in on that one."

"What about Anita? Aren't you still planning to take her?"

"I was, but now she's going to do something for me that is so essential to this operation that it will make her a heroine in her mother's eyes when she finds out what Anita did for Dan and I."

"I take it Anita knows nothing about this change in plans, as yet."

"No. I plan to tell her Monday evening when the three of us are together."

"How about explaining that to me," Jessica remarked, almost sarcastically. "Then we'll both know...won't we?"

"I'm sorry," he said apologetically, "I'm jumping the gun."

"That's okay. I'm used to it by now. Go ahead."

Looking across the pool, Neal observed that guests were gradually beginning to sit down for dinner. "Let's start walking over there," he said, nodding in that direction. "I'll tell you on the way."

As they walked toward the table where Sandy Sterling and Norma Manning were already seated, Neal explained why he had been forced to change his original plan. "DEA director, Raymond Bronson, sent me a package containing a special camcorder. I was to use it to record Dan Hughes' testimony. Quite by accident, I discovered that when the support handle is attached, it activates an electronic tracking device that would lead them to wherever I used it. Their intent being to place Dan and I under protective custody until his testimony could be documented and sent back to Bronson."

"Dan would never come back here if he knew that," Jessica remarked.

"Exactly," Neal agreed. "So, to foil their plan, I'm going to ask Miss Cassidy to ride with us to Palomar Airport Tuesday morning where you and I will meet Jim Taylor and fly to Catalina. Using my car, Anita will return to my place and wait for me to tell her when to activate the camcorder."

"Then what?" Jessica inquired. "If she drives the car back to your house, how is she going to get home?"

Hesitating before they came to within hearing distance of her mother's table, Neal said, "She's not. I'm going to give her enough money to catch a cab to the Hilton Inn where she can relax for a few days while we finish our business with Dan Hughes on Catalina. From then on we'll just have to play it by ear."

"Easy for you to say," she joked. "You're the piano player."

When they reached the table where Sandy and Norma Manning were sitting, Neal turned on his charm before Sandy could speak. "May I have the honor of sitting between you two lovely ladies during dinner?"

"That's why the chair's empty," she snapped back, sounding a little perturbed. "Just what have you two been up to all this time?"

Norma remained intentionally silent, sensing that Sandy was becoming irritated with her daughter.

Before Neal could respond, Jessica interrupted him and said, "I was reminding Neal about the book-related comments Norma had made earlier this week, and suggested that he might want to sit between the two of you and discuss them. I have to use the ladies room."

"You're excused, my dear," Sandy remarked, as she patted the other empty seat beside her. "Run along now. This seat will be waiting for you when you return."

Jessica is a clever one Neal thought, watching the almost masculine gate of her buttocks disappear into the house. Then, picking up the scenario that she had cleverly laid out for him, he addressed both women, asking, "Okay, who's first?"

Norma seized the opportunity to kill any discussion about Neal's book. "I'm sure Ms. Sterling would agree that this gala evening is neither the time nor place to be discussing business. Personally, I'd much prefer to discuss the type of music Mr. Thomas wants to play after dinner."

Sandy recognized the wisdom in Norma's comment and said, "I agree. Mixing business with pleasure on this particular occasion is inappropriate. Now, let's concentrate on what songs you two are going to play."

Neal and Norma looked at one another as if waiting for the other to speak. "I'm going to leave the song selection up to Neal," Norma said, exercising diplomacy. "My classical background is better suited for following his lead. I'm sure we'll do just fine."

"I'm honored," Neal replied, "but I would like to sneak away for a few minutes of practice with you as soon as Jessica returns. Just a few chord progressions to get used to one another. Is that okay with you, Sandy?"

"Of course," she replied, noticing Jessica returning to the table. "Here she comes now, so go practice. We'll eat when you get back."

During their absence, Jessica and Sandy entertained one another by discussing Neal's obvious attraction to Norma and Jessica's involvement in what Neal was secretly planning to do the following Tuesday. Without revealing any specific details regarding the operation, Jessica confided in her mother that she was taking a few days off from work to provide technical assistance during the filming of a book-related incident.

"To insure absolute secrecy until the filming has been successfully completed," she explained, "I can't discuss it any further. Trust me, mother, I am in absolutely no danger, and will return home immediately after the filming is over."

Sandy remained silent, looking almost sad for a moment. "I'm not worried about you, my dear. I'm envious of your youth, energy and adventurous life. Any promise of that in my life ended the day your father died. Now, all I have is his business, this place and you. Please be careful. I couldn't stand to lose you again."

For the first time in many years Jessica felt tears begin to well up in her eyes. Grabbing a napkin, she dabbed them away and hugged her mother for several seconds. "No fear of that," she sniffled. "I'm too mean to die."

A minute later, in a rush of laughter and animated conversation, Neal and Norma returned to the Sterling's table, unaware of the emotional scene that had taken place only moments before. "Okay, you two," Neal said, giving Sandy and Jessica each a kiss on the forehead, "It's time to eat."

Their animated arrival seemed to neutralize the emotional breakdown that had occurred during Neal and Norma's conveniently timed absence, making it easier for Sandy and Jessica to recapture their happier mood. As they stood together in the buffet line, Sandy remarked,

"You two certainly seem to be having a fun time. Was it the music, or the wine?"

"A little of both," Norma replied. "We play well together…no pun intended."

Never having heard Norma even approximate a sexually suggestive remark before, Jessica giggled and said, "Try it, you'll like it!"

The jovial mood and entertaining conversation between the four friends lasted well beyond dinner and continued until an announcement was made encouraging everyone to gather in the living room for the evening's entertainment. When all the guests were gathered, Sandy came forward and introduced Neal and Norma, as they sat nervously at their respective instruments grinning at one another.

Having already agreed on their selection of songs, Neal played a few introductory bars of *Somewhere In Time* and waited for Norma to begin the melody. She began with such skillful phrasing that it prompted spontaneous applause that ended quickly for the rest of the performance.

I've never played better Neal thought while he and Norma passed the melody back and forth as if they had been performing together for years. As the final measure of the song arrived, Norma drew her bow slowly across the final note, as Neal's hands played the harmonic chord that ended the song, bringing with it a spontaneous round of applause from everyone in the room, and a barrage of requests.

While Neal and Norma kept the majority of guests entertained for the next hour, some of the audience adjourned to the patio bar to listen from a distance, opting to enjoy the soft ocean breeze that floated across the patio. Among them were Sandy and Jessica Sterling, whose primary interest focused on the budding relationship developing between Neal and Norma Manning. "I believe we may be witnessing a match made in heaven," Sandy remarked. "If they harmonize as well on Neal's book, as they do on playing music together, I'd say we have a best seller in the making."

Jessica mused over her mother's observation for a moment before venturing a comment. "I'll reserve my opinions until after we've resolve this research item he's asked me to help him with. It could dramatically alter Norma's ideas about developing the current manuscript into an ongoing series. Let's wait until I get back to make the final decision on which is the best way to proceed. I really believe there's a blockbuster movie hidden in what Neal is thinking about right now."

"I hadn't thought of it in that light," Sandy admitted. "I agree. We should wait."

"Be sure you convey that thought to Norma," Jessica suggested. "We sure don't want to ruffle any tail feathers."

"I'll handle Norma, my dear. Remember, she works for me."

As soon as Sandy and Jessica finished their conversation, music from inside the house stopped, and guests began returning to the patio to say goodbye and eventually leave. Neal and Norma were among them.

"The party's over," Neal sang, as he embraced Sandy, Jessica and Norma. "Thanks for everything. I can't remember when I've had a better time."

A moment of awkwardness followed, prompting Norma to remark, "Drive carefully. Please contact me when you're free to resume work on your book. Goodnight all."

"I'll see you tomorrow evening right after work," Jessica reminded Neal, waving goodbye and walking toward the house. "Get a good night's sleep. We've got a busy day ahead of us."

Left alone with Neal, Sandy kissed him on the cheek and said the only thing she could think of, "Take good care of Jessica."

Chapter 13

Prelude To Freedom

Monday morning arrived in a gloomy shroud of thick fog that blanketed the beach behind Neal's house, making it difficult to identify familiar objects through the window at the foot of his bed. A foghorn sounded somewhere in the distance, bringing back the memory of his favorite Humphrey Bogart movie, *Casablanca*, and its classic theme song, *As Time Goes By*. Prompted by its lyric, he struggled out of bed and made his unsteady way to the shower to hopefully regenerate his enthusiasm for what he had to do today.

It wasn't until warm water wet his head for several seconds that he started remembering what had taken place Saturday evening. All too vivid was the image of Norma Manning sitting gracefully at her cello playing like a skilled professional. Grateful that he hadn't been tempted to follow her home, he reached up and closed the hot water valve and waited for the cold shock that followed. Seconds later, shivered back to some degree of normalcy, he turned the water off and toweled himself dry, confident that he was ready for whatever the day had to offer.

As the morning wore on, housekeeping chores that he felt obligated to complete before his two female guests arrived were taken care of. With that behind him, and the early morning fog almost gone, he prepared a light breakfast and took a short walk on the beach to clear his head and organize his thoughts. When he returned, the first item on his agenda was to pack his suitcase with what he needed for his brief visit to Catalina, and the new camcorder he had just purchased to replace the one Raymond Bronson had sent him.

In the briefcase that had served him so well over the years, he placed Dan's Presidential Pardon, a copy of the DEA questions Dusty Lewis had delivered to him, and the Donaldson family portrait Anita Cassidy had loaned him, certain that they would play a significant role in restoring the lives of both Dan Hughes and Anita Cassidy the next day. It was the Donaldson family photograph that prompted him to check the time. Only then did he realize that he only had one hour to pick up Anita, who as yet, knew nothing about what she was letting herself in for.

Though tempted to include a copy of Walter Douglas' personal records to supplement the other paperwork he was taking, Neal reconsidered that option in favor of using them strategically in case Raymond Bronson or Dusty Lewis made any attempt to discredit Dan Hughes' testimony; an ace in the hole, so to speak.

After placing the baggage in the trunk of his car, he removed the DEA camcorder and took it into the house for safe keeping until he returned with Anita. Satisfied that all was in readiness, he browsed through the newspaper until it was time to leave.

Fortunately, traffic delays on his way to Anita's apartment only made him a few minutes late. Thus, it came as no surprise when he found her leaning against a tree in the front yard when he got there, apparently unconcerned about the time, or anything else for that matter. Her smile said it all.

Bubbling with enthusiasm, she got into the car, leaned over and kissed Neal on the cheek and said, "Man, am I glad to see you. I didn't sleep a wink last night just thinking about today. Aren't you excited?"

Being careful not to say anything that would pre-empt what he was saving for later on that day, he replied, "Well, seeing you so happy sure makes it all worthwhile. For that, I am very grateful."

As they traveled the short distance back to his home, Neal tried to remember whether he had ever mentioned anything specifically about what this day was all about. As far as he could recall, Anita's entire focus had been directed toward Neal's relationship with her mother. He wondered if she would become upset when she learned that she was only being used to activate the DEA's camcorder. *Wait until after she meets Jessica to bring up that subject* his instincts told him.

When Neal drove into his driveway Anita gasped, "Oh my, Mr. T. What a beautiful view. And you live here by yourself?"

"I do now," he said unemotionally. "My former lady friend and I lived here for a number years before she decided to pursue a career in the nursery business. She fell heir to a place near Ramona not long ago, so we both agreed she should give it a try. Working for the city was beginning to get to her."

"I can't imagine leaving this place," Anita remarked. "But the opportunity to achieve financial independence doesn't come along that often not to give it your best shot. No offense, but I can't say as I blame her."

"Neither do I," he said, chuckling a little. "Like the man said, that's life."

"Can we go out on the bluff for a little while? It's such a beautiful day."

"Sure can." He replied, being pleasantly agreeable. "My other guest will be along shortly. We can see her from there."

Anita had started to move in the bluff's direction, but stopped abruptly. "Other guest?"

Oops, I blew it Neal realized, as soon as the words left his lips. *No use waiting for Jessica now.* Putting his arm around Anita's shoulder, he escorted her out to the bluff and faced the inevitable. "Jessica Sterling is a friend of mine who, like yourself, ran away from home shortly after her father died, because she couldn't tolerate her overly protective mother continually interfering in her life, much like yours did. Without going into a lot of meaningless detail, I brought them back together again. Like I'm trying to do with you and your mother. Your situation, however, is much more complicated."

"How so? I thought you said you had it all figured out."

"I do," Neal replied, "but I need your help to pull it off."

"To do what?" she barked. "I don't know what the hell you're talking about."

Realizing that he had no other recourse than to tell her the truth, he said, "I have a friend named Dan Hughes. I've known Dan ever since he was a child. Unfortunately, he became involved in trafficking illegal drugs when he grew up. Eventually, he fled the country rather than being taken into custody, even though he was offered amnesty for his testimony against a notorious drug Cartel. As a good friend of his family, I am actively working with agents of the DEA to get Dan to testify against the Cartel in exchange for a pardon. Before Dan would agree to come back and testify, I had to figure out a way to do it without the DEA knowing where the filming would take place. Unfortunately, I just found out that their real plan is to take us both into custody when we attempt to do it. That's where you come in."

"You still haven't told me what I'm supposed to do?"

"Come with me," Neal said impatiently. "I want to show you something."

They had only walked a short distance toward the house when Jessica Sterling's Mercedes sports car pulled into the driveway. Opening the trunk she removed her suitcase and yelled, "Hey, wait for me!"

"Saved by the bell, eh Mr. T?" Anita remarked sarcastically.

"Never you mind, young lady," he scolded. "Your looking at one of the toughest ladies you'll ever meet, so mind your manners."

As Jessica approached, she eyed Anita and said, "I've got to hand it to you, Mr. T. You sure know how to pick'em." Thrusting her hand at Anita, she said, "You must be Anita Cassidy. I'm Jessica Sterling."

Observing the scowl on Neal's forehead, and his firm grip around Anita's arm, Jessica sensed something of a rift had developed between them. Attempting to flatter it away, she said, "Neal speaks very highly of you, my dear. I hope you realize how important your contribution to tomorrow's mission is. I'm very pleased to finally meet you."

"Likewise," Anita replied, glancing up at Neal. "Now, will someone please show me where the bar is and tell me what the hell I'm doing here?"

"Come on," Neal gestured, and headed for the patio. "That's the first intelligent thing you've said since you got here."

Not knowing what to expect, Jessica and Anita followed Neal obediently toward the patio entrance to the house. As they passed by the Jacuzzi, Anita remarked, "I don't know about you, Jessica, but my body parts are screaming for a hot soak later on. Care to join me?"

"Fortunately, I did pack my bathing suit," Jessica replied.

"So did I," Anita giggled. "Or, we could go skinny dipping, if that's okay with you, Mr. T."

"Hell, I'm the father of three daughters, you two. I've long since stopped being embarrassed by a naked woman." Thinking about it for a second or two, he added, "Hell, I might just join you."

Jessica was quick to pick up on his remark. "I dare you."

Trapped by his foolish words, Neal laughed and changed the subject immediately. "Let's get serious for a moment, Jessica, while I explain to Anita what she's going to do for us after we fly to Catalina tomorrow." Looking directly at Anita, he said, "I hate to admit this, but I'm afraid the success of our whole operation falls directly on your shoulders, young lady. After I explain it all, we can get some pizza and do the Jacuzzi, if you're still interested."

"It's about time," Jessica kidded. "Now, tell Anita what she has to do while I pour the wine. You can get your own drink."

When they were settled down in the living room, Neal picked up the DEA camcorder and began explaining to Anita what she was supposed to do the next day. "Tomorrow morning at eight o'clock, you're going to go with me and Jessica to Palomar Airport in my car. Then you're going to drive back here and wait until the telephone rings. Don't answer it. After five rings, I will leave a short message and hang up. That will be your cue to activate the tracking device hidden inside this camcorder by attaching the handle. Make sure it is screwed in all the way and tightly seated."

"When will you call?" Anita inquired. "And do you expect me to remain here until you return from Catalina?"

Neal realized he had been somewhat vague in explaining what each member of his team was to do. So, to make sure they understood the broader picture, he decided to summarize everyone's responsibility one last time. Focusing primarily on Anita, he said, "Tomorrow morning your mother is going to use her yacht to pick up Dan Hughes from Puerto Nuevo, a small fishing village in Mexico just south of Rosarito Beach. From there she will take him to her condominium on Catalina where Jessica and I will be waiting to film his testimony on my personal camcorder. When they arrive, I will call you. Do not pick up the phone. The message I leave will be your signal to activate the DEA camcorder. That's it in a nutshell."

"One question," Anita fired back, "How the hell did my mother get involved in this boondoggle? I don't remember her being the adventurous type."

"You'll find out differently very soon," Neal replied. "She's helping me because I asked her to."

"Please continue," Jessica interrupted. "We can discuss the whys and wherefores later. Right now I'm interested in knowing what prompted all this."

Hesitating a moment to organize his thoughts, Neal continued. "The day after I discovered the DEA's intentions were to take Dan and I into custody as soon as we made contact with each other, I decided to alter my original plan and use their bogus camcorder to my own advantage. I figured it would be good strategy to have them think we were filming at my house by having someone activate their camcorder here."

A moment of silence followed until Anita remarked, "It wouldn't take a PHD to figure out whom that *someone* might be, now would it Mr. T? I'm your patsy, aren't I?"

The room fell awkwardly silent for a few seconds, allowing Jessica to ward off an immediate response from Neal. "Wrong reference, my dear. I believe, trusted friend, is more appropriate. I'd be honored, if I were you."

"I'm sorry," Anita said humbly, after weighing Jessica's words. "This is all so confusing."

"Get used to it, honey. You haven't seen anything yet," Jessica chuckled, as she stood up to replenish her wine. "Why don't we finish this discussion in the Jacuzzi?"

"I'm for that," Anita chimed in. "I only have one more question, Mr. T, then I'll shut up."

"Fire away, my dear. You might just as well get it off your chest right now."

"When are you planning for me to meet with my mother?"

I can't duck that one Neal realized, struggling to come up with a realistic answer. "Right after I confront her with that picture you loaned me," he replied. "That's one of the reasons why I didn't want you to come to Catalina. Plus, It would give me an opportunity to tell her what you have contributed to this operation. Kind of building up points, if you will."

"How can I stay here if that camcorder is going to signal the DEA to bust in on me," she asked, with visible concern. "They'll think I'm a part of this crazy conspiracy."

"Mr. T would never put you in harm's way," Jessica remarked, interrupting Neal's reply. "I'm sure he isn't planning for you to be here when they arrive."

"I appreciate your concern, Anita" Neal replied, "but Jessica is right. I would never expose you to that kind of involvement. I have a plan that I'm sure will meet with your approval. One you will enjoy."

"I'm overdue for that," Anita responded with visible relief. "What did you have in mind?"

"After you drop me and Jessica off at the airport tomorrow morning, I want you to come back here, pack your suitcase and plug that camcorder into any wall socket. The power cord is already attached. When you leave here after my phone call, make sure the front door is unlocked so the DEA won't have to break in. I've already replaced that lock two times."

"Where should I go?" she asked, somewhat confused. "I won't have a car."

Empathetic toward her concern, he smiled and reached into his pocket. "Here's fifty bucks. Call a cab and go to the Hilton Inn. Stay there until you hear from me. You do have a cell phone, don't you?"

"No, I couldn't afford one."

Perplexed by what to do about that inconvenience, he finally came up with an alternative plan. "While you two go upstairs and change into your bathing suits, I'll call my friend, Maggie Jyles, over at the Hilton Inn and have her reserve a room for you until we returrn from Catalina. Go to her for anything you need until I get there. Charge everything to your room…my treat."

The two women looked wide-eyed at one another, prompting Jessica to laugh and say, "On second thought, maybe I should stay here to supervise this part of the operation, just in case."

"Never mind," Anita responded immediately. "I can handle my part very nicely, thank you."

Giggling like two teenage sisters, the two ladies grabbed their suit-cases and hurried up the stairs to change. While they were gone, Neal called the Hilton Inn and talked briefly with Maggie Jyles, who agreed to reserve a room and watch out for Anita until Neal returned. Shortly after making those arrangements, his two co-conspirators came down the stairs wrapped modestly in beach towels, still talking and laughing playfully.

"Lets go, Mr. T." Jessica said in a flirting voice, "This is not the worst thing that can happen to you!"

Uncertain as to what they actually had on under their towels, Neal went upstairs to put on his bathing suit, returning a short time later to find both women sitting naked in the partial transparency of the swirling water.

Determined not to succumb to embarrassment, he lowered himself into the bubbling water on the side opposite from them, sipping his drink and looking up at the twinkling darkness above.

"Chicken!" Jessica finally remarked to break the awkward silence.

"Double that!" Anita added, slurring her words a little. "You're destroying your image, Mr. T."

Amused by their candid perception of nudity being no more than an expression of physical freedom without sexual connotation, Neal stripped away his suit and flung it up on the deck. "Okay girls, who's first?" he asked flirtatiously.

Anita immediately burst out laughing and looked at Jessica, expect-ing a similar response, but was surprised when Jessica's eyes remained focused on Neal. Somewhat cautiously, she asked, "You weren't kidding the other day when you mentioned ménage a trios, were you?"

Smiling devilishly, Neal put his bathing suit back on before exiting the water. Standing briefly on the steps, he replied, "Maybe another time, ladies. Right now we have something more important to attend to. Pizza anyone?"

With the two women looking at one another like they had been left standing alone on the dance floor at their Junior Prom, Neal left them to privately shroud themselves in their towels while he went upstairs to put on something casual.

When all three had reassembled in the kitchen some time later, the smell of pizza cooking in the oven filled the air, as Neal stood at his little bar fixing another drink. "Anyone need a refill?" he asked, without looking up.

Still a little concerned over the abruptness with which Neal had left them during their brief time in the Jacuzzi together, Jessica asked, "Did we say or do anything to upset you while we were in the Jacuzzi?"

"Nothing you need to concern yourself with, my dear." he replied. "All you did was bring back a few memories that are best left forgotten. Trying to relive the past is a fool's pastime. It rarely results in anything but trouble or embarrassment, so please forgive me if I made you feel uncomfortable."

Much as she wanted to remain silent, the wine she had consumed finally goaded Anita into expressing herself. "Hell, Mr. T, all we can criticize you for is not trying!"

Jessica immediately threw her hand up over her mouth to keep from losing the sip of wine she had just taken. Rushing to the sink to get rid of it, she laughed and shouted, "Damn you Anita!"

Tickled by the spontaneity of Anita's off the wall remark, Neal walked over to where she stood and took her into his arms. "Young lady," he said, trying not to laugh, "I'm sure glad I'm not your mother."

Fortunately for all of them, it only took a few more minutes for the pizza to be done. Sizzling hot, he removed it from the oven and served it in the box it had come in, passing out paper plates and napkins during the process. "Excuse the fancy china," he joked. "It's all I have."

Conversation during the next half hour was initially limited to praising Neal for the delicious simplicity of the dinner he had chosen. However, as they each began to approach their stomach capacity, the subject of their individual responsibilities regarding the next day's operation began to creep back into the conversation.

"I'm curious, Mr. T. Who's going to turn that camcorder off once it's turned on?"

"Based on what I've been told by my source inside the DEA office, I'd say it's going to be my friend, Agent Dusty Lewis. I'm glad I won't be here to witness how he's going to react."

"Me either," Anita remarked, starting to yawn. "Thanks for putting me up at the Hilton, Mr. T. I haven't stayed overnight in a hotel since I was a little girl."

"Hopefully, it will be the beginning of a new way of life for you," Jessica said, also holding back a yawn. "I couldn't be happier for you."

Observing that both women were having difficulty keeping their eyes open, Neal suggested that they go to bed while he cleaned up the kitchen. "I'll set my alarm for seven a.m., and knock on your doors when I go to put the coffee on. Okay?"

Both agreed without comment and headed for their separate rooms, more than willing to call it a day.

A short time later, bathed in moonlight that was filtering through the gently moving curtains covering his window, Neal had only one thought on his mind as he heard the muffled sound of the girls getting undressed and climbing into bed: *So near and yet so far?*

Chapter 14

Good Friends Gather

Just as the sun cast its bright yellow glow over the eastern horizon, Neal Thomas was awakened from a restless sleep by the sound of water running in the guest bathroom. A few seconds of reflective thought suggested that either Jessica Sterling or Anita Cassidy – possibly both – were awake and preparing for the difficult day ahead. *The eager beavers* he thought, coming to a sitting position on the side of his bed.

Following his shower, the smell of coffee brewing made it clear that his two houseguests were making themselves at home. Satisfied that everything was under control, he dressed and joined them, observing that Anita was barefoot in Levi shorts and a T-Shirt, a fitting compliment to her un-brushed hair.

Jessica, on the other hand, wore an attractive khaki pantsuit, and had her hair neatly brushed and tied in a ponytail. *What a pair I have here* Neal thought, as he took his place at the table.

Ignoring her overly casual appearance when Neal walked in, Anita remarked, "Forgive me for not dressing up for your departure. I'll clean up after I get back from the airport. I wouldn't want Maggie Jyles, to think I just fell off a turnip truck."

"Whatever," Neal chuckled, winking at Jessica. "We'll get a bite to eat at the airport, so don't bother fixing us anything to eat. Come straight back here and wait for my phone message. I probably won't be able to make it until mid-afternoon, so stay put until that's over with. After that, you're on your own."

"Thanks a lot," she joked. "Where do you think I've been for most of my life?"

Unable to address that remark, Neal replied. "Have a good time at the Hilton. I've got a feeling you're life is going to change for the better in the not too distant future."

"I hope so!" she replied. "I've had it with the one I'm living now." Pausing momentarily, she added, "Just for the record, I want to thank you for everything you've done for me, Mr. T. Please be careful, you're the only real friend I've got."

"Make that two friends," Jessica remarked. "I never had a sister."

Time passed quickly from that moment on, each person preoccupied with what they had to take care of before leaving. When that hour finally arrived, there was little left to say or do, other than getting into Neal's car and proceeding to the airport. Arriving there was somewhat of an anti-climax, as they fondly embraced one another and parted company, leaving Anita to drive back to Neal's house to complete her task before moving on to the Hilton Inn, the only bright spot in her immediate future so far.

Fifteen miles off the Los Angeles coastline, Gloria Donaldson finished a third cup of coffee at her condominium on Catalina Island. Dawn was about to break, as she walked anxiously from room to room checking to make sure everything was in order to receive her guests later on that afternoon. Satisfied that all was in readiness, she secured the condo, put a key under the front door mat and rode a scooter bike to the Avalon Harbor pier. A small outboard motorboat that she had called for in advance taxied her to her yacht, *The Wayward Wind.*

Getting underway moved quickly, since the small crew had already been informed in advance about the nature of their journey that day. Standing alone on the weather bridge watching the crew release the yacht from its buoy, Gloria Donaldson wondered what Dan Hughes had done to command such loyalty from a man like Neal Thomas. Never having met Dan, she could think of nothing, so she put her questioning on hold and listened to the twin diesel engines move the yacht slowly out to sea on a southerly course toward Mexico.

Given the relatively calm ocean she was traveling on, and the early hour of her departure, Gloria estimated reaching Puerto Nuevo around eleven-thirty that morning. There was little left for her to do until then, so she went to the galley and ate breakfast, content that by the end of the day she would be enjoying a cocktail, while a strange mix of friends congregated at her condominium to film a question and answer session about which she knew very little. Though the scenario was contrary to the type of activities she was used to participating in, the mystery of it all excited her beyond anything she had experienced for a long time, never realizing that the end of that day would bring her the surprise of a lifetime.

Disappointed that the terminal building at Palomar Airport had no regular restaurant facility, Neal and Jessica contented themselves with soft drinks and snacks from a few vending machines while they waited outside for Jim Taylor's arrival. "I'll treat the three of us to lunch when we get to Catalina," Neal said, checking the time. "Jim should be here in a few minutes."

"I'm in no hurry," Jessica remarked, watching Neal's eyes searching the cloud- speckled sky. "You're not getting anxious about Jim not showing up, are you?"

"No. He would have called."

His reply had no sooner been expressed when the faint sound of an airplane became audible from beyond the western end of the runway. Turning in that direction, Neal saw the shape of a twin-engine seaplane turning inland on its approach to the airport. "Ah hah," he sighed with relief, recognizing the unique silhouette of *The Goose*. "Here he comes now."

"We're going in that thing?" Jessica asked with surprise. "I hope he's got parachutes onboard."

"Hey!" Neal cried out, as if insulted. "What's good enough for Jimmy Buffett is damn sure good enough for us."

"Is he flying it?" Jessica asked, giggling a little.

"Be nice now," Neal cautioned. "Jim's very sensitive about his Goose. Wait till you see the inside."

"I can hardly wait."

Following a graceful landing, Jim Taylor maneuvered his two-engine amphibian over near the terminal building and signaled for Neal and Jessica to come aboard. By the time they reached the plane, Jim had the engines idling and the passenger door open.

"Sorry I'm a little late!" Jim hollered over the engine noise. "I had to replace a wheel!"

Rolling her eyes at Neal, Jessica handed Jim her suitcase, grabbed his outstretched hand and pulled herself up into the seaplane, looking around curiously while Neal came aboard.

As soon as Neal was inside, Jim closed and secured the door. Turning toward Jessica, he said, "You must be Jessica Sterling. I suppose Neal has told you all about me, so I won't bore you with repetition. Come, let's get you seated."

Pleasantly surprised by the comfortable interior of the passenger cabin, Jessica picked out a seat by a window, and was about to sit down when Jim took her by the hand and said, "Please, come join me in the cockpit. You'll get a better view of things from up there."

Glad for Jim's expression of hospitality, Neal smiled and said, "Go ahead, Jessica. I've already had the pleasure. Besides, I need a little time to organize my thoughts before we meet Gloria and Dan."

Once strapped into the co-pilot's seat, Jessica looked with fascination at the duplicate display of instruments in front of her, while Jim maneuvered his seaplane away from the terminal and out onto the taxi runway. When takeoff clearance came from the tower, Jim pushed the twin throttles forward until both engines roared to full power, taking them quickly down the runway and out over the ocean to a rendezvous none of them would soon forget

Unaware that Neal Thomas had orchestrated a plan to divert the DEA away from the location where he had originally planned to pick up Dan Hughes, Dusty Lewis and two armed agents boarded a small attack boat at San Diego Bay's U.S. Naval Station. Their goal: to intercept Neal's operation and take Dan Hughes into custody, supposedly for all of their protection. With that purpose in mind, Agent Lewis directed the boat's captain to chart a course for the southern tip of San Clemente Island where Neal had told Dusty he would pick Dan up that morning.

Thanks to the unusual speed of the navy's attack boat, they arrived at the island several minutes before ten o'clock. As yet, Neal and Dan were nowhere to be seen. After an hour of uneventful waiting, Dusty ordered the captain to return to the Naval Station where he and his assistants got into his car and headed back to their office to wait in frustration for their camcorder to send them a signal that they could zero in on.

Wait till I get my hands on that bastard was all Dusty could think of, as he sat in his office powerless to do anything, wondering if he had purposely been deceived, or something had gone terribly wrong. Little did he know that at that same instant, three armed members of the Tidewater Drug Cartel, acting on information they had just received from an informant inside the DEA office in Virginia, were in a black limousine on Interstate I-5 heading north with another purpose in mind.

At approximately twelve o'clock noon that same day, Gloria Donaldson stood by the captain of her yacht as he brought it to a stop within a few hundred yards of the Mexican coastline at Puerto Nuevo. Looking through her binoculars, she focused on the figure of a man standing alone on a fishing pier that extended a short distance out into the water. Seconds later, the man raised his arms up over his head, forming a circle.

Walking excitedly out onto the wheelhouse afterdeck, Gloria signaled two men standing on the boarding platform to start the outboard engine on a lifeboat they had already lowered into the water. Moments later, they pushed away and headed for shore to pick up their anxiously waiting passenger and then headed back to the yacht. When they were almost there, Gloria left the bridge and walked aft to greet the man she had heard so much about, but had never met.

"Welcome aboard, Mr. Hughes," she said enthusiastically, as Dan climbed the short ladder onto the main deck. "It's a pleasure to finally meet you."

"Likewise," Dan replied, shaking her hand. "I could use a towel, if you've got one handy."

"Of course," she replied, aware that Dan's upper body was partially wet. "Come with me. I'll show you where you can dry off, while I go tell the captain to head back to Catalina." As they passed through the lounge, she remarked, "There's a bar over there. Help yourself to a drink if you're so inclined. I'll be back in a few minutes."

After changing into a dry shirt and freshening up a bit, Dan returned to the lounge and took advantage of the hospitality he had been offered, convinced that he had fallen into the lap of luxury.

Moments later, Gloria returned and decided to reward herself for having successfully completed her mission. Pouring herself a glass of wine, she sat down near Dan and asked, "Have you ever been to Catalina before?"

"Only in the movies," he replied, deciding not to open any doors into the sordid world of his past. "I'm afraid I'm just a good old country boy from Virginia."

"Yeah, and I'm the Virgin Mary," Gloria remarked doubtingly. "I'm afraid your past has proceeded you, Mr. Hughes. Neal Thomas, your benefactor, has already told me all about you."

"Why am I not surprised?" Dan said. "It seems everyone in San Diego knows all about me. I guess that's why I'm in this predicament, wouldn't you say?"

"Just be glad you've got Mr. T. running interference for you," she replied. "Right now, he's the best friend you've got on this planet."

"No one knows that better than me," Dan admitted, looking wistfully out over the wake churning up rapidly behind the yacht. "I'd probably be dead now, if it hadn't been for him. Strangely enough, I still feel like someone's chasing me."

Gloria smiled and patted Dan's hand with heartfelt empathy, as she stood up to return to the bridge. "Get some rest," she suggested. "We still have a ways to go."

Taking her advice, Dan mixed another drink and sought the sun-drenched luxury of the open deck just aft of the lounge. After spreading out his damp shirt to dry, he stretched out on a lounge chair and let his tired eyes close.

The flight from Palomar Airport to Catalina Island that morning was a relatively short trip for Jim Taylor. Having Jessica Sterling in the co-pilot seat, and Neal Thomas in the cabin planning his filming session, ate up the minutes until he could see Avalon Harbor waiting in the distance.

"Doesn't the island look beautiful lying there all by itself?" Jessica remarked, in awe of its isolation. "I'd love to live there."

"Be careful what you wish for, my dear," Jim remarked, as he banked his seaplane northward to take Jessica on a shoreline tour around the island. "A few days on this island is all I can take."

Neal, quick to feel the change in direction, came up to the cockpit. "What's going on, Jim?" he asked, sounding concerned. "Is there a problem?"

Jim smiled. "No. Just giving Jessica a down to earth glimpse of what island life is all about. She thinks it would be fun to live here."

"For a couple of weeks, maybe," Neal commented, reinforcing Jim's earlier remark. "What I can see from the bluff behind my house, or the deck of a cruise ship, is all the ocean I care to see."

Jim had just completed a turn around the southern tip of the island when he began reducing his speed to prepare for their landing at Avalon Harbor. Once down, he maneuvered over to a buoy where a harbor taxi was waiting to moor the plane and take them ashore. Walking down the dock, Neal suggested that they get something to eat before moving on to Gloria's condominium. Jim and Jessica were in quick agreement.

Approaching the same waterfront restaurant he remembered eating in on past visits to the island, Neal suggested that they have lunch there. As he pointed out, a view of the harbor would allow them to see the Donaldson yacht when it returned. Neal's point was well taken, so the three of them gathered at a table overlooking the harbor to eat and pass the time until Gloria's yacht arrived.

An hour later, Neal observed the bow of *The Wayward Wind* turn into the harbor and head for its anchor buoy. Elated that Gloria had made it back, hopefully with Dan Hughes onboard, he interrupted Jim's story telling to announce, "Hey, you two, our long-awaited cohorts have just dropped anchor. Shall we go down to the pier and greet them?"

After Neal paid the check, the three of them walked back to the harbor taxi landing to wait for Gloria Donaldson and Dan Hughes to come ashore. It was a pleasant wait. The afternoon sun and soft ocean breeze played on them while other people of all sizes and shapes walked up and down the pier in colorful attire, shopping and enjoying whatever they had come there for. It was then that Neal decided the time was right to call Anita Cassidy.

After dialing his home phone number, he waited for the message machine to come on and said, "It's time to go on vacation, Anita. Erase this message and go."

A short time later, as the harbor taxi approached the pier, loud yelling from an all too familiar voice attracted everyone's attention. "Hello there, Mr. T! We finally made it!"

The waving arms and laughing faces of Dan Hughes and Gloria Donaldson had finally arrived.

After the customary introductions and friendly embraces concluded the much- anticipated reunion, Neal looked around nervously to see if their gathering was drawing any unusual attention. Satisfied that everything was proceeding normally, he was quick to suggest that they proceed directly to Gloria's condominium to deposit their luggage and discuss details for filming Dan's testimony. Everyone but Neal groaned their disapproval, favoring unwinding a little before attempting anything that serious. Reluctantly, Neal put his personal feelings aside and agreed that they all needed time to unwind before getting started. "Okay, we'll do it tomorrow morning," he suggested. "Are you all in agreement with that?"

"Fine with me," Dan answered. "That will give me and Jessica time to review those questions the DEA gave you."

"He's got a very good point there," Jessica said supportively. "I'd like to read what Dan's being asked to swear to if I'm going to be asking the questions."

That settled, Gloria summoned an island taxi that took her tired group of thirsty heroes to her condominium to celebrate their alliance, and an event that would leave a lasting impression on all of them.

Since they were not involved in the conversation the other three were engaged in, Gloria and Jim made themselves drinks and stepped outside on the balcony.

"I'm damn glad I'm not mixed up in what's going on in there," Jim remarked. "I've got enough to worry about. I sure don't need the DEA breathing down my neck."

Staring at her yacht sitting peacefully in the harbor, Gloria said, "The only reason I'm here at all is because Neal has become such a good friend. He's sacrificed a lot for Dan Hughes. I only hope Neal isn't disappointed with the outcome of all this. Dealing with our government can be a scary business. Believe me, I know."

"Hey out there!" Dan's voice shouted from inside. "Come back in here. We've said all we're going to say about tomorrow. It's time to party!"

Surprised by the apparent ending of what Neal, Dan and Jessica had been discussing, Gloria and Jim returned inside just as Neal was putting some papers back in his briefcase. Unintentionally, Gloria caught a glimpse of what she thought was a framed, black and white photograph. Dismissing it as something totally unrelated to what the threesome had been discussing prior to their return, she walked over to the refrigerator, poured a glass of wine and addressed the group, "Now, let's discuss a little more about this party Mr. Hughes has just brought up. I for one am ready!"

"Me too," Jessica quickly agreed. "Who knows when we'll all be together again? Might as well have a good time as long as we're here."

"Roger that," Dan said, fixing another drink, "Why don't we call a cab and go to that waterfront café we passed on our way up here. I noticed they were advertising live music tonight."

"Good idea," Gloria added. "Since there aren't enough beds here to accommodate all of us, may I suggest that Neal and I spend the night on my yacht. You three can flip for the two bedrooms and the couch. How's that sound?"

Neal was about to suggest that Jessica go with Gloria and let the men stay there when Jessica commented "I like Gloria's plan. That way, you and Neal can pick up some food for us before we start filming tomorrow. That will give Dan and me some extra time to go over those questions again and agree on the answers."

With everyone in full agreement with her suggestion, Gloria called a taxi to get their dinner party underway, silently congratulating herself on how cleverly she had arranged for Neal to return to the yacht with her that evening.

Back in Neal's home in Carlsbad, Anita Cassidy had just finished packing her suitcase and was walking down the stairs when the phone rang. A quick glance at the clock told her it was mid-afternoon, the same time Neal had said he might call. Hoping it was him she sat down and waited for the message machine to kick in. Her heart was beating a mile a minute when Neal's voice spoke the words she was longing to hear – "It's time to go on vacation, Anita. Erase this message and go."

After calling a cab, she picked up the camcorder lying on the dining room table and screwed the handle all the way in until it was seated hard against the casing, wondering what series of events would follow its activation.

Not my concern she decided, as the sound of an automobile horn beeped in the driveway. Making sure that the front door was un-locked, she closed it gently and got into the taxi. "Hilton Inn, please," she told the driver, satisfied that she had successfully done what Neal had asked her to do.

The receptionist at the Hilton Inn reservations counter smiled pleasantly when she saw Anita Cassidy write her name on the registration form. "We've been expecting you Miss Cassidy," the attractive woman said, as she picked up her intercom phone and tapped in an extension number. "Hi, Maggie. Your guest is here."

It wasn't long before a woman Anita Cassidy had never seen before came out of an office marked *PERSONNEL MANAGER*. Approaching Anita, she smiled and offered her hand. "Welcome to the Hilton Inn, Anita. My name is Maggie Jyles. Our mutual friend, Neal Thomas, said you would be staying with us for a day or two, so make yourself at home and enjoy your stay." Pointing to the office she had just come from, she said, "I'll be in my office if you need anything."

Following a brief elevator ride, Anita carded the door to her room and entered what she had no right to expect. Sighing with delight, she walked quickly over to a large window that gave her a bird's eye view of the beautifully landscaped pool area below. Flopping backwards onto the large quilted bed that felt like a cloud, she thought, *I've died and gone to heaven.*

After faithfully monitoring their electronic tracking device for several hours without receiving a signal, Dusty Lewis concluded that something unforeseeable had gone wrong with the camcorder they had given Neal Thomas. He was about to call Raymond Bronson to give him the bad news when the mapping screen on the tracking device suddenly lit up, and a blinking locator light indicated that their camcorder had been activated at a Carlsbad location. Nervously excited, Dusty pushed the print button to document its location, then hurried into the outer office where he asked two of his agents to accompany him while they investigated that location.

Still angry over having been fooled into going all the way to San Clemente Island on a wild goose chase that morning, Dusty and the two agents sped up the freeway and took the exit closest to where the tracking devise showed the signal was coming from. After traveling several blocks in that direction, Dusty told the driver, "Turn right at the next intersection. We're only one block away."

As the agent made the turn, Dusty cried out, "I'll be damned! This street is leading us straight to Neal Thomas' house. I came to a party here not long ago. Pull over before he recognizes the car."

As the agent did as he was told, Dusty explained, "If we bust in on Thomas in broad daylight, we're going to scare someone in there into doing something stupid. As long as this light is blinking, we know they're in there filming. Let's just wait here until the light stops. That will be our signal to go in and arrest them all. Remember, I don't want anyone hurt if we can possibly avoid it. Is that understood?"

The two agents verbally agreed and settled back with Dusty to wait for their opportunity to arrive, ignoring the black limousine that had passed by while they were talking.

When almost an hour had passed, and the tracking indicator light was still blinking, Dusty grew impatient and suspicious that the filming that was supposed to be going on inside the house was taking an excessive amount of time. Convinced that he had no other choice than to investigate, Dusty and his two agents left the car and proceeded cautiously on foot toward Neal's house. They had only walked a short distance when they saw the unexpected presence of a black Cadillac limousine parked in the driveway with its front end pointed in their direction. Two other cars were there also, one of which Dusty recognized as Neal's. Immediately sensing that there was something nonsensical about what was taking place, Dusty whispered, "Keep out of sight. There's something about this whole picture that doesn't add up, if Neal Thomas is really inside using that camcorder."

Separating a few feet from one another, the threesome inched their way closer to the house under cover of approaching darkness to get a better look. What they were able to see through the windows was the shadowy movement of male figures moving swiftly from room to room, apparently in search of something. Motioning for his men to come closer, Dusty whispered, "Neal doesn't own a black limousine. He's tricked us into coming here so he can film Dan Hughes' testimony somewhere else, not realizing that there would be someone else coming here that's as interested in that testimony as we are."

"Like the Cartel?" one of the agents whispered back.

"That's what I'm thinking," Dusty replied, moving closer to the agent to give him further instructions. "Go back and park our car in the driveway to block the entrance. Leave the lights off. Then call for emergency backup from the local police. Tell them you want a helicopter sent in to light up this house. When the chopper gets here, turn on all my car lights to identify our location and blind anyone trying to leave. Then come back here. Joe will cover the back of the house until the police are in place, especially on that bluff back there."

After Dusty's car was moved into the driveway, Dusty huddled with the other agent and said, "While you cover the back, I'll stay here and make sure they can't get to the limo. Hopefully, we won't have to use our weapons."

Unaware of the activity that was going on outside Neal Thomas' house, Miguel Ramirez and two of his Cartel henchmen frantically searched for any information that would lead them to where they had been told Dan Hughes might be hiding; a man they had been sent to California to kill before he could testify against them. Hampered by the growing darkness, they finally resorted to using flashlights to conduct their frustrating and unrewarding search until the blinding light from a helicopter's spotlight betrayed their presence.

Panicked by its sudden appearance, and a speaker demanding their immediate surrender, the three intruders rushed from the house in an attempt to flee in their limousine, only to find that it was being used to shield armed officers. Hopelessly outnumbered, Ramirez and his two cohorts threw down their weapons in a gesture of surrender, and waited angrily until armed policemen took them into custody.

Soon after the police left the scene with their captives, Dusty and his two agents went into Neal's home to assess any damage that may have occurred. Except for the papers that lay scattered about and the drawers of tables and desks that were left open, there didn't appear to be any serious damage. Feeling the urge, he told his two agents to wait in the car while he used the bathroom. When he finished, he unplugged Ray Bronson's camcorder to take with him, locked the front door behind him and walked down the driveway, mulling over the irony of what had taken place there that day. Smiling a little, as he settled into the car, he thought, *well Mr. T, I guess I owe you one.*

Located not far from Avalon Harbor's main pier and popular sunning beach, Antonio's restaurant commanded a postcard view of the harbor, making it a popular gathering place for residents and tourists. As a prelude to having dinner there, Gloria Donaldson invited the group to have cocktails onboard her yacht, which everyone agreed would be a fitting tribute to Dan Hughes' safe return.

While waiting for the taxi bus to arrive, Neal was struck by the coincidence that, since it had been Gloria's idea for him to spend the night on her yacht in the first place, wouldn't that provide him with an ideal opportunity to show her the photograph Anita Cassidy had loaned him. More than likely, the crew would opt to spend their night on shore, once they learned that Neal was spending the night on the yacht. Convinced that fate had contrived the opportunity, he removed the picture from his briefcase, wrapped it in his bathing suit and placed it in the same bag that held his toiletries.

The winding trip down into town provided just enough diversion to keep everyone's attention focused on the lighter side of life, and the excitement of partying on Gloria's yacht. Once onboard, they were pleasantly surprised to find that the crew had prepared a large tray of hors d'oeuvres that sat on a table in the lounge. Artfully arranged, it consisted of a large bowl of crushed ice mounded with cooked shrimp, scallops, oysters on the half shell, and an assortment of attractively arranged chips and dips.

"Dig in, folks," Gloria remarked. "This is it until dinner."

No one was bashful, either there or at the bar. Background music added a touch of sophistication that even neighboring boats were quick to appreciate.

As the evening progressed, friendly visitors from boats anchored near *The Wayward Wind* came aboard and joined in the revelry until

Gloria finally rang the yacht's bell and announced that the party was being relocated to Antonio's Restaurant. Thirty minutes later all the visitors had left the yacht, leaving Gloria and her four friends to relax by themselves before they went to dinner. When they were finally ready to leave, Gloria suggested that Dan, Jim and Jessica take the harbor taxi ashore so she and Neal could return to the yacht after dinner using the yacht's motorboat. All agreed that her suggestion made good sense. So when the harbor taxi arrived, Dan, Jim and Jessica took it back to shore, expecting Neal and Gloria to follow close behind.

As soon as the harbor taxi was well on its way, Gloria started putting the leftover food away. When she finished, she joined Neal outside on the weather deck and remarked, "I'm really not that hungry, are you?"

Neal laughed a little and replied, "Funny, I was thinking the same thing."

"Why didn't you say something?"

Something in the tone of her voice caused Neal to think carefully before answering. "You seemed to be having such a good time, it never dawned on me that you'd want to skip dinner and stay here. After all, they are expecting us."

Reaching down and releasing the clip that held her cell phone, Gloria pressed in a number and waited. Seconds later she said, "Jim? This is Gloria. Neal and I have decided to trade dinner in for a moonlight swim, and a good night's sleep, so….. Wait a minute, what's so funny? ……Shame on you…you dirty old man…. Is that so…..Well you just tell those other characters that……What? In your dreams, Jimbo… Never mind, Neal and I will pick up breakfast tomorrow morning and meet you at the condo at ten o'clock…No! You two be nice to Jessica, or I'll….What did you say?…..Goodnight, Jim."

"Not quite the response you were looking for, was it?"

"He is s-o-o-o bad…but funny."

"I take it they had already deduced that we wouldn't be joining them."

"Pretty much so," Gloria admitted. "With the crew not being here, I should have known I'd be in for a lot of flack."

"We can still go."

"Oh no you don't!" Gloria said, half laughing. "Go get your bathing suit on. I need to cool off a little."

Neal had just entered the lounge and was removing his bathing suit from around the Donaldson family photograph when the cabin lights went out. A sultry voice in the semi-darkness whispered, "I have a better idea."

Temporarily blinded by the darkness, Neal placed his bathing suit and the picture on the couch beside him, as Gloria wrapped her arms around his neck, pulling her naked body against his. "Take your clothes off, silly," she said, unbuttoning his shirt. "We're going for a swim."

Fortunately, Gloria's yacht was large enough to require anchorage on the outer perimeter of other boats clustered in the harbor, making any activity onboard difficult to see at night. Using the nocturnal obscurity as a shield, Gloria took Neal by the hand and coaxed him down onto the aft boarding platform where she pushed him playfully into the water and followed him laughing like a child.

The water was cold and deep. In less than a minute they were forced to return to the boat where she had laid out heavy towel bathrobes to cover their shivering bodies. Refreshed by their childlike disregard for what others might have considered a dangerous and irresponsible act, both returned to the lounge, turned the lights back on and relaxed with a drink until their body temperatures returned to normal.

As the evening wore on, and the awareness of their mutual nakedness began to build up a need for more intimacy, Gloria took the initiative and sat down on the couch next to Neal, kissing him passionately. The continuation of their feverish foreplay, however, caused the framed picture he had placed there earlier to fall off onto the wooden deck, shattering the glass and startling them both. In her haste to recapture the intensity of their passion, she reached down to push the broken frame out of the way and punctured her finger. "Damn it," she cried out in pain. "Where the hell did that come from?"

Sitting up abruptly, she grabbed the napkin from under her wine glass and pressed it against the small wound in an effort to stop the bleeding, staring down angrily at the broken frame lying in pieces on the deck. "Oh my God!" she suddenly gasped, after recognizing the people in the photograph. "Where did you get that?"

Drained of the passion that had suddenly been cut off like a garden hose, Neal sat up, took a large swallow of his drink and replied, "From your daughter. Whom, I might add, has picked a most inopportune time to show up."

Equally shaken by the incident, and almost afraid to question him further, she gasped, "From my daughter!"

Taking her hand in his, he explained, "Your daughter gave it to me, hoping I could find the right time and place to tell you that she's sorry for all the heartache you've had to endure since her father died." Taking a few seconds to let the shock subside, he continued: "Obviously, this is neither the right time, nor the right place to tell you all this, but sometimes fate steps in and forces our hand to make sure that what needs to be said, gets said. That broken picture on the floor finally accomplished that for me. Sorry if I've upset you."

Emotionally numbed by Neal's untimely admission, Gloria continued to stare blankly at the Avalon Village lights reflected on the calm water of the harbor.

"Where is Anita now?" she asked nervously.

"At the Carlsbad Hilton Inn."

"Alone?"

"Yes. The Personnel Manager is a friend of mine. I've asked her to look out for Anita until I finished filming Dan Hughes' testimony tomorrow."

"Then what?" she asked, as she left the couch to apply a Band-Aid to her finger.

"I honestly won't know until after the filming tomorrow."

"Would you mind a suggestion?"

Pleased that she seemed to be regaining a portion of her former self, Neal stood up to make a fresh drink and remarked, "Go ahead, I'm listening."

Slumping back against the couch for a moment, she said, "Jim Taylor's a terrific man, and a good friend of mine, but he has a business to manage and should be home managing it."

"I couldn't agree with you more. However, I don't want to hurt his feelings. After all, he did fly Jessica and me over here."

"You won't," she assured him. "Just tell Jim that I've volunteered to take you, Dan and Jessica back to the Oceanside Marina on my yacht after the filming has been completed. I can make plans to reconnect with my daughter from there. Jim knows all about my past, and will be happy as hell to learn that I'm finally planning to do something for someone other than myself. Looking at the situation from a personal point of view, I think it's about time."

Impressed by the commitment Gloria had made, Neal said, "Jessica has her car at my place, so she's free to do whatever she wants when we get back. Dan, however, has to stay under wraps until after the videotape tape has been reviewed and approved by the DEA. Otherwise, that pardon I have in my briefcase won't be worth the paper it's written on."

Mulling that thought over for a moment, her face suddenly took on a happier glow. "Well then," she said, slurring her words slightly, "we'll just have to leave his ornery ass here. He can stay in my condo until you get word that he's a free man. No one here knows who the hell he is, so he can relax on the beach and enjoy himself. It sounds to me like he could use a little R&R after what he's been through."

"How about us? Don't we deserve a little of that?" Neal remarked, suggestively. "It seems that everyone we know is making out, except us."

Aroused by his comment, Gloria sat her glass down and flipped off the lights again. Turning around in the soft glow of the harbor lights that partially veiled what she was doing, Gloria let her robe fall on the deck. "I can do something about that," she whispered.

Chapter 15

Justice Is Served

The unmistakable sound of seagulls squealing in the early morning air awakened Gloria Donaldson from a restless sleep despite the exhaustive intimacy she and the softly snoring man next to her had shared throughout the night.

Tell me I'm not dreaming she mused, as bits and pieces of what she struggled to remember began to fall into place. The reality was, in less than twenty-four hours she would come face to face with her only child, a daughter who had run away from home rather than live under the stringent rules her mother thought were in her best interest.

Trying not to wake Neal, she slipped into a bathrobe and tiptoed out to the weather deck. Standing uneasily on the gently rolling surface, she finally stretched out on a lounge chair and tried to envision what she would say when she and her daughter met for the first time in what seemed to be a lifetime. The thought was mind-boggling.

"Shall I make a pot of coffee?" Neal's unexpected voice questioned from the lounge door behind her. "My head says I could use a cup or two."

"Thanks, mine too. It's on a shelf in the galley. Make mine black."

Though the sun felt good on Gloria's exhausted body, the thought of her daughter being so close convinced her to join Neal inside to discuss the matter further.

"I think I had better call my crew and tell them to get back here by noon so the yacht will be ready to leave as soon as you complete your filming. I also have to call the Oceanside Marina and let them know I'm coming. I know the Dock Master. I'm sure he will find me a place to tie up for a day or two."

As soon as Neal activated the coffee pot, he took a seat beside Gloria and said, "I promised Anita that I would call her as soon as I had talked with you. Is there anything you want me to tell her before you meet her?"

Making no effort to avoid his inquiring eyes, she replied, "Before I answer that question, tell me what you know about my daughter. I know so little. What's she like? Is she pretty? Does she have a job...a boyfriend? Where does she live?"

The gurgling sound behind him signaled that the coffee was ready. While pouring, he considered Gloria's questions and replied, "Taking your questions in order; she's well-mannered, and probably a lot smarter than she lets on. She's unusually attractive, in a refined sort of way. And unlike other women in her profession, is soft-spoken, and very rarely cusses. I've never heard her use the *f* word."

"I'm glad to hear she's retained some of her upbringing," Gloria commented, smiling anxiously. "I would hate to think that all the money her father and I spent on her education was for naught. Sorry, please go on."

"She tends bar at a little place in Carlsbad called the Village Pub. She's well liked, but as far as I know, doesn't have a steady boy friend. And doesn't appear interested in having one."

"She's not gay, is she?"

"I hardly think so, based on how she kisses me. Much like her mother."

"You haven't...?"

Neal laughed and assured her, "No, I think she's adopted me as the father she lost years ago." Remembering what his friend, Allen Henderson, had confided in him at the Sawmill Club, he continued: "I think you should be aware that Anita goes by the name of Cassidy, not Donaldson."

"That was the last name of the man she met and married while in college." Gloria moaned remorsefully. "Our mother/daughter relationship began to deteriorate right after Anita's father made the young man an offer he couldn't refuse." Pausing a moment she added, "I'm afraid the aftermath of that emotional upheaval was what killed my husband and caused Anita to run away."

"Is that what you want me to tell Anita when I talk to her today?"

Looking as if she were about to cry, her quivering lips replied, "I honestly don't know what I want to say to her."

Empathizing with her dilemma, Neal patted her on the shoulder and suggested that he would be willing to act as an intermediary when Gloria brought his group back to the mainland. "I will call Anita today and pave the way for your reunion, assuring her that you are genuinely interested in seeing her again. Is that your wish?"

From the way she kept looking at him, Neal couldn't tell if she had heard his suggestion until her lips parted and whispered, "Yes."

"Okay, then lets get our act together and get this show on the road. We've got a lot to do today, so let's get dressed and get on with it."

Smiling at his expression of decisiveness, she remarked, "You first, Mr. Fixit. I'll start with getting my crew back onboard."

Back in the kitchen of Gloria Donaldson's condominium, Jessica Sterling took the fresh pot of coffee she had just brewed and filled the cups of her two male companions, Jim Taylor and Dan Hughes. Thinking out loud, she laughed and said, "Do you think it's too early to call our love birds and remind them not to forget our breakfast? I'm starving!"

"Knowing Mr. T, I'll bet he's still playing footsy with Gloria," Dan commented, also laughing. "Can't say I blame him. She looks pretty cool to me. What do you think, Jim?"

"I'm not paid to think this time of day," he joked in reply, "Knowing Gloria, you're probably right."

As they talked and speculated on when Neal and Gloria would actually show up, Dan's cell phone started to chime. When he answered, Neal's voice said, "Gloria and I are at Antonio's getting ready to order breakfast. Anyone got a problem with scramble eggs, sausage and hash browns?"

Dan repeated the menu to the others, all of whom returned an eager thumbs-up. "Sounds good to us, Mr. T.," Dan remarked enthusiastically. "Throw in a six-pack of beer while you're at it, will you? Jessica and I need a little hair of the dog."

Forty-five minutes later, a cabby driving an island taxi arrived with Neal and Gloria carrying six foiled plates of food and a six-pack of beer. Their arrival was greeted with genuine enthusiasm, which soon evolved into probing questions about how the twosome and threesome had spent their respective evenings.

"Well, for one thing," Jim began, "after we left the yacht yesterday, we did go to Antonio's for dinner. We weren't there but a few minutes when I recognized two old buddies I flew with in Korea standing at the bar, so I went over and asked them to join us. I guess our war stories were getting a little too much for Dan and Jessica, so after they ate, they said good night and left. I'm a little fuzzy as to what happened after that. Thank God the taxi driver recognized Gloria's last name when I finally decided it was time to call it a day. There was only one light on when I got here, so I assumed they had both gone to bed, leaving me the couch. Funny thing about that, I noticed that only one of the two bedrooms had been slept in this morning."

Dan who was quick to add a little humor to the situation by post-scripting Jim's remark. "Hey, man, you snooze, you lose."

The rest of their breakfast together was flavored with laughter and tales of good times, paving the way for Gloria to relieve Neal of having to tell Jim what she was planning to do after the filming was finished that day. "Since we are all in such a good mood," she began, "I would like to tell you some wonderful news that Neal shared with me last night."

After the blank stares and cartoon-like animation that so often depicts surprise in comic strip characters subsided, Gloria continued: "I have a daughter who ran away from home when she was in her early twenties for reasons that are best left to history. I haven't seen nor heard from her in over ten years. Neal told me last night that he's been in contact with her, and has arranged for us to meet as soon as we're finished here today. For this reason, I have volunteered to take Neal, Dan and Jessica to the Oceanside Marina on my yacht, so that Jim can fly back home and get on with his life. I think we all owe Jim a debt of gratitude for what he's done to help Neal repatriate Dan Hughes."

All were quick to applaud the news, and quickly set about cleaning up the condominium while Neal arranged the staging area where the filming was to take place. After all the furniture was in place, Neal mounted his new camcorder on its tripod and placed it between and off to the side of the two seating stations, so he could swivel it to film whomever was speaking at the time. Uniquely, the camcorder came with a small and powerful floodlight attachment that had a brightness control setting on it, adding to its versatility. Satisfied that all was in readiness, he stepped out on the balcony with Gloria to get a breath of fresh air, while Dan and Jessica argued over how he should answer several of the questions. Suddenly, Neal's cell phone chimed. Visibly surprised, he flipped the lid open and answered, "This is Neal."

"Hi, Mr. T. This is Ginger Spyce," a familiar voice on the other end acknowledged. "Are you alone?"

Gloria could faintly hear the female voice asking that question and politely left Neal alone.

"I am now," he replied, suspecting that she was not the bearer of good tidings. "Is anything wrong?"

"Forgive me for interrupting whatever your doing, but something has happened that I felt you ought to know about right away."

"You're forgiven, dear. Now, what has happened?"

"Well, you've sure got this office in an uproar. That trick you played on Dusty has bounced from California to Virginia and back. Director Bronson doesn't know whether to throw you in jail, or give you a medal."

"No offense, Ginger, but can you get to the point."

"Yesterday, Dusty and two agents were sent to San Clemente to apprehend you when you picked up Dan Hughes, not knowing that you had activated the camcorder Bronson gave you and left in your house to fool them into thinking you were there."

"Well it worked, didn't it?"

"It sure did," Ginger replied, starting to laugh.

"What's so funny then," Neal asked, unaware of the irony that was to follow.

"When Dusty and his men finally got to your place they found it being ransacked by members of the Tidewater Drug Cartel. Dusty thinks they were looking for information on Dan Hughes' whereabouts so they could kill him. They were taken into custody immediately and are now in jail waiting extradition back to Virginia. The head honcho is a guy by the name of Miguel Ramirez. Ever heard of him?"

Neal felt a chill race up his spine. "He's the guy that Dan Hughes used to work for before he broke away from the Cartel. I met Ramirez when I went back to attend a funeral for my best friend, Billy Newman. Dan was living in Virginia with his parents at the time."

"For what it's worth, Dusty and Raymond Bronson think they have enough evidence to indict everyone on the list that Dan Hughes gave you before he went into hiding. However, I did overhear Bronson tell Dusty that he still wants answers to those questions he gave you to use as backup at the hearings."

"What about Dan? What do I tell him?"

"Wherever he is, tell him to stay put until Dusty and Bronson have a chance to review the testimony. They will give you instructions after they have reviewed the answers."

"What's your read on all this, Ginger?" Neal asked, still somewhat leery about trusting the DEA. "I can't afford to take any unnecessary chances and get my ass locked up."

"Well, for whatever it's worth, Bronson thinks your the real world's next 007, but he can't afford to express himself publicly. My advice is, get the camcorder disc here as fast as you can and keep Dan Hughes under wraps till Dusty contacts you." Pausing for a moment, she added, "And remember, you didn't get any of this information from me."

"Absolutely not," he assured her. "And thanks so much for calling. I know Dan will rest easier knowing he's almost a free man. He won't forget you."

We're almost there Neal thought, as he yelled back into the condo, "Hey Dan, come out here for a minute. I need to talk to you."

After getting a cold beer from the refrigerator, Dan started toward the patio, patting Jessica on the rear end while she was attempting to restore the couch where Jim Taylor had spent the night. "Nice buns," he joked, dodging a playful slap.

"What's up Mr. T?" Dan inquired, as he stood gazing out over Avalon Harbor.

"I just received word from a friend inside the DEA that Miguel Ramirez and two of his henchmen were taken into custody by DEA agents yesterday after they broke into my house, apparently looking for information on your whereabouts."

"They never give up," Dan remarked, shaking his head in frustration. "Ramirez is the reason I'm standing here right now. Someone inside the DEA told him where I was in the Bahamas. That's why I fled to Mexico."

"Well, according to my source, Ramirez won't be worrying anyone much longer. All we have to do is get your testimony to the DEA as a backup to the information we've already given them."

"Where the hell am I going to stay in the meantime?" Dan asked. "I'm running out of money."

"Right here," Neal replied with a grin. "Gloria has offered you this place for as long as it takes the DEA to review your testimony. Once we get their okay, you're a free man. If you need cash, I'll give you back some of what you gave me. What's fair is fair."

Emotionally moved by what Neal and his friends had gone out of their way to do for him, Dan replied, "Well then, I guess we had better get on with it before I make a fool of myself."

Without mentioning Ginger's name, Neal shared the information he had just received with everyone when he re-entered the condo, emphasizing how important it was to proceed immediately with filming Dan's testimony, so that plans to leave the island could be set in motion as soon as they were finished. All agreed.

Taking her place behind the interviewer's table, Jessica began with a swearing-in statement. Then, one by, she addressed each of the questions the DEA wanted answered. For the most part, they related to the source from which items in Dan's surrendered collection of evidence came from, including names, places and, in some cases, photographs.

The last question was one that Dan knew was coming, but waited until that moment to un-nerve Jessica when she asked, "Are you now, or have you ever been associated with a man by the name of Walter Douglas?"

Using the pre-arranged hand gesture that Dan and Jessica had agreed to use when either of them wanted Neal to stop the camcorder, Dan stroked his chin.

Recognizing the signal, Neal immediately stopped filming. "What's wrong?"

Dan remained silent for several seconds, then replied, "I thought this testimony had to do with the Tidewater Drug Cartel. What's Walter Douglas' name doing in here?"

"I don't know," Neal replied, not wanting to reveal anything about the information Mary Jo Tyler had sent him.

"Well I'm not answering any questions that aren't relevant," Dan remarked angrily.

"Take it easy, Dan," Neal replied in an effort to calm him down. "Just say Walter was a friend of yours who passed away recently."

"What?" Dan shouted, whirling around. "What do you mean... passed away?"

"Just that," Neal replied. "I thought you knew."

Dan remained silent for a moment. "How the hell could I? I haven't heard from Cliff Bennett since I left the Bahamas."

Recognizing an opportunity to put the whole matter to rest, Neal said, "Don't worry about it. I'll erase that last question and have Jessica close the taping with a statement that will officially end your testimony. If the DEA asks why you didn't answer the last question, I'll have an answer for them they won't want to hear."

Dan appeared to have accepted Neal's advice, as he walked sullenly over to the refrigerator and grabbed another beer. Neal, glad that the mention of Walter Douglas hadn't progressed any further than it did, packed up his equipment while the others put the furniture back in place.

"I'm going to miss you guys," Dan admitted, sounding a little melancholy. "When are you planning to leave?"

"I'm going to call my captain right now and tell him to have the yacht ready to leave in two hours," Gloria answered immediately. "That will get us to Oceanside before dark, if that's okay with everyone."

Hearing no objections from Neal or Jessica, Jim Taylor said, "Fine with me. You can drop me off at The Goose on your way out."

With a departure time agreed to, everyone except Dan Hughes began packing to be ready to leave whenever Gloria called the taxi. Recognizing that time was of the essence, Neal made quick work of packing and then invited Dan to step out on the balcony. Holding out his hand, he said, "Here's two-hundred bucks to tide you over until I get home. Call me when you start getting low and I'll send you some more. In the meantime, I'll get my friend, Ron Barns, to duplicate the camcorder disc so I can personally deliver a copy to the DEA. I'm not going to tell them where you are until I have a sworn statement that you are a free man. I will call you as soon as I have that confirmation. Then we'll make plans to get you home. Agreed?"

Smiling softly in a way that Neal had never seen before, Dan took his hand and said, "Roger that, Mr. T." Then, as an after thought, he added, "If and when this whole matter gets settled, I'm going to send you a round trip ticket to Virginia to help me celebrate. We're going to have a party that will put the New Orleans Mardi Gras to shame. That's a promise."

Appreciative of Dan's expression of gratitude, Neal smiled and tried to make light of it. "You'd better check with your dad first, my friend. You're going to have a lot of explaining to do when you get home. Now, go make us a couple of drinks while I make a quick phone call."

"Coming right up,"

After Dan left the balcony, Neal took out his cell phone and pressed in the Hilton Inn number. Several seconds later, the front desk clerk answered, "Hilton Inn."

"Maggie Jyles' office please. Neal Thomas calling."

"She's out of her office right now, Mr. Thomas. Is there anything I can help you with?"

"I'm trying to get in touch with Anita Cassidy," Neal replied, becoming a little anxious.

"Oh, she's out by the pool. I'll connect you."

Several rings later, a sleepy voice answered, "Hi, this is Anita."

"Hi yourself," Neal said jokingly. "This is Mr. T. Did I wake you up?"

"No, I'm outside catching some rays by the pool," she replied, lazily. "Where are you?"

"Still on Catalina Island. We're getting ready to leave for Oceanside on your mother's yacht. Are you feeling okay?"

"Sure. Why do you ask?"

"Because I have something very important to tell you," he replied hesitantly.

Following a moment of awkward silence, Anita second-guessed what he was going to say, and asked, "You've talked with my mother, haven't you?"

Reassured that she had her wits about her, he answered, "Yes I have. And she wants to see you as soon as we can arrange a convenient time."

"I'm not going anywhere," she giggled. "Why don't you both come by here when you get back. Might as well get on with it while everyone's in a good mood."

Neal weighed her logic and agreed. "I'll call you when we reach the marina. Maybe you and Maggie Jyles can come up with something that will make your mother's arrival a little easier on both of you."

"Good idea, Mr. T, I'll get in touch with her right away."

By the time Neal had shut down his phone, the others were inside patiently waiting to leave. "Are you ready to get this show on the road?" Gloria asked.

"As ready as I'll ever be," Neal replied. Turning to Dan, he said, half kidding, "Try not to get into any trouble while I'm gone, will you. We've almost got it made."

"You worry too much Mr. T," Dan replied, grinning like a kid. "Go do your thing. I promise to be a good little boy."

Conversation during their ride to the Avalon pier was animated and filled with laughter, coming to a climax when Jim Taylor almost fell into the water in an attempt to board his seaplane. Once the entry hatch closed behind him, the harbor taxi driver maneuvered over to the mooring buoy and set Jim free to start his engines.

Minutes later, as Neal, Jessica and Gloria waved goodbye from the afterdeck of her yacht, Jim's seaplane sped across the harbor inlet and lifted gracefully into the mid-afternoon sky. Then, much to their surprise, the seaplane lowered its left wing and made a 180-degree climbing turn, bringing it back over the yacht. In a gesture of farewell, the wings dipped up and down several times before leveling off to resume its southeasterly course to San Diego. Jim Taylor was on his way home.

Compared with events everyone onboard Gloria's yacht had experienced over the past forty-eight hours, the relaxing trip to Oceanside seemed somehow anti-climatic, until Neal decided it was an opportune time to tell Gloria about his conversation with her daughter that day.

After inviting her and Jessica to have a drink with him to celebrate the successful completion of Dan's dramatic return, he turned toward Gloria and said, "That phone call I made just before we left your condo was to your daughter. She had made me promise to call her after you were informed of her whereabouts, and how you reacted to the news."

"And you told her…?"

"That you were gratefully relieved to learn that she was alive and in good health. You even expressed a sincere desire to meet with her after our business with Dan Hughes was taken care of."

"You're quite the diplomat, Mr. T. You should be in politics. Anything else?"

"As a matter of fact, she did invite all of us to visit her at the Hilton when we get back. She seemed very anxious to see you."

"I think that's a wonderful idea," Jessica commented. "I was in a similar situation with my mother until Neal re-united us. Trust me, you'll never regret it."

Realizing that there would be a transportation problem when they arrived at the marina, Neal suggested that they take a taxi to his house. "Jessica's car is there," he explained, "so she's free to do whatever she wants. I'll take Gloria to the Hilton for her reunion with Anita, and take her back to the yacht…whenever."

"Sounds good to me," Jessica remarked. "I can call my mother from Neal's house and let her know that we're all safely home."

With the Oceanside Marina closing rapidly in the distance, Gloria excused herself and went to the bridge to call ahead for docking instructions, growing more anxious by the minute over her impending reunion. That, however, seemed secondary in importance to the good news that docking space had been reserved for her in a slip belonging to an owner who had gone on a fishing expedition to Cabo San Lucas.

After Gloria and her crew had secured the yacht, she and Jessica went to Gloria's quarters to change into more suitable attire for the evening ahead. During their absence, Neal did the same and ordered a taxi. That done, he called the Hilton Inn, to tell Anita that meeting with her mother was less than a couple of hours away. Seconds later, an excited voice answered. "Is that you, Mr. T?"

"Yes, it's me. I have good news."

"You'd better have!" she remarked, excitedly. "I'm as nervous as a sinner in church. How's my mom?"

"The same. We just docked at the Oceanside Marina. We'll be over to see you after Jessica and I pick up our cars at my place. We should arrive at the Hilton in about an hour and a half."

"I'll be waiting for you in the lounge."

Encouraged by Anita's happy voice, Neal stepped back inside to mix a drink while he waited for the taxi to arrive. Soon, the captain and his two-man crew greeted him, as they left to eat dinner at one of the several restaurants around the marina's harbor. A short time later, Gloria and Jessica returned to the lounge and suggested that they wait for the taxi onshore. They had no sooner arrived at the head of the dock than the taxi's familiar roof light came into view and stopped at the head of their slip.

The driver, a short, middle- aged Hispanic man with a bearded round face, wore an old golfer's cap and smiled a lot, exposing a gold-capped front tooth. His comic appearance and broken English provided much in the way of amusement, keeping the threesome entertained for the thirty-minute duration of their trip to Neal's driveway. Thus, it was mutually agreed when they arrived that the driver had more than earned a generous bonus for his services, which Gloria insisted on paying.

Still laughing and joking about the experience, they proceeded down the rest of the driveway. As they neared the front entrance, Neal noticed a piece of paper Scotch-taped to the front door. Angered when he couldn't open it, he cursed, "Damn it!" I told Anita to leave this door unlocked."

While Gloria and Jessica stood watching him read the note, his lips gradually curled into a smile. Curious, Gloria asked, "What's so funny?"

Knowing they probably wouldn't understand it's meaning without an explanation, he handed the note to Jessica who read it out loud. "Congratulations, Mr. T. I'm sure you're very pleased with yourself. We are too. Call me when you get back. Signed, Dusty"

While Neal removed a spare key from his wallet to unlock the door, the two ladies looked bewildered at one another. Gloria finally asked, "You are going to explain all this, aren't you?"

Prepared for the break-in that Ginger Spyce had already told him had taken place, Neal replied, "Let's get inside first."

Flipping on the switch that controlled a shaded lamp just inside the door, Neal was surprised to see that, except for a few pieces of furniture that looked out of place, everything appeared to be as he and Jessica had left it. The camcorder that he had instructed Anita Cassidy to activate, however, was missing. *Dusty took it*, he assumed, as his eyes noticed a stack of documents sitting on the dining room table. Before he could begin to explain what Ginger Spyce had told him earlier, Jessica remarked, "Okay, we're inside now. Things look pretty much the same as they did when we left. So would you please explain why we're tiptoeing around like we were breaking in?"

"Evidently, someone else did," Neal informed her, and went on to explain. "It would appear that Dusty Lewis put the place back in order before he took Miguel Ramirez and his accomplices off to jail. His way of settling what he thinks he owes me, I guess."

"May I use your phone, Mr. T?" Jessica asked. "I better call mother and let her know that I'm on my way home."

"Help yourself. You've been here before."

"You're not going to the Hilton Inn with us?" Gloria asked with surprise.

"I've already met your daughter, Gloria. She's a lovely young lady. Besides, this reunion belongs to you two. Believe me, I can tell you that from personal experience."

"Then I suggest we get a move on," Neal advised. "We don't want to keep Anita waiting."

Following a brief conversation with her mother, Jessica gave Neal and Gloria a hug goodbye and left, eager to return to the comfortable solidarity she had become used to as second in command of Sterling Publishing.

Now that there was just the two of them, Neal invited Gloria to have a drink with him, unaware of the surprise that Anita and Maggie Jyles had arranged for Gloria's arrival.

All that was left of the pleasantly sunny day that Neal and Gloria had enjoyed earlier that day was a pinkish glow over the western horizon that highlighted a dark gray silhouette of Catalina Island. The sky overhead had already turned to deep blue and was beginning to twinkle with stars when Neal turned off Old Coast Highway into the Hilton Inn parking lot. Smiling at each other apprehensively, they kissed and left the car, walking as if they were approaching the end of something, rather than the beginning.

"Anita told me to take you directly to the lounge," Neal said before entering. "Don't ask me why, I haven't a clue."

"Doesn't matter." She remarked, feeling her heartbeat quicken. "We're here, so let's make the best of it and enjoy the moment."

They had no sooner entered the lobby than a wave of laughter and lively music swept over them as they approached the lounge entrance. Stunned by what she had walked into, Gloria froze and cried out, "Oh my God!"

Held in the air by balloons over a small banquet table was part of a sheet with large letters taped to it that read – *WELCOME HOME MOM.*

Left speechless by what was taking place, Gloria grabbed Neal's arm to maintain her balance, straining through her moistening eyes to identify the two attractive women who were walking toward them.

Neal, on the other hand, recognized them immediately. "The woman on the right is your daughter," he whispered. "The other one works here."

Observing that her mother seemed mesmerized by the greeting that she and Maggie Jyles had arranged, Anita took the initiative and offered her hand. "It's been a long time, Mom. I can't tell you how much I've looked forward to this moment."

Brushing the hand aside, Gloria put her arms around Anita and hugged her tightly, whispering softly in her ear, "The feeling is mutual, sweetheart."

The joyous outburst from customers all over the lounge were so emotionally charged that Anita could no longer maintain the sometimes icy persona she had become identified with. Bursting into tears, she held onto her mother tightly and cried uncontrollably.

When cheers and clapping finally subsided, the two ladies separated long enough for Anita to introduce Maggie Jyles who took Gloria's hands and said, "My pleasure Ms. Donaldson. I'm honored to have been able to help Anita prepare for this moment."

Looking at Neal, Maggie suggested, "Why don't you escort Ms. Donaldson over to the table I've reserved for us, Mr. T. She must be exhausted."

Over a delightful dinner flavored with what seemed to be an endless supply of champagne, the three women talked ceaselessly about everything imaginable until Neal finally interrupted with a reminder that it was getting late. Looking at Anita, he told her that he still had to get her mother back to the yacht before he could go home. "I have a busy day ahead of me tomorrow," he explained, "but you two have all day to figure out where you're going from here. Personally, I think that decision is best left to the two of you."

Looking at her daughter, Gloria admitted, "He's right, you know. Why don't you sleep on it and call me in the morning. We can have lunch together and talk about your future. In any event, I think you should check out of here tomorrow so you don't leave Neal with a big bill to pay."

"This one's on me," Maggie spoke up. "Compliments of Miss Hilton. She can afford it. Spend the night here and I'll drive you home tomorrow."

"Thanks, for everything, Maggie," Anita said, sounding tired. "I think I'll go back to my not-so-lonely room now and enjoy a good night's sleep for a change." Embracing her mother one more time, she said, "Good night, Mom. Call me tomorrow morning before I check-out."

Sensing that Anita was emotionally tired from all that was being planned for her, Gloria reached across the table and took her hand. "A trip of a thousand miles starts with a single step, my dear. I can assure you it will be well worth the taking. Now, walk with me to Neal's car. He's waiting to take me back to the marina."

After thanking Maggie for her generosity and promising to return, Neal escorted Gloria and Anita to the parking lot where he gave Anita a fatherly embrace and a kiss on the forehead before opening the door for Gloria and taking his place behind the wheel. As the engine idled, he heard Gloria tell Anita, "You have no idea what this day has meant to me. I only wish your father could have been here to see what a beautiful woman you've become. Get some rest, dear. I will call you in the morning. We have much to talk about."

Less than an hour later, Neal dropped Gloria off at the marina and picked up his luggage, politely declining her invitation to share a nightcap. "Thanks for all you've done to help me save Dan Hughes from a lifetime of running," he said before leaving. "Someday I hope I can make it up to you in a manner befitting your grace and charm. You are a true friend."

Minutes later, all that remained of the only man she had ever had feelings for, other than her late husband, were the taillights on his car disappearing in the distance. Unconsciously, she sang in a whisper, "We'll meet again, don't know where, don't know when..."

Chapter 16

And The Beat Goes On

Awakened from a restless sleep the next morning, Neal's first thought recalled the note Dusty Lewis had taped to his door before leaving with his prize catch of Miguel Ramirez and his Cartel thugs. Now that his involvement with Dan Hughes was temporarily on hold, it seemed reasonable that he should contact Dusty to determine what, if anything, he should be doing during the interim.

Following a light breakfast, Neal called the DEA office. As usual, he was pleasantly greeted by the seemingly amused voice of Ginger Spyce, who transferred the call immediately to Dusty's office.

"It's about time you checked in, my elusive friend," Dusty said, sounding a little agitated. "Have you got Dan Hughes' testimony with you?"

"What? No hello, how are you, good job?"

"Never mind all that," Dusty persisted. "Have you got that testimony?"

"Didn't your mother teach you any manners?" Neal teased. "Of course I have it. That's why I'm calling."

"Good. Can you bring it to my office this morning? Bronson is worrying the hell out of me about when he's going to get it."

"I'll try to be there by noon. Maybe we can grab a bite of lunch someplace."

"We'll talk about that when you get here. Right now I need that testimony."

"Okay, okay," Neal shot back, "You'll get the damn disc when I get there."

Reflecting on Dusty's abruptness and lack of congeniality after he hung up, Neal poured a final cup of coffee and took a walk out on his bluff to calm himself. As he reached the bluff's edge, a thought came to him that reinforced his decision to ask Ron Barns to make him a copy of the disc in the event that something happened to it while it was in Dusty's possession. Walking back to his house he poured what was left of his cold coffee on a withering plant and prepared to leave.

Neal's watch read almost 10:30 a.m. when he took the Del Mar exit off the freeway that led to Ron Barns' house. As soon as he appeared in the doorway and mentioned Dan's name, Ron laughed and asked, "Aren't you ever going to get rid of that guy? "What is it this time?"

Taking the camcorder disc from his briefcase, Neal handed it to Ron and replied, "Before I turn this over to the DEA, I want you to make me a copy so I'll have something to cover my ass if anything happens to this one."

"What's on it, if you don't mind my asking?"

"The answers to a bunch of questions the DEA needs to authenticate the evidence I gave them when Dan disappeared a couple of months ago. It's a crazy story. I'll tell you all about it after I drop this disc off at their office. Hopefully, I'll be back here sometime this afternoon."

"Whenever," Ron remarked, as he went about the duplication process. When he finished, he handed them to Neal and said, "I saved it on my computer. So if you ever need another copy, I'll be able to burn one."

Thanking Ron, Neal turned to leave, but hesitated a moment. "How about dinner at Bully's this evening? My treat. We can have a few pops and I'll tell you what's been going on in my dull and uneventful life."

"I can hardly wait," Ron replied, with a touch of sarcasm.

Despite slowly moving traffic on southbound I-5, Neal arrived at the DEA office at approximately 11:45. All eyes were on him when he entered, prompting a silly question when he approached Ginger Spyce. "Is my fly open?" he whispered, with feigned concern.

Struggling to contain her laughter, Ginger managed to keep a straight face and replied, "Not my job. I'll let Agent Lewis know you're here. He can tell you."

Neal laughed and sat down. "How have you been?" he inquired.

"Compared to what?" she shot back. "This office has been nothing but a mad house ever since you pulled that camcorder switch on Agent Lewis."

Neal looked smugly in the direction of Dusty's office, and said, "Seems to me that switch got him more than he bargained for, all things considered."

Looking up from her computer keyboard, Ginger was about to say something, but was cut off by Dusty's voice on her intercom, "You can send Mr. Thomas in now."

It was her turn to smile, as her eyes drifted back to her computer screen. "You heard the man, Mr. T. Your turn in the barrel."

Neal got up and walked over to the door leading into Agent Lewis' office with the distinct feeling that there was more on Dusty's mind than the camcorder disc in his briefcase. Prepared to defend himself against a bombardment of questions, he opened the door and entered.

Dusty remained silent until Neal was seated across the desk from him. "I was on the phone with Director Bronson before you got here," he finally explained. "Ray wanted me to thank you for what you did. Personally, the wild goose chase you sent me on did piss me off a little, but the clever use of the camcorder Bronson sent you did lead to capturing Miguel Ramirez. I also learned from Ray that Ramirez has made a plea bargain in exchange for a reduced sentence, if he's convicted. That, we feel, is a certainty, given the testimony you say you were able to obtain from Dan Hughes. Do you have it?"

Surprised by the formality Dusty was exhibiting thus far, Neal opened his briefcase in a way that blocked Dusty from seeing the duplicate, placing the original on the desk in front of him.

Examining the disc curiously for several seconds, Dusty rose and walked over to a television CD player that sat on a credenza nearby. After sliding in the disc, he returned to his desk and waited. Seconds later, the inside of Gloria Donaldson's condominium appeared on the screen, with Dan Hughes and Jessica Sterling sitting at tables facing each other, just as Neal had arranged them the previous day. When the camcorder zoomed in on Jessica, she addressed it and began talking:

"My name is Jessica Sterling. As a former agent of the Drug Enforcement Agency, I swear under oath that the testimony you are about to hear is based on questions prepared by that agency, and are being answered under oath by Mr. Dan Hughes, suspected member of a drug trafficking organization known as the Tidewater Drug Cartel. Specifically, these questions relate directly to evidence collected by Mr. Hughes, and are being asked for the purpose of validating their authenticity. That said, I will now proceed with the questioning in the same order they were prepared."

Following the question and answer session, Dusty removed the disc and returned to confront Neal. "I was instructed to review the entire session to verify that all the questions had been answered, and were in enough detail to be used in a congressional hearing."

"And your opinion is…?"

"I'll say one thing in your favor, Mr. T. No one can argue with the quality of your presentation. That was good strategy putting Jessica Sterling in the driver's seat. How long have you known her?"

He's digging for something, Neal thought, as he hesitated for a moment to phrase an answer that would place Jessica above reproach. "She and her mother are friends of mine. Jessica left the DEA recently to take a job working for her mother's publishing company. They've recently commissioned me to finish a book I've been working on."

"A book!" Dusty exclaimed. "What kind of book. What's it about?"

"You know I can't tell you that, Dusty. It's proprietary."

"Fiction…non-fiction? What?"

Got him, Neal mused, as he wallowed in the glory of his own self-satisfaction. "It's a fiction adventure novel using bits and pieces of real life experiences and the people who were involved," Neal finally admitted. After watching Dusty squirm a little, he said jokingly, "Don't worry, names have been changed to protect the guilty."

"That's the innocent, Mr. T," Dusty corrected.

"Whatever," Neal remarked, looking at his watch.

"Got someplace to go?"

"Well, I'm supposed to meet my best friend, Ron Barns, in a half an hour," Neal replied, hoping to finalize their meeting. "We're having dinner at Bully's later on."

"Tell him I said hello, will you. I remember talking to him at your last party. He's quite a character."

"That's for sure," Neal said, standing to say goodbye. "Are we through here?"

Dusty came around to the front of his desk and said in a hushed voice, "Tell Dan Hughes that, as far as the DEA is concerned, he's free to return home. Unofficially, his pardon is being processed, as we speak. Director Bronson assured me of that before you arrived here today."

"He'll sure be relieved to hear that," Neal responded with a sigh of relief.

"I'm glad it worked out this way," Dusty remarked, shaking Neal's hand. "That little trick you played on us with Bronson's camcorder bagged a guy we've been after for quite some time."

Before Neal left the office, Dusty held him back for a moment and said, "Oh, one more thing…tell your friend, Mr. Hughes, that if we ever catch him messing around with drugs again, I'll put him under the jail for more time than he's got left."

"I'll give him the message."

At the same time Neal Thomas and Dusty Lewis were reviewing the camcorder disc Neal had brought him, Gloria Donaldson was on her yacht at the Oceanside Marina placing a call to her daughter at the Hilton Inn.

Anita Cassidy, faithful to her promise to remain at the Inn until her mother called, had just finished taking a shower, and was cuddled up on her bed watching television. To her, the thought that life was about to take a seriously complicated turn was frightening, adding to the anxiety she experienced when the phone rang. Nervous, almost to the point of nausea, she picked up the receiver. "Hello?"

"Good morning, dear," the happy voice of her mother began. "I hope you had a good night's sleep. Mine was dreadful."

That makes two of us, Anita reflected. "Good morning, Mom," she replied, trying to hide the apprehension she was experiencing. "I'm afraid mine wasn't much better. Nervous, I guess."

"Understandably so, considering the circumstances," Gloria remarked. "Are you hungry?"

"Are you?"

"I have an idea, if you enjoy the ocean," Gloria replied, maneuvering toward a suggestion.

"Try me," Anita responded affably for the first time. "I don't scare easily."

"Neal Thomas' friend, Dan Hughes is staying at my condominium on Catalina Island for a few days. He's a nice guy and would probably enjoy the company, at least for a little while. I'll call ahead and invite him to have lunch with us. We can come back here when we've finished and spend a quiet evening together at the marina."

"Only one problem," Anita mentioned, "I don't have a car."

Gloria laughed and replied, "That's the least of your problems, my dear. I'll send a taxi for you. When can you be ready?"

"Right now," she giggled with delight. "Here's the address."

With Dan Hughes' exoneration now a certainty, Neal left the DEA's office and headed up I-5 to Ron Barns' house, unaware of the plans Gloria Donaldson had made with her daughter that day. Ron greeted him with enthusiasm and insisted that they play a few games of pool before going to Bully's. Neal was only too happy to oblige and went immediately to the kitchen to mix a drink. When he returned to the pool table area, he heard Ron's voice call out from the bathroom that he had had a calling, and would join him in a few minutes. Using that brief period as an opportune time to tell Dan Hughes what he had learned from Dusty Lewis that afternoon, he stepped out on the front porch and made the call. Moments later, Dan answered.

With measured excitement, Neal explained what had taken place at the DEA office less than an hour ago. Dan replied, "I'm ever grateful for what you've done for me, Mr. T, but I have an inbred fear of believing anything the government says it's going to do for me. So, that said, guess who's coming to see me today?"

"This is no time to be playing games, Dan," Neal replied with some irritation toward Dan' negative attitude. "Who the hell knows you're even there?"

Using a little more diplomacy than he was used to, Dan said, "Your lady friend, Gloria Donaldson, and her daughter."

"What for?" Neal asked, shocked out of his irritability.

"Gloria thought a cruise out here would give them time to adjust to one another, so they asked me to have lunch with them before they return to the marina later on this afternoon."

"There's your first ticket back home, my friend. Do you want me to call Gloria and arrange it?"

"I can handle that, but I need a place to stay until I can book a flight back home."

"Hell, I've got two empty bedrooms. You can stay with me."

"Better yet, make a reservation for me at the Hilton Inn. That way I won't be interfering with your schedule. Besides, I'm due for a little R&R after what I've been through. And so are you."

"Whatever floats your boat," Neal replied. "I'll call Maggie Jyles and have her reserve a room for you. You remember her, don't you?"

"Do I ever," Dan replied. "She saved my ass from getting locked up one night when I was staying at the Hilton Inn."

"She's a manager now, so behave yourself. Call me tomorrow morning and we'll get together for a drink. Okay?"

"Make that two, Mr. T. I don't fly too well on only one wing. And thanks again for all you've done. I really do appreciate it."

Steps away from where he had just finished talking with Dan Hughes, Neal heard Ron lining up balls on his bumper pool table in preparation for their game. Ironically, before they began the break, a white sedan belonging to Johnny Holland and his new wife, Tammy, pulled up in front of the house. Eager to participate in the game, sides were chosen, leaving Neal and Johnny partners against Ron and Tammy, an arrangement particularly pleasing to Ron, because he relished coaching Tammy on how to line up her shots.

After an hour, and several drinks all the way around, the score between the two sets of partners was tied at two games each. Not content to leave it that way, Ron coaxed Neal and Johnny into playing one last game to break the tie. Neal and Johnny reluctantly agreed. Thus, the opening shots fell to Johnny against his wife, which normally would have put Tammy at a disadvantage. To compensate, however, Ron placed his finger on the side cushion where he wanted her ball to hit, and left it there until she shot. Having been consistently success-ful in making his opening shot, Ron's finger was well placed, angling Tammy's ball off the cushion and into her goal at the opposite end of the table. She squealed and laughed with delight, as Ron took another swallow of his gin martini and grinned with pride.

Though their opponents' first ball down advantage was a difficult one to overcome, Neal and Johnny eventually managed to reduce the playing field to two balls apiece, with Ron having the next shot against Neal. Though neither of the two opponents had a clear shot at their goal, Ron saw an opportunity to shoot one of his balls at the other and leave both of then in line for a clear shot at his goal. With a touch he had trained himself to make over the years, he accomplished what he had set out to do. Tammy had it made.

Unable to bust up his opponent's skilled positioning from where his two balls lay, Neal was forced to shoot the one that offered him a bumper shot that he was skilled at making. He was not disappointed, although the ball did teeter on the edge of the goal before finally fall-ing in.

What to do now, he pondered, as he circled the table looking for possibilities. Only one had a fifty-fifty chance of succeeding – a slam-bang, two cushion corner shot he hoped would hit Ron's clustered balls, sending at least one out of play. Unfortunately, he miscalculated the two-cushion angle, which sent his ball flying off one of the center bumpers and into his opponent's goal, costing him two penalty balls and the game.

After the laughter and kidding stopped, Ron drained the last drop of gin from his pint-size glass jar and rattled the ice in a gesture of vic-tory, hollering, "It's Bully's time!"

Earlier that same day, while Neal and Dusty Lewis were finalizing their review of Dan Hughes' testimony, Anita Cassidy stepped from a taxi at the Oceanside Marina and walked down the dock alongside her mother's yacht. As she approached the boarding platform, Gloria ap-peared on the open deck behind the wheelhouse and waved her aboard, smiling excitedly. Moments later, the two women embraced while a crewmember released the mooring lines and jumped back onboard. As the twin diesels began to churn water off the stern, *The Wayward Wind* eased out of her borrowed slip and headed for the open sea carrying a mother and daughter who's lives would never be the same again.

Having already contacted Dan Hughes to let him know that she and her daughter were on their way, Gloria invited Anita into the lounge to enjoy a glass of wine with her while she made her first attempt to discuss Anita's future.

"Now that we finally have a little time to discuss some things that need addressing," Gloria began, "why don't you start by telling me what you've been doing all these years."

Anita's eyes wandered wistfully out over the yacht's wake, as she thought, *where do I begin?* Deciding to generalize rather than getting into the sordid details of events she had made a personal commitment to forget, she replied, "I've had jobs as a waitress, bartender, receptionist, baby sitter, truck driver. You name it. I've done it. With a couple of exceptions, that is."

"And they are…?"

"I've not done drugs or indulged in promiscuous sex. Not that I'm a virgin, or gay. After all, I was married once, if you'll remember."

"Yes, I remember, and for whatever it's worth, I've regretted interfering in your life ever since. I thought it was in your best interest, but I was wrong."

"Well, there was a plus side to all of that," Anita remarked, aware that her mother was deeply regretting what she had done. "You saved me from motherhood, and a possible lifetime of total commitment to raising children, which I was ill-prepared to take on at that age. All things considered, you did me a favor, though I was too young and stupid to realize it at the time. So don't beat yourself up over the past. The future's what I'm more interested in. I'll need your help with that."

"What kind of help are you looking for?" Gloria asked. "Financial aid, a higher education, a job recommendation?"

Reflecting on what Neal Thomas had told her about the trust fund she was heir to, Anita manipulated her reply to give her mother an opportunity to discuss it. "I've had a lot of time to think about that," she began. "I've reached the conclusion that, if I had the money, I would like to spend my time helping homeless children here and around the world get clothing, medical aid, food and emotional support, free of government intervention or control. Based on what our so-called disaster relief program has done for the homeless victims of our own national disasters, I believe I could accomplish more."

"That's a noble pursuit, my dear," Gloria commented, "One that would almost demand soliciting contributions from other sources. Have you considered that?"

"Are you kidding?" Anita replied, suddenly becoming more animated. "From what I've overheard about what goes on at Grampa's Sawmill Club, it seems like a pretty good place to start."

"That's an all male, private organization my dear, with their own set of rules. Soliciting them would be like trying to break into Fort Knox."

Calming down a bit to present her bizarre proposal, Anita smiled and uttered a child-like laugh, replying, "Mom, I'm well aware of what goes on in those cottages on the other side of the lake. If the men who go there are as vulnerable as I think they are, then they're pretty ripe pickings for a charitable contribution to a worthwhile cause, wouldn't you think?"

Realizing that her daughter was a lot smarter than she had given her credit for, Gloria asked, "What do you mean, what goes on in those cottages?"

Anita fell silent for a moment while she poured each of them another glass of wine, observing that Avalon Harbor was only minutes away. When she returned, the memories of her youth came alive. "When I was in my early teens, I used to hide in the game room closet and listen to Daddy and Gramps talk about the Sawmill Club. The more they drank, the sillier they became. Inevitably, Gramps would bring up the subject of what he had done to keep his men satisfied during their weeks of isolation there. Two and two still makes four, Mom."

Gloria looked stunned, and shivered at the thought that Anita might know, or suspect, that she was in any way involved with supplying female services to the cottages she had managed following her husband's death. Maintaining her composure, she reacted defensively and said, "Your father's death placed a tremendous financial burden on me for a number of years, but I managed to get rid of it by doing whatever was necessary to pay it off. I won't go into details, but it may interest you to know that my efforts in that regard made me one of the wealthiest and most powerful women in San Francisco. As far as your personal goals are concerned, I admire your candor, and intend to help you achieve them in any way I can. We'll discuss it further after we pick up Dan and have some lunch. I'm starved."

It wasn't long before the harbor taxi arrived and carried them to the mainland where another taxi was waiting to complete the trip up the winding road up to Gloria's condominium.

Dan Hughes had already packed his bags and was standing on the balcony having a drink when he heard the door to the condominium open. Seconds later, a voice called out, "Dan, we're here!"

Recognizing Gloria Donaldson's voice, Dan left the balcony to greet her, but stopped short when he discovered two women standing in the entranceway. Before he could say anything, Gloria interrupted. "Dan, I want you to meet my daughter, Anita."

"Leave it to Mr. T. to send only the best," Dan remarked, offering Anita his hand. "Hi, I'm Dan Hughes."

"The pleasure is all mine, Mr. Hughes. Mother filled me in on your background on the way over. I'm surprised you're still alive."

"To tell the truth, so am I," Dan laughed.

"Me too," Gloria added, visually sweeping the room. "I must say, you've taken good care of the place. I'm impressed."

"Thank you for letting me stay here," Dan replied. "I don't know many people who would have gone to this much trouble for a stranger. I'll never forget you for it…either of you."

"Well then, let's make sure you don't," Anita giggled. "I'm famished!"

The taxi that Gloria and Anita arrived in was still waiting outside when the party of three left the secured condominium and directed the driver to take them to Antonio's restaurant. Much of their conversation during lunch jumped back and forth on the subject of what each of them intended to do when *The Wayward Wind* reached the mainland. Gloria was the first to comment. "Anita and I still have a lot to talk about with regard to her future. Hopefully, she will choose to accompany me back to San Francisco where we can redirect her energy toward the humanitarian goals she wishes to pursue. There's a challenging future for her there, if she wants it. What are your plans for the future Mr. Hughes?"

Looking somberly down into his glass of beer, Dan replied, "Up until the time Mr. T. came along, I wasn't sure I was going to have a future, given the life I've been living. All things considered, I think I'll go back to Virginia and see if my dad will give me back my old job in his real estate business. That is, after I pick up my boat in the Bahamas. I can live comfortably on it and have my privacy too. Fortunately, the family home is located on an inlet off the James River. I've got a lot of friends back there. It will be good to see them again."

Reflecting on where life had taken her after she ran away from what most kids could only dream about, Anita offered an unexpected statement of her intentions. "I'm definitely ready for a transition. I've scraped the bottom of the barrel long enough. It's time for me to return to the land of my heritage." Pausing reflectively, she smiled and looked at her mother, singing softly, "I left my heart in San Francisco. High on a hill, it calls to me…"

One hour later, while the crew of *The Wayward Wind* was preparing to up-anchor and return its human cargo to the Oceanside Marina, Neal Thomas parked his car in Bully's parking lot and entered the restaurant. Ron Barns was seated at a corner table in the dining room, along with Johnny and Tammy Holland.

"Here partner!" Johnny called out, pushing a full drink across the table. "These two wanted to say thanks for that last shot you made."

"Didn't make," Neal corrected. "I never thought it would jump the table like that. I really blew it."

"You had fun didn't you?" Ron asked, grinning like a Cheshire cat.

"Of course," Neal replied begrudgingly, "if you go along with that line of horse hockey that says, it's not whether you win or lose, its how you play the game. What a crock!"

"Look at it this way, Mr. T," Tammy interrupted, slurring her words a little, "you didn't lose…we won!"

"You sound like a Washington politician, honey." Johnny remarked, roaring with laughter. "You should be on a congressional investigating committee or something."

Ah, now the door is open, Neal thought, as he seized the opportunity to announce his own good news. "Not to belabor the subject of winning, my friends, but I have some news along those lines that I'd like to share with you."

The three grew silent as they looked at one another with registered surprise. "You're not going back to work are you?" Ron asked, knowing that Neal had mentioned it on occasion.

"No," he replied, "but as Ron is aware, I have been working secretly with the Drug Enforcement Agency to get my friend, Dan Hughes, a pardon in exchange for his testimony against the Cartel. I'm happy to report that the pardon has been officially issued, and Dan will be going home soon to begin a new life with his family."

"And this has been going on under our noses all this time?" Tammy asked with surprise.

"Ron knew," Neal admitted. "But for obvious reasons, I could only tell those who had a need to know."

Looking at her watch, Tammy said, "I wish Johnny and I could stay here a little longer to hear more about this mystery you've kept a secret all this time, but we have to attend a timeshare meeting. It's been fun, but we really must go. See you next Tuesday."

"Shall we have dinner?" Neal asked Ron, after Johnny and Tammy disappeared out the door. "It's on me."

Ron thought about it briefly and then replied, "Let's make it another night. I think I'll adjourn to the high bar and drink a cold glass of beer before calling it a night. Care to join me?"

Before Neal could respond, the waitress who had been serving them approached and said, "There's a woman sitting at the low bar who says she knows you, and wants to buy you a drink. Are you interested?"

Having overhearing the conversation, Ron grinned. "Go ahead. I'll see you next Tuesday."

After Ron left to take a corner seat at the high bar, Neal gave the waitress his credit card and said, "Keep my tab running until I see who this woman is. I'll settle up with you when I leave. Okay?"

"Knock yourself out, Mr. T. I'm not going anywhere."

Neal had only walked half the distance to the low bar when a smiling face he recognized immediately came into focus. It was Norma Manning. Pleasantly surprised, he sat down beside her. "When the waitress said there was an attractive lady sitting at the bar who wanted to buy me a drink, I thought someone was pulling my leg. I never expected to see you here."

"Why, because you don't find me attractive?"

"Just the opposite, I'm afraid…and talented. An addictive combination for a man of my tastes."

"Oh, and just what are they, if I may ask?"

Avoiding the suggestive direction the conversation was headed, Neal tried to change the subject by asking, "What brings you to Del Mar?"

"You didn't answer my question," she persisted, "but I'll let it pass for now. To answer yours, I'm attending an editor's conference at the Del Mar Hilton and decided to have dinner here for old times sake before returning to La Jolla. Would you care to join me?"

"Why not. I had planned to have dinner here anyway. Thanks for asking."

Nodding to her waitress that she was moving to the dining room, Norma picked up her briefcase and led their way to the corner booth Neal had just left. After they were seated, Neal said, "You mentioned coming here for old times sake. Does Bully's have some special significance for you."

"My former husband and I used to come here after spending a Sunday at the track," she replied. "I don't get up this way very often so I decided, why not? What's your excuse?"

Pointing in the direction of the high bar, Neal replied, "That guy I just left is my best friend. We were supposed to have dinner here tonight, but the couple we shot pool with this afternoon decided to join us for a drink, which delayed things a little. When they left, you showed up. So, Ron went to do what he does every Tuesday after we finish shooting pool – drinking and playing liars poker with the bartender."

"Why don't you ask him to join us?"

"He couldn't care less. Besides, I'd like to ask you a few questions about my book."

Briefly interrupted by the waitress stopping by to take their dinner order, Norma explained that she was making good progress with the editorial process and hoped to have a draft for Neal's review in a few days. "I hope you're not sensitive to editorial changes," she remarked sensitively. "My commitment to any author is to make them as good as they can be. It's my job."

"I wouldn't expect anything less, and I'm sure Sandy Sterling feels the same way. Actually, I'm only sensitive about a weak drink. So change whatever you believe is in the best interest of the book, and to hell with my sensitivity."

Dinner followed shortly thereafter, made pleasant by a mix of talk about music and questions regarding the outcome of Neal and Jessica Sterling's trip to Catalina. Eventually returning to the subject of Neal's book, Norma finally brought up the subject of its future development and promotion. "While you've been involved in repatriating your friend Dan Hughes, Sandy Sterling has been in contact with producer types she knows in the movie industry. She's convinced your story can be adapted to a film series similar to *Indiana Jones*, for example. So don't be surprised if she approaches you on that subject the next time you two get together."

"What are your thoughts along those lines?" Neal asked, suddenly excited by the movie possibility. "Certainly you have an opinion."

"I'm an editor, Neal, not a producer. Even though I see certain similarities between how you develop your story and how the film industry develops theirs, my advice, for whatever it's worth, is to follow the instincts of your mentor and write accordingly. You're fortunate to have such an enthusiastic publisher."

"And editor?"

"We wouldn't be having this conversation if I wasn't. Unfortunately, it will have to end there," she added apologetically. "I really must be going. Don't be surprised if you have a message from Sandy Sterling when you get home tonight. She's anxious to talk to you."

Following a gesture to give him money for her part of the bill, Neal reacted by saying, "Dinner's on me this evening, my dear. And thanks for your counsel. Let me walk you to your car. It's dark outside."

Minutes later, Neal returned to the restaurant to pay his bill and apologize to Ron Barns for not having spent more time with him.

Observing a trace of lipstick on Neal's lips, Ron grinned and asked, "Does she taste as good as she looks?"

Chapter 17

All's Well That Ends Well

For the first time in many weeks Neal Thomas enjoyed the luxury of sleeping soundly through the night. It wasn't until a gusty wind from off the ocean rattled his bedroom window that his eyes finally cracked open. Basking in an emotional calmness he hadn't enjoyed for some time, he laid there thinking about his chance meeting with Norma Manning the night before and remembered her mentioning that he might have received a telephone message from Sandy Sterling. Hastening to shower and get ready for the day ahead, he felt a sense of relief at not having to deal with Dan Hughes the first thing this morning. It wasn't until he glanced at his message machine while fixing a pot of coffee that he was reminded of how quickly that could change.

Not until after I've had a cup of coffee, he decided, trying to second-guess the identity of the callers. Several minutes later, as the coffee-scented vapor drifted up from his mug, he reluctantly activated the recorder. There were three messages:

"Message one…Hi Neal. Paula here. It's important that I speak with you as soon as possible. I hope all went well with you and your Dan Hughes business. I'm home most evenings during the week, so give me a call. Bye."

Something in the sound of Paula's voice registered a sense of urgency that Neal was unaccustomed to hearing. Grabbing a pen from a utility mug nearby, he scribbled a reminder on the phone pad: *Call Paula this*

269

evening – important! Troubled by the first message, he pushed the *PLAY* button again, hoping for something less worrisome.

"Message two… Mr. Thomas, Sandy Sterling. Please call me as soon as you return from Catalina. I would like to meet with you to go over a book-related topic that I believe has great potential. I look forward to hearing from you soon. Jessica said she was quite impressed with Dan Hughes. That worries me."

Smiling and shaking his head with amusement, he couldn't believe how his emotional pendulum had swung from mild contentment to one of anxiety. He pushed the *PLAY* button one more time.

"Message three… Hi, Mr. T, it's Dan. Gloria Donaldson and her daughter just dropped me off at the Hilton here in Carlsbad. Maggie Jyles checked me into a nice room, so give me a buzz when you can and we'll get together for a drink later on. She'll probably want to join us, so be prepared. In the meantime, I'm trying to book a flight to the Bahamas so I can pick up my boat. See you soon."

So much for peace and quiet, Neal thought, as he poured another cup of coffee and walked to the bluff behind his house to consider what to do next. He hadn't been there long when he heard his cell phone chime back in the kitchen. "Damn!" he cursed, upset for not remembering to bring it with him. The fifth ring had already sounded when he picked up and panted, "This is Neal!"

"Ginger Spyce. Are you alone?"

"For the moment," he replied, sensing she was being cautious. "What's up?"

"Where is Dan Hughes right now?"

Her question sent a shiver running down Neal's spine. It would only have been asked if she had reason to believe that Dan was not as free as he thought he was. "Why, is anything wrong?" he questioned.

"I don't know, but for whatever it's worth, Director Bronson has ordered Agent Lewis to personally deliver that camcorder disc you gave him yesterday. Dusty's on a flight back to Virginia, as we speak."

"I don't think that has much significance except to guarantee its safe delivery," Neal replied. "Bronson probably doesn't want to take any chances on the disc being lost or stolen. Just a precaution is my guess."

There was a slight pause before Ginger made a comment that bothered him. "Then why did Dusty become so upset and irritable when Bronson gave him the order? He's flown for the agency before, and actually enjoyed it."

"Did he make any calls before he left," Neal asked, starting to feel a little uneasy.

"Only one, but it was from his cell phone, so I don't know who he called. Could have been his wife."

Thinking about how cautious Ginger had sounded when she first called, Neal asked, "Why did you ask where Dan Hughes was?"

Again, there was a slight pause before she answered. "Don't ask me why, but I don't think Dan Hughes is as free a person as that pardon says he is. If I were you, I'd tell him to watch his back until the Tidewater Drug Cartel is out of business, and Miguel Ramirez and his thugs are all in prison. Call it feminine intuition, but I think there's more going on here than meets the eye. Pass that on to Dan."

"I will," Neal assured her, "along with a couple of other things he may have forgotten about. Thanks for the heads-up."

Checking the time, Neal decided to return Sandy Sterling's message, hoping that what she had to say would give him a more positive lift than the one Ginger had dropped on him. Despite every effort Neal made to dismiss it from his mind, Dusty Lewis' bizarre reaction to Ray Bronson's order still wouldn't go away, as he dialed the Sterling Publishing Company number.

Fortunately, the wait was short-lived. The receptionist had immediately forwarded his call directly to Sandy's office. "Thanks for returning my call so promptly," she greeted him. "You must be quite relieved to finally put Dan Hughes' problems behind you. That's all Jessica and Norma Manning can talk about."

Rather than dampen her enthusiasm with a negative response, Neal decided it would be more to his advantage to keep his future relationship with Dan Hughes a sideline issue, and redirect his energy toward the publication of his book. To that end, he replied, "I feel confident that Dan's situation has been satisfactorily resolved to a degree that will allow me to keep my attention focused on our mutual interests. In that regard, what did you want to talk to me about?"

"Tomorrow night I'm having a dinner party for some friends of mine from Hollywood. They're here in La Jolla shooting film clips for a movie they are producing. I thought it might be an informative experience for you to meet them, and get a feeling for how books are developed into movies. Norma Manning and Jessica will also be there. Can you make it?"

Without a moment's hesitation, Neal answered, "Yes. What time?"

"I told everyone six o'clock."

"Fine. I'll be there...and thank you?"

Though Sandy's invitation came as a welcome break in the hectic routine he was starting to become used to, Ginger Spyce's phone call still lingered in his mind like a bad dream, prompting him to call Dan and suggest that they get together as soon as possible. Dan reacted positively and told Neal to come over whenever he felt like it. "I'll be out by the pool when you get here, Mr. T. Things are finally starting to fall into place."

Let's just hope they continue to do so, Neal thought, as he locked up his house and drove toward the ocean. On the way he thought about how to approach Dan on what Ginger had just told him. *Proceed with caution* came to mind.

In another part of town at approximately the same time, Gloria Donaldson and her daughter stood talking in front of Anita's apartment while the taxi driver removed her suitcase. When he sat it down next to Anita, Gloria turned to the driver and said, "Wait here for me, I'll be right back."

When the two ladies reached the privacy of Anita's apartment, Gloria searched around in her handbag and pulled out several hundred dollars, and said, "This will help until you settle up with your landlord and quit your job. Let me know when you're ready to leave for San Francisco and I'll arrange for your ticket. Ship your personal belongings through UPS and I'll store them at my house until we can get you relocated to a place of your own."

Anita, overwhelmed by the speed at which her life was suddenly changing direction, asked, "Are you sure this is what you want, Mom?

I damn sure don't want to put you through all this and then find out we've both made a big mistake."

"The mistake would be not correcting the one that's already been made, my dear," Gloria remarked, confident that bringing Anita back to San Francisco would give her future some meaning. "I want to help you make your dreams come true. You'll thank me some day. Now I must go."

After embracing Anita affectionately, Gloria smiled and kissed her daughter goodbye. Then she quickly descended the stairs, waved from the waiting taxi and told the driver to return to the marina, happy for what Neal Thomas had brought back into her life.

Like a travel magazine advertisement, Dan Hughes epitomized the picture of rest and relaxation when Neal found him lying on a lounge chair at the Hilton Inn swimming pool. He had an exotic drink in one hand, and a house phone plugged into an outdoor jack nearby, a clear indication that he was still mixing business with a glass of pleasure. "You certainly blend in well with the local scenery," Neal remarked, as he looked around the pool area and sat down. "Any trouble getting a flight back?"

"Yeah," he replied irritably. "According to a CNN weather report this morning, there's a Category 2 Hurricane building up in the Atlantic that's headed straight toward the Bahamas, and increasing in strength every hour. Flights in and out of Southern Florida have been cancelled, and they're already encouraging residents to prepare for an evacuation order to avoid the Katrina-type disaster that hit them last year. There's no way I can get my boat out of the islands now. And I damn sure can't afford to stay here until it blows over."

Recalling what Ginger Spyce had told him about Dusty Lewis being out of town for a few days, Neal said, "Your welcome to stay with me until it passes. I could use the company. At least your dad will rest easier knowing you're out of harm's way."

Dan thought about that option while Neal picked up the phone and ordered a drink. When he finished, Dan said, "On one condition…"

"And that is…?"

"You let me buy your ticket back to Virginia to help me celebrate my homecoming. It never would have happened if it hadn't been for you."

"And someone you haven't met yet," Neal added.

Dan looked puzzled for a moment, and asked, "Who's that? I thought there was only you, Gloria Donaldson and that guy with the seaplane...Jim Taylor."

"Basically, yes," Neal agreed. "But who do you think provided the information that allowed me to outfox the DEA?"

Dan shook his head in a gesture of comic ignorance and admitted, "I haven't got a clue."

"Dusty Lewis' receptionist, Ginger Spyce." Neal revealed. "We'd both be under the jail if it hadn't been for her."

Rising up quickly to a sitting position, Dan looked squint-eyed at Neal and said with surprise, "You had an informant in the DEA's office? How in the world did you pull that off?"

A moment of truth had arrived, Neal realized as he considered his answer. "I told Ginger she would be well rewarded for risking her job, and possible prosecution, for keeping me informed as to what went on between Dusty Lewis and Director Bronson. Especially after I had turned all your evidence over to them. It never dawned on me that the committee reviewing the case would consider it insufficient evidence without your sworn testimony. It was Ginger who tipped me off that Dusty and his men planned to intercept both of us when Jim Taylor and I attempted to pick you up on San Clemente Island as we originally planned."

Dan settled back in his chair, the furrow in his brow displaying deeper concern. "I had no idea we had a silent partner. Like you say, she saved both our asses." After thinking about the seriousness of what Ginger had done, Dan asked, "How much of that hundred thousand dollars I gave you do you still have?"

"About seventy-five."

"Give her thirty-thousand." Dan said without hesitating. "I'll give you half of that back when you come to my homecoming party. Fair enough?"

"Fair enough."

While Dan picked up the phone and called the bar to have two more drinks delivered, a smartly dressed woman emerged from inside the Inn and approached them. "Now here's a pair to draw to," the woman said in a friendly way. "Are you two enjoying yourselves?"

"Maggie Jyles!" Neal shouted, and got up to greet her. "Give me a big hug. You look wonderful,"

As the two embraced, Dan remained on his lounge chair and asked, "Is this a work-related visit, or can you join us for a drink?"

"Thanks, but no thanks," she replied, sounding conservatively disappointed. Looking directly at Dan she said, "Our receptionist just received an anonymous phone call from a man speaking broken English who wanted to know if you were registered here. She told him that it was hotel policy not to give out that kind of information without knowing who the caller was, and the reason for calling. She reported the incident directly to me, adding that the man yelled at her using some awfully foul language before hanging up. Any idea who that might have been?"

Dan looked immediately at Neal. "Well, Mr. T, it looks like you just bought yourself a roommate." Picking up his towel, he turned toward Maggie and said, "Sorry girl, I'd better get the hell out of here before someone comes snooping around looking for me. As far as the hotel is concerned, I was never here. You okay with that?"

Maggie agreed and hugged him goodbye. "Take care of yourself."

In less than thirty minutes, Dan had gone to his room, packed his bags and returned to the lounge. Neal was waiting at a table with the two drinks Dan had ordered from the pool. "Take it easy, sport," he remarked, remaining calm over what had happened. "Finish your drink. I've already settled up with the bar, and Maggie has already deleted you out of the Inn's computer."

Dan collapsed in the chair opposite Neal. "And I thought I was a free man," he sighed. "Bullshit! Now it's the Cartel breathing down my neck."

Realizing that Dan was becoming more uncomfortable with each minute that passed, Neal suggested, "Let's go. You'll be more at ease when we get to my place."

Though the drive to Neal's home only took twenty minutes, it seemed like an hour to Dan. Remaining thoughtfully quiet for most of it, he finally spoke when they entered Neal's driveway. "Sorry if I over reacted back there. That telephone call Maggie told us about kind of freaked me out. I'm still not comfortable being back in the States. I felt the same way after being in the Caribbean for weeks at a time. I'll snap out of it once I get home."

"What are you going to do about your boat?" Neal asked.

"I won't know until after the hurricane hits. I have friends down there that I can call to find out if I still have a boat. But based on what happened along the Gulf States during Katrina, it might just end up on somebody's roof. Let's turn on the television as soon as we get inside. CNN will probably be tracking it by the hour."

At least nobody's broken into the place, Neal thought as he inserted his key into the front door lock. They weren't inside but a few seconds when Dan remarked, "Do you realize that this is the first time I've ever been inside your house, Mr. T?"

"Hadn't given it much thought, but I guess you're right. Welcome aboard."

Setting their luggage aside for the moment, Neal walked into the kitchen, put a bottle of vodka on the table and said, "Help your self. There's mix in the refrigerator. I'll turn on the news."

After looking through the sliding glass doors that led out onto the patio deck, Dan ventured outside and admired the view. Glancing briefly at his wristwatch, he called back to Neal, "It's almost six o'clock. What's the CNN channel?"

"Thirty-one. There's a commercial on," Neal shouted back. "Have a seat while I fix a drink and open up some chips."

Dan returned inside and sat opposite the television, waiting anxiously for a weather report. The commercials ended just as Neal returned to an image of Anderson Cooper leaning into driving rain. It was obvious from the palm trees in the background that the approaching hurricane had been increasing in intensity over the past few hours. Struggling to maintain his balance, Cooper reported that wind velocity had increased to a level 3 intensity, forcing a mandatory evacuation order into affect for the greater Miami area, and Southward into the Keys.

"The path seems to be in a westerly direction between southern Florida and Cuba," Cooper commented. "Pictures taken in the Bahamas earlier today showed widespread damage to housing and boats in that area."

"Well, I guess that pretty much kills any chance of getting my boat out of there," Dan remarked, sounding discouraged. "There's no way airlines could still be operating in that kind of weather."

"Better than losing your life," Neal remarked. "Let me fix you another drink and we'll see what we can come up with. All is not lost."

While Dan sat dejectedly weighing the options that were still available, Neal took his glass and went into the kitchen. It was then that he saw the reminder note he had written on the phone pad – *Call Paula this evening – important!*

Checking the wall clock he thought, *I'll give her a little time to get home from work.* Returning with Dan's drink, Neal sat back in his recliner and said, "You know, Dan, if this were my problem, I'd fly home and worry about what to do about my boat when I got there. After all, there's not much you can do about it here, or there, until the hurricane decides where it's going. But at least you'd be home where you've got friends and family to help you work it out."

Dan thought about what Neal had proposed for a moment and said, "Now that makes sense, Mr. T. No use beating myself up over something I can't do anything about. What I should do is forget about it for now and relax in that Jacuzzi of yours."

"Excellent idea!" Neal agreed. "Go upstairs and unpack your suitcase. Don't worry about a bathing suit. Wear your under shorts and grab a towel out of the bathroom. In the meantime, I have to make a phone call. I'll turn on the Jacuzzi and join you there in a few minutes."

"Roger that!" Dan said in a more jovial tone, as he made his way up the stairs.

Feeling as though he had given Dan a more positive outlook on where things were going, Neal walked into his studio and called Paula Dillon, totally unprepared for the reason why she wanted to talk to him.

"Hello. This is Paula," an almost un-recognizable voice said from the other end.

"Hi, It's Neal. I just received your message. Anything wrong?"

There was a pause, one that hinted of impending unpleasantness. "I wish I didn't have to tell you this over the phone," she said awkwardly, "but your life is so unpredictably hectic I have no other choice."

"Tell me what?"

Again there was a pause, as if she was having a difficult time trying to phrase her response. It finally came in a shattering statement he was unprepared for. "Shortly after the last time we saw each other, Mike and Ellen had a party at their house for his fellow doctors and their wives. I met one of those doctors, a nice looking older man whose wife had died of cancer over a year ago. We enjoyed talking and before the evening ended he invited me to dinner the following evening."

"What's his name?" Neal interrupted.

"Dr. Peter Bennings." She answered nervously. "May I continue now?"

"Sorry, please continue."

"Thank you. I know how easily you are distracted." After clearing her throat she said, "While you were off chasing after Dan Hughes, I've been seeing Peter on a regular basis, trying to make up my mind if I liked him well enough to become seriously involved."

"As in having sex?"

Pausing only briefly, Paula realized that Neal was not going to make it easy for her to be nice, so she said, "Okay, Curly, if that's the way you want it. Yes, we're having sex. And I have a diamond engagement ring on my finger to prove it. Any more questions?"

Sinking heavily back into his chair, embarrassed and ashamed of his behavior toward the one person who had always respected and admired him, he replied, "I truly am happy for you, Paula. Congratulations. I guess the shock of hearing you say it made me angry for a moment or two, but I'm over it now. When's the wedding, if you're not too upset to tell me?"

"I'm not," she said more calmly now. "I never could stay mad at you for very long. I'll let you know when Peter and I decide on a date. You will come to the wedding won't you?"

"Why of course," he replied more affably. "I'll even play the piano… if Peter doesn't mind."

"Are you kidding? He's a piece of cake. Just like you. I guess that's what attracted me to him."

With little else to say under the circumstances, Neal decided it was time to call it quits. "Well, I guess I better go check on Dan Hughes to make sure he hasn't drowned in the Jacuzzi. He's staying here until he can book a flight back home. Hopefully for good this time."

Paula laughed and said, "Don't count on it, Curly. Sounds to me like you two are joined at the hip. Tell him I said, Hi."

It took a minute or two for the reality of what Paula had revealed to him to sink in. *What's over is over*, he thought, walking despondently back into the kitchen to drink away the emotional vacuum he felt inside. Looking out the window he saw his counterpart's naked torso relaxing in the Jacuzzi as if he hadn't a care in the world. *Talk about a couple of losers*. "Don't go anywhere. I'll join you as soon as I put my bathing suit on."

Dan's reply was just as silly. "Not the way I'm dressed, Mr. T."

When Neal came down the stairs the next morning, it came as somewhat of a surprise to find Dan already awake and talking on the telephone in his studio. Rather than eavesdrop on his conversation, he continued into the kitchen and began preparing breakfast. Shortly thereafter, Dan joined Neal and said he had been able to make a reservation on a flight to Norfolk the next morning, leaving at ten o'clock.

"What's your hurry?" Neal asked, surprised by Dan's sense of urgency.

"I woke up early this morning and got to thinking about what Maggie Jyles told us about that fowl-mouthed bastard calling the Hilton to ask if I was registered. That tells me that the Tidewater Drug Cartel is still trying to find out where the hell I am, so they can get rid of me, not knowing that my testimony has already been recorded and..."

"Shit!" Neal shouted as he put a generous helping of scrambled eggs and a couple of sausages on their plates, still mumbling curse words.

"I don't care for any, thanks," Dan joked. "I've had more than my share of that recently."

Placing the two plates on the table, Neal didn't begin eating right away. Watching Dan dig in, he said, "That would go along with what Ginger Spyce called to tell me about yesterday morning. And I just kissed it off!"

"Kissed what off?"

"Ginger told me that Dusty Lewis went ballistic when the Director of the DEA ordered him to personally deliver that camcorder disc we made on Catalina Island a couple of days ago, instead of mailing it."

"Isn't that his job?"

"Not if he had something else in mind."

"Like what?"

"Come on, Dan. Think about it."

Dan stopped eating and concentrated for a moment, his forehead gradually wrinkling into a frown that forced him to reply. "I'll be damned," Dan said in a whisper. "Dusty Lewis is a double-dipper?"

"I don't want to believe it, but certain observations recently make me wonder."

"For instance…?"

Neal got up and poured them both another cup of coffee. When he returned and sat down again, he continued, "When I first told the DEA that they should let me record your testimony at an undisclosed location, and under my personal supervision, Dusty was against it. Director Bronson, on the other hand, thought it was a very clever idea. He even sent me a camcorder to use, but failed to mention that it had been modified to include an electronic ground-positioning device. That's how they were going to find out where we were recording your testimony. They had planned to move in at just the right moment and get both of us. When I found that out, I used it against them by leaving it here and having Anita Cassidy activate it when I called her from Catalina. I had already purchased a new camcorder to use over there. That's the disc I gave Dusty Lewis."

"That still doesn't make Dusty a bad guy," Dan remarked. "Just a typical Government Agent who thinks he knows what the hell he's doing, and gets pissed when someone proves he doesn't. But then again, he did apprehend Miguel Ramirez and his boys."

Neal laughed and said, "Yeah, but that was just a lucky coincidence. He thought he was going to catch you *and* me. What he was really after was the disc in the camcorder Bronson sent me. Without it, Bronson couldn't prove their case against the Tidewater Drug Cartel, which your testimony would certainly guarantee. The more I think about it, the more I'm inclined to suspect Dusty Lewis of playing both ends against the middle. He wanted to destroy that disc before the DEA could use it against the Cartel. Getting rid of the Cartel would cut off a big chunk of his income."

"You don't have to remind me of that, Mr. T." Dan remarked. "I've been there and done that…remember?"

"Which is all the more reason to believe that Ginger Spyce observed behavior in Dusty that validates my suspicion that he's playing with a marked deck."

"How are you going to prove it?" Dan asked.

How could I have forgotten that, Neal pondered, as the memory of a recent incident suddenly came to mind. "Only one way to find out," he said, leaving the table and disappearing into the garage.

Now, where did I put that damn thing? "Ah hah," he grunted, after locating the charcoal starter in which he had hidden the papers Mary Jo Tyler had Faxed him. Returning to the kitchen, he removed the Ziploc bag and spread them on the table in front of Dan. "Recognize these?"

Dan's eyes got as large as two hard-boiled eggs when he realized what he was looking at. "Where the hell did you get these," he snarled, trying to hide the fact that he knew what they were.

"Let's just say a mutual friend gave them to me," Neal replied cunningly. "It shouldn't take long to verify whether or not Dusty Lewis' name is in here. That should answer the question you asked me a moment ago."

Dan went immediately to the page where last names beginning with the letter <u>L</u> were listed. There were only a few, but the nickname *Dusty*, parenthesized behind one of them, stuck out like a fly in the punch bowl.

Dan massaged his eyes for a few seconds, then looked up wearily at Neal. "You know what will happen if this information gets into the wrong hands, don't you?"

"There's only one name I'm interested in, "Neal replied calmly. "I just want you to know that we have an ace in the hole, if push ever comes to shove. I don't intend to let the DEA flex its muscle at us after all we've done for them. I'm sure Ray Bronson would be happy as hell to learn about what's going on in his organization if anything happens to that disc. Just for the record, I had a copy made and mailed it to your father just to be on the safe side."

Dan shook his head and commented. "Why not? Might as well get him in the loop too."

While Dan returned upstairs to shower and enjoy a much-needed shave, Neal cleaned up the kitchen, and was about to call Ginger Spyce when his cell phone chimed. It was Sandy Sterling. "I called the Hilton

Inn a few minutes ago to invite Dan Hughes to dinner tonight, but the clerk said there was no one there by that name. Has he disappeared again?"

"We should be so lucky," Neal joked in reply. "We decided it would be safer for him to stay here after the Inn reported they had received an anonymous call asking if he was registered there. He's upstairs taking a shower. Do you want to talk to him?"

"No. Jessica mentioned that he would be company for her, so bring him along. I think she finds him interesting. Dress is casual."

"I'm sure he'll want to come, even though he has a flight out of San Diego at ten o'clock tomorrow morning."

"He can sleep on the plane. Where is he going, by the way?"

"Back to Virginia. His father and sister live there."

"Good. I'll see you both at six o'clock."

Looking noticeably refreshed, Dan came down to the kitchen a few minutes after Neal hung up the phone. He was dressed casually in shorts, a colorful short-sleeved shirt, and beach sandals. Whistling a tune that was unfamiliar to Neal, Dan went straight to the bar and said, "I can't tell you how good I feel about going home tomorrow, Mr. T. Especially with that pardon in my suitcase. I just hope nothing happens to screw it up. I'm tired of running."

Rather than dwell on the negative side of the DEA's internal affairs, Neal opted to surprise Dan with Sandy Sterling's dinner invitation. "Jessica's mother called a few minutes ago and asked me to bring you to a dinner party she is having this evening. Interested?"

"Hell yes I'm interested!" Dan said enthusiastically. "I can't think of anyone I'd like to spend my last night on the West Coast with than Jessica. She sure is a live one. Just make sure I get to the airport on time. I'll sleep on the plane."

Neal laughed. "That's what her mother said. Go ahead and take a walk on the beach. We don't have to be in La Jolla until six o'clock. In the meantime, I want to call Ginger Spyce about that matter you and I discussed yesterday."

"Can I take a drink with me?"

"Yeah. Mix it in that covered coffee-mug on the bar so the Beach Patrol won't bother you. And take your cell phone…just in case."

While Dan was gone, Neal contacted Ginger Spyce at the DEA office and invited her to lunch the next day, using the excuse that it was a small payback for her services.

"Shall I go to that same restaurant in Balboa Park where we met the last time?" she asked in a hushed voice. "I can arrange to take two-hours personal leave, if that will help any. Agent Lewis is still back in Virginia."

"That will be fine. See you tomorrow at noon."

Since Dan had left the house for a while, Neal went immediately to the garage and took thirty thousand dollars from his grandfather's suitcase and returned to the kitchen. Using a large Ziploc bag, he arranged the bills in an even number of bundles, binding each one with a rubber band. As he had hoped, they fit perfectly when he closed the bag, allowing for safe storage in his briefcase until he met Ginger the next day. *That's that,* he thought, returning to the kitchen.

With little to occupy his time until Dan returned, Neal looked over at the unopened- mail basket on the counter top and decided he had pushed that unpleasant chore aside for long enough. Pouring another cup of coffee, he went to his studio and began the envelope-by-envelope process of reading junk mail and paying overdue bills. When he finished, the trash basket near his desk was nearly full, and a stack of stamped envelopes representing his monthly commitments was ready for the mailbox. The walk out and back was invigorating, prompting him to continue on to the bluff behind his house where he could see the faint outline of Catalina Island on the horizon. The memory of what had taken place there suddenly came back to mind, causing him to question what Dusty Lewis was doing at that same moment?

Inside his office at DEA Headquarters in Virginia, Raymond Bronson sat across the table from Agent Dusty Lewis, watching with curious eyes as his attractive assistant played a disc that Lewis had delivered only minutes ago. Its significance lay in the fact that the disc contained crucial live testimony of Dan Hughes authenticating the source of every item of evidence that Neal Thomas had turned over to the DEA many weeks prior. Because of its importance in their effort to bring charges against the Tidewater Drug Cartel, very little conversation passed between Bronson and Lewis until the presentation ended. It was Bronson who opened the dialogue.

"I wish Neal Thomas, was working for us," Bronson remarked, as he went over to the CD player and unloaded the disc. Speaking to his assistant, he said, "Mark this confidential and place it in central lockup. No one is to have access to it without my permission. Is that clear?"

"Yes, Sir!" the assistant replied.

After she had left the room, Bronson sat down heavily at his desk and put his hands under his chin as if he were too tired to hold his head up. Seconds later, he looked wearily over at Dusty and said, "You're to be commended, Lewis. I'm afraid I've misjudged you, much as I hate to admit it."

Dusty felt a monumental wave of relief pass over him, but resisted showing it for fear of giving away how emotionally upset he had been. "If you don't mind my asking, Sir. What did you misjudge?"

"Your ability to differentiate between responsibility and friend-ship when you found out, like me, that Neal Thomas was a whole lot smarter than either of us had given him credit for. Your persistence gave us Miguel Ramirez, and two of his goons." Hesitating a moment to catch his breath, Bronson continued, "Make no mistake, that effort, and getting the disc here, will finally give us what we need to get rid of the Tidewater Cartel once and for all . Dan Hughes' testimony is what's important now, and to hell with the past."

"That pardon will finally set him free," Dusty remarked. "He's got it made."

"Not if the Cartel gets their hands of him," Bronson shot back.

"You honestly think Miguel Ramirez will give us enough informa-tion to prevent it?"

"Our people have interrogated him thoroughly enough to assure me that Dan Hughes has earned the right to go wherever he wants to, as long as he's smart enough to stay away from that bunch of bastards. If he doesn't, he's toast."

Again, there was a period of silence that followed Bronson's remarks. As he walked over to a window and looked wistfully up at storm clouds gathering in the distance, he said, "If I were you, I'd hop an early flight back to California, and get on with my life before it changes into some-thing ugly. Your work is finished here."

Dusty stood and waited for Bronson to turn around and face him, still hearing his words hanging in the air like a whistle warning. "I'm glad this investigation has worked out the way it has, Ray. I've been thinking about requesting a transfer to another division. The type of work I'm doing here is having a telling affect on my marriage, and I know Katie would welcome the change. Things haven't been all that good between us lately."

Bronson left the window and walked over to Dusty with his hand extended. As soon as he took it, Bronson said, "You'd be wise to listen to her. As I said, your work is finished here. Get out before it gets messy."

Later on that evening, as he sat in the airport waiting to catch a red-eye flight back to San Diego, Dusty thought about his meeting with Director Bronson and couldn't answer the question he had been asking himself all day: *Did I quit, or get fired?*

While Neal stood at the top of his bluff watching Dan Hughes approaching from the beach below, he wondered if Dan was as free a man as he thought he was. *Maybe from the DEA,* he conceded, *but what about the Cartel?* Putting his thoughts behind him as Dan reached the top of the stairs, Neal asked, "See anything interesting down there?"

"Yeah, as a matter of fact, I did," he replied, unfolding his hand to let something shiny fall from one finger. It was a necklace. Holding it up in front of Neal's face, he asked, "Anyone you know lost one of these recently?"

Upon closer inspection, Neal knew instinctively it was a valuable piece of women's jewelry. "Not that I know of," he admitted, straining to remember who he had seen wearing a similar one. "Where did you find it?"

"Anchored around a large beach stone half buried in the wet sand," Dan answered, still baffled as to how it could have gotten there. "Who would be foolish enough to wear this into the ocean?"

"A woman with a little too much to drink, possibly," Neal speculated. "I see guys with metal detectors roaming this beach all the time. You'd be amazed at what they find."

They were about to leave the bluff when the figure of a woman standing knee-deep in the ocean triggered the recollection of a similar scene Neal had witnessed several months ago. That woman, however, had removed her clothes in the privacy of the fallen sun to hide her nakedness while she wandered into the water, submerging herself several times before returning to the beach. *Could that have been the same woman who lost this necklace?* Neal asked himself. It seemed an almost impossible coincidence, yet something about the locket kept nagging at him that he had seen it before.

"Here, take this thing," Dan remarked, as they walked back toward the house. "I can see that it means more to you than it does to me. Let me know if you ever find out who lost it."

While Dan left to clean up for their evening out, Neal went into his studio and hung the lost necklace from his note board, hoping that its presence there would eventually remind him of its owner. When he heard the upstairs shower cut off, Neal bathed and dressed for dinner, totally ignorant of the far-reaching influence the evening would eventually have on the rest of his life.

There were only a couple of automobiles parked in front of the Sterling's impressive home when Neal and Dan arrived. One glistened with the luxurious look that only a freshly polished, black Cadillac limousine could exude.

Dan couldn't resist a humorous comment. "If that limo is any indication of what we're about to get our butts involved with, I'd say we're going to be hobnobbing with the upper crust this evening, Mr. T. Maybe we should park across the street and walk in."

Neal had to laugh. "Nah, I think I'll park behind it so old Bessy won't feel neglected."

As the two men walked into the front entrance, they were greeted by the butler, Ivan Olofson. Following a friendly exchange, he directed them to the patio where Sandy's other guests had gathered.

It was a small group, making it easy for Jessica Sterling to notice Neal and Dan when they made their entrance. Taking the initiative, she came over to welcome them. Smiling devilishly at Dan, she offered her hand. "Welcome. Haven't we met before?"

Laughter and jokes of a personal nature ensued, until Dan mentioned that he could use a drink. As Jessica turned to show him the way, she gave Neal some friendly advice, "Mother saw you come in. You'd better go over there and let her introduce you to her friends before you do anything else. Norma Manning is also with her."

Taking that as a reminder of social protocol, Neal made his way over to the table where Sandy Sterling and Norma Manning were being entertained by several men he had never met before. One of them nodded to Sandy that another guest had arrived. When she stood to greet Neal, he could tell by her gracious smile and demeanor that she was glad to see him. After a cordial embrace, she proceeded to introduce him to each of the other men, all of whom were friendly and welcomed him enthusiastically.

In way of further introduction, Sandy added, "This is the man I mentioned earlier who has written an unusually exciting fiction adventure novel. Sterling Publishing is currently editing it for publication. Neal also plays the piano beautifully, which I'm sure my friend and Chief Editor, Norma Manning, will attest to. Right Norma?"

"For an un-schooled musician, he ranks up there with the best of them," she replied, "I'm sure we can talk him into playing for us later on. Right now the poor guy needs a drink." Getting up and offering her chair, she said, "Sit down and get acquainted while I get you one. Vodka Tonic?"

Grateful for her thoughtful gesture, he nodded his approval and sat down, wondering where Dan and Jessica were. His curiosity was short-lived when one of the men, a slender, medium height man with graying curly hair, opened conversation by asking, "Ever heard of Futurama Pictures, Mr. Thomas?"

Neal challenged his memory for a moment before admitting, "No, I seldom go to movie theaters any more. Too easy to sit at home and watch them. Why? Are you guys in the movie business, Mr...?"

"Mitchell...Mark Mitchell," the man replied. "Actually, we're in the screen writing end of it. Simply put, we take an author's story and compress it into a two hour movie, sometimes longer, depending on its complexity and location."

"That's why they're here," Sandy explained. "Mark's in charge of screenplay development. I sent him a preliminary copy of your story to get his reaction. He called me from Hollywood a few days ago and said he liked the story and wanted to meet the author. I arranged this little get together so you could discuss the possibility of making it into a movie, after the book is published."

While the group was preoccupied with reviewing various details relating to the story, Norma Manning returned with Neal's drink. After looking at the others, she said, "Excuse me for interrupting, gentlemen, but I believe all of you could use a refill."

All agreed, and took a short break to replenish their drinks, and talked among themselves about storyline-related subject matter.

When they returned, Mitchell directed his attention toward Norma, and said, "I understand from Sandy that you are currently editing the draft of what she sent me. Can you give me an estimate of when you'll be finished?"

Norma thought about her progress to date and replied, "With Neal's help, I believe the book can be ready for publication in a month." Placing a fixed stare on Neal's blank expression, she smiled and added, "That is, if we can keep him from getting mixed up in other people's business for that long a time."

One of the other two men laughed. "Hell, that's what we call research, Norma. Getting mixed up in other people's business is how we get our material."

It was Sandy's turn. "Trust me, we'll keep his nose to the grindstone."

Amused by what was going on, Mitchell looked over at Neal and said, "Of course you realize that, sooner or later, you'll have to visit Hollywood to review our production in order to validate its adherence to your book. That, Mr. Thomas, is a twenty-four hour a day commitment that will include travel, and a disruption to your personal life for a while. Are you prepared to accept all of these inconveniences?"

Now it was Neal's turn to laugh. "What personal life?" he replied. "I haven't had one of those since I got married and had kids. Now I'm divorced and too damn old to remember what a personal life is. On top of all that, my estranged lady friend just informed me that she's met someone who has asked her to marry him, and she accepted. So I ask you, what kind of personal life are you talking about?"

The remark brought a chuckle from everyone there, especially Norma Manning, who remarked, "Welcome to the club, Mr. T. Looks like we'll be seeing a lot of each other from now on…in a working sense, that is."

As he paused momentarily to take a swallow of the drink Norma had fixed for him, Neal couldn't help but wonder if its potency hadn't been purposely intended. To confirm his suspicion he handed his near-empty glass to her and politely asked for a refill. "Anything that good deserves a second chance," he said with a grin. "I can't fly on just one wing."

During her absence, Neal took the opportunity to explain to the other men that his friend, Dan Hughes, was leaving for the East Coast the next day, and would no longer have a disruptive influence on his so-called personal life. "I've known Dan since he was a pup," he explained, "He was wild then, and still is to some extent. But I truly believe he's turned a crucial corner in his search for a meaningful future."

Though no one was paying much attention to the weather, Sandy noticed that the late afternoon sun was slowly disappearing into a thickening marine layer rapidly rolling in on La Jolla, prompting her to suggest that everyone adjourn to the family room until dinner was served.

"Where are Jessica and Dan?" she asked Neal, as Norma approached with his drink.

Overhearing the question, Norma remarked, "I believe they're having a private discussion about Dan's future plans. Apparently, Jessica became a little disgruntled when Dan mentioned that he was flying back to Virginia tomorrow morning."

"Is that true, Neal?" Sandy asked, obviously surprised. "We all assumed he would be staying here a little longer, since you've invited him to stay with you."

"So did I," Neal admitted, "but an anonymous phone call he received at the Hilton Inn made him nervous. Understandably, he decided to return home as soon as he could book a flight. After what he's been through, I can't say as I blame him."

"And I suppose you're taking him to the airport?" Norma asked.

Feeling as though he was being un-necessarily cross-examined, Neal replied, "He is my guest. I can't very well ask him to catch a cab."

The moment of awkward silence that followed began to make Neal feel as though he had interfered with some anticipated activity that

Sandy, Norma and Jessica had looked forward to after the group of screenwriters left for Hollywood. Out of curiosity, he turned toward Sandy as they were about to enter the house, and asked, "Did I miss something here? I thought I was invited to this dinner party so I could meet your friends and discuss my book. Why all of this sudden concern over Dan leaving tomorrow?"

Before Sandy could respond, Norma interrupted by commenting, "Unless you're blind, you must have observed that Jessica has very strong feelings for Dan, especially following their time together on Catalina Island. She had looked forward to spending a little more time with him, now that he is staying with you. I don't blame her for being a little upset."

Here I am in the middle again, Neal thought, as they entered the house and learned from Ivan that the men were gathered around the family room bar. Before entering, Neal stopped and tried to clarify the situation. "Look ladies, Dan and Jessica are perfectly capable of working this out by themselves. They don't need our interference. If you want my opinion, Dan's departure tomorrow is the best thing that could happen to Jessica. So lets go find your friends and give her and Dan a little privacy to iron out their differences." Attempting to ease the tension with a little humor, he smiled foolishly, and said, "After all, they're not married!"

Reluctantly accepting his rationale, Sandy and Norma accompanied Neal into the family room where they joined Mark Mitchell and his cronies engaged in telling liquor-flavored jokes and gossip from the Hollywood rumor mill.

Moments later, having temporarily settled their emotional differences, Dan and Jessica entered the room to join the others. A short time later, Ivan the butler announced that dinner was ready whenever the group wished to eat, which prompted Mitchell to remind Norma about Neal entertaining on the piano.

With fresh drinks all the way around, the boisterous group relocated to the living room. After some coaxing applause, Neal sat down at the grand piano and began playing a mix of popular ballads and soft jazz favorites. It was during his changeover to *Gone With The Wind's* classic theme song that Mark Mitchell leaned over to Norma Manning and whispered, "When did you say his book would be ready?"

Whispering back, she replied, "Don't mention this to Neal, but I'll probably have my editing done by the end of next week. Why do you ask?"

"I mentioned the story to a director friend of mine before coming down here. He expressed an interest in reading the screenplay. So send me a copy as soon as it goes to press."

Recognizing that Mark was being genuinely serious about his request, she said, "I'll deliver it personally."

Waiting politely until after Neal had finished the song he was playing, Ivan the butler returned and encouraged everyone to eat. "Before it gets cold!"

For the better part of the next hour, the congenial group forgot about business and amused themselves by talking about their contemporary lives and backgrounds. For reasons of his own, Dan Hughes remained understandably quiet until one of the screenwriters asked, "Tell me, Mr. Hughes, what's your connection with Sterling Publishing?"

Dan's momentary struggle to put together some believable reply prompted Jessica to come to his rescue, rather than let him embarrass himself in front of strangers. "Dan and I met in the Caribbean while we were both there on business," Jessica explained. "His small airplane made an emergency landing on the beach near where I was staying."

"What an adventure," one of the screenwriters remarked, looking over at Dan. "Were you injured?"

"The nose gear broke when I landed, knocking me unconscious for awhile," Dan replied. "Jessica saw the accident and looked after me until my friends could come and get me."

"Thanks to Mr. T, Dan and I were re-united only three days ago," Jessica explained further. "I never dreamed I'd see him again after he left that island."

With his eyes growing heavier by the minute, and having to get up early the next morning, Neal decide it was time for he and Dan to head up the freeway. "I hate to leave such charming company," he said, struggling to hold back a yawn, "but Dan and I had better be getting on home, or I'll never get his ornery butt on that plane tomorrow."

"That goes triple for us," Mitchell added, "We have a two hour drive back to Hollywood, if the traffic behaves." Turning to Neal, he shook his hand and said, "I enjoyed your music. And I look forward to receiv-

291

ing a copy of your book when it's published. Sandy and Norma will keep you informed on how we are progressing along those lines."

About that time, a middle-aged man in a dark suit entered the room from the kitchen. As he passed by, he smiled and waved, then left.

"That's our limo driver," Mitchell remarked. "A damn good investment for this time of night." Then they said goodnight and left, leaving Neal and Dan to do the same. Following a hug or two, Sandy bid them all goodnight and quietly disappeared upstairs.

Sensing that Dan and Jessica would appreciate a moment of privacy before they parted, Neal took Norma by the hand. "Come on, I'll walk you to your car. Those two need to be alone for a couple of minutes before we leave."

"So do we," Norma whispered back, suggestively "It's nice and dark out there."

Back at Neal's house Dan lit a cigarette and fixed a drink, mentioning to Neal, "Let's take a walk out on the bluff while I smoke this thing. I need to throttle down a little before I hit the sack."

Figuring, *why not*, Neal also mixed a drink and walked side-by-side with him out to the bluff. Moments later, Dan looked wistfully out over the ocean and said, "It's a good thing I decided to head home tomorrow, Mr. T. I'm afraid Jessica was expecting more from me than I'm prepared to give."

"I was afraid it was going that way," Neal commented. "You made the right decision, though. Long distance romances rarely amount to anything more than running up a phone bill, and somebody getting his or her heart broken. Who needs that?"

Putting out his cigarette, Dan flicked the butt toward the ocean and coughed. "I told her I loved her," he admitted reluctantly. "But then I got to thinking; I would never fit in with the kind of life she lives. I'd be like tits on a boar hog. I should have kept my big mouth shut, I guess."

"Don't beat yourself up over it, Dan. I know Jessica well enough to know that she's not going to sit around pining over you for very long." Laughing over the obvious differences in their backgrounds, Neal continued: "Can you see yourself sitting behind a desk at Sterling Publishing Company for the rest of your life?"

Dan coughed again. After grunting out a laugh, he replied, "What the hell would I do, empty the waste paper baskets?"

Not very long after the two men returned to the house, Neal laid awake for a few minutes remembering the embrace he and Norma Manning had shared before parting that evening. His lips curled into a grin as he re-thought the arousal he had experienced when she fondled him below the waist, and mouthed his tongue, suggestively. Finally closing his tired eyes, he thought, *that's what dreams are made of.*

Chapter 18

Picking Up The Pieces

Dan Hughes was already in the shower when Neal's alarm clock sounded the next morning. It was six o'clock. While he waited for Dan to finish, Neal mulled over what he had to do that day and realized that taking Dan to the airport and meeting Ginger Spyce for lunch were the only two commitments he had. *Finally, a little time of my own,* he thought, as the hall bathroom shower stopped running and Dan returned to his room.

Several minutes later, dressed casually for the day, Neal found Dan talking on his cell phone in the kitchen when he came down the stairs. Based on his frequent reference to names that he recognized, Neal concluded that he had contacted his father.

"That's right, Dad, my flight arrives in Norfolk at six p.m. your time," he said, rolling his eyes at Neal. "Yes, I'm alone," he continued… "No, it's still in the Bahamas…I'll talk to you about that when I get home…Yes, I'll tell him…See you tonight…Bye."

After shutting down his cell phone, Dan shifted his eyes to Neal. "Pop says hi, and wants to thank you for all your help. He says he's expecting you to visit us after things settle down a bit. No excuses."

"That's very kind of Henry. I could use a little getaway time whenever you say it's okay." Reflecting on the past for a moment, he asked, "I've wondered… whatever happened to Vicki Daniels. Does she still live at the beach?"

295

Dan thought for a moment and replied, "As far as I know, she does. I'll look into it and give you a call after I get back." Reflecting on the past again, he remarked, "You thought a lot of Vicki, didn't you, Mr. T?"

"Damn right I did," Neal admitted, smiling reflectively. "A man my age doesn't forget a woman who gave him the kind of attention she did. Please convey my fondest regards if you happen to see her."

"Roger that," Dan assured him, glancing at his watch. "Shouldn't we be leaving for the airport about now?"

"Unfortunately, it's that time, my friend. Grab your bags and we'll get you airborne."

Several minutes after they drove onto the freeway, Dan said, "When you have lunch with Ginger Spyce today, please pass on my gratitude for all the confidential information she provided. You and I could have ended up in the slammer had it not been for her. I only wish I could have met her. Is she attractive?"

Neal smiled, knowing what was always on Dan's mind when it came to women. "Let me put it this way," he replied, intentionally teasing his imagination, "If I were to introduce you to her right now, you wouldn't be getting on a plane in a couple of hours."

"Hmmm," Dan grumbled, rubbing his chin, "Maybe I should have stayed a few days longer."

"And you would tell Jessica Sterling what?"

"Hmmm," he grumbled again, and then laughed. "I'm too young to die, Mr. T. Get me the hell out of Dodge!"

There was little time to waste on meaningless conversation when Neal came to a stop in front of Delta's baggage check-in station, other than, "Have a good flight, and tell Henry I'll be in touch. And do me a favor...stay out of trouble!"

As was his way, Dan just grinned and said, "How can I? It's my middle name." In seconds he was gone.

Because it was nearing the end of summer, traffic en route to Balboa Park was less congested than Neal had anticipated, allowing him an early arrival at the Del Prado Restaurant. Judging from the number of customers who had already gathered there, only about half the tables were occupied. Because the nature of his meeting with Ginger Spyce was of a private nature, the waitress was able to seat him at a corner table where being overheard would be less likely. Placing his briefcase within easy reach, he ordered a chilled bottle of wine and perused the menu.

A minute or two later, while his attention had been distracted by a familiar melody of background music, an un-noticed female approached his table and whispered, "Little Jack Horner sat in a corner, thinking, that song I can play."

Amused by her novel approach, Neal stood up and gave his guest a friendly embrace. "What a treat it is to see you again, my dear. How have you been?"

Ginger seated herself immediately and poured a glass of wine. "Considering the news I have to share with you, I'd say, pretty damn good," she replied pleasantly. "And you?"

"Well, I just put Dan Hughes on a plane back to Virginia, so you can imagine how good that makes me feel. Now, what news have you brought with you?"

Sneaking a quick glance around the immediate area, she said softly, "Your friend, Dusty Lewis, just returned from delivering Dan Hughes' testimony. I don't know what Director Bronson said to him back there, but Agent Lewis has processed a request for a transfer to another department outside the DEA. Now why would he do that?"

Rather than reveal what he suspected was Dusty's motivation for making such a sudden move, Neal chose to camouflage it under the cloak of departmental politics and replied, "I think Dusty has hit the ceiling of advancement in your department, and is searching for something more challenging. Probably a wise move at his age."

Ginger's brow took on a reflective wrinkle, as she offered a speculative comment, "I seem to recall a remark his wife made at our office party last Christmas. She implied that she was not too happy with the demands the DEA was putting on its employees. Especially the excessive time they were spending away from home. Maybe that pot finally came to a boil!"

"That could very well be part of the problem," Neal remarked, relieved he didn't have to express his opinion on the matter. "I'll miss seeing him occasionally."

"What am I, burnt toast?" she asked, feigning a pout. "Aren't we going to remain friends?"

"Depends," he answered, reaching for his briefcase.

"On what?"

"Your reaction to what's in this briefcase."

Ginger's expression went blank with puzzlement. Shifting uneasily in her chair, and gulping down a swallow of wine, she asked, suspiciously, "You're not getting kinky on me are you, Mr. T?"

"Not hardly," he laughed. "It's just a token of thanks for keeping Dan and me appraised of what Dusty and the DEA were up to when I was making plans to get Dan out of Mexico. Your information allowed us to secretly record his testimony on that disc Bronson wanted. Without it, the DEA would never have been able to indict the Tidewater Cartel."

Peering into the briefcase after Neal opened it, Ginger's eyes grew wide with surprise when she saw the Ziploc bag bulging with money. "Oh…my…God!" she gasped. "How much is in there?"

"Thirty-thousand dollars, to be exact," Neal explained. "Enough to build a good retirement income if you invest it wisely. It was Dan's idea."

Ginger still hadn't moved, her eyes remaining fixed on the money. Then, as if someone had put drops in her eyes, Neal noticed they began glistening with tears, overflowing down both cheeks. Noticing their waitress approaching, he handed Ginger his napkin and closed the briefcase.

"Are you all right, miss?" the waitress asked, visibly concerned.

Ginger quickly regained her composure and wiped her eyes dry. "I've never been happier in my life," she sniffled, winking at Neal. "When's the last time a dirty old man proposed to you?"

Momentarily caught off guard by Ginger's reply, and the blank look on Neal's face, the waitress began to laugh, and continued to do so intermittently throughout their ordering. When they finished, she took back the menus with eyes still wet from laughing, and said, "Congratulations, I think you make a darling couple."

The hour that followed passed quickly with pleasantries, laughter and the comfort that comes from the promise of a lasting friendship. Even their waitress, who still had her doubts about what was going on, acknowledged their so-called engagement with another bottle of wine, compliments of the house.

Since it was already three o'clock, Ginger made the decision not to return to work that afternoon. She felt uncomfortable having consumed so much wine, and wanted to put the money in the bank. Recognizing that she was exercising good judgment, he advised her to go outside, phone her office and wait for him in the parking lot.

Several minutes later Neal left the restaurant and saw Ginger standing by her car waving at him. By the time he reached her, she had already gotten in and rolled the window down. "I hate saying goodbye this way," she said, giggling a little. "After all, we are engaged now."

Neal laughed. "We sure had that waitress in a tizzy, didn't we." Opening his briefcase, he withdrew the plastic bag containing the thirty thousand dollars and handed it to her. "Put this in your glove compartment and keep it locked until you get to the bank." Looking around cautiously, he asked, "Don't you have something you can hide this in until you get inside the bank?"

"My bowling ball is in the trunk. I can use the bag."

"Perfect! Now get out of here before one of the security guards gets suspicious."

"What, no kiss goodbye?"

Neal smiled, and leaned his head into the open window, thinking, *I thought you'd never ask.*

Cupping his face with both hands, she met him full on, holding her lips on his for a few seconds. "I wish I could give you more, Mr. T. Hopefully, we'll meet again some sunny day, as the song goes. Until then, take care of yourself. Give my best wishes to Dan when you see him again. He's a good-hearted man."

Following Ginger's departure, Neal remained at the spot where she had left him for a few moments, watching with squinted eyes as her car disappeared in traffic. A feeling of emptiness suddenly chilled him, as he turned and walked back to his car with one re-occurring question on his mind, *now what?*

At his home in Del Mar, Ron Barns was relaxing in a recliner playing computer solitaire when he noticed a car parking in front of his house. He recognized the white, 4-door sedan immediately as belonging to his closest friend, Neal Thomas. Checking the time, his eyebrows raised with curiosity. It was neither a pool-shooting Tuesday, nor had

Neal given him prior notice that he would be stopping by that after-noon. *What's he up to now*, Ron questioned, as he watched Neal cross the lawn and enter the house. "Are you lost, or just bored to death?"

"Neither," Neal replied, as he proceeded directly into the kitchen to mooch a drink from the bottle of vodka Ron kept on top of his refrigerator. "First off, I took Dan Hughes to the airport early this morning to catch a ten o'clock flight back to his home in Virginia." Returning with his drink to take a seat near Ron, he continued: "Then I had lunch with a friend of mine from the DEA office in San Diego."

"Dusty Lewis?"

"No, his secretary, Ginger Spyce," Neal explained. "I had to give her a package that Dan Hughes wanted me to deliver. There's more to the story, but I'll spare you the details."

Ron laughed and shook his head. "You never cease to amaze me, my friend. Aren't you ever going to slow down and smell the roses?"

Neal took a sip of his drink and looked wistfully out over the lagoon in the distance. "I'd probably drop dead if I did, but there is good news."

"Oh, really!" Ron remarked, in his classic response to the unbelievable. "That's a switch. May I ask what it is?"

Reflecting on the evidence that Dan had mailed him before he fled the country, Neal explained: "Dan's a free man now. That disc you copied for me the other day is now being used to bring indictments against the Cartel ringleaders, and was the bargaining chip that put him on that plane this morning."

"That's all well and good, my friend, but what did you get out of all this?"

Neal thought about the money stored in his grandfather's travel bag sitting inconspicuously on a shelf in his garage and replied, "The satisfaction of having saved a friend's life, and the wonderful friends and other people who have benefited from it along the way, myself included."

Ron continued flipping cards busily from one place to another on his computer screen until a musical note signaled that another game had been added to the thousands of games he had already won. Smiling at the results, he said, "I seem to recall you saying, on occasion, if you can't eat it, drink it, or screw it, it ain't worth much. Still feel that way?"

Neal was careful to respond ambiguously, recalling the many times he had uttered that phrase in the past. "To some degree, but not always," he answered, "Depends on what you're eating, drinking or screwing, I guess."

"You're a sly old fox," Ron conceded. "Truthfully now, what else is going on in that crazy head of yours? How's the book coming along?"

During the ensuing hour, Neal explained, chronologically, how the book he had begun over a year ago had progressed to its current status, including the results that evolved from the dinner party he and Dan Hughes had attended the previous evening.

"Now that Dan is finally on his way home, I guess I'll be working full time on getting my book published. Those screenwriters from Hollywood seemed very interested in getting their hands on the published version."

"Here we go again," Ron remarked, finally shutting down his computer and standing up. "What do you say we launch this new adventure at Bully's? I'm buying."

Though he knew it would be a much smarter choice to go home, Neal couldn't deny his friend's offer to join him for a drink at a place they had been frequenting for years. Besides, there was nothing at home that demanded his attention for a change, other than reading the day's mail. *That could wait until tomorrow.* "Sure, why not?" he replied. "Save me a seat at the high bar."

On the East Coast at approximately that same time, the Delta jetliner carrying Dan Hughes had just touched down at Norfolk International Airport.

In his black Cadillac sedan, accompanied by an attractive lady friend sitting on the front seat next to him, Henry Hughes waited for his son to exit the large baggage claim area. It had been almost a year since the two men had seen one another, so there was some degree of anxiety attached to the long-awaited homecoming. For that reason, Helen Farmer had agreed to accompany Henry to the airport to act as a buffer when the two men finally came face to face.

"I've never seen you quite this nervous before," Helen remarked. "Is there something bothering you?"

"The weather, I guess. Dan's boat is still down in the Bahamas where hurricane Louise is headed."

"Surely he's not crazy enough to attempt going down there with an evacuation order in affect."

Henry's head turned slowly in her direction, his tired eyes gazing over the top of his glasses. "You don't know my son. He *is* that crazy."

About that time, several of the doors exiting the baggage claim area near Henry's car swung open, and a steady flow of people poured out heading in all directions. It didn't take long for Henry to recognize the grinning face of his son among them, walking hurriedly toward the car with a suitcase dangling from each arm.

After popping the trunk lid open, Henry left the car to greet Dan, hugging him affectionately and helping him stow his luggage. Before getting back in, he took Dan aside. "I brought Helen Farmer along for company tonight, so be careful what you say. I haven't acquainted her with all the gory details of where you've been, and what you've been doing. For her sake, the less she knows the better. Okay?"

Dan laughed goodheartedly, "Don't worry, Dad, I won't embarrass you."

For most of the trip home, conversation between the three adults concentrated on family and business matters which Henry purposely orchestrated so that Dan would not have to be exposed to questions Helen might ask about his past. She, on the other hand, was not about to be denied the opportunity to satisfy her own curiosity. Exercising that prerogative, she addressed Dan directly. "Pardon my asking, but I don't get the connection between you owning a boat in the Bahamas, and flying home from California. Do you have business in both places?"

Noticing how quickly Henry had shot an almost irritating look of disapproval in Helen's direction, Dan concluded that she had probably crossed a threshold of inquiry that his father wanted limited. So rather than getting into the specifics of that dilemma, Dan replied, "I went to California to research a piece of timeshare property that my father had invested in some years ago. I stayed with an old friend of the family by the name of Neal Thomas, a retired engineer who lives on the ocean near that same piece of property. He's the guy who drove me to the airport this morning."

Satisfied that Helen had believed his son, Henry took over answering the other half of her question by explaining, "I also have property in the Bahamas that Dan frequents periodically when clients show an interest. He has a boat their for entertaining those clients."

"Great fishing," Dan added in support of the lie. "That's why we're watching the progress of hurricane Louise so closely. Losing that boat would be very costly."

Helen seemed to buy into the explanation, changing her line of inquiry to one of a more personal nature. "What are your plans for the future, now that you've returned to the nest?"

Observing that Henry had exited the highway and would soon be entering the residential area where Helen lived, Dan condensed his reply into one that was intended to be open-ended. "Dad has mentioned to me that he would like to semi-retire, now that I'm available to assume more responsibility. So I've decided to try and help him do that. All things considered, I think it's time I thought about settling down. I'm sure he's happy to hear me say that."

"Amen, brother," Henry sighed with relief. "I wish your mother was alive to hear those words."

Dan laughed. "Can't you just hear her – I'll believe *that* when I see it!"

When they entered the driveway to Helen's home a few minutes later, Helen insisted that there was no need for Henry to walk her to the door and said goodnight. Waiting until she had safely entered her home and the lights came on, Henry backed out and headed for home, content for the first time in years that there just might be a light at the end of the tunnel.

Driving down Camino Del Mar on his way to meet Ron Barns at Bully's, Neal Thomas wondered how close Dan Hughes was to arriving in Norfolk. He smiled with contentment at the thought that Dan was finally free of the past that had threatened his life on several occasions, and could look forward to a normal relationship with his family and friends again.

I hope Dan follows through with that part, Neal thought when he parked in the lot next to Bully's and joined the bustling, late afternoon gathering at the bar. Ron was already there, and had a drink waiting for Neal when he arrived. Familiar faces of others who had come to be known as *the regulars* were also present, each expressing their pleasure in seeing Neal again. It was during this mayhem of cross-conversation that Neal felt Ron tap him on the shoulder and nod in the direction of the front door. Turning in that direction, he saw Russ Chandler following close behind Judy Bass, as they proceeded straight-faced past the high bar, down the main aisle and out onto the open patio.

"They must be feuding again," Ron remarked. "Rumor has it, things are not going too well with them lately. She retired recently, and apparently regrets having done so."

"Did they ever get married, or are they still living separately?" Neal asked.

Ron shrugged his shoulder, implying that he didn't know. "Just be glad you had your fling with her and got out when the getting was good," he commented. "Those in the know say Judy caught Russ with another woman recently and is definitely not a happy camper."

Remembering the brief but torrid affair he had with Judy when Russ crossed over the *don't go there* line once before, Neal wondered why she continued to put up with his philandering. Still attractive and physically well preserved, she was a good catch for someone looking for a serious relationship.

From where he was seated, Neal could see Judy on the patio facing Russ. Both their expressions were emotionless, frequently looking away from one another as if in search of someone. At that very moment, Judy's eyes turned toward the high bar and established point-to-point contact with his, locking on like a radar signal from a guided missile. The soft smile that followed caused Neal concern that she might make an attempt to approach him. Finishing his drink with one large swallow, he excused himself on the grounds that he was tired and needed to get home.

Ron and the others expressed their disappointment with his sudden decision to leave, but sympathized with his wish to get home before dark and toasted him on his way.

Neal had just about reached the front door when a waitress he had known for years called out to him. "Mr. T! Hold up! I have a message for you."

While he stood in the halo of light over the front entrance, she rushed up and handed Neal a note. "You old fart, what have you been up to?" she asked suspiciously. "Judy Bass asked me to give you this note." Shaking her head and giggling, she turned and left.

Waiting until he was inside his car to open the folded paper napkin, he read the note: *Give me a call sometime. Russ needs another wake up call!!*

Amused by the clever phrasing of her discreet solicitation, Neal waited until he passed by one of the trashcans in the alley to get rid of it. *Thanks, but no thanks*, he mused. *Once was enough.*

The Village Pub parking lot was almost full when Neal arrived there late that same afternoon hoping to find Anita Cassidy still there. He was in luck. She had just come out of the back door when he rounded the corner. Lowering the window, he shouted, "Timing is everything! Can I give you a lift home? I really don't need another drink."

"Then why'd you come here in the first place?" she replied, coming nearer. "Where's your buddy?"

"I put Dan on a plane for home this morning," he replied, sensing some irritability. "I'm here because I was interested in how you and your mother were getting along. Sorry if I caught you at a bad time. You okay?"

Without responding, she walked around to the passenger door and sank heavily into the front seat beside him. "Sorry if I snapped at you, Mr. T." she said apologetically. "This has been one hell of a day. Thanks for the lift."

Neal remained quiet for several minutes, hoping that his offer of a ride home would intimidate a response. They were coming up on the street where she lived when Anita rolled her head toward him and said "The Pub gave me a week's notice today."

"Why?"

"The owner's daughter just graduated from Nursing School. She wants to work at The Pub until she can find a nursing job in North County."

"What's the problem? Isn't your mother expecting you to come to San Francisco in two weeks anyway? You'll have a week to ship your stuff home and get the hell out of here."

"That's true, but the lease on my apartment isn't up until the end of the month, and I'll lose my deposit if I leave before then. I need that money to pay off my bills."

Conscious that Anita hadn't yet fully comprehended what being Gloria Donaldson's daughter meant to her financially, he asked, "How much is the deposit?"

"One month's rent. That amounts to seven-hundred and fifty dollars!"

Rather than mock her emotional-concern over such a paltry amount, considering the money she was soon to inherit, Neal said, "Buy me that drink I don't need, and I'll tell you what we're going to do about that. Got any Vodka up there?"

"Does a bear poop in the woods?" she replied, laughing for the first time. "As Clint would say…Make my day."

As soon as they entered her apartment, Anita went straight to the kitchen cupboard and brought down a half-empty bottle of vodka that had been there since Neal's last visit. Pouring a double shot over a glass filled with ice, she added tonic and sat it on the table in front of him. "I'll be right with you," she said, obviously in a better humor. "I need a glass of wine."

Neal nodded, envious of the innocent sexuality she exuded with every movement.

Moments later, she sat down across from him and said, "So tell me, Mr. T, just how do you propose to fix this mess I'm in?"

Having already pieced together what seemed to be a reasonable plan, he replied, "First of all, I want you to finish out your week as pleasantly as you can. Say your goodbyes, and don't tell anyone where you're going."

"Just like that? No party? No nothing?"

"Exactly," Neal replied with steadfast resolve. "One week from to-day you're going to be Anita Donaldson for the rest of your life. Anita Cassidy will only be a memory. It's as simple as that. So, start preparing yourself for that day right now."

"You're serious, aren't you?"

"Dead serious," Neal replied. "Where you're headed you can't afford to look back. Your future is all that's important."

"What about my rent deposit? I'm not Anita Donaldson yet."

"I'll give you the money. Call it a loan, or a going away present… whatever. The important thing is, get back to San Francisco where you can build a new life for yourself. How many people have that as an option?"

"Not many," she replied. "By the same token, how many people are lucky enough to have you as a friend?"

It was time to go. The vodka was beginning to generate thoughts of violating a basic code of behavior for men his age: *Don't make a fool of yourself.*

After discarding what was left of his drink, Neal took a few swallows of water, and said, "I better get going. I have a busy day ahead of me tomorrow. Call me when your week is up. I'll find a place for you to stay until you leave for San Francisco. When will you need the seven-fifty?"

"The day I leave," she replied, her eyes starting to tear a little. "I have enough in the bank to pay my bills and close out the account. I'll call my mother tomorrow so she can make plane reservations for me. I'll call you when I have the details."

Realizing how emotionally upsetting it must have been to be pressured into this situation, Neal reacted as if it were happening to one of his own daughters. "On second thought," he reconsidered, "why don't we…"

"We?" she responded, with a marked expression of surprise. "What's on your mind, Mr. T?"

Pacing the floor for a moment, Neal suddenly spun around and said, "Wouldn't it be simpler if you stayed at my place until you leave for San Francisco. You've already paid this month's rent. So finish out your week at the Pub, ship your personal belongings to your mother's place and stay with me until your ticket arrives. She can send it to me via my e-mail address. I'll drive you to the airport."

Unprepared for such generosity, Anita remained silent until she could grasp the consequences of accepting it. "Do you think my mother would approve?" she finally asked. "This is certainly not the time to arouse any suspicions about *our* relationship."

"You leave your mother to me," Neal advised. "I'll make sure she understands that my intentions are in your best interest."

Anita giggled. "Are you sure of that?"

From the bottom of her apartment stairs, Neal turned and waved goodbye to the smiling face of a woman whose mother he had been sexually intimate with only a couple of days ago. Almost embarrassed by the thought, he waved back and said, "Call when you want me to pick you up. Good luck!"

"Thanks, Mr. T. Keep that Jacuzzi of yours nice and hot!"

It was pitch black when the headlights on Neal's car searched their way up his winding driveway. The uncomfortable feeling that came from an empty stomach reminded him that it had been ten hours since he had lunch. Content with being finally alone, he immediately set about making a sandwich to eat while he watched the evening news and opened his mail.

He had only eaten part of the sandwich when a live CNN news report from Miami Beach, Florida broke in on local broadcasting to announce that Hurricane Louise had been upgraded to category 3, based on information they had just received from airplanes tracking the storm near the Bahamas.

For a moment, Neal sat almost mesmerized by the camera shots that were being shown to dramatize the storms growing intensity. The two thoughts that came to mind immediately were Dan's expressed concern about his boat, and a necklace he had found half-buried in the sand yesterday. The same necklace that now hung from a large thumbtack on his office note board. Still intrigued by why it seemed so familiar, he set the food aside and walked to his office to take another look, hoping it might remind him of where he had seen it before. Though he had taken the time to restore the chain and locket to their original luster, the locket itself was too fragile to attempt to open, so he thought, *Maybe I should take it to a jeweler.*

Returning to the living room, he put the rest of his half-eaten sandwich in the refrigerator, turned off the television and climbed the stairs to his bedroom thinking, *I'll do that tomorrow.*

Chapter 19

Glimpses Of The Future

Oddly enough, the first thought that came to mind when Neal Thomas opened his eyes the next morning was, *I wonder if I got any phone messages yesterday?*

Normally a twice-a-day ritual, he attributed the oversight to the distracting events associated with Dan Hughes' sudden departure, and the necklace Dan had found on the beach the day before he left. Though the discovery held no clue to whom it might have belonged, something about its size and shape kept insisting that he had seen it before. Mildly concerned that his power of recall was not functioning as well as it had in the past, he was certain that, in time, it would return. Meanwhile, the incident had no direct bearing on what he had planned today, so he showered and dressed for some long-overdue domestic activity that needed taking care of.

As was his habit, he glanced briefly at the phone when he entered the kitchen to see if the message diode was blinking. Typically, it was. Trying to avoid its annoying presence while preparing breakfast was like ignoring a pesky fly, so he stopped and pushed the *PLAY* button. *"You have one message"*:

"Message one: Neal, this is Norma Manning. Please call my office. I have some information for you. Hope all is well…Bye."

Neal progressed as far as making a pot of coffee when the phone rang. "It's alive!" he shouted with irritation, as he picked up the receiver. "This is Neal."

"Hi, Daddy, this is Karen," his oldest daughter's voice greeted him. "How are you?"

"Karen who?" he teased.

"Your oldest and most beautiful daughter," she teased back, "or have you forgotten you have one?"

"Not much chance of that. How are Derek and young Bobby doing?"

"You can ask them yourself, if you're not busy next Sunday. We're planning a family get-together here at our house. Can you make it?"

"I wouldn't miss it for the world. What time?"

"About three o'clock. It's a pool party, so don't forget your swim suit."

"I won't, dear. Thanks for calling."

Except for the occasional squawking of seagulls circling the beach, the next half-hour remained undisturbed so Neal could relax and enjoy his breakfast while reading the newspaper. A glance at the wall clock a few minutes later, however, indicated that the Sterling Publishing Company business day had started over an hour ago, reminding him that if he wanted to remain in Norma Manning's good graces, he had better call her right away. After a few bars of canned music, she answered. "Thanks for returning my call so promptly," she said. "Has Huckleberry Finn left yet?"

Amused by her storybook characterization of Dan Hughes, he replied, "Yes, I'm pleased to report. I put him on the plane yesterday morning. He wanted to get back home before Hurricane Louise arrived."

"I thought Louise's current path was toward the Bahamas."

"It is," Neal agreed, "but Dan's boat is still there. Knowing him, he'll try to rescue it if the storm suddenly turns north and doesn't make landfall."

"I hope he doesn't do anything foolish," Norma commented, "I'd hate to lose such an amusing character that way."

Surprised by her almost motherly concern, Neal laughed and said, "He'll be okay. He has a guardian angel looking over him. Now, what was it you wanted to talk to me about?"

"I've finally finished editing your novel," she replied, "but before I can release it to our publishing department, I need you to sign off on my changes, as well as approve the hardcover jacket artwork and personal profile information. I was thinking we could have lunch somewhere and wrap this whole thing up."

Amazed by Norma's progress report and what she was expecting of him, Neal had no other choice but to agree with her suggestion. "Where and what time?"

"The Marine Room at the La Jolla Beach and Tennis Club. One o'clock. My treat."

"I'll be there."

Walking out onto his patio deck to determine how badly the lawn needed mowing, Neal shrugged his shoulders and returned inside, thinking optimistically, *there's always tomorrow.*

It was high noon in Virginia when Henry Hughes and his son, Dan, climbed aboard Henry's twin-engine cabin cruiser to enjoy a welcome home lunch at a local marina called Knotts Landing. Though it appeared small from the outside, the inside was surprisingly spacious, offering a water view dining room, a well-equipped kitchen and a cozy bar.

As soon as Henry eased the boat's bumpers up against the dock, Dan jumped down and secured the bow and stern lines, his mind seemingly preoccupied with what was happening to his own boat in the Bahamas.

Once Henry had shut down the engines, he joined Dan on the dock and said reassuringly, "If it eases your mind any, Helen Farmer just called to tell me that the twelve o'clock weather news has reported a slight change in Hurricane Louise's direction. She thought you would appreciate knowing that there's a good chance the eye of the storm might miss the Bahamas all together."

"That is good news," Dan admitted with some sign of relief. "Lets just hope it isn't headed up this way."

Inside the restaurant the usual gathering of locals who enjoyed the luxury of mixing business with pleasure had already gathered. Fortunately, Henry had called ahead and reserved a table facing the scenic inlet. After they were seated, an attractive waitress came over to take their orders. In a southern accent you could cut with a knife, she stared at Dan and said, "Bless my soul! Is that you, Dan Hughes? I thought you had fallen off the planet. Good to see you again."

Flattered by the attention, Dan took quick notice of her nametag and replied, "Good to see you again too, Melissa. I'll have a bourbon and Ginger Ale for starters."

"How about you, Mr. Hughes?" she asked with flirting eyes. "What tickles your fancy today?"

"A glass of Chardonnay will do just fine, thank you. We'll order lunch later."

"Fine. "Y'all sit tight, ya hear. I'll be back in a minute."

Dan watched her hips roll all the way to the bar. Turning toward Henry, he remarked, "Southern fried chicken! Ain't nothing like it anywhere. Sure is good to be home again, Pop."

In less time than Henry had anticipated, Melissa returned with their drinks. "Enjoy," she said melodically. "Flag me down when you want to order."

Her quick departure provided Henry with the opportunity to discuss what had been on his mind ever since he got up this morning. "Is it too soon to ask what you intend to do for a living, now that you're back home? Permanently, I hope."

As if he had read his father's mind, Dan looked across the rippling inlet and replied, "I was serious last night when I told Helen Farmer that I wanted to help you retire. After all, I was your best salesman at one point in time. It's time we switched places so you can travel and enjoy yourself. I've had my fill of it."

"What about your boat? You're not going to give up on it, are you?"

"No. But I have to wait until Hurricane Louise makes up her mind about what the hell she's going to do. Once she does, I'll know how to proceed with getting my boat back. The *Foxy Lady* is a valuable asset in our kind of business, Dad. We're talking first class entertainment here. And, she'll come in mighty handy for researching that waterfront property poor old Shark Hadley left me."

"You boys ready for another," Melissa asked, interrupting Henry before he could answer.

"One more, then we'll eat," Henry replied abruptly.

Following her departure, Henry leaned over toward Dan and whispered, with some aggravation, "When were you going to tell me about this Shark Hadley property? We've never discussed it."

Dan feigned mild amusement, as he drained his glass and replied, "Truth is, I had forgotten all about that piece of property until I ran across the deed while searching through a box of old records this morning."

"And...?"

"I remembered showing it to Neal Thomas when he came back to Billy Newman's wake months ago. We joked about the feasibility of building a high-end condominium complex on it, including a fancy restaurant, a bar, and a golf course. I thought it was a crazy idea at the time, but now... I'm not so sure."

Out of the corner of his eye, Henry noticed Melissa returning with their drinks, and cautioned Dan, "Let's talk about this after lunch. I don't want anyone to overhear what you have to say."

After agreeing to meet with Norma Manning for lunch, Neal proceeded directly to his office and turned on his computer, the intent being to have something in hand when he and Norma met that would express his own ideas of how the book summary and personal profile should be written. Looking at his watch an hour later, he realized he was running out of time if he wanted to change his clothes and make it to La Jolla on time. Quickly printing a copy, he put it in his briefcase and changed into attire more suitable for the restaurant she had selected.

The drive to La Jolla brought back pleasant memories of days when Neal used to meet with his fellow scuba divers on weekends to explore the underwater beauty of the waters off La Jolla beaches. *A world like no other*, he thought as he wound his way down La Jolla Shores Drive and followed the familiar side streets to The Club.

Norma was waiting to greet Neal when he entered the Marine Room. She led him to an ocean view window where a large bottle of white wine sat chilling in an ice bucket. "I hope you took the afternoon off," Neal joked when he seated her. "That's a lot of wine."

"How else would I celebrate my achievements?" she replied. "As for taking the afternoon off... well, let's just play that one by ear."

As the meeting progressed, Norma revealed that she had committed herself to hand deliver a published copy of his novel to Mark Mitchell at Futurama Pictures. "I guess that's why I've been pressing you so hard recently," she admitted. "I don't want their interest in making a movie to cool off."

After refilling both their wine glasses again, Norma reached down and opened her briefcase. Removing a thick, letter-size manuscript, she handed it to Neal and said, "This is my edited version of your book. Read it carefully and mark anything you would like changed. When we both agree it's what we want the world to read, it goes to press. When can I expect it back?"

Overwhelmed by the urgency her question seemed to demand, Neal rested back against his chair and thought about the important commitments he had made with people who were counting on him. Anita Cassidy was one, but not until she was ready to move in with him. Realistically, however, he couldn't treat her presence there as something that would hinder his work in any way. All that seemed to remain was his daughter's party...a *few hours on Sunday*.

"Can you give me a week?" he asked. "I just can't drop everything I'm doing right now."

A smile formed on Norma's lips as she refilled both their glasses for the third time. "You know, taking the rest of the day off has some appeal, now that you've given me what I was hoping for. Care to join me for a walk on the beach after lunch?"

"No reason not to," Neal replied. "It's been a while since I walked the beach down here."

"Good. You can follow me home. I live just a short distance from here."

By the time they had finished lunch, the bottle of wine was empty, but the glow it left lingered well past their arrival at Norma's bungalow. It was a cute little place that looked like it might have been built back in the early forties. Neal grinned as he parked on the street nearby, noting how much it resembled the quaint little house in Oceanside where segments of the movie *Top Gun* had been filmed. Inside was much the same, neat and well kept.

"Make your self at home while I use the powder room," she remarked. "There's a bottle of wine in the fridge. Pour us a glass."

For an instant, something about the setting in which he found himself seemed almost surreal. Like he had been suddenly transported to an alien place where nothing was familiar. *Maybe it was the wine.* Amused by his bizarre feelings, he filled two glasses and looked aimlessly around at the furnishings, realizing for the first time that they totally contradicted his former perception of her being a more formal and well-organized person. Oddly, that was further contradicted when she returned wearing a short sleeve blouse, cut-off jeans and beach sandals.

"Your turn," she said, motioning to the small bathroom behind her. "I'll wait for you on the porch."

Heeding her advice, Neal stepped into the same bathroom, grateful as hell for her having prompted him to do so. Upon his return, a glance in a full length mirror near the front door reminded him that he was over dressed for a walk on the beach, so he removed his shoes and socks, rolled up his trousers and took off his shirt.

"Now that's more like it," she remarked, as he stepped out onto the porch.

"Shall I lock the door?"

"Yes please. I have my keys."

Minutes later while walking in the wet sand at low tide, Neal asked, "Do you think Sandy Sterling will be upset because you took the afternoon off?"

"Nope. She left that decision entirely up to me. We have a good working relationship. The important thing is, are you sure you can complete your review in one week?"

Neal was quick to reply, "Oh yes. That's firm. I also have drafts of how the author bio and story summary should read. They're in my briefcase. So don't let me forget to give them to you before I leave."

"I won't. Except for artwork, we have everything we need. I'm sure you'll be pleased with the finished product."

"I'm sure I will."

As they approached the lifeguard stand that Norma used as a land-mark to turn her daily walks around, she began to laugh. "What a waste of good wine. Hell, I'm almost sober!"

"Me too," Neal admitted, enjoying her humor. "Shall we turn around?"

"Might just as well. Look what's coming."

Following the direction her hand was pointing, Neal saw a thick gathering of fog beginning to eclipse the sun as it sank slowly toward the horizon. After circling the lifeguard stand, he said, "That stuff reminds me of a few scuba diving trips I took to Mexico years ago. We won't be able to see a thing by the time we get back to your place."

"Where in Mexico?"

"Just south of Ensenada at a place called Punta Bunda."

As they continued to walk, the fog pushed its way steadily toward the shore, eventually turning the air directly over their heads into a misty blanket of gray. Convinced that Neal would be crazy to drive home under those conditions, she suggested he stay the night. "I can promise you clean sheets."

Neal laughed as they approached the house and replied, "I hope you've got another bottle of wine in there. Clean sheets are just a bo-nus."

When they finally reached Norma's cozy little nest, the view looking back through the front door ended there. Beyond the steps was a solid wall of gray, except for the faint glow of streetlights that had purposely been turned on earlier due to the fog.

When Neal attempted to turn on the lights, Norma's soft warm hand prevented it. Instead, she turned on her CD player and slid in a disc featuring Peter Nero at the piano. "Let's get our wine first and watch the growing darkness cover us. Wouldn't that be fun?"

"Being kept in the dark is nothing new to me, my dear," Neal joked in reply. "But never quite like this. Go get the wine."

As time passed the darkness inside and outside the house became one. The only light Neal could see was from the refrigerator when Norma went to refill their glasses. When the door opened on her third trip, the light illuminated her enough to reveal that she had gotten undressed. After returning with their refills, she took Neal by the hand and led him into her bedroom. Removing his clothes, she pulled him down gently onto the freshly scented sheets she had boasted changing, saying in a whisper, "It's time to collect your bonus."

It was mid-afternoon when Henry Hughes and his son finished their lunch in the marina restaurant at Knotts Landing. Henry, somewhat un-nerved by Dan's sudden interest in a piece of property he had inherited from an old fisherman by the name of Shark Hadley, signaled their waitress to bring him the check so he could discuss the subject further in the privacy of his boat on their way home. Aware that Dan was attracted to Melissa, and she to him, Henry asked Dan to warm up the engines on their boat so he wouldn't think up some excuse to linger.

Reluctantly, Dan finished the last of his drink and did as he was told. On his way out, however, he and Melissa did pass one another. Heads nodded and laughter was exchanged before they separated. Jealous of the boldness with which the younger generation conducted their personal relationships, Henry could only shake his head with envy, as he watched the rhythm of her movement deliver its message.

On their return trip to the estate, Dan took the helm to sharpen his skills at navigating the creek again, while Henry relaxed in a deck chair preparing to reopen their brief conversation regarding Dan's inherited property on Back Bay. "Other than Neal Thomas, does anyone else know about the property Shark Hadley left you?"

Dan searched his memory for a moment and then replied, "Donna Sanders is the only person who has ever been there. She couldn't find the place again if her life depended on it. She was strictly along for the ride when I took Mr. T there after Billy Newman's wake. As far as I know, the only persons who knows I own that property are the guy who notarized Hadley's will, and the clerk at the Tidewater Land Office."

"Where is Donna now?" Henry asked, still searching for information.

"I haven't got a clue, and couldn't care less," Dan answered, sounding a little disgruntled. "To her, I was just a ticket out of Dodge...and good riddance."

In the distance Dan could see the large dock that paralleled the shoreline in back of the Hughes' estate. They were home. Before docking, Henry asked one more question: "When can we take a look at this property?"

What's he up to? Dan thought, as the bumpers rubbed up against their wooden dock. Leaving a window of time to get his life back in order, he replied, "Right after I get my boat back from the Bahamas, one way or the other."

Sounds of water running in the bathtub adjoining Norma's bedroom opened Neal's eyes to a headache he hadn't experienced in a long time. Added to what tasted like a large ball of cotton in his mouth, the outlook for an eight-hour day of serious reading didn't look very promising. *Damn wine, I should know better*, he thought, as he searched the floor for his clothes.

"Lose something?" a voice giggled, as Norma's towel-draped body entered the room.

"Yes...my mind," Neal answered painfully. "Where the hell is it?"

"Try that empty wine bottle in the kitchen," she remarked, still unable to contain her laughter.

"I could say it's all your fault, you know."

"Yeah, like I held you down and had my way with you...right?"

"Yeah, something like that."

"In your dreams, big boy. It takes two to tango. Now, go take a shower while I fix coffee and dress for work." Hesitating briefly, she asked, "Or did you have something else in mind?"

Having finally located all of his clothes, he began dressing and replied, "I'll take a shower when I get home. I don't want to make you late for work."

"Is that a yes?"

"No!"

"Chicken!"

Neal laughed at her playfulness and thought, *I believe you would.* Thinking about the consequences of her implication, he replied, "Somebody around here has to work!"

Standing on the sidewalk near their cars minutes later, Neal handed Norma the drafts of the work he had prepared, and said, "Here's the information I told you about. I'll start reviewing your manuscript as soon as I get my head screwed on straight. In the meantime, thanks for making me feel like a kid again. I'll call you in a week, or sooner if all goes well."

"Make that two kids, Mr. T. I had a ball."

Moving slowly northward in the heavy traffic that morning, Neal had difficulty accepting the reality of having slept with an entirely different Norma Manning than the one Sandy Sterling had originally introduced him to. The Dr. Jeckle and Mr. Hyde syndrome came humorously to mind. *Talk about a split personality.*

Though tired and hung over, the sight of his driveway entrance and the thought of a relaxing soak in the Jacuzzi brought a sigh of relief. As soon as he entered the house, he stripped naked and headed for the patio with the telephone remote clutched in his hand in case someone called.

Five minutes later, with the fantasy of his previous night's adventure still fresh in his mind, the phone rang. It was Anita Cassidy. "Just a reminder that I'll be a homeless woman in a few days. Are you still okay with what we're doing?"

Neal quickly checked the date on his watch and said, "Relax, everything is just fine. How's the packing coming along?"

"More work than I expected," she replied, sounding tired. "I've been busting my buns every night to get my things packed. There isn't much, but it's all I have. UPS is picking up the boxes at the end of the week."

"Have you called your mother?"

"Yes. She's sending me an Internet reservation via your e-mail address for a flight out of San Diego leaving next Monday at three o'clock. It should arrive late this afternoon. Any problem with that?"

"None at all. When do you want me to come and get you?"

"Pick me up at the Pub Friday around six o'clock. There'll be party going on, so be prepared to stay for a little while, if you don't mind."

"I'll be there," he assured her. "You call the ball."

"Thanks, Mr. T. See you tomorrow."

She's finally going home, Neal thought, shuddering that such circumstances should ever befall any one of his own three daughters.

Still tired, but grateful that the intensity of his hangover had all but disappeared, he shut down the Jacuzzi and returned the remote to its stand in the kitchen. Having had little to eat since his lunch with Norma Manning the previous day, he put on a pot of coffee and prepared breakfast to give him the energy he needed to begin the book review Norma had asked for.

The fog that had engulfed the Southern California coastline late yesterday afternoon had now retreated several miles out to sea. The sun was pleasantly warm, and a soft breeze made it enjoyable to begin reviewing Norma's manuscript in a lounge chair he had moved out to the bluff. Resigned that any phone calls he received would of necessity have to be recorded, he began the process, eager to learn if Norma's editorial expertise was as proficient as her sexuality.

Though he periodically dozed throughout the six-hour self-imposed reading schedule he had set for himself that day, Neal did manage to maintain a high level of interest and enthusiasm over what Norma had done to correct his sometimes unprofessional use of grammar, phraseology and punctuation. In addition, he was relieved to see that she had also managed to maintain a fundamental conformity to the storyline and character development he had tried so hard to establish.

Damn she's good, he thought, folding over the page corner to mark where he had stopped …*at everything!*

After leaving the lounge chair he had sat in for most of the day, Neal glanced at his watch and decided it was not too late to get a little exercise by mowing the lawn and trimming some neglected shrubbery.

One hour later, literally soaked with sweat, he finally put away his tools and took a shower. Casually dressed in clean clothes, he returned to the kitchen to fix a drink while he watched the news and read his mail. He had just clicked on the TV when a CNN update on Hurricane Louise appeared. The screen was divided into two pictures; one in the broadcasting studio, the other showing live coverage by Anderson Cooper reporting on location from Miami. Based on the hurricane's animated movement and Cooper's wind-whipped commentary, Louise was changing her direction dramatically toward northern Florida, with some speculation that it might eventually turn out over the ocean.

Curious as to whether Henry or Dan Hughes might be watching the same weather report in Virginia, Neal checked the time and determined that it was only a little past nine o'clock East Coast time. Relocating to the kitchen, he placed the call. Several seconds passed before the other end picked up. "Hello?"

"Dan! This is Neal Thomas."

"Mr. T! Must be some telepathy going on. Dad and I were talking about you just this afternoon. Hold on, I'll get him on the other line."

In seconds, Henry joined the conversation and asked Neal, "Have you been following the news on Hurricane Louise?"

"I've got CNN on right now," Neal replied. "That's why I'm calling. Anything new back there?"

"Only that she's passing north of the Bahamas," Dan commented. "She might be heading further north than originally predicted, thank the Lord."

"We're praying Dan's boat gets spared," Henry remarked. "I have a feeling we're going to need it one of these days."

"Why? Are you two going into the fishing business any time soon?" Neal joked.

"Not if I can help it, Mr. T." Dan responded with a laugh. "But we do have something else in mind."

"Care to expand on that," Neal asked.

"It's a little too early for that," Henry interrupted, "but we will need your help when we get further along with what Dan has in mind. We'll keep you informed on our progress. How is your book coming along?"

"I'm reading the editor's manuscript as we speak," Neal replied. "I have to return it to her in a week, so I'm going to be pretty busy for the next few days. I'll get back with you when I'm finished. In the meantime, I'll keep tracking Louise with you, Dan. I hope all goes well with getting your boat back. Please stay in touch."

I wonder what those two are up to? Neal questioned when he clicked off the television and climbed the stairs to his bedroom. *You don't want to know* was his final thought for the day.

Only a few miles from where Neal Thomas had ended his day, Anita Cassidy struggled to do the same thing, but without much success. Everything she owned, except what was needed to get her through the next few days, she had shipped to her mother's address in San Francisco. *I could have stayed at Mr. T's,* she thought repeatedly, as the balmy night air flowed intermittently across the bed she would never see again. *Will this week never end?* she asked herself, as effortlessly the day finally did.

Chapter 20

Lost And Found

While eating breakfast the next morning, Neal revisited the conversation he had with Henry and Dan Hughes yesterday. He questioned why Henry seemed reluctant to discuss what he and Dan were thinking about doing after Dan got his boat back. *Why would they need my help?* That's the more important question, he thought. But rather than waste any more time wondering what those two were up to, he finished his breakfast and resumed review of Norma Manning's manuscript indoors, rather than on the bluff.

Unlike the previous day, Neal managed to stay awake for the full six-hours of reading he had scheduled for Thursday, stopping only to use the bathroom, grab a snack and refill his water glass. It was now 3:00 p.m.

Satisfied with what he had accomplished, he put the manuscript aside and took a walk out on the bluff to stretch his legs. As he stood at the top of the beach access stairway, his eyes caught sight of a woman in shorts standing knee deep in the water a few yards from shore. Overcome by a strong desire to determine if she was the same woman he had seen naked at almost the same spot a few weeks ago, he descended the stairway and walked to the water's edge where she had entered. "Excuse me!" he yelled. "My name is Neal Thomas. Can I talk to you for a moment?"

Turning abruptly to see who had yelled at her, the woman saw Neal waving and started walking toward him, stopping cautiously in the water a few yards away. "Do I know you?" she asked, shielding her eyes from the water's glare.

"I don't think so," Neal replied, "but I need to ask you a question if you don't mind."

Looking puzzled, the woman advanced a few more feet and stopped. "What's your question?"

"Have you lost anything in the water around here recently? I noticed that you seemed to be looking for something."

Still looking puzzled, she replied, "Why do you ask?"

"A visiting friend of mine found a piece of women's jewelry near this spot a few days ago. I thought you might be the person who lost it. I live up there on the bluff."

"That's very thoughtful of you sir," the woman replied, looking at him less suspiciously, "but whatever you found isn't mine. Sorry."

Disappointed, Neal apologized for bothering her and said goodbye.

Arriving home a few minutes later, he stood in his studio pondering over the mystery of the orphaned necklace, still convinced that it held some special significance for him, but gave up when the pieces of his puzzlement wouldn't come together.

Uneventfully, Friday finally arrived. After spending most of it reading and re-reading the corrections he had made to his book, Neal glanced at his watch and was pleased to see that it was nearing the time when he had promised Anita Cassidy he would join her for her last day at the Village Pub. Finding the owner of the necklace would have to wait.

There were no parking spaces available when Neal arrived at the Village Pub minutes later, so he parked in a restaurant lot nearby and walked back. Several familiar faces gave him a friendly greeting as he tried to enter. "Sorry Mr. T," one of them spoke up, "they're already up to capacity, but a bunch of the boys from down the street said they were leaving after they said goodbye to Anita. Shouldn't be long now. Here, have a drink."

Neal sniffed the open end of what looked to be a clear plastic bottle of *Arrowhead* drinking water and recognized the familiar scent of vodka. Amused by the innovation, he took a courtesy swallow and handed the bottle back. "I didn't know you could get this from a spring," he joked. "Thanks for the sample."

Several minutes later, a group of six laughing men exited the Pub's rear entrance and started across the parking lot. One of them remarked in passing, "Cassidy's in rare form today, man. I hope she's got a ride home."

"She does," Neal assured him, curious as to what was going on inside.

Surprisingly, the body count had reduced itself to not more than twenty people, making the addition of Neal and the smokers safely below the capacity limit. Though busy hurrying back and forth behind the bar, Anita was immediately conscious of the new arrivals and made a special effort to serve them. When she finally faced Neal, she remarked, "Only a little while longer, Mr. T, and I'm all yours! Bud Light?"

Nodding yes, he thought, *they're sure going to miss you around here, baby doll.*

For Neal, the next thirty minutes passed in slow motion until Anita suddenly climbed up on the bar and shouted a ten second countdown to end her final day at the Pub. Then, to the uproarious applause of everyone in the place, she threw her arms up over her head and shouted, **"I'm outta here!"** Moving like a chorus girl in an old western movie, she walked the entire length of the bar blowing kisses to everyone, and then climbed down, her eyes wet with tears.

After a short recovery period in the ladies room, Anita emerged dry-eyed and smiling, as she went back behind the bar to get the suitcase she had put there when she came to work that day. Nodding to Neal that she was ready to leave, she waved one last time and accompanied Neal to his car, glad that that part of her life was now over.

Having already had the pleasure of spending the night at Neal's house when he and Jessica Sterling were planning Dan Hughes' rescue from Mexico, Anita entered the living room as if she were visiting an old friend. Neal sensed it and remarked, "You know where everything is. Make yourself at home while I fix us both a drink. This has been quite a day for both of us."

Taking him at his word, Anita went immediately upstairs and changed into more casual attire, hoping for a walk on the beach later. By the time she returned, Neal had their drinks prepared and was laid back in his easy chair with the television on.

"There's no place like home, is there Mr. T," she commented, while choosing the comfort of his couch on which to relax. "What's on?"

"I was hoping the evening news might have an update on the progress of Hurricane Louise," he replied. "Dan Hughes has a boat in the Bahamas that he wants to bring home, but he's afraid it might get wiped out in the storm."

"Do you think that guy's ever going to be able to live a normal life?" she asked, shaking her head doubtfully. "I've never met a man who could get into trouble by just opening a door."

Neal laughed at her amusing analogy, and answered, "I guess that would depend on what's on the other side."

Before conversation could continue, the first segment of CNN news came on with studio coverage of Hurricane Louise's progress. Based on the animated direction the eye of the storm was taking, it now appeared to be unmistakingly traveling in a more northerly direction, and was being pushed out to sea by an unusual formation of high-pressure moving toward the southeastern seaboard.

"Based on what little I know about the weather, it looks like Danny Boy can breath a little easier now," Anita broke in. "Hopefully, his boat weathered the storm."

"I sure hope so. He's probably making plans to go get it as we speak. In the meantime, can I fix you something to eat? I'm hungry."

"I was wondering when you were going to get around to that. What's on the menu?"

"I've got a pepperoni pizza in the fridge."

"I'd love it. Can I fix you another drink?"

While Neal began un-boxing the pizza and heating the oven, Anita mixed a vodka and tonic for him, and refilled her wine glass before sitting down at the table to keep him company. "Have you checked your e-mail lately?" she inquired. "Maybe my ticket to San Francisco has arrived."

"By golly, you're right," he replied excitedly. "Let me get this pizza in the oven and we'll check it out."

Moments later, Neal escorted Anita into his studio and turned on the computer. After gaining access to AOL, he clicked the tool bar and watched his mail appear. Scanning what first appeared to be nothing but *SPAM*, he found an e-mail subject that read: *Flight Reservation Confirmation Attached*. In seconds, the information was printed and lying in the tray. "Here it is, my dear," he said, handing her the printout. "Your ticket to a brand new life."

Surprised that she just sat there with a blank expression on her face, he realized that she was staring at his note board. "What is it?" he asked, suddenly concerned. "Are you all right?"

"Where did you get that?" she replied, pointing to the necklace that hung there. "That necklace! Where did you get it?"

"Dan Hughes found it on the beach the day before he left for Virginia. Neither of us have any idea who it belongs to. Why do you ask?"

"It's my mother's," she sobbed, covering her face with her hands.

Unable to believe what he just heard, Neal went to her side and attempted to console her. "You must be mistaken," he said, handing her his handkerchief. "It couldn't be."

Freeing herself from his grasp, she reached for the necklace and held the locket in her left hand for a moment, examining it like a jeweler would. Then, with the fingernail of her right index finger, she counted clockwise to the three o'clock location of the tiny red gems that encircled its case and pushed that stone very carefully. To Neal's utter amazement, the locket's hinged cover popped open. Captured inside was the still recognizable portrait of Randy Donaldson, Anita's father.

"Daddy gave it to my mother on their first wedding anniversary," she explained. "Here, hold it. I'll be right back."

While Neal sat there wondering what to make of this bizarre situation, Anita went to her suitcase and brought back the frameless photograph of her family that Neal had returned to Anita when he came back from Catalina with her mother. Though slightly scratched when the glass was accidentally broken, it was easily recognizable as the same photograph Neal had seen in her apartment the first time he went there.

"See," she said excitedly, pointing to her mother's neck. "She wore that necklace to every important social event I can remember, even daddy's funeral. She was obsessed with it."

"How do you think she's going to react when you return it?" Neal asked almost certain of her answer.

The first sign of a smile slowly began to appear on Anita's face, as she pondered her reply. "As you may have already discovered for yourself, Mr. T, my mother never loses control of a situation, or herself, for that matter. But my guess is, her armor's going to fall off like a G-string and she'll cry like a baby…I hope."

"Not a pretty picture," Neal remarked. "Remember, she is your mother."

"I know. I'm just kidding," she apologized. Sniffing the air, she asked, "By the way, how's our pizza doing?"

"Damn!" Neal blurted out, leaving quickly for the kitchen. "Thanks for the reminder."

"I'll join you as soon as I put this necklace in my suitcase," she said, following close behind. "I still have questions about all this."

Fortunately for Neal, Anita's timely statement about the pizza prevented it from burning up in the oven. He was slicing it into pieces when she entered the kitchen, prompting him to ask, "What's your question?"

"Knowing how much my mother prides herself with being on top of things, I can't imagine her wearing her most prized possession into the water. What was she thinking?"

Rather than complicate matters further by mentioning her mother's sundown skinny-dipping adventure when the loss apparently occurred, Neal replied, "There was a period of time during my working years here in California when I was one of five partners who owned vacation property in Mexico. We used to go down there on weekends to party. Three of the partners were single women, and actually wanted to live there when they retired. On one such weekend I went swimming with some of our guest's children to act as lifeguard because the surf was unusually rough that day. The water was cold, so cold the children decided to lie in the sun. While my back was to the ocean, a wave snuck up from behind and sent me tumbling ass over teakettle onto the beach, minus my wedding ring. My fingers had shrunk so much it literally fell off when the wave hit. Try explaining that to your wife."

After Neal placed the box of sliced pizza on the table and sat down, he sensed that Anita was still questioning her mother's apparent carelessness in not taking off the necklace before entering the water. To end the pointless speculation he said, "Look, what difference does it make now. Ask her how she lost it after you get home, if it's still bothering you. Otherwise, enjoy the moment and forget about it. There are a lot more important things to be concerned with once you return to San Francisco."

"You're right. I am making too much of this. Great pizza, by the way."

Amused by her sudden switch from *the ridiculous to the sublime*, he mentioned, "My oldest daughter Karen is having a family get together at her house this Sunday. Would you like to go?"

"That's very thoughtful of you, Mr. T. I'd like that very much if you're sure she won't mind you showing up with a stranger."

"Don't worry about that," he laughed, "I'm the one they think is strange."

While Neal cleaned up the kitchen, Anita finished the rest of her wine and asked him if he had any plans to visit San Francisco any time soon. He gave it some thought and replied, "The most pressing issue I have right now is to finish reading my editor's comments on the book I've written. Beyond that, I haven't given the future much thought, although I would enjoy seeing your mother again, after you get re-acquainted with one another. That in itself is going to take some time."

"I've thought about it a lot lately," she admitted. "Going back to live with my mother after the way I've been used to bumming around is going to take some getting used to. I hope she has a sense of humor."

"Keep yours and you'll do just fine."

Not wanting to get involved in a situation over which he would never have any appreciable influence, he side stepped the subject by addressing his immediate objective. "I hope you won't mind entertaining yourself tomorrow. I'll have to read all day to meet my one-week deadline. But tomorrow night we're going out to dinner to celebrate your return to San Francisco, and a long overdue reunion with your mother. Would you like that?"

"Who wouldn't?" she replied, overwhelmed by his fatherly enthusiasm. "And don't worry about me tomorrow. I think I'll spend the day on the beach. I haven't done that in quite a while."

Content with watching television together for the rest of the evening, Anita called it quits at eleven o'clock and went to bed, leaving Neal to watch the news for an update on the progress of Hurricane Louise. It came as an unexpected surprise to see the storm's eye moving progressively northward into the crescent shaped shoreline between the cities of Orlando, Jacksonville, Savannah and Charleston. *Looks like Dan's got it made* he thought, as he turned off the television and climbed the stairs. *I'll call him in the morning and find out what his plans are.*

The smell of coffee percolating in the kitchen when he opened his eyes the next morning made Neal aware that Anita was up and about, eager to begin her day. Following her lead, he moved quickly to join her. "I'm not used to this kind of service," he remarked, as he entered the kitchen. "Did you sleep well?"

"Like a baby," she replied, searching the cabinets for two cups. "How about you?"

"Likewise. It must be your presence."

"I'll take that as a compliment," she laughed, handing him a cup of coffee.

Following the silence that came from their brief preoccupation with the newspaper, Anita asked, "What time are you planning to take me out to dinner this evening?"

Neal put his paper aside and considered her question thoughtfully for a moment, and replied, "I've made a special effort this week to hasten the end of my book review so I can take care of other interests. Barring any unforeseen interruptions, I'd say I should finish by two o'clock this afternoon, giving us an hour to freshen up a bit before we leave. I have a couple of friends I would like you to meet before we go to dinner. Is that okay with you?"

"You're the driver, Mr. T. I'll be ready whenever you are," she replied, with a noticeable spark of liveliness Neal hadn't noticed before.

"You're happy, aren't you?" he commented. "I can see it in your eyes."

"Very happy, thanks to you," she said, lowering her eyes. "I've been lost for years and suddenly found again. I hope we'll always be close friends."

"Thank you, my dear," he said, struggling to smother an upwelling of emotion. "Looks like I've been blessed with another daughter."

Recognizing the sensitive path their conversation was taking, Anita lightened it with a little humor. "Don't go gushy on me now. I won't be able to eat my breakfast. What are we having, by the way?"

"Mexican style scrambled eggs, turkey bacon and a piece of sourdough toast!"

"Will you marry me?"

Neal recognized her attempt to humor him, and laughed uncontrollably for a few seconds before replying, "Be careful what you wish for, honey. I may be old, but my battery still carries a charge."

It was Anita's turn. "Jumper cables?"

And so it went for the next thirty minutes. One joke after another until breakfast was over, and Neal settled down in his studio with the door closed to finalize his review. Anita, in support of that effort, cleaned up the kitchen and left for the beach, thinking as she walked along the water's edge, *I wonder if mother and Mr. T ever...?*

Sitting at his desk in the Hughes Realty Company offices in Suffolk, Virginia, Dan Hughes' attention shifted back and forth between weather updates on Hurricane Louise, and a map of the Back Bay area he had obtained recently from a local land office. His interest in the maps was to help him locate and plot the size and location of the property his benefactor, Shark Hadley, had willed him prior to his accidental death.

Based on weather reports Dan had tuned into throughout the day, Louise had been downsized to a tropical storm. CNN's forecast was predicting a gradual northeasterly direction that would eventually dissipate over the ocean, sparing the Bahamas and the Atlantic States from the wind and flood damage that was predicted earlier in the week. Satisfied that he could now begin making serious plans to rescue his boat from its hiding place in the Bahamas, he turned off the television and began thinking about what he had to do that day to prepare for that eventuality. He hadn't gotten very far when his cell phone chimed.

Aggravated that his concentration had been broken, he grabbed it and flipped the cover open. "Hello."

"Is that you Dan? This is Neal Thomas. How are you?"

"A lot better since Louise changed her direction," he replied, sounding less agitated. "I was just mulling that over in my mind when you called."

"Have you made any plans yet?"

"No, but your call has triggered an idea."

"And that is…?"

"How would you like to go to the Bahamas with me?" Dan replied. "You promised to come back here to attend my welcome home party. Ever been to the Bahamas?"

Just thinking about what Dan was suggesting caused Neal to get up and pace the floor. "Are you serious?" he asked, half laughing. "I've got Anita Cassidy staying here. Her mother has talked her into returning to San Francisco and I'm taking her to the airport on Monday." Pausing to collect his thoughts, he added, "Then there's my book. I have to deliver my review of the editor's comments next week. Who knows what else is going to happen?"

"Then how about after I get back?" Dan persisted. "Hell, take some time off and enjoy yourself. I'll give you a call when I return so we can make some plans. Dad is really going all out for my welcome home party. He's going to be disappointed if you can't make it."

Torn between the certainty of knowing what a good time he would have, and the uncertainty of not knowing where his future as a writer was headed, he decided that discretion was the better part of valor, and replied, "I'd love to go with you, Dan, but there's just too much on my plate right now. Call me when you get back from the Bahamas and we'll work something out. Henry will understand. I should have it all sorted out by then."

"Okay, if that's the way it has to be," Dan remarked disappointedly. "I'll take Cliff Bennett along. He's always good company."

"Good choice," Neal said, relieved that he now had the time to get his life back in some kind of order for the first time in weeks. "Be sure to call me when you get back. And please explain my predicament to Henry."

"I will."

Neal had just finished writing a reminder comment on the final chapter of Norma Manning's review manuscript when he heard someone enter the kitchen. Assuming it to be Anita returning from the beach, he tidied up his desk and went to greet her. "Did you have a good time?" he asked, admiring her figure. "You've picked up some color."

"That's not all I picked up," she giggled. "Look what I found."

Neal recognized it immediately as a medium-size abalone shell stripped of its muscle. "I used to belong to a scuba diving club when I was married," he explained, examining it closely. "I still have a few of them around here as reminders."

"I noticed," she remarked. "That's why I brought it back with me. So you'll be reminded of me every now and then."

The simplicity of her gesture caught Neal by surprise. All he could think of to say was, "Thank you, my dear, though I need no reminders of you. I'll clean it up like the others and put it over the fireplace where I can say good morning to you every day."

"Mother was right," she said, running quickly up the stairs. "You do have a way with words."

While Anita showered and dressed for dinner that evening, Neal mixed a drink and called his daughter to give advance notice that he was bringing a guest to her party the next day. Karen, being the liberal she had always been, said, "Bring whomever you want, Daddy. We'll treat her just like one of the family. If she can handle us, we can certainly handle her." Hesitating a moment before saying goodbye, she asked, "You're not involved with this woman, are you?"

Neal laughed and replied, "Her name is Anita Donaldson and she's leaving for San Francisco on Monday to live with her mother, whom I have dated I might add."

"Sorry," she said, with a hint of embarrassment. "See you two tomorrow."

It wasn't long after Neal finished talking with his daughter that Anita reappeared in slacks, a cleavage-enhancing blouse and sandals. Her hair, unlike he had ever seen it styled before, was gathered attractively on top of her head, and held there with a decorative comb. "Wow," he remarked, as she descended the stairs. "Where's your friend Anita?"

Flattered by his reaction, she replied, "She's upstairs lying in a heap on the bedroom floor. I'm her sister."

Her quick-wittedness made him laugh, as it had in the past. "I'm going to miss you around here young lady," he remarked. "I really envy your mother."

While they lingered in the kitchen, Neal explained briefly what their evening together would include. "Before we go to Bully's for dinner, I'd like to introduce you to a couple of my very best friends. They're both characters, but I think you'll enjoy them. Are you game for that?"

"I'm not dressed for church, Mr. T. Make me some memories."

John Pauly was a live-alone widower and liked it that way, having raised and educated eight children. Neal made his first stop at John's ocean-view condominium to introduce Anita to this full-blooded Irish-man whom Neal had met through Walter Douglas, when Walter vacationed there several times a year.

As usual, John was resting in his easy-chair watching Jerry Springer when Neal and Anita appeared and knocked on his door. Unaware that Neal had a young lady with him, because Anita was partially hidden by the half-open door, John bellowed out, "Come on in you old fart! The door's open!"

Anita giggled, as she walked closely behind Neal, amused that Pauly still hadn't noticed that Neal wasn't alone.

Equally amused, Neal waited until they were almost in front of him before acknowledging her presence. "John, I'd like you to meet my friend, Anita Cassidy. She used to tend bar at the Village Pub."

Startled when she stepped out from behind Neal, John rose clum-sily to his feet, looking wide-eyed and confused. "Damn it, Neal," he scolded, "Are you trying to scare me into an early grave?" Looking at Anita, his face softened into a devilish smile. "And just what is a pretty young lass like yourself doing hanging around with the likes of him?" he asked. "Can I offer you a drink? I know what he wants."

Looking sheepishly up at Neal, she replied, "I'd love a glass of wine, if you have it."

"Why of course I have it," John replied confidently. "Come into the kitchen with me and I'll pour you a glass. That character you're with knows where the vodka is. What's your preference, my dear? Red or white?"

"White, please."

Though he had been warned against drinking alcohol because he was a borderline diabetic, John always seemed to find an excuse to break the rules, especially when he played host to an attractive woman. "Diabetes be damned!" he said in a whisper. "I think the pleasure of your company is reason enough to take a wee nip myself. I haven't had a drink since Neal was here last. I'd say I'm deserving, wouldn't you?"

Not wanting to offend John by responding negatively to the verbal gymnastics he was going through, she replied, "I don't have diabetes, Mr. Pauly. It's strictly your call."

"Ah, you're a cagey one," John remarked while he began pouring orange juice over his double shot of Jack Daniels. "Now, if I may be so bold as to ask, what is a good-looking lass like yourself doing in the company of that old man over there."

Neal had just fixed his own drink when he heard John's question. "Talk about the pot calling the kettle black," he remarked, winking at Anita.

Recognizing from the language being exchanged between the two men that they were used to kidding one another, Anita decided to join the game. "Neal has offered me lodging for the next two days, and then I'm flying on to San Francisco to visit my mother."

"Does she know about this?" John asked, his Catholic eyes growing bigger by the second.

"Oh yes," she replied in a ho-hum manner. "She and Neal are old friends."

John shook his head in dismay and motioned for them to join him in the living room. Turning the television sound off, he asked Anita, "Are you traveling alone?"

Amused by John's roundabout way of determining if she and Neal were going to be alone together those two nights, she replied, "I'm afraid so. I'm on the unemployed list as of yesterday, so Mr. T. offered me sanctuary until Monday."

John remained silent for a moment or two, his eyes moving back and forth occasionally between the two of them while he sipped his drink. Then he smiled and said, "He's been a good friend to me also. I'll miss seeing him as frequently as I used to."

"What's that supposed to mean?" Neal asked, surprised by the implication.

John got up and fixed Anita another drink and one for his self, assuming Neal would get his own. When they all returned to the living room, he explained: "Arguing with eight grown up children who have decided that I'm too old to be living alone is a tough battle to win. So I finally gave in and notified my landlord that I would be moving out by the end of the month. My daughter in Rancho Santa Fe has made arrangements for me to live with her and her family for a while. Like it or not, it's a done deal."

Not expecting this turn of events, Neal took consolation in the fact that John would continue to live in the general area. "Just be glad you've got a family that cares that much about you, John. It makes all of the sacrifices you made for them over the years worthwhile. I really admire them for what they're doing. We'll still see each other now and then. In the meantime, Anita and I have one more stop before dinner, so we'll say goodbye and let you get back to Springer. Thanks for the drinks."

Backing out of the condo's guest parking space, Neal watched his friend wave goodbye and walk back inside. As they drove way, he turned to Anita and remarked, "I hope I'm that lucky."

"Where to now, Mr. T?" Anita inquired, as Neal headed south on the freeway.

"Since we were going to be eating in Del Mar anyway," he replied, "I thought you'd get a kick out of meeting my best friend, Ron Barns. He's a retired computer programmer who worked for the same company I did. Both of us retired around the same time."

"Married?"

"Divorced."

"Children?"

"Three; a son and two beautiful daughters."

"You mentioned earlier that he was somewhat of a character. Can you expand on that before we get there?"

Neal laughed, not because of the question, but the phrase it brought to mind. "Ever heard of that old saying, a picture is worth a thousand words?"

"My dad used to say that whenever he was having a hard time trying to explain something to me."

"Exactly. You'll see what I mean when we get there."

Moments later, Neal took a right turn at the corner market that led to Ron Barns' house, and proceeded up the street to the next corner. "Voila!" he exclaimed. "We're here!"

"What's that supposed to mean?" she asked, curiously viewing the odd looking bungalow they were parked in front of.

Unable to keep from laughing at the expression on her face, Neal explained, "That's it, my friend Ron's place. Come on, I want you to meet him."

Reluctantly, Anita got out of the car and followed Neal to the sliding door entrance, still questioning what manner of man she was about to meet. One step inside convinced her it wasn't going to be Donald Trump.

Because he had turned down his hearing aid, Ron Barns was unaware that he had visitors, until Neal hollered, "Hey Ron, you've got company!"

"Well, well. Mr. Thomas, I do believe," Ron said, unaware that Neal was in the company of an attractive female. "To what do I owe this unexpected visit?"

Taking Anita by the arm, Neal led her around the mountain of computer equipment that had hidden her presence, and said, "I want you to meet my friend, Anita Cassidy. Soon to be Miss Donaldson."

Because of an old injury that prevented him from bending his right knee, Ron remained seated, and said, "My pleasure, Miss Cassidy, but shouldn't that be Mrs. Donaldson? Who's the lucky man?"

Still bewildered by the untidiness that lay all around her, Anita politely replied, "Cassidy is an alias I took when I ran away from home years ago. Monday I am returning to San Francisco to live with my mother, and will revert back to my family name of Donaldson. Mr. Thomas is a friend of my mother's, and is responsible for reuniting me with her." Looking up at Neal adoringly, she added, "I wish I could take him with me."

"There's a lot of people around here who wish you would," Ron joked. "But then again, there are many who'd be disappointed if you did, especially his family."

"She's meeting them tomorrow," Neal remarked. "Karen is having a family get together at her house tomorrow and invited Anita to come along."

Ron shook his head and smiled. "I can see you're a glutton for punishment, young lady. But you sound like you can handle that bunch. I can assure you of one thing, you will have a good time." Looking at Neal, he said, "Where's your manner's, Mr. T. Go fix the lady a drink."

Before Neal could react, Anita took Neal by the arm and said, "Thanks, but we're on our way out to dinner, Mr. Barns. Plus we had a couple over at Mr. Pauly's house. We really should eat before having anything more to drink."

Ron laughed. "Well, at least one of you has some sense. Go and have a good time. I'll see you next Tuesday, Neal. Goodbye, Anita, and good luck in San Francisco."

Neal and Anita were in the car driving north through Del Mar when Anita remarked, "You and your buddy sure bring new meaning to the old phrase – *opposites attract*. You sure hit the nail on the head when you said Barns and Pauly were a couple of characters. I'll never forget that pair."

As one of the most popular restaurants in Del Mar, Bully's was expected to be crowded on a Saturday around dinnertime. And it was. The number of people waiting to get in, as Neal and Anita came up from the parking lot, was at least six couples deep. Disappointed and hungry, Neal and Anita mutually agreed that, between the influx of vacationers and patrons of the Del Mar Downs racetrack, dining in Del Mar was out of the question.

"There's a Mexican restaurant just north of the seawall in Carlsbad we could go to, and its closer to my place," Neal mentioned. "How does that sound?"

"I love Mexican food!" Anita replied excitedly. "Let's do it."

Though Fidel's had people waiting when they arrived, they were seated outside fairly soon. Eager to quench their thirst, Neal ordered a pitcher of margaritas to enhance their appetites and fill the time gap until their food arrived. Once it did, they wasted little time in enjoying different flavors of the combination plate recommended by their waiter.

Thirty minutes later, full and giddy from the tequila, Anita suggested that they work their dinner off by walking the beach. Neal agreed, but suggested that they drive to the south end parking lot where it would be less congested. They arrived just as the late afternoon sun began its plunge into the ocean and the sky gradually began turning pink.

As the early morning news that day had predicted, the tide was high and the surf not recommended for swimming, which encouraged Anita to suggest that they remove their shoes and leave them in the car if they were going to walk on the sand. That accomplished, they started to walk, agreeing that one round trip would be enough.

They had just reached the halfway mark on their initial trek when they observed a young man and woman in street clothes staggering around in the backwash of a rip current. Apparently, they had been drinking and were splashing around in the water playfully, totally ignoring the sudden upwelling of a wave that was about to break over them.

"Those two shouldn't be out there, "Anita cried with alarm. "They're drunk!"

Neal was about to shout to warn the couple but he was too late. The six-foot wave curled and crashed, burying them both in a blanket of turbulent surf with only their flailing arms and legs visible. Being the stronger person, the man eventually was able to stand up, as the receding backwash rushed past his legs, threatening to sweep him back into the ocean at any second.

Being the weaker of the two, the young woman had already succumbed to the rip current and was being quickly swept away, as the young man stood helplessly by, screaming her name.

Instinctively, knowing he only had seconds to react, Neal pulled his wallet and car keys out of his pockets and thrust them at Anita, hollering, "Go back to the car and call 911 on my cell phone! I'm going after that girl!"

As he ran by the young man who was now out of the water and sobbing on the wet sand, Neal yelled, "Go get rid of any booze you've got and wait here with that blanket!"

Sighting in on her weakening effort to stay afloat, Neal stripped off his shirt and pants and plunged into the out-rushing water of the rip current, swimming aggressively like he had when he was a young competitive swimmer. The current was strong, and helped him to reach the young woman before she gave in to exhaustion. Approaching her with caution, he said, "Lay your head back and put your hands on my shoulders. Don't try to grab hold of me. You're going to be just fine."

Using every ounce of strength he had, Neal turned their bodies parallel to the beach and breast-stoked his way out of the rip current. Once free of it, he used the surf's inward flow to coast toward the beach until it was ready to break. As they approached the dangerous point where he could feel the surf ready to curl, he said to the woman, "I'm going to roll you over on your back and tread water so we can keep from being dragged into the wave when it breaks. If you can, start kicking when I tell you to. Okay?"

There was no answer.

Damn it, she's passed out, he thought, struggling to keep her afloat. Then he felt what he was waiting for. The water rose when the next swell passed beneath them, raising the two bodies up and down like a cork, as it curled and crashed on the beach ten to fifteen yards ahead of them. *The next one's it*, he decided.

Quickly moving the woman's limp body so it faced the next wave, he kicked frantically to keep her vertical while he wrapped his arms around her waist just below her breasts. Then it came. The wave lifted and lowered their two bodies simultaneously like a horse on a merry-go-round, as the wave Neal had been waiting for passed by and lowered them gently onto the sandy bottom. With little time left before the next wave rolled in, he dragged the woman's limp body backwards onto the beach and quickly began CPR, while the woman's companion covered her motionless body with their blanket, whimpering like a child. Seconds later, in a gushing of booze-scented vomit, the woman regained consciousness and her eyes opened.

As Neal helped the coughing woman roll over onto her hands and knees, he could see Anita Cassidy running toward them, shouting, "The Paramedics are on their way. Is she all right?"

"Just water-logged," he assured her. "She'll be okay in a few minutes, but the medics will want to examine her. We can go as soon as they get here."

"Thanks, mister," the young woman's male companion remarked, his lips still quivering from his dunking in the cold water. "You saved Dawn's life."

After several more dry heaves, the exhausted young woman gathered the blanket around her shivering body, and rolled over into a sitting position. Brushing back the wet disheveled hair that hung down over her sand-covered face, she spoke for the first time. "That goes double for me, mister…?"

"Thomas," Neal filled in. "Don't try to talk right now. Just rest until the paramedics get here."

"Here they come now," Anita said, pointing to a large red vehicle with flashing lights approaching rapidly on the sand.

By now, a small crowd of curious passersby had gathered around the rescue scene, busily chattering with curious speculation on what had happened. The crowd parted immediately to allow access, as three men approached from the truck and asked who had summoned them.

"I did," Anita spoke up. "My friend, Mr. Thomas, saw these two people get knocked down by a large wave. The girl was swept out by a rip current, and would have drowned if Mr. Thomas hadn't gone out to rescue her."

"She was unconscious when I finally got her back to shore," Neal explained. "But I administered CPR and managed to get her breathing again. She swallowed a bit of water, but threw up most of it when she regained consciousness."

"What about the boy?" the chief medic asked.

"He was strong enough to keep from being pulled into deeper water and made it back to shore on his own," Neal replied. "He was scared more than anything else. The girl wasn't that lucky."

"How do you feel, young lady?" the chief medic asked, turning toward Dawn. "Do you want to be examined by a doctor?"

"Hell no!" Dawn exclaimed adamantly. "I'm in enough trouble as it is. My parents are really going to be pissed."

Agitated by the scene he had all too often been called to investigate, the chief medic turned to Neal and asked, "How about you, Mr. Thomas? Are you okay?"

"I'll survive." Neal replied. "I'm just sorry you guys had to be called down here. I guess this kind of nonsense is pretty much par for the course around here."

"You don't know the half of it," the medic replied, turning to leave. "I only wish those two were young enough to get their asses spanked when they get home. Take care."

As soon as the paramedics left, the small crowd dispersed. After the young couple that had caused the incident finished gathering up their beach paraphernalia, the woman came over to Neal and said, "It took a lot of guts for a man your age to do what you did. I only wish that wimp I'm with had half as much. Thanks for saving my life. I shall never forget what you did here today. And if I ever have any kids, they won't either." Kissing Neal on the cheek, she smiled and said, "Goodbye, and God bless you."

Chilled to the bone and totally exhausted, Neal put his shirt and pants back on and said to Anita, "I don't know about you, but I could use a drink and a few minutes in my Jacuzzi."

"Funny you should mention that, Mr. T," she replied, handing him his wallet and car keys. "I had the very same thought."

Later on, after Neal and Anita had relaxed in the Jacuzzi for nearly half an hour, Neal turned on the eleven o'clock news and waited for the latest report on Hurricane Louise, while Anita excused herself and went to bed.

As was predicted earlier that day, the storm had changed direction and was now heading harmlessly out over the Atlantic Ocean. That raised a question in Neal's mind as to what immediate steps Dan Hughes was taking to retrieve his boat from the Bahamas. *Should I have gone with him*, Neal asked himself, ever mindful of his financial obligation to Sterling Publishing Company. *Stop dreaming* his conscience commanded, re-directing his thoughts to treat his trip to the airport on Monday as a convenient opportunity to drop off his comments on Norma Manning's changes. He smiled, as he turned off the television and climbed the stairs, remembering in detail the intimacy they had enjoyed. *It will be nice to see her again.*

Chapter 21

Of Things to Come

The next morning arrived with all the promises that blue sky and an eighty-degree temperature forecast could promise. The previous day's excitement had given Neal and his attractive houseguest a bonus of an extra hour's sleep, making their invitation to his daughter's party that afternoon all the more exciting to look forward to as the day progressed.

To show her appreciation for his hospitality, Anita insisted that Neal shave and shower first so she could use that time to surprise him by preparing breakfast. After carefully examining the contents of the pantry and refrigerator, she decided to use a can of *Roast Beef Hash* as the base for a dish she had seen her father prepare when she was a teenager.

Though her father had used ground up leftover meat and boiled potatoes, she discovered essentially the same ingredients in the *Mary Kitchen* hash, so she opened the can and began the process. After dicing and slow cooking a piece of onion she found hiding in a corner of the fridge, she added the hash, sprinkled it liberally with black pepper, and turned it over with a spatula occasionally to cook off the grease.

"I don't know what you're cooking down here," Neal remarked, as he entered the kitchen, "but if it tastes as good as it smells, I'm going to love it."

Anita grinned and replied, "Are you ready to eat? The finishing touches only take a minute."

"Go girl. I'm ready."

Placing half of the hash on a dinner plate, she lightly layered it with blended cheese, sprinkled on some hot sauce, a little Italian Seasoning, covered it with a paper plate, and placed it in the microwave for a few seconds to melt the cheese. Steaming with delicious aroma, she placed the un-covered dish in front of him and waited for his reaction.

The scented vapor that floated up into his nostrils and closed his eyes brought a big smile to his face. "This must be paradise," he sighed, picking up a fork to sample his serving.

"And...?" she asked, hedging for a comment.

"Fit for a king!" he replied, taking another taste. "Hurry and fix your plate so we can both enjoy this while its hot."

Following breakfast, the remainder of time leading up to leaving for Neal's family get together was spent reading the Sunday newspaper, watching television and preparing for Anita's departure to San Francisco the next morning. While Anita was preoccupied with laying out her travel clothes upstairs, Neal made sure that his briefcase contained Norma Manning's review manuscript, and the notes he had jotted down while reading it. He had just finished securing the briefcase when the phone rang. It was Gloria Donaldson. "Hello, Neal," she said, somewhat somberly. "I'm calling to verify that you received Anita's flight schedule. Is she there?"

"Yes, she's upstairs," he replied. "Hold on, I'll tell her you're on the line." Going to the bottom of the stairs he yelled, "Anita! Pick up the phone in my bedroom! It's your mother!"

In seconds, Anita rushed to the table next to Neal's bed and picked up. "Hi Mom! I'm so glad you called. How are you?"

"Better, now that I know you'll be on that plane tomorrow," Gloria replied. "I miss you."

The tone of her mother's voice didn't sound quite normal. Bothered by it, Anita asked, "What's the matter, Mom? You don't sound like you feel very good."

"I'm just tired," she admitted reluctantly. "We'll have plenty of time to talk about that when you get here. I just wanted to let you know that all your things arrived safely, and we've got one of the large spare bedrooms all fixed up for you."

"I could have done that when I got there, Mom. Get some rest. I'll be home before you know it."

"I will, dear. Tell Neal goodbye for me. My limo will be waiting for you at the airport. Be careful, and have a good flight. See you tomorrow."

Suddenly despondent, Anita went downstairs and approached Neal. "Something's bothering my mother, Mr. T., I can hear it in her voice."

Caught off guard by Anita's sudden shift in mood, Neal admitted that he had noticed it too, but wasn't going to mention it. "Your mother is a busy woman," he said. "She's probably suffering from the emotional strain of getting her grown up daughter back after all these years. That would sure have a traumatic affect on my life."

"Yeah, I guess it would," she admitted, accepting his male reasoning. "Maybe I'm just pre-supposing a bit. She even said she misses me."

Time passed slowly from that point on, each person preoccupied with their individual thoughts regarding the world of unknowns that lay beyond that day. The clock, however, knew not of those concerns and gave silent warning that it was time to leave for Karen and Derek Stone's barbeque, a family event that Neal had not participated in for quite some time. Hopeful that the mix of new personalities she was soon to meet would help Anita dilute the effect of her mother's phone conversation, Neal took her by the arm and escorted her to his car, remarking humorously along the way, "Trust me, it will be a laugh a minute."

Not far from Virginia's Atlantic Coastline, where the Bennett's Creek estate of the Hughes family nestled in seclusion, Henry and Dan Hughes relaxed in their home's family room, each preoccupied with what Hurricane Louise's timely exit meant to them individually. For Henry, his real estate business had escaped the potential damage that a destructive hurricane could have brought to his multi-acreage holdings, costing him untold thousands of dollars in cleanup.

Though Dan Hughes had shared his father's concerns, the hurricane's unexpected change in direction solved his problems, and replaced it with a timely opportunity to fly to the Bahamas. There, with the assistance of the man who had helped him flee the murderous cartel initially, he could reclaim his boat and return home. That one-week return trip would be ample time for his friend Neal Thomas to get his affairs in order so he could join the Hughes family for the reunion Henry had already begun planning for.

That reunion, unbeknownst to Neal Thomas, would also expose him to the bold new plan Dan Hughes had conceived to develop the Back Bay property he had inherited into a multi-million dollar resort and condominium complex. Given Dan's past involvement with the Tidewater Drug Cartel, and the inability to trust anyone as a result of it, only his mentor, Neal Thomas, had the technical background, aesthetic temperament and trustworthiness that Dan needed to guide him in the presentation and development of such a project. As he sat roughing in the square-footage of the project's main elements, one worrisome question kept running through his mind – *is he going to be available?* Only time could provide the answer.

Rounding the street corner leading to the Stone residence, Neal smiled and spoke to Anita as if she were one of his own daughters sitting there. "Now don't be nervous," he advised, "The people you are about to meet are as easy-going as any you will ever run into. If anything, they'll probably smother you with attention. Just roll with the punches and have a good time"

"After tending bar all these years, I doubt there's anyone in your family that even comes close to what I've had to deal with on a daily basis. I'm actually looking forward to a family get together for a change. They were always fun when I was a kid."

The front door had been intentionally left ajar when they reached the entranceway. Without hesitating, Neal pushed it open and entered with Anita following close behind.

That a party was going on became immediately apparent, judging from the jumbled mix of excited talk and laughter that was coming from the kitchen. Despite everyone's preoccupation with whatever they were doing when Neal and Anita appeared, several guests stopped long enough to wave, and express a variety of greetings that included: "Daddy's here" – "Hi Pops" – "The entertainment just arrived," and "Whose your lady friend, Mr. T?"

Observing the overwhelmed look on Anita's face, Neal's oldest daughter, Karen, left the sink where she had been helping one of the men prepare snacks. Approaching her father, she said, "Hi Daddy," and gave him a quick kiss before turning to Anita. "And you must be Anita Donaldson. Welcome to the Stone family house of chaos," she laughed, "I'm Karen."

After they shook hands, Karen winked at her dad and said, "Get her something to drink, will you Daddy? I'll introduce her to the rest of the family."

Marveling at how comfortably relaxed Anita had suddenly become, Neal made his way out onto the patio deck where his son-in-law was barbequing his traditional chunk of tri-tip steak and sipping a glass of quality scotch. "Hi, Pops," he greeted Neal. "Karen told me last night that you've had a young lady staying at your house for a couple of days. Is she a relative?"

Neal laughed at how quickly the rumor-mill started tongues wagging whenever an older man was suspected of having an affair with a younger woman. "No," he replied, "but I'm flattered to be considered guilty of what the relationship suggests. The reality is, she lost her job and had no place to stay. Since she's leaving for San Francisco tomorrow, I told her she could stay at my place. Hell, she's like one of my daughters."

"What's her profession?" Derek asked, becoming more and more curious about the woman he had yet to meet.

"She was a bartender at the Village Pub. I've known her since she started working there. Her last name was Cassidy then."

"What do you mean, *was*?"

Neal's drink was almost empty by now, so to condense the story to an abbreviated reply, he said, "She ran away from home soon after her father died, and changed her last name to Cassidy. It's a long story, but I recently reunited her with her mother, who just happens to be one of the wealthiest women in San Francisco. Get the picture?"

Derek smirked. "Yeah. It's all about money, isn't it?"

Watching him drink the last of his scotch, Neal said, "I need a refill. Can I get you one too?"

"Thanks, Pops. From the looks of this meat, I'm going to be here for awhile."

Walking past the familiar faces of his family and friends, all of whom delayed him temporarily from completing his mission, Neal finally made it to the bar. While he was preoccupied with fixing his and Derek's drink, he heard the familiar voice of his former wife, Janet, address him from behind, "Can you spare a minute? I have some information I think you ought to be aware of."

"Sure," he replied, turning in her direction. "I'll meet you on the patio as soon as I give Derek his drink."

Janet was standing alone by the pool watching the children playing in the water when Neal walked over and asked, "Now, what is it you want to tell me?"

"Have you received a letter from Walter Douglas' attorney yet?"

"You mean Harvey Kline?"

"Yes. He's been Walter's attorney since he graduated from law school and is in charge of administering Walter's will. When was the last time you read your mail?"

"A couple of days ago, I guess. What's this all about anyway?"

Janet shook her head in frustration, remembering how forgetful he had been at times when they were married. "Walter left everyone in our family a sizeable amount of money. So I suggest you read your mail when you get home."

Dumbfounded by what she had told him, Neal couldn't help but laugh at the irony of it all, and remarked, "Knowing Walter, I guess he figured if he couldn't take it with him, he might as well give it away."

"I thought it was very generous of him," Janet commented. "Of course it's going to take awhile to actually receive the check, so don't run out and buy a Cadillac tomorrow. When I questioned Harvey about when we'd get the checks, he said probably late December, or early January."

Neal took a large swallow from his drink, looked wistfully up at the scattered clouds overhead and said, "May the good Lord take a liking to you, old buddy. Many thanks."

Not having seen him for several weeks, Janet asked, "How is your book coming along, by the way?"

"It's finished, except for incorporating my editor's comments," he replied. "There's a film company in Hollywood that thinks it might make an exciting movie. They're going to review the published version and get back to us. In the meantime, I'm planning a trip to Virginia as soon as Dan Hughes gets his boat back from the Bahamas. Henry is planning a big welcome home party for Dan, and wants me to attend."

Janet's eyebrows suddenly began to bunch together in a frown. "You'd better think twice about getting mixed up with that bunch again." she remarked seriously. "Nothing good will come of it, that's for sure."

It's time to join the others, Neal thought, realizing he was venturing into a sensitive area as far as Janet was concerned. Looking at his watch as a ploy to avoid an argument, Neal said, "Thanks for the heads-up on Walter's will, but I had better check on Anita before this family destroys whatever plans she may have had to have children of her own.

I'll be in touch."

Just the opposite had occurred. Neal's re-entry into the den portion of the Stone home found Anita the center of attraction in a laughter-filled, story telling session of her experiences as a bartender. His fear that she would feel like the fifth wheel on a four-wheel buggy couldn't have been more wrong. So he refilled his glass and listened, glad to see that she was relaxed and having a good time with her captive audience. Moments later his cell phone chimed, forcing him to relocate to the patio. It was Norma Manning.

"I hope I'm not interrupting anything," she began. "I wanted to confirm that you were stopping by the office tomorrow to drop off your review of my comments."

Neal smiled to himself, knowing how eager she was to report to Sandy Sterling that the book was only a few days away from going to press. "I have to drop a friend off at the airport tomorrow morning," He explained. "I should be at your office between nine and ten o'clock, if that's convenient."

"Perfect!" she replied excitedly. "I'm looking forward to it."

From where he was standing Neal could observe Derek Stone lifting his signature barbequed tri-tip steak onto a wooden cutting board and carrying it into the kitchen. *Ah, dinner will soon be served*, he thought, as he followed close behind Derek to rejoin the others. As he suspected, the group had grown to include a few friendly neighbors and their children. Most had gathered in the living room to hear one of the guests play his guitar, while Karen and her two sisters, Susan and Laura, helped set up the buffet. The finishing touch came when Derek placed the steak platter at one end of the table and yelled, "Dinner is served!"

Traditionally, the children were served first, followed by grown-ups who congregated in small groups at tables on the pool deck, or near the outdoor fireplace. Several of the older boys, however, were still playing water ball. Judging from the variety of skimpy bathing suits the girls who had teamed up with them were wearing, food was hardly a priority.

Amused by the seemingly innocent activity that was taking place, Neal fixed his plate and joined Anita on the fireplace patio where she had thoughtfully reserved him a chair. As if reading his mind, she smiled and asked, "Oh, to be young again. Is that what's going through your mind, Mr. T?"

Neal smiled back and replied, "The way young women talk and act these days I probably wouldn't make it past my twenty-first birthday."

"Then I guess it's a good thing women don't think like men," she came back quickly.

Before Neal could think of an appropriate response, a woman across the table from him remarked, "I read an article in the paper this morning that said researchers have discovered a gene in women that supports the theory that women actually do think differently than men. They believe the gene is a motherhood related phenomenon."

"That would make sense," Anita remarked supportively. "That's why our bodies are made differently. Why not our brains?"

Rather than get involved in a discussion that, as yet, had not been validated by scientific fact, Neal tried to be supportive by injecting a little humor. "Doesn't that support the common theory that women can see things in a man that no one else can?"

"I guess so," the woman replied. "Why else would a woman have an affair over the Internet? Or fall in love with a man in prison that she'd never met before."

"It's safer that way," Anita commented, giggling a little. "You get all the hearts and flowers, but none of the physical abuse. Sometimes fantasizing about a relationship can be almost as satisfying as the real thing."

"Maybe so," the other woman said, "but I'm inclined to go for that warm, cozy, body snuggling up against me on cold winter mornings."

Before the conversation could develop into a verbal shooting match between Anita and the woman across the table, a voice from the open

door that led into the living room yelled, "Hey Pops. You've got an audience in here. They want to hear you play a few numbers."

"Go ahead, Mr. T," Anita said encouragingly, "I'll join you as soon
as I finish eating."

Glad for the opportunity to escape further discussion on a subject
that wasn't going anywhere, Neal dropped off his empty plate in the
kitchen and continued on into the living room. To his surprise a mixed
group of his family members, and those of several neighbors, had gathered there to listen to Derek and his friend play their guitars. When
Neal joined the gathering, everyone clapped and encouraged him to sit
down at the grand piano and join in the fun.

Glad not to be the center of attraction, Neal found a great deal
of enjoyment in playing accompaniment for the melody-picking guitars, rather than the serious concentration required of a soloist. The
audience's reaction was equally rewarding, expressing itself in the un-
noticed appearance of Anita Donaldson listening at the entrance to the
living room.

When the song the three men were playing ended, and a moment of
silence lingered, Anita seized the opportunity to make a request. "Blue
Moon?" she asked shyly.

Surprised by the uncommon request from someone too young to
remember that age-old classic, Derek said, "It's all yours, Pops. We'll
chord it."

Fingering a brief introduction, Neal began the main melody wondering all the while what had prompted Anita to request a song that
dated back beyond her years. *What does it matter*, he thought. *I'll ask
her later.*

One by one, people began leaving as the evening wore on. The classic excuse of having to work the next day was the main reason, which
prompted Neal to bring up Anita's early morning trip to the airport.
Reluctantly, she agreed that getting a good night's sleep took precedence
over the hangover she would have to deal with if she drank any more
wine. The sweet sorrow of parting was that everyone there, including
some of the younger ones, came to her with open arms and wished
her well, inviting her back unconditionally whenever it was possible.
Though she tried her best to fend them off, a few tears ran slowly down
Anita's cheek when Karen Stone took her in her arms, as if she were a

child of her own, and said, "You're one of us now, girl. Come back any time."

Because he understood how much emotional strain Anita had been under for several days, Neal let her unwind for a minute or two before he asked, "What ever prompted you to request *Blue Moon* this evening? You're way to young to remember that song."

"It was my father's favorite," she replied, beginning to smile again. "He'd sing it whenever he thought no one was listening. As my mother used to say, he couldn't carry a tune in a bucket."

Buttered toast and coffee were waiting for Neal when he came down to the kitchen Monday morning. From the corner of his eye he noticed Anita's suitcase sitting by the front door. "Looks like you're planning on going somewhere today, young lady." he joked. "Thanks for fixing this. We'll be on our way as soon as I eat. Are you nervous?"

"Like a cat on a hot tin roof...and scared," she replied. "More for my mother, I guess. I just hope she's ready for this."

"I know the feeling." Neal admitted. "I felt the same way the morning my widowed mother dropped me off in front of the city library to catch a bus for Indian Town Gap, Pennsylvania."

"What the hell for?" she asked, her brow creased with confusion.

"To begin my two-year hitch in the United States Army, thanks to my friends and neighbors – as the induction notice read. But then again, that's another story."

"I can imagine."

"We'll save that one for some rainy day in the future. Right now, I need to get my briefcase and take you to the airport. Are you ready?"

"As I'll ever be."

Forty-five minutes later Neal took the Terminal 2 exit off Harbor Drive and drove to the curbside check-in for Anita's flight. Because of increased security restrictions, and constant patrolling to keep traffic moving, there was little time for a long-winded goodbye. Suitcase in hand, and a smile getting bigger by the second, Anita stuck her head in the window and said, "I love you, Mr. T. Thanks for everything."

"Call me tonight to let me know you got there safely."

"I will," she promised.

Entering the elevator at Sterling Publishing Company, Neal's mind was still harboring the emotional residue from Anita's last words to him – *I love you, Mr. T.*

Wondering when and if he would ever hear those words from a woman again, he punched the button and listened to the canned music until the doors opened. The volley of activity that greeted him brought back the reality of why he was there.

"Neal Thomas to see Norma Manning," he informed the studious looking receptionist.

"Good morning, Mr. Thomas," she said quite formally. "I'll check to make sure she's still in her office." A moment later she returned looking a little flushed, and said, "You may go right in. The door is open."

Walking the few steps it took to reach Norma's office, Neal sensed that eyes were following him. Wondering why, he proceeded to walk right in, not expecting the door to close quietly behind him. Surprised by the sound it made, he turned and found Norma standing there with a flirtatious look on here face. "Your place or mine?" she asked, winking like a chorus girl in an old western movie.

When Neal burst out laughing, she could no longer maintain the silly ruse and reacted the same way. It did not, however, lessen her intent, as she stepped into his arms and flattened her body against his with a kiss he had only too recently been seduced with. "Too bad we don't have time for this right now," she said, straightening her clothes and hand-brushing her hair back in place. How've you been, Mr. T?"

Amused by her sexually playful antics, he replied, "Fine, until now. Are you in heat or something?"

"That's for me to know, and you to find out," she replied, while reopening her office door. "Now where are those comments of yours? We have work to do."

Back and forth for the next hour, Norma and Neal exchanged agreements and disagreements regarding the comments she had made about various aspects of his book and its presentation. Though some concessions on both their parts were made, the end result was unanimous; the book was ready to process for publication. It was just after this important decision was made that Sandy and Jessica Sterling appeared in the doorway. "Well, what's the verdict?" Sandy asked. "Are we, or are we not, going to press?"

Smiling smugly at one another from across the desk where crumpled balls of paper bore testimony to the work they had accomplished that morning, Norma looked at her boss and said, "He's a tough nut to crack, Sandy, but we're there. We can start publishing as soon as the art work is ready."

Both Sterling ladies clapped their hands and hugged one another in open excitement before Jessica remarked, "Looks like a celebration is in order."

"Right after the first book rolls off the press," Sandy suggested. "We'll need the time to get our advertising campaign organized. Great work, you two."

The ride home that morning was one of jubilance, a time to sit back and smell the roses of literary accomplishment. The fantasy of thinking that it might be the first stepping-stone on the pathway to a future filled with celebrity, adventure and financial security made him light-headed for a moment. *I need to share this wonderful day with somebody.*

Too emotionally charged to give it much serious thought, he decided to wait until the first royalty check arrived before prematurely jumping to any conclusions. To be overly optimistic at this point would be a mistake, he reasoned. *Only time could provide the justification.*

For the first time since his one-time lover, Paula Dillon, had moved away, Neal experienced a rare feeling of loneliness as he entered his home. Desperate for something to take his mind off of it, he turned on the radio and stepped outside to bring in the mail, all of which turned out to be either advertisements or bills. Tossing them aside to be read later, he started upstairs to change the sheets on the bed where Anita Donaldson had spent the night when the phone rang. Ironically, it was Anita fulfilling her promise to call.

"I'm glad I caught you at home, Mr. T," she began. "I'm at mother's place right now trying to get settled in. Poor mother, she's not feeling well, and had to send the limousine to pick me up at the airport. I'm taking her to the doctor tomorrow to have some tests run. Hopefully, it's nothing serious. Are you okay?"

To lift her spirits, he replied, "I am now. I was just on my way up to change the sheets on your bed when you called. Should I wash them?"

She laughed heartily, and replied, "In case you hadn't noticed, I'm too old to wet the bed any more, Mr. T. But you might just as well get them ready for your next guest. I'm sure she'll appreciate it."

Amused by her subtle jealousy, Neal said, "Thanks for calling, Anita. Tell your mother I hope she feels better real soon."

"I will."

Again, Neal started for the stairs to strip the sheets from the guest room bed when the phone rang again. "Damn," he cursed, "What now?"

"Hi, Neal. This is Jim Taylor."

Neal's jaw dropped with surprise. "Jim! Where are you?" he shouted over what sounded like airplane engines.

"I'm about to leave for Catalina," he replied. "Do you want to join me?"

With nothing but boredom to look forward to for the next few days, Neal asked, "How long are you planning to stay?"

"Two or three days...whatever."

"Sure! I'll meet you at Palomar Airport in an hour."

"Take your time. I'm in no hurry."

Excited by the spontaneity of what was taking place, Neal packed an over-night bag with a few days clothing and clipped on his cell phone. After he called the only neighbor he communicated with to ask him to pick up his mail, he locked up the house and left for the airport, purged of the fleeting moment of loneliness he had experienced earlier. *Now it's my turn.*

By the time Neal arrived at Palomar Airport, Jim Taylor was landing his twin-engine Cessna and taxiing toward the terminal. After passing through the security checkpoint, Neal proceeded to the area where Jim had parked and climbed into the aircraft.

There was a broad smile on Jim's face when Neal buckled into the co-pilot's seat. "I still don't know what prompted me to call you today," Jim admitted. "Maybe going back to Catalina brought back memories of our last day together, especially when Gloria Donaldson told me my services were no longer needed. How is the old girl, by the way?"

Rather than try to explain what he had learned from Anita Donaldson over the roar of two engines, Neal replied, "I'll buy you a drink when we get to Catalina and tell you all about it. It's quite a story."

"Fair enough," Jim said, as he pushed the throttles forward and sped down the runway, shouting, "Catalina, here we come!"

THE END
Maybe

CPSIA information can be obtained at www.ICGtesting.com
Printed in the USA
LVOW041056111111

254533LV00002B/275/A